HARVEST AMERICAN
Writing

THE
CHOIRING
OF THE
TREES

Books by Donald Harington

The Choiring of the Trees

The Cockroaches of Stay More

Let Us Build Us a City

The Cherry Pit

Lightning Bug

Some Other Place. The Right Place.

The Architecture of the Arkansas Ozarks: A Novel

THE
CHOIRING
OF THE
TREES

A NOVEL BY

DONALD HARINGTON

A HARVEST/HBJ BOOK

HARCOURT BRACE JOVANOVICH, PUBLISHERS

San Diego   New York   London

Requests for permission to make copies of any
part of the work should be mailed to:
Permissions Department, Harcourt Brace Jovanovich, Publishers,
8th Floor, Orlando, Florida 32887.

Library of Congress Cataloging-in-Publication Data
Harington, Donald.
The choiring of the trees: a novel/Donald Harington.—1st ed.
p. cm.
ISBN 0-15-117550-0
ISBN 0-15-617099-X (pbk.)
I. Title.
PS3558.A6242C5   1991
813'.54—dc20   90-4989

Designed by Alex P. Mendoza

Printed in the United States of America

First Harvest/HBJ edition 1992

A B C D E

For Llewellyn Howland III
Once a great editor; still a great friend

The novelist wishes to thank Bob Razer, librarian, his perennial advocate among Arkansas readers, who once upon a time invited the novelist to serve as a judge for the essay contest of the Pulaski County Historical Association, one entry to which was a biography of a courageous Arkansas woman who sought to rescue an Ozarks mountaineer condemned to the electric chair. The author of that entry (which alas did not win the contest despite the novelist's admiration for it) was Marcia Camp, who further assisted him by furnishing the original manuscript of that Arkansas woman's memoirs, and by suggesting that he should convert the woman from a novelist, which she was, into an artist, which she is herein.

Most of the people in this work of fiction are as "real" as the places. The governor of Arkansas during 1913–1917 was George Washington Hays, who may actually have been as bad or as good as he seems to appear here, and he was replaced in 1917 by Charles Hillman Brough, who was better. The state penitentiary at Little Rock was a place called The Walls, and conditions there were just as terrible as the novelist has attempted to depict them here.

Steve Chism offered the novelist access to numerous materials that enabled him to stick close enough to the facts to give this story the semblance of life and truth. And copy editor Douglas Woodyard took the novelist's words and gave them syntax, style, and sense.

The mind, that ocean where each kind
Does straight its own resemblance find;
Yet it creates, transcending these,
Far other worlds, and other seas,
Annihilating all that's made
To a green thought in a green shade.

—Andrew Marvell
"The Garden," stanza 6

Constable said that the superiority of the green he uses for his landscapes derives from the fact that it is composed of a multitude of different greens. What causes the lack of intensity and of life in verdure as it is painted by the common run of landscapists is that they ordinarily do it with a uniform tint. What he said about the green of the meadows can be applied to all the other shades.

—Eugène Delacroix
Journals

At sundown, when they led him to the chair, Nail Chism began to understand the meaning of the name of his hometown, Stay More. Down through the years, citizens have theorized about the origin of the name, but Nail Chism had always taken it for granted: it was just a name, like you call a tree a pine: you don't wonder if the tree's name is a behest too, telling you to yearn or to long or something. But now it suddenly dawned on Nail that the name of the village of his birth and rearing might contain some kind of message, urging him not to go to the chair but to hang around awhile and see what the world was a-coming to.

How could he do that, in the last few yards of walking space left to him? Now they were trying to budge open the rusty iron door that led into Old Sparky's room. The hinges needed grease, and the thing hadn't been opened since they had cooked that colored boy, Skip, on Halloween. Fat Gabe spoke: "Chism, lean your shoulder into that. That's the ticket, here she goes." The iron door creaked open. The guests had already come into Old Sparky's room from their designated door.

But there weren't twelve of them. Nail Chism stopped thinking about the meaning of the name Stay More just long enough to squint into the dark room and take a head count. There weren't but nine, including Fat Gabe and Short Leg, his guards, and Bobo, at the switch. The law said you were required to have twelve witnesses. Nail himself had been brought in to stand witness for Skip the colored boy, and before him for that mother-killer Clarence Smead, who sure enough had at least eleven other witnesses besides Nail.

Could this be a sign? Could it be that the presence of only nine witnesses indicated that it wouldn't happen, that Nail would stay more? Or maybe they just hadn't all arrived yet? Or maybe in the dark corners he'd missed one or two? Maybe they'd have to wait awhile for the others to show up, and that would be long enough for Nail to determine if they really intended to go through with it, before he made up his mind to do what he had to do, if it was clear that he wasn't going to stay more.

What he had to do, at the last minute, if it became clear they intended to make him sit and tried to tie the straps, was take as many as he could with him. Beneath his dirty gray jacket, on a string around his neck, hidden by his jacket collar being buttoned, was the blade: a common steel table knife purloined two weeks ago from the mess hall, and then slowly sharpened on the concrete floor, hour upon hour, silently, until it was pointed like a dagger and razor-sharp on both sides. He was going to get Fat Gabe first, then Short Leg, and then take their guns out of their holsters and shoot the rest of the witnesses. He was going to save Bobo for last, right after shooting the warden. He wanted to watch Bobo sweat. He wanted to be sure that Bobo was sober enough to understand what was happening to him, and then he would make Bobo sit down in the chair and get a few low-voltage jolts of his own medicine. He would make Bobo learn a few things before he died.

Jimmie Mac the preacher stepped up to him and said, "Brother Chism, have you managed to say any prayers?" Jimmie Mac's breath frosted like smoke in the cold air. Nail shook his head and wondered in what order of execution he would have to kill Jimmie Mac. Maybe right before the warden. Right after he did the lady.

The lady, wrapped in a double-breasted melton coat but wearing a simple hat without feathers or anything fancy, wasn't supposed to be there. The law said you got twelve witnesses, and all twelve had to be men. You couldn't invite your mother or your sister or your girlfriend. It wasn't decent to make a woman sit through such a thing, to make her hear the hollering and the sizzling, to make her watch the twisting and jerking, to make her smell the awful stink of roasting flesh. It was sure to make her puke, or swoon, or both.

But this lady worked for the newspaper. She had sat beside Nail when they watched Skip get it, and when Nail himself had screamed at Bobo, "Goddamn you, Bobo, turn up the juice and leave it on!" she had put a hand gently on his arm to calm him down. The hand she had rested on his arm held a drawing-stick, a charcoal pencil she'd been using to make a sketch of the black boy, and in resting her hand on his arm she'd accidentally left a mark of charcoal on the back of his hand, and he had worn that mark for days and days before washing it off, as a reminder of what he'd watched, and what she'd done. She was a cool customer. Probably she wasn't even a lady. She probably cussed and drank and even smoked cigarettes when nobody was looking. Her red hair wasn't as long as a lady's hair ought to be. She drew good pictures, and Nail had never even heard of a lady artist. Maybe he would shoot her between the warden and Bobo.

The warden, Mr. Burdell, stepped up beside Jimmie Mac and said, "Okay, McPhee, you can say a short prayer for him."

"He aint repented," Jimmie Mac told the warden.

"Skip the prayer, then," Mr. Burdell said, and turned to Nail. "Chism, you got any last words?"

"Yessir, I do," Nail said. "How come there aint but nine witnesses?"

Mr. Burdell looked around the room, moving his lips and his index finger as he counted. He spoke the last two aloud: ". . . eight . . . nine . . ." He hesitated, then grinned. "Ten, counting you, Chism. Aint you gonna witness this yourself? And if you want to count Ole Sparky hisself, there, that makes eleven." Fat Gabe and Short Leg laughed at their boss's wit.

"That's still one short," Nail protested.

Mr. Burdell stopped grinning and looked tired and irritated. He said, "It don't make no difference."

"It aint legal," Nail said. "Also, it aint legal to have that lady there."

The warden turned to the woman and smiled. "Miss Monday," he said. "Are you legal?"

She did not return his smile. She shook her head.

The warden glowered fiercely at Nail and said to him, "Okay, Chism, it's cold in here and the sun's fixin to go down, and it's gittin real cold. Let's git this over with. You want to say anything important? You been actin like you're just out on a stroll to a picnic or something. You gonna be a real good boy and take this peaceful-like and easy, huh? Or do you want to start hollerin a bit and git it out of your system?"

Nail looked down at his hands. The trees were singing, *Stay more, stay more.* His hands were still bound together with cuffs. They would have to unlock the cuffs in order to strap his arms to the chair. In the instant between, he would reach inside his shirt for the razor-sharp dagger. He was conscious of the woman sketching his picture in her drawing-pad. With his head shaved smooth as an egg, he wasn't much of a sight. The picture she'd drawn of Skip had made him look old and scared to death, although he was just sixteen and real brave for a colored boy. Nail wondered if the picture she was drawing of him was honest.

"Any last request?" Mr. Burdell asked him. "You aint got time for a cigarette."

3

Nail inclined his head toward the woman. "Could I see the pitcher she's drawin? That's all."

Mr. Burdell walked over and leaned down and spoke to Miss Monday. She said something to the warden. He returned and spoke to Nail: "She aint finished with it yet."

"Could we jist wait jist a second, till she's done?" Nail requested.

Mr. Burdell grunted, and hauled out his pocket watch and opened the gold cover of it. He stared at it for a time. He glanced at Miss Monday, and then at Nail. "Law says you got to be dead before the sun disappears," he said. He walked back over to where Miss Monday was sitting, and stood behind her chair, watching her draw. He looked back and forth between her drawing and Nail's face, as if he were comparing the two. Nail tried to look pleasant. He stared straight at Miss Monday, and from time to time she raised her head from her work and looked him right in the eye for a long moment. She was a pretty girl, even if she was cold as ice. Her eyes were sort of greenish . . . it was hard to tell in this light. Her skin was the palest, whitest flesh he'd ever seen. Red hair, green eyes, white skin: she was a picture herself.

While he posed in the last minutes of his life, he planned every move that he would make, trying to guess exactly what they would do while they were still able, before he took over. Fat Gabe would unlock the handcuffs. Short Leg would push him down into the chair. Fat Gabe would commence strapping his left arm while Short Leg would reach for the strap to do his right, and at that instant Nail would whip out the blade and slash it across Fat Gabe's throat in one left-to-right motion that, continuing, would bring the point of the dagger in line with Short Leg's heart, where Nail would thrust it forward, reaching in the same blink of an eye for Short Leg's holster . . .

Oh stay more! sang the trees, and Nail sang back, *I'm doing my best!* And apart from the singing the only sound in the cold, darkening room was the skritch-skritch of the woman's charcoal pencil as she drew on and on.

off

Up on the lilting mountain far above the village is a farmplace so old the trees still sing of it, but nobody else does. The trees, a fat maple and a gangling walnut, left to grow for shade a hundred years ago when they were already old, about the time Nail Chism was born, don't really talk each other's language, but they sing a tune together, a kind of soughing ballad, a ditty maybe just of fragrances, leaf-smells in the sunlight that drop an octave in the moonlight, heard or smelled attentively by owls who roost there, and a nightingale, wondering at a treesong about people named Chism, whose farmplace it was when sheep still grazed the orchard grass, yarrow, and sweet-scented vernal, now grown to scrub, tangled with emerald vines and turquoise nettles. The leaning house behind the tilted white-paling gate was lived in for a few years just recently by some young people from another state who raised goats and marijuana, distant echoes of the sheep who had once grazed there and the corn whiskey moonlighted in the hollow down below.

Nail Chism helped his older brother Waymon and his kid brother Luther in the making of Chism's Dew when the moon was right, but neither brother helped Nail in the keeping of the sheep, who were his alone, or even in the shearing of them, when the moon was right, in its waxing. There were a hundred and sixty acres on the Chism place: eighty downhill plowed to corn for the making of vernacular bourbon, eighty upland sown to timothy, meadow foxtail, white clover, and fescue, with a good bit of parsley mixed in among the yarrow and the sweet-scented vernal, to feed Nail's flock, which numbered rarely less than a hundred or more than two hundred, including three or four rams to service.

The colors of the pasture grasses rose from deep jade and Kelly to light Nile and spring green, and each midsummer Nail sowed the bare spots of the fields with a bushel of mustardseed, the mustard adding sulphur to the diet of the sheep and adding yellow-green to the colors of the pasture, intensifying them in keeping with the heat of the sun and Nail's keeping. The rape was sown in July and August for a fall feeding.

Rape, a primitive cabbage, Brassica cousin to mustard, is a purplish shade of green at its base, but the leaves are an intense phthalo green (pronounced without the *ph*, which reminds me of the one they used to tell about Nail in his schooldays: the new schoolmarm steered clear of questions that might get an argument out of him, and she wouldn't protest when he told her right off that he didn't intend to spell "taters" with a *p*, regardless of what the book says). Two pounds of rapeseed sown to the acre is enough; too much rape will cause the sheep to bloat. Some folks who didn't like the word "rape" called it colza, but the rest of us never knew what they were talking about.

But it is the other kind of rape that dwells at the heart of this story, so it won't do to confuse the issue by describing all that rape out in Nail's pastures. He also grew a lot of turnips, because his sheep liked both the tops for forage and the pulverized roots as a main treat in the winter, and turnips never got anybody thrown into the penitentiary. The turnip top is a light, whitish green, not very intense, cool, a gentle shade that belies its pungent taste. Of course Nail never broadcast the turnip seeds but grew them separately in a fenced-off garden.

He grew a different kind of turnip for his mother to cook for greens with sowbelly, or mashed up like taters, or baked into a pie (yes, with sorghum sweetening, turnip pie is the best there is). In the Ozark Mountains garden truck is generally the womenfolk's work, and some people raised an eyebrow at Nail Chism out yonder under his felt hat in the garden patch a-chopping weeds out of the ingerns, or onions, but most folks just said that was the *least* of his peculiarities, and better to let it go.

The sheep were his principal peculiarity. Not that sheep were so rare in the Ozarks (they weren't at all in those days), but that a genuine shepherd was. If a man wanted to make a dollar or two every April from selling the wool, he'd keep a ewe (anybody who had one pronounced it "yo") out behind the house where the dogs couldn't get it. He wouldn't think of eating it; nobody ate mutton, let alone lamb, in the Ozarks, where "meat" meant only pork, nothing else. (Pork can be salted and cured and preserved, but mutton cannot.) When the ewe got too old to be sheared, fourteen or so, and hadn't died of natural old age, its owner would just let it go to rot or rust through neglect, and bury it, or take down the fence separating it from the dogs.

Nail Chism was the only man anybody knew, or even heard of, or read in the papers about, who kept a whole pastureful of sheep, and he spent most of his time, when he wasn't tending the vegetable patch or helping his brothers with the whiskey still, living with the sheep and watching

6

after them. We could hear him up there a mile off calling, "Sheep! sheep! sheepsheepsheep!" He knew everything there was to be known about sheep. He knew how to get the yolk just right—for anybody else, that meant the yellow part of an egg, but Nail would explain it was the soapy or greasy stuff on the fleece: too little yolk, and the sheep wasn't getting the right mix of greens or else had been sired by an inferior ram, and the fleece would be dry and coarse; too much yolk, and twenty pounds of sheared fleece would weigh only four pounds after the first washing.

Every April, Nail Chism rented from Willis Ingledew's livery a wagon, which he loaded with fleece to the sky, or at least to the lowest tree branches, and drove to Harrison, a week's journey there and back, where he got the best dollar for his "crop." Some folks wondered why Nail Chism even needed to join his brothers in the manufacture of illicit vernacular bourbon (those weren't their words for the stuff) if he made a downright good living year in and year out from what he got at Harrison for his fleece. The answer, if you troubled to ask him, was simply that the Chisms had been making the best drinking-whiskey in the Ozarks ever since Nail's grandaddy had come from Tennessee back in 18 and 39.

It was a family tradition, which Seth Chism had elevated to just about the acme of quality and repute and had instilled in his sons from the earliest they'd been able to plow the corn or fire the biler. Nail, Seth's middle boy, had been made superintendent of the biler at the age of fourteen and had become a professional moonshiner long before the day he became a captive audience for a traveling peddler, name of Eli Willard, who was trying to unload a pair of Cotswold lambs he'd been swapped for out of something in Kentucky.

In those days the village reached its top size, the closest Stay More ever came to being a real town, with the Ingledews running a big three-floor general store as well as the post office and the gristmill, and getting competition from no fewer than three other general stores; there was almost a genuine Main Street of the kind associated with the motion picture called a western (although the surrounding countryside looked nothing at all like the stark badlands of the westerns: it was too green, had too many shades of green, was too lush and too uplifting, the hills rising steep and pastured and forested and bluffed), and along this Main Street there were two doctors' offices and two dentists as well as Jim Tom Duckworth's law office and at least three blacksmiths with the latest tripod gear-driven quickblast forges, and even, by the time this story really gets going good, a bonafide bank waiting to be robbed, and around the corner you'd find such things as Murrison's sawmill and William Dill's wagon factory, making some of the best horse-drawn vehicles still competing with the just-arrived automobile.

Eli Willard hadn't yet discovered the automobile when he arrived in the thriving village with two Cotswolds in the back end of his wagon (a William Dill spring-platform model he'd bought at the factory his last trip to town, and reputedly driven to Connecticut and back without a broken wheel). Everyone in the Ozarks who did have sheep had a breed called American Merino, but the Cotswold, unbeknownst to Nail, who knew nothing about sheep at that point, is superior to the Merino for the production of wool.

The peddler Eli Willard was not in the business of purveying livestock; he just happened to have the two lambs this trip around, which actually was devoted to the selling of musical instruments, everything from parlor organs to Jew's harps. For thirty-five cents Nail also bought from him a harmonica, a fitting accompaniment to sheep-raising. It was an M. Hohner Marine Band Tremolo Echo, and Nail taught himself how to make it tremble and to make it echo, when he wasn't too busy teaching himself how to keep Cotswolds happy and healthy and reproductive. The trials and errors of this operation, had they been known to the other people of Stay More, would have made for all the jokes anyone would ever want to tell on Nail Chism, but he suffered his self-education in absolute privacy, and he practiced "Fisher's Hornpipe" and "Billy in the Low Ground" and "Sook Pied, Sook Pied, Come an' Git Yore Nubbins," in complete seclusion from any ears except those of his sheep, who seemed to appreciate him and would sometimes blaat along.

What did he look like? He was very tall, the loftiest of the Chism brothers, at six feet three inches, and muscular without seeming strong, with a shock of very light brown hair, not quite blond as the newspapers would describe it, stuck up in what folks chose to call his sheeplick. He had blue eyes. The *Arkansas Gazette*'s drawing of him in December of 1914, by their staff artist Viridis Monday, does not fairly represent him, with that head shaved of its prematurely whitening locks (he was not yet twenty-eight) and that splendid physique looking frail beneath its prison clothes. Only the eyes in the Monday drawing seem to be the Nail Chism that most of us remembered: pale, gentle, comical, inquisitive, curious, and brighter-than-you'd-like-to-think: certainly not the eyes of a man on his way to the electric chair. Nail Chism was nobody's fool. And yet there were those who liked to think that he was everybody's fool.

One of those was his brother-in-law Sewell Jerram, of Jasper, the county seat, some ten miles north of Stay More. Sewell, or Sull as everybody but his mother pronounced it, had been born in Stay More but thought of himself as a town boy, although Jasper back then was already what it still is: the smallest county seat in the state of Arkansas, with just a few hundred people, and being a town boy in a small village didn't leave Sull Jerram conspicuously different from a country boy; an outsider from, say, Little Rock wouldn't have been able to tell them apart. But Sull Jerram didn't know anything about farming, and the three brothers of Irene Chism, when Sull was courting her, got considerable amusement out of observing Sull's ignorance of country ways and customs.

Irene Chism was but a half-sister to Nail and his two brothers. Her mother, and senior by only fifteen years, was Nancy Nail Coe, whose father Jethro Nail, one of the first settlers of Newton County, had married a Choctaw Indian girl, making Nancy Nail a half-breed, and thus Irene and her brothers Waymon, Nail, and Luther were quarter-breed Indian, although the only thing about Viridis Monday's portrait of Nail to indicate such Indian ancestry is his somewhat long nose and his intense but blue eyes beneath their heavy, crowding eyebrows.

Nancy Nail had been taken to wife at the age of just fourteen by a Stay Moron named Columbus Coe, but she had been widowed at the age of sixteen, when Irene was an infant, and had inherited a homestead of eighty acres northeast of Stay More, which she was determined to manage on her own and succeeded in running—cornpatch, pigpen, cowlot, and orchard—for nearly a year before asking her neighbor, Seth Chism, for a little help with the heavy lifting. Seth was covetous of that cornpatch, a few acres to supplement his own, which all went to the making of his whiskey, and he proposed marriage to the young widow Nancy Nail Coe not so much out of desire for her as need of her cornpatch and her help running the still.

Waymon Chism was born just under two years after Irene, and they grew up together until Nail joined them. The three were in their teens, and had been joined by Seth and Nancy's last-born, little Luther, before their parents explained to them how it had come about that Irene was

9

only a half-sister, not a full sister. That made no difference to Waymon, and the only difference it made to Nail was to explain to him how Irene was sexually different from the three brothers: she had only half, or less than half, of whatever between-the-legs equipment the boys possessed. But then Irene began to acquire more than twice as much above-the-waist equipment, and Nail began to watch as his sister was courted by the town boy Sull Jerram.

Nail was Irene's favorite half-brother, the one she had given most of her attention and care in his upbringing, the one she (lacking a sister or a girlfriend) trusted with her secrets, and the one she chose to chaperone her whenever Sull Jerram came to call. In those days a girl never ever went off anywhere alone with a boy, not even walking together from the schoolhouse to home, not even walking together from Willis Ingledew's store to Jerram's store (owned by Sull's brother) down the road. It just wasn't done. A girl had to have someone else with her, even (lacking a sister or a girlfriend) her kid brother.

Country boys understood this, and nobody expected to get a girl alone by herself, or to find a girl alone by herself, much less, finding such a one, to speak to her. You had to be content to spark her as best you could with somebody eavesdropping, or at least with her sister or someone in the same room, or sitting on the next log, or walking a few paces behind. Maybe eventually, after you'd proposed to her and she had accepted and the date had been set for the wedding, you might get a chance to sit with her out on the porch or in the dogtrot for an hour or so without anybody else in sight, because the others would stay politely behind the door.

Maybe town boys didn't understand this. Sull Jerram always seemed annoyed when Nail tagged along on what passed for dates between Sull and Irene. Of course Sull was a good bit older: he was already twenty-five, they said, when he first came to Stay More to call on Irene when she was just sixteen, and presumably he'd had some experience with some of the town girls who didn't have the sense to keep from finding themselves alone with him. Lord knows what those town girls did. The stories were enough to turn your ears pink. It's very doubtful a person from Little Rock could see a bit of difference between a Jasper girl and a Stay More girl, except the former might be wearing shoes, but probably not. People wondered why Sull Jerram didn't just stay in Jasper.

10

But Irene Chism was a very pretty gal, and her above-the-waist fixtures were full and high and firm, and, as Nail would have been the first to tell you, she had a voice that could have beguiled the Devil himself: sweet and musical and colorful. Her voice was almost as if she were touching you and patting you and stroking you and sliding herself all over you. Possibly Sull Jerram didn't care about her voice, but he sure cared enough about all the rest of her to spend every minute of his free time trying to get Nail to wander off and leave them alone for half an hour.

And Sull Jerram seemed to have an awful lot of free time. Nobody knew for sure what he did for a living. Nobody asked him. People who visited Jasper from time to time reported that "he's jist one of them fellers who hangs out at the courthouse": not the old men who sit on benches in the shade of the courthouse yard all day long telling lies, and not the lawyers who seem to hurry from room to room telling bigger lies, but the men who are just loitering in the lobby or the hallways, leaning up against the wall talking to one another in hushed voices as if they were cooking up lies that could be translated into money.

"Yeah, I reckon ye could say Sull's cookin up mischief," Jim Tom Duckworth told Seth Chism when Jim Tom dropped by to get his demijohn refilled. Jim Tom was Stay More's own native-born lawyer, our representative to the courthouse, our spokesman and champion before the bar of justice. "But jist *whut*-all mischief he's into, I couldn't tell ye. I do know that he's aimin to see if he caint git hisself elected ass-essor, and I tell ye, once a man gits to be ass-essor, next thing you know he's runnin fer treasurer, and then watch out if he don't run fer sherf, or even jedge."

Whatever Sull Jerram was running for, it didn't claim any of the attention he devoted to pursuing Irene Chism, or to trying to get Nail to leave them alone for a little bit. Nail couldn't be bribed. He couldn't be threatened. He could be cajoled, that is, he would politely listen to cajolery, but he wouldn't necessarily respond to it.

The first words Sull Jerram ever spoke to Nail Chism were: "Go tell yore momma she's a-lookin fer ye."

And young, green Nail actually took several steps in the direction of carrying out this request before it dawned on him that it was a trick, a foolery of words; Sull and Irene were laughing at him. Some time later Nail was wary when Sull told him he'd seen a man just back up the road a little ways giving away puppies. "Hurry, and you'd catch him," Sull suggested, and Nail was almost out of sight, this time, before he realized it was just another trick.

Once, eventually, Sull Jerram told Nail that he and Irene and Nail, just the three of them, were going to walk up to a glade on the side of Ledbetter Mountain where there were a lot of snipes. A snipe is a kind of bird, Sull explained, although Nail wondered why a town boy would claim to know more ornithology than he himself knew, and he knew there weren't any snipes, not of the sandpiper sort, in the vicinity of Ledbetter Mountain. Sull explained that these snipes only migrated through at certain seasons, and there was this glade up yonder where them snipes liked to visit. Sull gave Nail a towsack made of burlap. "Now what we're gonna do is," Sull explained when they got to the glade, "is me and Irene are gonna go over thar in that bresh and wave our arms about and flush 'em out of thar, and you stand over yere with this yere sack, and when they come a-runnin, you jist herd 'em into the sack. See?"

"Birds don't run," Nail said. "They fly."

"Not these yere snipes," Sull said. "Now you jist do like I tell ye, and we'll have us a mess of good eatin fer supper tonight."

Nail watched them disappear, or almost. It is very bad luck to watch someone walk all the way out of sight. He had never seen anybody walk out of sight, least of all his sister Irene, who had rarely ever been out of his sight before, except when she'd gone out to the bushes on a call of nature. Maybe, he thought, waiting and turning aside so as not to watch them disappear, she's on another call of nature, kind of.

They did not return, nor were there any snipes or other birds, except a pair of prothonotary warblers. After half an hour Nail began to look for Irene and Sull, and then to call for his sister, but he got no answer. That night she apologized for the trick Sull had played on him.

"Where did you'uns go?" Nail asked. "What didje do?"

"Oh, honey," she said in her musical voice, "sometimes I jist need to git away from you." She asked him not to tell anybody else what had happened.

He was careful not to let her out of his sight again, and he was within earshot when he heard his mother start in to faulting Irene for being "knocked up," whatever that was. He listened. His mother began hollering.

Then she called for him, and he came, and she said, "Nail, chile, you was sposed to keep a eye on her and Sull, and watch 'em, and pick gooseberries, and take keer of her."

"I did," Nail lied.

His mother slapped him. It was the first time she had ever hit him in the face. His pappy had clobbered him frequently, but never before had she slapped his face. Irene protested in tears that it wasn't Nail's fault, that Sull had pulled one on him, that there wasn't no call to hit Nail for what Sull had done. But Nail didn't hang around to listen to the rest of it. He fled up the mountainside to a cavern by a waterfall and stayed there, meditating on the injustices of life in this world.

He didn't go to the wedding. It wasn't much of a thing anyhow, although his brothers told him of all the food he'd missed out on, pies you'd never heard of before. Nor did he join the shivaree that was thrown to tease the newlyweds. He couldn't stand the sight of Sull Jerram, and any man with any sense at all should have been able to tell from Nail's eyes that he couldn't stand the sight of him and wanted him off the earth, but Sull was a town boy and all he saw in Nail's eyes was a dumb, sullen kid.

Irene Chism Jerram miscarried her baby and never had any children after that. The years went by. Sull was elected assessor, and folks said the only thing that kept him from running for sheriff was he was too trigger-happy. Irene lived in Jasper but would come home about twice a year for a long visit until Sull came to get her. One of the times he came to get her, or tried to, was in an automobile, the first car to get that far. Eli Willard had driven the first automobile to appear in Stay More, but he hadn't been able to drive up Right Prong, because there wasn't any road, just a trail; when Sull Jerram tried it, there wasn't any road either, but he was mad to get Irene back and he drove over some boulders and plowed down some saplings to get up to the Chism place and spooked the livestock and, according to Seth Chism, spoiled a whole batch of sour mash a-brewing at the hooch plant. Irene wouldn't go with him. He stayed for a few days, arguing with her, trying to persuade Nancy or Seth to talk some sense into her, and, finally, appealing to Nail himself.

"You're the only one she listens to," Sull told Nail. "She don't listen to me nor nobody. You tell her that she caint spend the rest of her life up here on this mountain."

"Why caint she?" Nail asked. He wasn't a kid anymore and was half a head higher than Sull Jerram and still remembered as if it were yesterday the tricks Sull used to pull on him.

"Why, because, she's, don't you see? she's my wife, and if she wants to be my wife she's got to live in Jasper." Sull paused and studied Nail's eyes. "Don't that make no sense to ye? Do you want me to say it again?"

"If I was you," Nail said, "I'd git that piece of machinery back down the mountain while it will still roll. Come tomorrow, you might not find any wheels left on it."

But Sull Jerram did not go back to Jasper. Someone said he'd spent the night down at the Whitter place, and folks laughed and said the Whitters was probably the only ones who'd give him a bed, he was that low, *they* was that low, the Whitters. Some years before, not long after the turn of the century, the only criminal Stay More ever had, in its peaceful history, had come from that family. Ike Whitter had killed a man and terrorized the sheriff himself before a lynch mob led by John Ingledew ganged up on him and stopped him and lynched him. But Ike's father Simon Whitter still ran the farm and kept his head high and apologized to no man for having sired the only bully, felon, and cutthroat in the history of the village, and some of Ike's younger brothers threatened to become as wayward as he had been, while his baby sister Dorinda was growing up into a turtledove who, it was said, would drive men to rash deeds and early graves.

After a few nights at the Whitter place, Sull loaded all the Whitter boys into his vehicle and took them into Jasper to see the sights. Dorinda would have gone too, young as she was, if she'd had her way about it, but not even the Whitters, low as they were, would have condoned a young girl going off to the county seat with a married man and nobody to chaperone her but her brothers.

Dorinda threw a tantrum that almost cost her the friendship of her best girlfriend, who was me. The south benches of Ledbetter Mountain were all that separated the Whitter place from the Bourne place, and my dad Saltus Bourne was all that separated Simon Whitter from being the poorest farmer in Stay More. This isn't my story, and I'm not going to say anything more about my father, except that he and Simon Whitter were friends only because nobody else would have anything to do with them, just as people used to say of me that I was Dorinda's only friend because neither

14

she nor I was able to find anyone else as cheap or as bad or—they said this too—as beautiful as ourselves.

Oh, she was beautiful, there's no dispute of that, and those who wondered how a man as grossly repulsive as Ike Whitter could have had a baby sister as magnificent as Dorinda were the same who said that Saltus and Fannie Bourne must have adopted me. But I'm not going to say much else about myself, except that I was Dorinda's best friend, off and on, for all the years that this story took place. We always sat together in school at the same double-desk, even when Miss Blankinship kept on holding Dorinda back a grade after promoting me, because Dorinda simply didn't want to learn how to read, or couldn't, and we always put our arms around one another at recess, and kept them there, and in the days of our growing up and filling out we always compared ourselves in every little detail and told each other that you are more pretty than me.

Now, that day Sull Jerram took her brothers to Jasper and wouldn't take her, she had a fit and cussed and broke up some things in our playhouse. The back of her father's forty met the back of my father's forty at a basso profundo oak tree way up on the ridge of Ledbetter Mountain, and beneath that oak we'd long ago carried some planks of scrap lumber from Murrison's and stacked and nailed them against one another in a shelter against the wind and rain and winter chill, and inside that small space we had our secret home with a few shards of china and mostly stoneware, some chipped glasses and rag napkins, dolls we'd outgrown now and cast-off calendars for the years from 1908 to 1911, when we'd still been children. Dorinda was not a virgin. Sure, I've heard the jape that by definition hereabouts it's a five-year-old girl who can outrun her brothers, and Dorinda was way past five and had six brothers. Ironically, it was the only one of the six brothers who was younger than her. We had invited him to the playhouse, Lewis, when he was just ten, I was nearly twelve, and Dorinda was already twelve. Although she was older than me, I had "accomplished" one thing she had not: I had lost my virginity, and without the help of any brothers, for I had none. He was a cousin, and twice-removed at that, named Every Dill, a year older than me, a year ahead of me in school, and a virgin himself. It had been almost happenstance, not premeditated, one night when I'd been left alone at his folks' cabin while they and my folks and sisters and everybody else went off to a funeral. Nothing I'd care to go into here, except to say that Dorinda

15

knew about it and envied me it, and now was determined to lose hers too, even if to her own brother Lewis. He was the first boy ever to go inside our secret house, and Dorinda had dared me to do it with him since I already had experience, and I'd taken the dare but lost my nerve while he was trying to position himself atop me, and she'd said, when I got cold feet, that she'd do it herself, and Lewis didn't care which one of us it was, so long as he had a hole he could enter. Of course he wasn't old enough to make babies, but he was sure old enough to do it, in the sense of what they actually placed inside of what, and how they moved, and how long it lasted, and the noises they made. I watched, but they seemed to forget I was there. Watching them do it, I wondered if I had looked like that and sounded like that and smelled like that when I had done it with my cousin Every.

There was one big difference, I learned later. I had fooled around that one time with my cousin Every out of curiosity and pleasure and maybe even something approaching love. But Rindy had done it for revenge. She was bloody, and she showed the blood to her mother and told her parents who had done it, and Simon Whitter thrashed poor Lewis nearly to death, and later Rindy told me and laughed and said that was her way of getting even with Lewis because he was his mother's favorite and got extra dessert when she didn't.

So when Dorinda told me, much later, that she wanted Sull Jerram, wanted him real badly, my first reaction was to ask, "What's he done to ye that ye want to git back at him for?"

She laughed and said no, she wanted him because he was a big grown man and would really know how to do it and make her feel good. "Rindy," I said in exasperation, "he's married to Irene Chism, and has been for years and years, and besides he's old enough to be your father." She didn't care, and for a long time I thought it was just his automobile she lusted after, the same way, years later when automobiles became common, that most silly girls (myself included, once) couldn't tell the difference between a boy and his car.

Whatever it was that Sull Jerram took her brothers to Jasper for, they began spending most of their time there, hanging out, if not in the actual corridors of the courthouse, somewhere in the vicinity where mischief was a-cooking. Sull Jerram ran for the office of county judge in 1913, and Irene

16

moved back to Jasper and lived with him during the campaign. Now, I don't know about other states, but in Arkansas a county judge is just a kind of administrator, not a magistrate, no, not in any way a legal arbitrator; all he judges is whether or not a road ought to be fixed up or a new roof put on the jail. But he's the most powerful politician. Dorinda's brothers scoured the county on Sull's behalf, and some folks said that they used coercion and bribery and ballot-stuffing. Most of Stay More voted for Sull's opponent, and Sull didn't like us for it, and he never let us forget it after he was elected.

That election made him into "Judge" Sull Jerram at the same time it offered him a way to get rich. It was the same general election when most of the counties of Arkansas voted dry, six years in advance of national Prohibition. Newton County had always been dry, and always would be, so there was always a good local market for Chism's Dew, and always had been, and there still is. When the first Chism came from Tennessee in 1839, he didn't intend to break any laws or make a lot of money, he just wanted to do what he knew how to do: make good sour mash drinking-whiskey. There was a time when Seth Chism had some trouble in the 1870s with the government for the manufacture, possession, and sale, but apart from that the Chisms had been moonshining through four generations with impunity, free hands, and honesty. No sheriff of Newton County would come near the Chism place, as long as the product was sold on the premises, which it always had been, or at least not any farther from the premises than "downtown" Stay More, where, in the autumn, a man could buy a pumpkin from little Luther Chism on Saturday afternoon and find a refilled jar or jug inside of it.

Chism's Dew had a reputation beyond the boundaries of Newton County, and there were even Little Rock politicians, lawyers, and bankers who obtained quantities of it for their personal use and to entertain guests, but the Chisms had never made any effort to market their commodity outside of Stay More . . . until the 1913 state "drought" created a demand, and the politicians up at Jasper saw a way to get rich from it. At the same time Sull Jerram became county judge, a friend of his got elected the new sheriff, a fellow from somewhere over in eastern Newton County named Duster Snow, who had worked his way up from assessor and surveyor, with a couple of years as a deputy revenue marshal, so he knew the liquor trade inside

17

out. We got a new county clerk and a new county treasurer, and Judge Sull Jerram found himself presiding over a gang of courthouse liars and ruffians and mischief-makers who lost no time in cooking up a surefire scheme for getting rich: marketing Chism's Dew to the outside world.

Judge Jerram was still Seth Chism's son-in-law, which didn't entitle him to a better price than anyone else—he paid the same two dollars per gallon—but he began to buy up every last drop that Seth and his boys could make, as fast as they could make it, and Sull had it hauled off to Jasper, where it was loaded onto a big newfangled vehicle called a motor-truck and taken off to Harrison. The Chisms ran out of containers; every jug and gallon demijohn in Stay More had been rinsed and refilled and sold to Sull Jerram, and all the jugs and demijohns that he could bring in from Jasper, Parthenon, Spunkwater, Swain, Nail, Deer—whatever community might have a few—he rounded them up and the Chisms filled them and they found their way to Harrison. When all the jugs and demijohns in Newton County had disappeared, they began to use bean pots, cream pitchers, stone jars, wash pitchers, chicken fountains, soup tureens, punchbowls, compotes, gravy boats, even slop jars or thundermugs.

The Chisms ran out of corn. Or, rather, the Ingledews' gristmill could not furnish any more cornmeal, having ground up everything the Chisms had raised. My father even made a little pin money selling the hard-dent corn out of his corncrib, and so did everyone else, until all of that was gone, and there were a lot of hungry hogs and chickens that winter. Sull Jerram arranged with whoever was buying the finished product in Harrison to start supplying the raw product, and the motortruck that was transporting the load of containers into Harrison would return with a load of corn or cornmeal.

What the Chisms didn't know then was that Sull Jerram and his court-house gang were buying the Chisms' whiskey for two dollars a gallon and sending it to Harrison, where they were getting four, five, and then six dollars a gallon for it.

But one night in the spring of 1914, the Boone County sheriff and his deputies stopped that motortruck at the Boone County line and confiscated a whole load of whiskey, arrested and jailed the driver, and kept the motortruck. Sull Jerram's entire bootlegging operation came to a halt. Our new sheriff Duster Snow talked to the Boone County sheriff, but the latter was incorruptible. Judge Jerram tried to work out a deal with the Boone

County judge, but the latter was, while not incorruptible, unswayed by Sull's terms.

Seth Chism, visiting his daughter Irene and her husband the judge at their new Jasper house, had been impressed with their improved standard of living. He himself had built a new barn, put a new roof on his still, replaced his thirty-five-gallon pot still with a hundred-gallon copper still, and replaced the old bedrock furnace with a snail shell furnace, all with the profits from his increased production. And his wife Nancy took to wearing Sears, Roebuck dresses to church. Seth appreciated these improvements, and he was sympathetic when he heard about the confiscation of the motortruck, and he said he'd talk to his boy Nail when Judge Jerram suggested that Nail might be willing to transport a load of whiskey inside his wagon of sheep's wool, which was going to Harrison anyway.

Nail said he didn't have any room, that his fleece wagon was loaded down with fleece and the axles would break if he took on a cargo of concealed whiskey. He was just telling the truth. He didn't really object to his brother-in-law's bootlegging, although he had resented the extra time he'd had to spend working the still, time spent away from his sheep, who needed him, especially now that shearing time had come. Nail liked making whiskey, and he liked drinking it, and he liked selling it, or he liked seeing his father sell so much of it that the farmplace was getting some improvements. But he just couldn't see his way to risking a broken axle or two by carrying a load of whiskey inside the load of fleece.

"You're jist afraid of gittin caught," Sull Jerram taunted him.

"No, I aint afraid of that," Nail protested. "Who'd stop me anyhow?"

"What's wrong with makin two trips?" Sull wanted to know. "Or twenty, if you have to?"

"Yeah," Seth said to his son, "you don't have to take it all at once, and you could bring us back a load of corn."

So Nail agreed to take a load to Harrison inside his load of fleece, although he'd be delivering only half as much fleece as the wool agent was expecting, and he'd have to explain that to the wool agent, and he'd have to deliver and unload the whiskey beforehand. He took his kid brother Luther for company and whatever help he might need, the two of them riding side by side on the buckboard the long trip, Nail telling the boy tales or entertaining them both with his harmonica, playing "Red Wing," "Turkey in the Straw," and "Paddy on the Turnpike."

They didn't have any problems on the trip into Harrison; but coming home, with the wagon piled high with sacks of cornmeal, a wheel broke and came off, and while they were trying to repair it, a sheriff's deputy rode up and offered some help and then observed, "Thet shore is a mighty heavy load of corn you'uns is haulin. Whar ye headin with all such as thet?"

Luther, who was fifteen, answered politely, "Stay More," before his brother could nudge him into silence.

The deputy laughed and said, "I hear tell Newton County is plumb out of corn. The eatin kind, that is." The deputy helped them fix the wheel, and then he said, "I jist hope you fellers aint aimin to bring none of this here corn back to Boone County in another form. The sherf is real sot in his ways and he'd th'ow ye in jail so hard you'd never git out."

They drove on and crossed back into Newton County. On the last stretch of road between Parthenon and Stay More they met Judge Sull Jerram in his automobile. Sull didn't stop. He only waved, and he had a girl with him. The girl was Dorinda Whitter, on her way to Jasper at last. A cloud of thick dust billowed out from the rear end of the Model T and obscured the disappearance of the couple.

"Rindy," I said to her later, "you were jist out of your fool haid. Don't you know that everbody in Stay More is talkin about ye?" I guess I knew better than anyone else, except Miss Blankinship, just how dumb Dorinda could be.

"You should've seen them boys over to Jasper," she said. "They hung their mouths open like they never seen a pair of tits before! And I jist wiggled my bosom at 'em! And Judge Sull, he jist took me ever place like he owned the town, and I do believe he does!"

There were some folks, later, who speculated that Nail Chism had had a crush on Dorinda for a long time. If that was true, he was certainly keeping it to himself. As far as I know, he never spoke to her before that June. Some folks were inclined to wonder if he had been "following" her, or at least itching for her. The fact that he was, at twenty-seven, still a bachelor did not of itself raise any eyebrows; we had plenty of single men in Stay More. It ran in families, even: all of the sons of banker John Ingledew were unmarried, six of the most eligible and handsome bachelors in town, and not one of them could get up his nerve to court a girl, let alone propose to one, and all six of them were past marrying age, except for maybe Raymond, the youngest, and I had my eye on him and was cooking up ways to get him to speak to me, or at least notice me. Nail Chism wasn't like the Ingledew brothers, who were congenitally so shy of any female they couldn't talk to their own sister Lola; at least Nail was able to talk to Irene . . . and he did talk to her and asked her if she knew that Sull Jerram was fooling around with Dorinda Whitter, and Dorinda not but thirteen. Irene told her brother that all she knew was what everybody else seemed to be talking about.

Nail found Sull at the courthouse, and right there in the lobby, within earshot of lawyer Jim Tom Duckworth and Sheriff Duster Snow and whoever else was paying them any attention, Nail told Sull, "I aint runnin any more goods fer ye."

"That so?" Sull said. "Got skeert bad this run, huh?"

"Naw, but me and Luther did have a little talk with a Boone County deppity."

Jim Tom and the Sheriff moved a little closer, to hear better, but Nail didn't elaborate upon his conversation with the deputy. Sull said, "Well, Nail, son, I'm sorry to tell ye, but you aint got any choice. Everbody's dependin on ye to run that stuff."

"Find somebody else to depend on," Nail said calmly, but he was beginning to get angry.

"Aint nobody else with a wagon full of wool," Sull said.

"I want ye to stop sparkin Dorinda," Nail said.

Sull laughed. "You sweet on her?"

"Naw, but I'm sweet on Irene, and I don't want ye treatin her like that."

"Yo're welcome to Irene," Sull said. "Nobody else wants her."

Nail hit Sull. According to Jim Tom, who told it later around Stay More, Nail just clenched a fist and lifted it faster than anybody could watch and caught Sull under the chin with it and lifted him about a foot off the floor and slammed him up against the wall. Just one punch, and Sull sort of peeled down the wall and into a heap on the floor. Nail turned and walked off, and Jim Tom and Duster Snow lifted Sull into a chair and worked him over to get him awake, and to pacify him Sheriff Snow said to Sull, "I'll have a little talk with ole Seth fer ye." And that night the sheriff

21

came to Stay More for the first time and rode his horse up to the Chism place up there on the mountain and sat on the porch with Seth Chism until well past dark, and even spent the night, at Seth's invitation.

The next morning, as the sheriff was saddling his horse, Nail Chism came down from the pastures where he'd spent the night with his sheep, and walked right up to Duster Snow and said, "Sheriff, you and Sull aint about to make me run any more goods fer ye."

"We'll jist see about that, son," Duster Snow said.

"Yeah," said Seth Chism to Nail, "you'd best listen to what I got to tell ye, boy. We don't want to make Mr. Snow mad. He could bust up our still, ye know."

Nail became very angry. "Go ahead and dust it, Buster!" he snarled at the sheriff, but corrected himself: "Go ahead and bust it, Duster! You bust our still, and I'll tell the federal law the names of everbody who's been runnin liquor to Harrison."

"Reckon yo're under arrest, boy," Duster informed him. The sheriff arrested Nail on a charge of assault and battery against the county judge, Sull, and took Nail into Jasper and put him into that big stone jail that's still there, off the square. Jim Tom tried to bail him out but couldn't get Nail to meet the condition: to retract his threat to expose the bootleggers to the federal law. So the sheriff let Nail stew for a week in the jailhouse. Jim Tom said the courthouse politicians, of which he was not one himself, were scared of Nail. The politicians, especially the county judge himself, were scared Nail might carry out the threat, he might try to contact Raiding Deputy Collector John T. Burris of the U.S. Revenue Service, or (they hoped Nail was too ignorant to know of the existence of the legendary Burris) he might at least have a chat with Isaac Stapleton, Stay More's own former deputy collector and onetime assistant to Burris, recently retired from a long career of working downstate busting up stills in Perry and Scott counties. If Stapleton told Nail how to contact Burris, that might blow the lid off the bootlegging operation.

Nail said he wouldn't have minded staying in the Jasper jail, awful as it was, except that there was nobody to take care of his sheep. His brothers Waymon and Luther visited him, and he tried to explain to them how to do the many little jobs that a shepherd must handle in the month of May, but it was clear that Waymon and Luther didn't know anything about sheep. The law couldn't keep Nail in the Jasper jail forever, and Jim Tom

22

convinced Sull and the courthouse gang of politicians of that, so they "released him on his own recognizance," whatever that meant, but first the entire courthouse gang took him into the jury room and sat around the table with him and talked to him for half the night, and then Sull Jerram told him they would let him go if he'd keep his mouth shut.

But Nail refused to make any promises.

———

"Oh, Latha, he *loves* me!" Dorinda exclaimed to me one morning in June on our way to school. It was the last week of the seventh grade for us, and Miss Blankinship was quitting after that, and we'd get us a new teacher the next year, and we could hardly wait to see her go, and meanwhile the weather was beautiful and cool for that time of year, although it was very dry and hadn't rained since May 4th and wouldn't rain again for the rest of the summer.

"Who does?" I asked. I wasn't sure but what she might have heard some of the gossip about Nail Chism having a crush on her, as his motive for hitting Sull Jerram.

"Sull!" she said. "The *judge*! He told me so! Well, he didn't come right out and use that *word*, but he said to me, says, 'Rindy, sugar babe, you shore make my ole heart beat *fast*!' and guess what? He plans to up and leave that Irene for good!"

"Rindy honey sister sweety dear," I said as nicely as I could, "you have just got to be *careful*. I know in my bones that a feller like Sull Jerram just wants to get *under your dress*."

"So?" she said. "I aint skeert. He'd do it real nice, and I'd even enjoy it myself, I bet ye."

"And you'd find yourself swole up with a woodscolt!"

"Then he'd dist *have* to marry me!"

"He's already married, you fool!"

But trying to talk some sense into Dorinda Whitter was like teaching a kitten to eat apples. She didn't give a hoot what the world thought of her, and I doubt she cared for my opinions either. When we were still children, she had said to me, "You're whole lots smarter than me, and that's how come I lak ye so, but dist don't never try to tell me what to do." No use trying to convince her that she was pretty enough to get the best husband in the country if she'd only take her time and behave herself instead of chasing after the first man with an auto to come to town. Sure, Sull Jerram was handsome and sightly, and smart and smooth, and now he was rich to boot, but I wouldn't have gone into the bushes with him if he'd had three silver balls!

A few days later, after school let out, Dorinda and I were taking a shortcut up through the woods toward our playhouse on the south slope of Ledbetter Mountain. There's an old cowpath runs up through that copse of chanting walnuts, and we were just tripping along one behind the other up that cowpath when here come Nail Chism, nearly running over us, except he wasn't running, just walking the way he did, with long, gangling strides.

"Howdy, girls," was all he said, and grinned bashfully in that woman-shy way that bachelors have.

Rindy and I were so astonished to find somebody on that old cowpath in the woods that we didn't say anything, and he walked around us and went on his way, and we went on ours, but Rindy kept looking back over her shoulder, as if he might have turned, and once when she did that I challenged her: "You think he's follerin us?"

"Shhh," she hushed me, and whispered, "I *know* he's follerin us!"

I said, "Why would he do that?"

"Shhh! Why do you *think*, you silly?!" she whispered, and said, "Ess go!" and began running. We ran all the way up the hill out of the woods and into the meadow and kept running until we reached our playhouse. We got ourselves inside of it, and Rindy knelt at the one little window and peered out, panting and watching, panting and watching. I looked around me, at the poor interior of our old playhouse, and realized that we had outgrown it and would soon be having to give it up.

"Nail Chism wouldn't foller us," I declared.

"You don't think so?" she demanded. "Then tell me who's that, Miss Smarty! Santy Claus?" She pointed, and there, down at the edge of the woods, edge of the meadow, far off, stood a man. He was just looking up the hillside toward our playhouse. My heart skipped a couple of beats. Was it Nail? He wasn't close enough to tell for sure, and you couldn't tell by his clothes: the men all dressed alike in blue denim overalls and a store shirt and a felt hat. Even those courthouse politicians dressed that way. He just stood there, looking in our direction. We waited. I said to her that whoever it was, he wouldn't come up to our playhouse and bother us, because there were two of us and we could handle him, but I think I was just talking to myself, not to her.

Finally he disappeared back into the woods. We stayed in the playhouse for a long time, but we were too old for play, and when we left it, we were leaving it for good. Dorinda asked me if I'd come spend the night with her. Sure, I said. "Go ask your mother," she said. I said she could come with me while I asked my mother. She said no, she'd go on home and do her chores and tell her mother to set out another plate for supper, and for me to just come on whenever I was able.

I went home and told my mother I wanted to spend the night at Dorinda's. My mother didn't mind, but I had to slop the hogs and milk the cow before I went. I did, and then I went to Dorinda's.

The Whitter place was set back up into a hollow on the west side of Ledbetter Mountain: just a two-room log cabin that had a couple of sleeping-lofts and a shed behind the kitchen, which was Dorinda's room. There were several horses tied to cedar posts in the front yard, and I assumed they were just the riding-beasts of the Whitter boys, but then I remembered the Whitters were too poor to own more than one horse.

One of those horses belonged to Doc Plowright, and he was inside. Another belonged to Hoy Murrison, who was a Stay More sheriff's deputy, and a third was that of Alonzo Swain, our justice of the peace. While I was there, some other horses arrived, with men on them.

When I said to Mrs. Whitter, "Did Rindy tell ye, I've come to stay the night?" she looked at me as if I'd said I was flying off to the moon, and she ignored me while she told the new arrivals, "Doc and Hoy is with her in yonder house." And the new arrivals climbed the porch and went in. Then she looked back at me, not as if I'd said I was flying off to the moon but as if I had returned from it, and she seemed to recognize me, and said, "Latha, hon, my baby has been ravaged."

Then she began to cry.

———

Sheriff Snow sat with me on the edge of the porch. He asked me to tell him what time it was I'd seen her last, and I said I'd just have to guess, it was maybe 4:30 P.M. He asked me to tell him what we'd been doing, and I told him we'd been to our playhouse. He asked where the playhouse was. Dorinda and I had sworn each other to eternal secrecy that we would never tell anyone else about the location of our playhouse, and I couldn't tell Sheriff Snow. I think I told him, "Up yonderways," and gestured vaguely toward the east.

"Did you see anybody else up in that vicinity?" he asked, pronouncing it *vi*-sinitty. There was a man, I said. He was a right far ways off and I couldn't see him too well, and I didn't know who he was. "What was he doin?" the sheriff asked. Just standing there, down below, a good ways off, staring toward our playhouse. And then he went away. "You didn't see him good enough to tell who he was?" the sheriff persisted. I shook my head and shook it again. "You didn't think it was maybe Nail Chism?" he suggested.

"What makes you think it was Nail Chism?" I wanted to know.

"You let me ast the questions, gal," he said sternly. "Did you think it could've been him?"

It could've been, I allowed.

He asked me to tell him my full name and exactly where I lived, and then he said to me, "Do you understand what awful thing was done to thet pore girl?" I nodded my head, uncertainly because I didn't know if he meant did I know what rape was or did I understand how awful it had been. Sheriff Snow said, "Iffen I was you, and anybody ast me who done it, I'd tell 'em Nail Chism." I started to protest, but the sheriff said with conviction, "He was the one who done it, no doubt about it. No doubt whatsoever. He's already confessed. Now you jist tell 'em he's the one you saw if anybody asts ye. Hear me?"

They wouldn't let me see her. Doc Plowright gave her something to calm her down and make her sleep, and she slept a long time. I didn't get to see her until several days later, when Jim Tom Duckworth drove me in his buggy (with my older sisters Barb and Mandy as chaperones) into Jasper to the courthouse. "Do you gals know what a grand jury is?" Jim Tom asked us. We said we didn't, although Barb often was ready to claim she knew everything. Jim Tom explained, "This here grand jury aint gonna find nobody guilty, or even innocent neither, as far as that goes. There's twenty-three of these fellers and they jist sit and listen, as long as it takes, and it aint really a trial, jist a kind of preliminary trial to find out if we have to have us a real trial. I don't know why they're called grand, tell ye the honest truth. Aint nothin grand about 'em, they jist sit and listen, and some of 'em fall asleep, and some of 'em are kind of drunk to start with, and they aint a jury at all with the power to decide pore Nail's fate, they'll jist see if they think he needs to be in-dited. 'In-dited' means you aint guilty of nothin, you've jist been accused of somethin that maybe you didn't do. So, Latha, gal, I'd jist 'preciate it iffen ye'd tell those fellers exactly what ye tole me: that you couldn't tell if it was Nail or not."

I wasn't called until late in the afternoon, and, just as Jim Tom had said, by that time many of the so-called grand jurors were already asleep or drunk or just not paying much attention to me. Before my turn came, I got to watch the rest of it. I watched with wonder as my best friend was led into the room, wearing her only good Sunday dress but walking as if it pained her to move, and wincing at every step. I listened with wonder as she told what had happened. And I began to question whether she was capable of giving the performance that it seemed to be. It seemed to me somebody else was speaking through her mouth.

She pointed at me when she said, "I left Latha yonder and started out towards our place, stayin far as I could git away from the woods where we'd seen Nail dist before. But to git to our place, I had to go through this yere kind of thicket of ellum saplins, and there he was! He dist jumped right out at me, and he says, 'Now, don't ye holler, or I'll crack ye on the haid with this yere rock.' And I seen he had a sharp-pointed rock about this big in one of his hands. He says, 'Now I tell ye what I want fer ye to do, and ye better do it, or I'll break yore haid open with this yere rock.' And he reached in his pants and pulled out his thing, which was this long, and he stuck it straight out at my face and said, 'Now, Rindy, you better suck on this, and not stop till I tell ye, or I'll bash in yore haid.' And I said, 'Nail Chism, you couldn't make me suck on that thing if you gave me a million dollars,' and he said, says, I think he said, 'You dist better, iffen you know what's good fer ye,' and he grabbed my hair and pulled my head up against his thing and tried to get me to open my mouth, but I wouldn't so he took that rock and tapped me real hard right on top of my haid, I've still got the bump right here, see? and it nearly knocked me out and I said 'Oh!' and when I said 'Oh!' my mouth opened up like this, and he poked that thing right inside and then he commenced running it in and out of my mouth, and I was so dizzy from gittin cracked on the haid I didn't think to bite him, and he dist kept on jabbin it into my mouth on and on until all of this hot wet stuff come gushin down my goozle . . ."

The so-called grand jurors were all wide awake and paying very close

27

attention, and some of them were fidgeting in their chairs, and one of them, I swear, was letting some spittle dribble down his chin. Mr. Thurl Bean, the prosecutor, asked, "Was that *all* he done?" as if it hadn't been enough.

"Oh, no!" Dorinda said. "That was dist the start. He had dist started. He says to me, says, 'Now it's my turn to do you,' and he made me lie down and lifted up my dress and mashed his mouth right down between my legs and started in to lickin me up and down and all over, right here. He done that for a good long while till he was satisfied, and then he taken his thing and put it where his mouth had been and give a real hard push, but . . ." (Dorinda seemed trying very hard to cry, and not doing it convincingly) ". . . but I'd never been done like that afore, and he couldn't git it in easy. He kept on and kept on, a-pushin and a-shovin that thing, and had my back up against this ellum saplin, and he took a deep breath and grunted hard and somethin broke, and there was blood, and he had that thing, this long, all the way up in me, as fur as he could git . . ."

When it came time for Jim Tom Duckworth to ask her questions, Jim Tom wanted to know only two things: One, he said, was she real hundred-percent sure about that sharp rock business? because it seemed to Jim Tom, "and you grand gentlemen of the jury has got to agree, that a big stout powerful feller like Nail Chism wouldn't need no sharp rock to threaten her with, he could manage her with his bare hands, or leastways with that there bowie knife that he always carried on his belt, so jist what is this here rock business?" And Dorinda swore it was a sharp, heavy rock, this big. Well, secondly, was Dorinda absolutely certain that she "had never been done like that afore," because, after all, here she was, what? *thirteen* years of age, "and as everbody knows that's kind of old not to have no experience whatsoever in the loss-of-virginity business, at least not where I come from, which is Stay More, same place where she comes from, and her with six brothers . . ."

"Objection!" hollered Mr. Thurl Bean, and began to rant that it was a crime to say such things, and the defense attorney had better watch his mouth or he'd find himself in-dited for public indecency and obscenity, and Mr. Bean didn't know about Stay More, but where *he* came from, Mt. Judea east of here where folks is God-fearing and moral and law-abiding, it wasn't at all uncommon to find virgins who were fourteen or even fifteen.

Doc J. M. Plowright of Stay More was called to testify. He had been one of our two physicians as long as I could remember, since he'd assisted at my birth and looked at me when I'd had measles and diphtheria and impetigo. He had, he said, examined the young lady immediately after the alleged misfortune had occurred, that is to say, as soon as Simon Whitter had come and got him, less than an hour after the said violation had happened, and he found her in a condition of near-shock as a result of the imputed assault and discovered that "she still had, no doubt about it, some feller's jism a-tricklin down her laig, and she had a sure-enough lump on her haid like from a rock bouncin offen it, and yes, it sure did look like her maidenhead had been took, she sure wasn't no virgin no more, and the blood was still fresh all over the gash."

"Gash?" said Mr. Thurl Bean, and became indignant. "You mean that monster there done went and inflicted a *cut* on the pore gal?"

"Naw," Doc Plowright said, turning crimson. "I was jist referrin to her slit, I mean, her, you know, her natural openin."

When I was summoned, I had to put my hand on the Bible and take an oath, and give my name and age and address, and please tell the court how long I'd known the victim. Then Mr. Thurl Bean asked me to tell what had happened that afternoon in my own words to the best of my ability and recollection, and I told everything I knew, except the precise location of our playhouse. When I finished, Mr. Thurl Bean said, "Now, gal, this yere man that you saw from the winder of yore dollhouse, is he a-settin anywheres in this room?"

I looked around. "He could be," I said.

"Which'un is he?" asked Mr. Bean.

I pointed at Jim Tom Duckworth. "It could've been him." I pointed at Nail Chism. "Or it could've been him." Then I pointed at Judge Sull Jerram, who was sitting in the audience, and left my finger sticking in his direction. "But for all I know, it was jist as likely *him*."

He asked me some more questions, trying to get me to say for sure that it was Nail, and making me tell over again that it had been Nail we'd seen in the woods not long before. But he couldn't get me to swear that it was Nail who had been looking at our playhouse, and as I was leaving the stand to return to my seat, Sheriff Duster Snow said to me out of the side of his mouth, "You forgot what you was tole." He looked fierce.

Finally Nail Chism was put on the stand. His wrists were fastened together with handcuffs, and nobody had bothered to comb his hair for him, so it stuck up and out in several sheeplicks. He seemed very sad, and I thought at first that maybe he had done it and was feeling guilty about it.

But he denied everything. That cowpath, he said, was the way he used every afternoon to get from his sheep pastures up on Ledbetter Mountain down into the village. Every afternoon this time of year, when the weather was nice, he'd go down to the Ingledew store and sit on the porch with the other fellers, whittling and spitting, just passing the time, you know, and watching the world go by, and swapping dogs and knives and tales, they've been doing that in Stay More ever since there was a storeporch to set on. He had gone straight from his sheep pasture down to Ingledew's, and sure he had seen the two girls, Dorinda Whitter and Latha Bourne, on that cowpath, and to the best of his recollection he had said howdy to them and gone on. He sure had not doubled back and waited to rape Dorinda. That was a baldface lie, and he didn't know why a sweet young girl like her would make up such a story, or, if she wasn't making it up, why she'd try to put the blame on him. She didn't have anything against *him*, now, did she?

"Not before," said Mr. Thurl Bean, and then he said, "Mr. Chism, let me ast ye a question: do you lak women?"

"What-all kind of question is that?" Nail wanted to know.

"Answer it. Do ye or don't ye?"

"Why, shore, same as the next feller," Nail replied.

"Maybe more'n the next feller," Mr. Bean put in. "You bein a bachelor-feller and unmarried and all. Would ye say that you've got a normal *desire* for the fair sex? Don't ye git to feelin some *passion* ever wunst in a while?" Nail just stared at him, not knowing how to reply. "Or is it true," Mr. Bean said, "that you have been known to obtain carnal gratification from one of yore sheep, now and again?"

"Objection!" said Jim Tom Duckworth, and he began to holler that the prosecuting attorney had better watch his mouth and not go imputing imputations against his client that were not substantiated by bonafide facts, and that maybe those folks over around Mt. Judea got their jollies from screwing ewes, but Stay More people had better sense, not to mention taste.

The judge, or magistrate (he wasn't Judge Villines, our circuit judge, but just a j.p.), had to pound his gavel for order, and then he sustained Jim Tom's objection and instructed the prosecutor to make an effort to stick to the facts.

Mr. Thurl Bean eventually gave up trying to prove that Nail Chism was a sex maniac, and asked Nail if it was not true that he had publicly accosted Judge Sewell Jerram yonder right here in the halls of this seat of justice and told said Judge Jerram to leave his said girlfriend Dorinda alone.

"I never called her my girlfriend," Nail said.

"But you tole said Judge Jerram yonder to leave her alone."

"Yeah, 'cause he's married to my sister and hadn't no business foolin around with Dorinda."

"Or maybe ye was jist jealous," Mr. Bean said, and without giving Nail a chance to deny it he turned and said, "Thar you are, grand gents of the jury, thar is yore motive: Nail Chism was sweet on that gal, he was green as a gourd with jealousy, and he let it be known, and then he went and done that vile abomination unto her."

Jim Tom Duckworth called as witnesses the men who gathered every afternoon on Ingledew's storeporch, one of whom, Fentrick Bullen, testified, "I could set my watch by the minute that ole Nail comes down to the store of an evenin, and he was right on time. He never had no dalliance."

One by one the sitters of the storeporch, fifteen in number, testified that Nail Chism had arrived at the store at exactly his usual time. But the grand jury voted, ten to nine, with four abstentions (two drunk, two asleep), to indict Nail Chism for sodomy, perversion, assault, battery, and sexual violation of a female beneath the age of consent and against her will. Trial was set for August.

The next time I saw Dorinda was not at our playhouse (we never went there again, at least not together) but on the front porch of my house, one afternoon when she came over, bringing with her the 1914 Sears, Roebuck and Company Consumer's Guide, which had been loaned to her by somebody in Jasper. She said she wanted my help in picking out a couple of dresses and a pair of shoes. It wasn't play-like picking either, not the kind of wishing I did whenever I could see one of those catalogs. She had ten dollars actual cash money. I'd never *seen* that much real money in my entire life.

"Where did you git it, Rindy?" I inquired.

"They gave it to me," she said.

"Uh-huh," I said, and I waited a long time for her to elaborate. She began to leaf through the pages of the catalog, sighing and cooing at the pictures of dresses, and sometimes asking me to read for her what it said under the picture. After doing this for a while, I said, "They *who*?"

"Mr. Snow and them," she said.

"The sheriff gave you ten dollars?" I asked. "What for?"

"To pay for my dresses and shoes, silly," she said. "Don't ye know, I've got to go to that there trial, come August? What does it say under this yere one?"

" 'Made of finest quality white lawn.' How's the knot on your head?"

She raised her hand and felt the top of her head. "It's gone, I reckon. What's 'lawn'?"

"Sheer linen. Did you really git raped, Rindy?"

"Yep, I did. What does this one say?"

" 'A handsome white India lawn wrapper.' You don't want that one, it'd be too hot for August. Was it really Nail?"

"Then what about this one?"

"That's taffeta silk and would make you look like a whore. Honest, did Nail really rape you?"

"Latha, ladybird lollypop, we swore we'd never ever tell a story to each other. Didn't we? So don't you git me to tell ye a story."

In July most of Nail Chism's sheep took sick and began to die. He was in that stone jail at Jasper, and although Waymon and Luther visited him and described to him the sheep's symptoms, their diarrhea or scours, their choking and catarrh, their pining and staggers, Nail was helpless to do aught but instruct Waymon and Luther in comforts and solaces that didn't even cure the sheep of whatever was ailing them, and it takes a shepherd to comfort and solace. But the best shepherd can't produce rainfall, which is what we desperately needed. The sheep were thirsting to death, and so was the grass.

In August the men who sat on Willis Ingledew's storeporch complained of the drought, and the heat, and they spent some time speculating about the upcoming trial, and they devoted only a small bit of discussion to what was happening far across the sea: some duke had been murdered in Austria, and the Russians and Germans were starting a fracas, and the English and French were getting into it too. The Jasper newspaper carried very little national news, let alone international news, and throughout that month of August, as the Germans invaded Belgium and the French invaded Lorraine, nobody in Stay More knew that the whole world was starting the Great War to End All Wars.

On a Monday in August the men on the Ingledew storeporch rode their horses or their mules, or drove their spring wagons if they had them, sometimes with families in them, to Jasper for the trial, to watch if not to participate. Jim Tom had explained to them it wouldn't be any use for all of the storeporch crowd to keep saying the same thing over and over, that Nail was there at his usual time; three or four repetitions of that testimony were all that the court would tolerate.

I rode in with Jim Tom again, and this time my father and mother came along too, although it turned out they couldn't get into the courthouse, it was so crowded. My father had been impressed that the county sheriff himself had paid us a visit the night before. Duster Snow had even had supper with us, unexpectedly, because he arrived at suppertime and Momma had to be polite. After my father and Duster had eaten (in those days the custom was always that the women and girls would wait until after the menfolk had finished before having their own supper), the sheriff said he wanted to talk to me while I ate; maybe he figured I couldn't talk back to him with my mouth full.

Before I was separated from my parents at the courthouse, my father squeezed my arm very hard and said, "Gal, don't you go and bring no embarrassment upon us. You do what the sheriff tole ye to do, hear me?"

I knew I would be punished for it (and I was, later), but I disobeyed my father and the sheriff: I refused to tell the court that Nail Chism was the man I had seen looking at our playhouse. Judge Villines himself started in to asking me questions, helping out the prosecutor, but I swore the man I saw looking at our playhouse was not Nail Chism.

Fat lot of good it did. Dorinda Whitter sat there in her pure-white Sears, Roebuck lawn dress and told her story again as if she had been rehearsing it every spare minute of July, with somebody helping her rehearse; as if she had been practicing how to cry, and she did a real good job of crying. There was a lot of crying in the audience when she cried. And a lot of gasping. And more than one of the jurors had spittle dribbling down his chin. There were just twelve men this time, and none of them were sleeping or drunk, at least not while testimony was given and the sum-mations were made, all in one afternoon. Juries in those days were never sequestered overnight, and a rumor went around that Sull J. held a quiet little party that night at his house, two blocks from the courthouse, with plenty of Chism's Dew, ironically, I thought, and that certain of the jurymen had been present and had imbibed freely and had made up their minds then and there before they returned the next morning and required only forty-five minutes of deliberation to find Nail Chism guilty.

When Nail was asked by Judge Villines if he had anything to say before sentence was passed upon him, he said, "I jist want to ask one question: is there *ary* man, woman, or child in this here courtroom who honestly believes I raped that girl? If so, stand up and look me in the eye."

For a full minute not one person stood, except Nail, who was already standing, towering over every man. Then, finally, the prosecutor and Sull Jerram nodded at each other and seemed to agree to rise up together, and those two stood. Then the foreman of the jury stood up. Three other jurymen rose, that's all. After a few moments Judge Villines himself stood.

Maybe she was too dumb, but Dorinda herself never did think to stand up.

Judge Villines, still standing, along with those half-dozen others, said, "Nail Chism, it is the sentence of this yere court that you be committed to the custody of the Arkansas State Penitentiary in Little Rock and that there you be put to death according to law. May Gawd have mercy on yore soul."

On the storeporch at Ingledew's, in the days following, the men talked of the drought, and that ruckus in Europe, and not so much the guilt or innocence of Nail Chism as the exceptional speed of the trial ("Like them courthouse critters had made up their minds in advance," one said) and the exceptional severity of the sentence. Nobody from Newton County had ever gone to the electric chair. It was an awesome fate, and not fully understood, since there was no electricity in Newton County—Jasper itself was still several years away from the first primitive attempts at electrifi-cation. The closest anybody could conceive of a lesson to explain it was getting lightningstruck, like old Haskins Duckworth, who couldn't move one side of his face and was bald on that one side but was still alive, they thought. The only time anybody had been convicted of rape, not in my lifetime but back in the last century, they'd simply cut off his testicles and let him choose whether to sing soprano or stop going to church, and he chose the latter.

August is an awful month in the best of years, but that August the trees stopped singing, or they murmured dirges. Only the weeds and wildflowers throve: there was still yellow in the sneezeweed, coneflower, and goldenrod, the penstemons and great mulleins still held their heads high, and the wild bergamot and verbena must have found moisture in the air, but there was little green, just dusty shades of olive, drab shades of terreverte, faded shades of green ocher.

But the day they took Nail Chism off to Little Rock, it rained. Not a real toadstrangling pourdown but enough to settle the dust and sprinkle the dirt on the hogs' backs. Not enough to save Nail's sheep, who all died before he was scheduled to. In a bad drought, when people have a hard enough time feeding themselves, they tend to stop feeding their pets, and all the dogs of Stay More, hungry, began to run down the last of Nail's lambs and to fight over the remains.

For the rest of the summer until school started I was confined to the house for disobedience ("grounded" in those days meant only what happened to you when you'd overdosed on Chism's Dew). I didn't see Dorinda again until school started, and we had a new teacher, Mr. Perry, who insisted we sit by grade, not by friendship, and I wouldn't have sat with her by either.

Once at recess she tried to talk to me. "Latha, how come everbody acts like I done somethin wrong? How come it's my *fault* I got raped?"

I just looked her in the eye for a while before I asked, "*Did* you get yourself raped?"

"Yes!" she yelled, and the other pupils stopped what they were playing to look at us. "Honest! I did! It hurt! It hurt me *real bad*!" She burst into tears. Whether or not she had faked her crying in the courtroom, she wasn't pretending now.

"What's the trouble here?" Mr. Perry said. He was new, and no one had ever told him.

"She hurts," I said, and that's all I said.

on

"Lady, that's enough now," Warden Burdell said, and he held out his hand toward her as if asking her for the next dance. She stared at his hand, a chubby, gnarled, knobby, and hairy paw with dirt beneath each of the fingernails. It required a moment for her to realize that he was holding out his hand to be given the sheet of paper on which she was making her drawing, but she was in no hurry to hand it over to him. She had enjoyed these minutes of reprieve that her art had procured. Not that she had any wish to delay the execution of a convicted rapist, especially not one who had brutally abused and raped a child, but that this man's last request, to see her drawing, had been an acknowledgment of the existence of her art. Nobody commented on her art—well, scarcely anybody other than her sister and Mr. Fletcher, the managing editor, who gave her these assignments and felt, doubtless, duty-bound to make some remarks about her work: "Good likeness," "Clever lines," "Fancy," "Shows feeling," or "It'll do."

She wanted to give her drawing of Nail Chism a final glance before handing it over to Warden Harris Burdell. Something wasn't right. The ears perhaps; they really did stick out that much, but the shaved head seemed to exaggerate the protuberance of the ears into almost a caricature, and she did not want to seem to be making any sort of mockery. Actually, Nail Chism had been an exceptionally good-looking man when first she'd seen him, sitting beside her at the execution of the Negro Skipper Thomas. Chism had had his full head of hair then, although its yellow was already prematurely frosting white in places, and he'd worn some red bruises on his cheeks and temples as if he'd been in a fight . . . or been beaten.

Too, his heavy eyebrows, a darker blond than his hair had been, grew thicker as they met each other above the bridge of his nose, and this seemed to give him a coarse look, and to accentuate the effect of the shaved head. She had been especially careful with the skull, not to strain the shading of its bumps and general shape, because it was a fine cranium, almost Grecian. But what difference did such subtle shading make? The printed picture, on page 5 or 6 of tomorrow's *Gazette*, wouldn't retain the subtleties of her chiaroscuro.

She tore the sheet from its pad and handed it over to Warden Burdell.

He took it and stared at it with a frown, as if seeing a Cézanne for the first time. Then he grinned his penitentiary smirk and said, "Hey, Chism, I caint show you this. It'll give you the swell-head." But he turned the drawing around and held it up by the corners so that Nail Chism could see it, held it as if Mr. Chism's eyesight might be poor. "How 'bout that?" the warden asked. "Don't that make you look like Miss Monday has done went and fell in love with you?" The doomed man squinted his eyes as if indeed his eyesight were bad, and focused on the drawing, and the trace of a smile gave *sfumato* to the edges of his mouth. He said nothing, however. "Are you satisfied?" the warden asked, expecting an answer, and waited.

"I reckon I look pretty awful," the convict said. "I aint seen a mirror in a month. But leastways I don't have to worry about my hair shootin out ever which way, like it always done." He grinned.

"What do you say to the lady?" the warden prompted.

"Thank you, ma'am," Nail Chism said, looking her right in the eye again, the way he had throughout his sitting, or standing, rather. It had disconcerted her, and perhaps even slowed down the progress of the drawing, the fixedness of his stare, his eyes trying to tell her his whole life's story in these last minutes of it. "I'm much obliged to ye," he said.

She spoke, for the first time, not knowing exactly what to say: "You're welcome."

That should have been the end of the exchange, but Nail Chism continued it: "You gave me a few more minutes of life, ma'am. I hope you'll remember that. I hope it'll be some comfort to ye."

What could she say? He seemed to be expecting some response from her. The warden too was looking at her, waiting for her remark on that. She couldn't think of anything to say. "I'm just doing my job," she said modestly.

"HAW! I'M JUST DOIN MY JOB!" said Irvin Bobo, the executioner, and, in his bad idea of a joke, gave the switch a couple of practice jolts, which darkened the one green-shaded overhead light and made everyone except Bobo jump.

"Cut the shit, Bobo!" Warden Burdell said. Then he apologized to Viridis: "Pardon me, ma'am. He's drunk, as usual. I reckon I'd git drunk too, I had to throw that switch on a feller. But Bobo's impatient, and I don't blame him, we're all standin around talkin like it's a goddamn tea party. Come on, boys, let's get him to sit."

For a second there Viridis thought he was referring to Irvin Bobo, as the one to sit. But then the two guards flanking Nail Chism, Gabriel "Fat Gabe" McChristian and James "Short Leg" Fancher, took the prisoner's arms and led him to the electric chair and backed him up to it, and sat him down in it. From the moment he had first come into the room, the prisoner had amazed Viridis Monday by his composure and poise, and now in his last moments he was not struggling at all. Mr. McChristian took a small key from a chain on his belt and inserted it into the handcuffs that bound the prisoner's wrists, and he unlocked and removed the handcuffs.

Only then did the prisoner begin to struggle. He seemed to reach for his heart to still it, he seemed to be trying to thrust his hand inside his jacket, but Mr. Fancher grabbed the hand and slammed it down on the armrest of the electric chair and began strapping it. Mr. McChristian quickly strapped the other hand. Then they strapped his ankles to the lower parts of the chair. Nail Chism went on twisting and struggling for just another moment before seeming to realize that he was trapped and could not get loose, and then he remained absolutely still, with his eyes closed, while they lowered the metal cap to the top of his head.

This was the third time Viridis had been through this ordeal, and she had asked herself which of the many long moments in the execution process was the worst. Someone else would doubtless have chosen the instant of the first jolt of electricity. Someone with imagination might have chosen the moment when the convict first catches sight of the waiting chair. But for Viridis, trying to empathize, it was the instant that the black hemisphere of the metal cap, cold as the room was terribly cold, touched the raw, bare scalp of the man. She noticed Nail Chism shiver.

"Our Father Which Art in Heaven," the Reverend James S. McPhee began to intone. "Jimmie Mac," as they called him, was not actually a minister of any particular church, or an ordained minister at all, but a railroad conductor who, with his wife Estelle, made a hobby of "bringing religion" to The Walls. Viridis had surreptitiously drawn his portrait more than once, not that she intended to publish it, but that McPhee was a character study in pious asceticism.

They never let Estelle McPhee join her husband to witness these executions, much as she agitated to be allowed to witness. She was a woman, and women were not allowed. Oh, she hollered and screamed that they would allow Viridis to attend but wouldn't let *her*, who was like a sister to these poor doomed sinners. They'd had some trouble explaining to Estelle that Viridis was a "newspaperwoman" and thus exempt from the restriction.

Actually, it had been Tom Fletcher, the managing editor, who'd arranged for Viridis to attend. Warden Burdell was in Mr. Fletcher's debt for a few favors regarding privacy of information, and Tom had used the privilege to get Viridis under the ban, and consequently to get some exclusive pictures of the condemned men in their last moments. Photographs were strictly forbidden, there was no getting around that.

Viridis wasn't actually a "newspaperwoman." Her reportage was graphic, not verbal, although she was not above, on occasion, such as now, doing double duty as reporter and illustrator, careful to get the correct names of all the witnesses and to record such things as the exact time, and what the prisoner said, and so forth. For an important execution, for a murderer such as that heinous Clarence Smead, who had butchered his parents, the *Gazette* sent an actual reporter along with Viridis (and her drawing of Smead weeping like a baby in his last moments had made the front page), but for some reason known only to the men whose fraternity the new science of "journalism" consecrated, the crime of rape was considered a lesser offense, perhaps excusable, even if it had been perpetrated upon a thirteen-year-old hillbilly girl of subnormal intelligence by a tall, brutal moonshiner. "He's all yours, Very," Tom Fletcher had said to her, informing her that the *Gazette* would not send a regular reporter to the electrocution of Nail Chism.

The two guards, McChristian and Fancher, moved to the side of the room where the witnesses sat. Warden Burdell moved to the wall where Irvin Bobo stood beside the switch. The prisoner was alone in his chair in a small room that suddenly seemed much larger because of his isolation, as if the walls and ceiling had expanded to make him smaller and lonelier. Viridis snapped her charcoal pencil in two, between her clenched fingers, and abruptly realized it was the only sound in the silence, and was embarrassed, as if she had broken wind.

"Ready, Bobo?" the warden said, and raised one hand.

Bobo nodded.

". . . for Thine is the Power and the Glory, Forever and Ever . . ." intoned Jimmie Mac, in hardly more than a whisper, but it was booming.

Viridis Monday had an uncanny sensation of hearing a kind of singing, a choir of voices, but they were not human voices. The sound seemed to be—and remembering it later, she couldn't account for the strange thought—the sound seemed as if the trees themselves (but there were no trees!) were singing. Later she would remember two questions occurring to her at that moment: Can trees sing? and What trees?

She could not answer either question.

The swelling sound of the song, or cantata, was punctuated by tympana, a drumroll, and in the instant that the warden's hand fell she realized that the drumroll was somebody knocking on a door and the warden was lowering his hand not to signal Bobo to pull the switch but to point at the door and say, "Somebody get that!"

Gabriel McChristian opened the door, which had been latched. Standing in the door was Michael O. Shoptaw, the turnkey, who said, "Scuse me, Warden, sir, but Governor Hays is calling up on the telephone."

"Who?" demanded Mr. Burdell. "Which telephone?"

"The governor, sir. That telephone in your office."

"Don't he know we're doing a execution?" Mr. Burdell said. "What's he want at a time like this?"

"Wants to talk to you, is all I know, sir," said Mr. Shoptaw.

"Caint it wait till we're done?"

"Sir, I'm just tellin you what Williams come and tole me. He says the telephone is ringin in your office and he answers it like he's sposed to, aint he? and it's the secretary of the governor, and says the governor wants to talk to you right now."

"Right now, huh?" said Mr. Burdell, and seemed to be deliberating. "Governor Hays himself, huh?" He looked around at the others in the room, waiting for someone to advise him. No one spoke. "Well, I reckon I better go see what he wants." No one objected. The warden turned to Bobo. "Bobo, you just cook him real slow till I git back, and make sure he aint done before I git here." Several people failed to laugh at the warden's wit, and he realized his joke had fallen flat, and retracted it. "Aw, I'm just kiddin you, Bobo. Stand back from that switch till I tell you. I'll be right back."

The warden marched out of the room. The turnkey followed. The condemned man opened his eyes, which had been closed as though in meditation. He stared right at her, at Viridis. She didn't know what to do or say. She smiled slightly, and wanted to say, See, you get a few more

40

minutes of life, not just from me. The trees she had been hearing singing, perhaps just in her head, had changed their tune: it was not a mournful carol but a hymn of joy. If it was the trees. If it was only inside her head. She wished Nail Chism would stop looking at her. Was he going to look at her the whole time they waited for the warden to return?

The others did not seem to know what to do. Gabriel McChristian and Short Leg Fancher chatted, too quietly for her to hear. Jimmie Mac was rubbing his hands together as if he had a bar of soap inside them and was washing them. Irvin Bobo reached inside his coat and produced a flat glass bottle, which he unscrewed and tilted up to his lips.

"Now, I wonder," said Jimmie Mac, "what-all that is about. Could be something important. Could be, even," he looked down at the convict and spoke the rest of the sentence to him, "could be the governor has granted you a stay, or something."

Nail Chism did not appear to hear him. He continued to stare at Viridis, seeming to see her for the first time. His eyes, she realized, were not as dark as she had rendered them. She put the drawing back on top of the pad and used a kneaded eraser to lighten the pupils of his eyes. His eyes were a kind of hazel-tinged blue. She wasn't too uncomfortable staring into them as long as she was examining them for the purpose of her drawing.

Suddenly his eyes grew enormously large, and his whole body jumped, and the green-shaded overhead light dimmed. Bobo had thrown the switch! She heard a frantic screech, and realized it was herself. She had thrown down the sketchpad and jumped up from her chair and lunged toward Bobo and the switch, and she found herself clawing at Bobo and the switch and protesting as fast as she could talk, too fast to be understood.

McChristian and Fancher were restraining her. "Take it easy, lady," the obese McChristian was saying to her. "The switch aint on. It aint on. Bobo was jist foolin! He jist give it a teensy little spark, jist fer a joke." To the executioner McChristian said, "Okay, Bobo, enough's enough, you better jist wait for the warden and don't be foolin around."

Viridis shook herself loose from the hands of McChristian and Fancher and looked at both of them indignantly, then gave Bobo her most scornful glower and asked, "What kind of monster are you?"

"Hey, lady, I was jist givin him a little sample," Bobo said. "He hardly felt it. But if ole Burdell don't git back here soon, I might jist let my hand slip and give him the full dose." Bobo fished out his bottle and took another swig, then offered it to Viridis. "Here. You act like a man, so be a man. You're the only *wo*-man that ever watched me. Kind of guts it takes to do that can shore stand a swaller of this stuff. Drink it."

Viridis shook her head and returned to her seat, picking up the sketchpad from the floor. The drawing was smudged. She'd have to do one side of the face again. Her charcoal pencil was broken in half; she had another in her purse, but they hadn't let her bring her purse into the execution chamber. She would use half the pencil as best she could, sharpening it with her fingernails. But first she took a scrap of newsprint out of her pocket and carefully wrote down exactly what Irvin Bobo had done and said. She intended to put it into the story if Tom Fletcher would let her write it.

The subject was still staring at her, but this time, when her eyes met his, Nail Chism smiled and said, "Thank you." Then he said, "You're very brave. You could have got yourself hurt."

"There's some things I can't stand," she said. It was the first almost conversational remark she had made in a long while.

Warden Harris Burdell returned and, forgetting there was a woman present, began to speak coarse profanity. He swore obscenely, and then he announced, "The goddamn governor has done gone and granted Chism a stay. Git the fucker out of the chair, boys, and throw him back in his fuckin cell." He turned and saw her. "Oh, shee-*it*, Miss Monday, I forgot you was here."

off

The last time I was in Little Rock, just a few years ago, for my sister Mandy's funeral, I took some time off to go out Arch Street and look for the house where Viridis Monday had spent all of her childhood and adolescence. My granddaughter Sharon drove me, at my request; she'll know why when she reads this. The house is still there, and the present owners have lovingly restored it to what must have been its original appearance, when the architect Charles L. Thompson designed it for bank vice-president Cyril J. Monday. I would guess that the original two colors of the house were a sort of tarragon with a trim of sage, and the present owners have taken pains to duplicate these colors exactly, giving the house its Victorian feeling of elegance relieved by fanciness and playfulness. It is a storybook house. Sixteen rooms, seven porches, two turrets (one with a domed cupola), a steeple, lots of wrought-iron trim and jigsaw decoration, fishscale shingles, miles of turned balusters and spindles, and maybe (I didn't count) two dozen roof pitches, no two of them alike. I learned that this is called Queen Anne—inappropriately, because it had nothing to do with the era or the personality of Queen Anne—and that its dominant characteristic is an avoidance of symmetry. The rooms shoot off and up in every direction, and one of them up there was Viridis' aerie: her studio and her bower.

Most such urban houses, on huge high lots with leaf-dappled lawns, were intended for large families at a time when large families were desirable, but Cyril and Elsie Monday had only five children; they would have had more, but Elsie's health was not good after the birth of Viridis, who was the first girl, fourth child. The last-born, also a girl, Cyrilla, was frail from infancy, although she outlived them all.

The house is a short, brisk hike from downtown Little Rock, not far from the governor's mansion. All its neighbors are distinctively individual but large and rambling houses of the 1890s and early 1900s. Although the Mondays had servants, a black couple who handled the yard work and kitchen work, Viridis told me, years later when she was filling in the pieces of her life for me, "I remember at an early age being placed in charge of them, in charge of the household, since my mother was either too ill or too indisposed to give orders to the servants. The black couple, a man named Samuel and his wife Ruby, called me Missy V, and they did not seem to mind taking orders from me, and I was careful never to give orders in a demanding or supercilious fashion."

Cyril Monday had originated in Malvern, Arkansas, and so had Elsie. Malvern was in the flat timberlands southwest of the capital, and Cyril, although he liked to claim that he was a "self-made" man, was the son of a prosperous lumber baron, who, however, had insisted that each of his sons attend "the College of Hard Knocks." So Cyril at seventeen became a driver for the stagecoach that ran from the depot to the resort spa at Hot Springs. One of his regular passengers was the Little Rock banker Henry T. Worthen, who took young Cyril under his wing, persuaded him to move to Little Rock, and gave him a job in his bank. Within five years Cyril had risen from clerk to teller to vice-president. "But never more than that," Viridis told me. "All of my growing-up years I had to listen to my father complain that he was not ever going to realize his ambition to become president of the bank. He was a very frustrated man."

Cyril Monday may have remained only a frustrated vice-president for all of his working life, but he was a very wealthy one, and he and his family were "comfortable"—a word then meaning without a care in this world, except that Elsie was often in poor health, and when she wasn't spending long periods in Hot Springs taking one "cure" or another, sometimes for addiction to drink, she was convalescing at home, not bedridden but spending most of the time in her garden, which covered nearly half an acre behind the Monday mansion. "In good weather, if I wanted to speak to my mother," Viridis told me, "I tried the garden first. If my mother wasn't there, she was in Hot Springs. I was seventeen and in college before it suddenly dawned on me that my mother had never had any friends."

Henry Worthen once suggested to Cyril Monday that he would never become president, of the bank or of any of the civic and fraternal organizations to which he belonged, unless and until his wife Elsie began to "entertain." Cyril Monday did not apologize for Elsie. Some women, he felt, were not cut out to entertain, and he himself was not fond of large dinner parties at which a fortune was spent on food that remained unappreciated because the eater was too busy either trying to keep stains off his or her clothing or else carrying on a conversation to pay any attention to what was being eaten.

Nor did the girls, Viridis and Cyrilla, do any entertaining in the form of inviting friends to come to the Monday mansion for food or play or casual conversation. Cyrilla was almost as delicate as her mother, and in fact she began at the age of twelve to accompany her mother on the regular cures to Hot Springs. What social life existed at all within the confines of the Queen Anne house was that of the three sons Matthew, Dallas, and Henry, who frequently invited their classmates to come and visit, to explore the countless cupboards and crannies of the endless house, to play croquet or badminton on the lawns, to shoot billiards on the third floor, to climb even higher into the fifth floor of the domed turret and shoot pigeons on the roof.

"I remember the house as being overrun by males," Viridis said to me. "When my mother and sister were gone to Hot Springs for long stretches, and my three brothers had three or more of their friends spending the night or longer, I had no one to talk to except my father, and he had very little time to listen to me, although we did spend much time together, evenings especially."

(It is hard for me to get out of the habit of thinking of "evening" as meaning "afternoon," as it always did in Stay More and the Ozarks. Evening was the time before supper, night was the time after supper, but to say that Viridis and her father spent their nights together is misleading . . . somewhat.)

Days, when she had any time free from managing the household, from meeting with the tutors who came regularly to give private lessons in voice, piano, French, and Spanish to her and her sister, from planning the lunches for her brothers and their friends, from dusting the spots that Ruby had missed, from shopping in the markets along lower Main, Viridis would climb the smaller north turret, not the south one the boys used as a pigeon blind, to the room that was her studio, which she had created at the age of eleven when one of the books she'd got from her Grandmother Monday at Christmas was *The Young People's Concise Doorway to the Fine Arts*, wherein she had learned what an easel is, a palette, a mahlstick, and the names of such colors as madder, alizarin, ocher, umber, sienna, and, her delightful discovery, viridian. "Neither my father nor my mother, who hadn't known it themselves, had ever told me the meaning of my given name, which had been bestowed upon me, my mother had said, because she had 'found it in a novel' and had thought it 'was pretty and

45

unusual.' My mother had not been able to remember which novel, and once I searched their library without finding it. My father couldn't even pronounce the name, or, if he could, he chose to mispronounce it roguishly to rhyme with 'paradise.' " She was destined to endure from other people its mispronunciations and misspellings (Viridas, Viredes, Vyradis, Veredis, etc.) all of her life.

She spelled it for me, and she told me it was pronounced properly Vera Dis, although she didn't mind that I had been saying it Verdus, which was the way Nail Chism had pronounced it too.

"I have too many eyes," I thought she said, but she was saying that she had a surplus of the letter *i* in her name, three of them, and I jokingly called her Three-Eyes when I was irritated with her, which was not often: she was fourteen years older than I, and I loved her dearly.

Sometimes I've wondered if she couldn't tell this whole story of her growing up and becoming a woman much better than I could do it. What follows I have put into her words, pretending it's what she spoke to me, but it wasn't then, that year I first met her, and it wasn't even over the many years following that I knew her and we would sit endless hours together rocking away on the porch while she told me the whole story of her life. No, what follows is a kind of combination of bits and pieces she told me over the years, and some other things I learned from other people who knew her, and parts of it, perhaps the best parts of it, not from what she or they said but from what she wrote, in her private diaries, which came into my hands after her death many years later. So yes, I will let her tell this:

———

That studio, up there in the top of that turret, behind that large northern light. No one (except my father) was ever allowed into it, and it became my cloister, my nunnery, my ivory tower, as well as my autodidactic academy. It is not true, as some newspapers have said, that I was self-taught. But Little Rock High School, a seven-block walk east of my house, offered no courses in art, just as it offered nothing in Spanish, French, voice, or piano. I had begged to be allowed to go off to Arcadia College, an Ursuline Academy for Young Ladies in Arcadia, Missouri; I knew nothing about it except that it offered classes in art and had a wonderful pastoral name; but my father would not let me leave Little Rock. So for most of the years of my adolescence I had to learn art from trial and error and what books I could find or order. At the age of eleven, and continuing until the age of . . . well, until I removed myself forever from that house, I used that little turret studio as a private place for working out my ideas about the making of pictures.

My father wasn't a miser, but he didn't throw his money around either, and when his children wanted something we had to beg for it and justify it and remind him several times and then promise to do something in return for it. I always managed to get what I needed for my studio: the easel, the palette, the mahlstick, and all the tubes of paint, and yards of canvas, and endless sheets of drawing-paper. Daddy did not approve of the expenditure; he did not want me to become an artist; for that matter, he didn't want me to "become" anything, other than grown-up . . . and he wasn't sure he wanted me to grow up. But Mother had her garden, and she would not let me help her in it. My father faulted her for that, and even yelled at her about it, but Mother would not accept help even from the Negro Samuel with the tender plants that she considered her real babies, in the garden. So the north turret studio was my garden, and the only green in it was what I painted. Daddy hoped I would outgrow it.

My only fond memory of Little Rock High School was that I achieved popularity among the other girls by painting for each of them an excellent copy of a Gibson girl as a reasonable likeness of themselves. I was the only "artist" any of them had ever even heard about.

When I told my father that I wanted to go away to the Chicago Art Institute to study art, he was horrified. Or, rather, he was at first very puzzled, because he didn't know there was such a thing as an art college that would accept women, and then, when I showed him the brochure, he was scornful, and only later, after I had got up my nerve to tell him that I definitely intended to go, did he become horrified. He stormed and shouted. He railed and ranted. He sulked. He plotted: he told my older brothers of my intention, and they, all in college themselves at that time (Matthew had gone to Vanderbilt, Dallas was at Southern Methodist, while Henry settled for the University of Arkansas), filled my ears with stories of college life, how difficult it was, how impossible for the "fair sex," who were always, if they could be admitted at all, viewed as ornaments, oddities, or odalisques.

"What's an odalisque?" Daddy asked my brother Matthew.

"A concubine," Matthew explained.

"Is that what you want to be?" my father demanded of me.

"If I could be one of the kind Ingres painted," I told him.

"Who?"

When I gave up my dream of the Chicago Art Institute and instead actually began to make plans to apply for admission to the University of Arkansas, and needed my father's signature on the application, he flatly refused and said he'd rather see me walking the streets. I did not particularly want to go to Fayetteville anyway; in that year, 1904, the University offered only two courses in art, both taught by a woman whose specialty was penmanship. At the last minute before the opening of the fall term, I applied for and was accepted at Conway Central College and Conservatory of Fine Arts, a women's school in the college town of Conway, less than two hours by train from Little Rock. Somehow I got my father to sign the papers, perhaps by my promise to come home every weekend. And I did: I caught the 4:15 every Friday afternoon and went back on the 6:45 every Sunday P.M. The house went to hell during the week. I tried to persuade Cyrilla to assume my duties as manager of the household, but Cyrilla, while willing, wasn't constitutionally strong enough and wasn't able to give orders or instructions to Samuel and Ruby. Daddy kept complaining that the house was going to hell.

There was one teacher, Miss Opaline Dearasaugh, at 4-C F.A. (as it was called, pronounced Fourcie Effie), who was reasonably talented at drawing and could impart the rudiments of watercolor technique, so my time there wasn't entirely wasted. But I reflected that the hours I spent in travel, going home every weekend, could have been better spent doing my homework and polishing my drawings, or, at worst, accepting one of the frequent invitations I received from the young men at Hendrix, a Methodist college in Conway. Most of the girls at Fourcie Effie were enrolled there because of its proximity to Hendrix, where they hoped to find an eligible swain. It did not take me long to discover that my classmates were less interested in the fine arts than in men, and that all of the girls were indeed ornaments, oddities, or odalisques.

Our first assignment in Miss Dearasaugh's class was to do a self-portrait, and I've shown you the pastel I did in the mirror and have kept, and which you have called, I thank you, beautiful. I took no great pride in my features, but men—or boys—seemed to be quick to notice me . . . although slow to do anything about it. A Hendrix premedical student named Jason Sample stopped me on the sidewalk in downtown Conway and introduced himself and apologized for his forwardness and asked me to allow him to be my escort for the Hendrix Christmas cotillion. I smiled sweetly and thanked him and declined, not on the grounds that I didn't know him and hadn't been properly introduced by a responsible party but that I didn't know how to dance . . . which was true. He smiled engagingly and told me that he didn't either, that the two of us could watch the others and use the event as an excuse to get acquainted, because all he wanted to do was learn my life's story. I smiled again and said that my life had no story. "Then I would like to start its story," he offered—and I loved that, the way he said that, and I wanted to say, Oh yes I'd love to go with you to the Christmas cotillion (any of my Fourcie classmates would have given an arm to have been invited), but I said that since the cotillion was on a Saturday night and my presence was required in Little Rock each weekend, I would have to forgo the kind invitation. Any other young man, after half an hour attempting such persuasion, would have abandoned the effort, but Jason Sample persisted, and at length I admitted that it just might be possible for me to get out of the trip to Little Rock, and the next day I wrote my father (I could have waited until the weekend and spoken it to him, but I thought a letter would be more effective) and told him I was going to the Hendrix Christmas cotillion. My father did not reply, nor did he mention it when he saw me that weekend, and I wondered if he had received the letter. I waited, and two more weekends went by without mention of the letter. As I was leaving Little Rock the weekend before the cotillion, I said simply, "I won't be home next weekend."

"Yes you will," my father said.

"No I won't," I said, and I was not. I went to the cotillion with Jason Sample, and I loved it. But Daddy came to Conway the next day and told me he was taking me out of school. And he did.

In the months and months following, Jason Sample wrote to me several times and asked if he could come to Little Rock to see me. I attempted to discourage him and told him it was unlikely that we could continue to see each other. He wanted reasons, he demanded explanations, and all I could do, eventually, was ignore him. Alone in my turret studio I was learning more about art than I had in Miss Dearasaugh's classes, and I did not miss Conway at all; it was such a provincial village compared with Little Rock.

49

By accident, in conversation, Daddy's boss Henry Worthen learned that I was interested in art, and he arranged for me to meet his "daubing cousin" Spotiswode Worthen, who was a legendary Little Rock eccentric, a strange old man in his seventies and virtually a recluse. Apparently, Henry Worthen was in charge of Spotiswode's financial affairs, and he thought it would be "useful" if his "unemployed" cousin agreed to give "lessons" to the daughter of his vice-president. Spotiswode Worthen had not given lessons during the previous twenty years, nor had he made any sort of social contact, and I remember how terribly rusty his voice sounded at our first meeting. He wasn't an unkind man, and he knew much about the entire history of Western painting up to but not including the time of the Impressionists, who, he felt, were demoralizing the visual culture of civilization. Do you know the Impressionists, Latha? No? Well, they had revolutionized the art of that time, but Spotiswode Worthen had no use for them. The last great painter, he believed, had been Fantin-Latour— a mediocre academic hack—but Bouguereau—a somewhat more talented hack—remained "promising," although he was in the last year of his life (Bouguereau, not Worthen, who would live two more years).

Spotiswode Worthen was the first "real" artist that I had ever known, although the few paintings of his that I was permitted to see did not impress me, except with their technical facility. His style was . . . oh, what can I call it if you don't know art? His style was constipated. It was hard and dark and fecal. Yet it was smooth and slick. But I tell you, "Spot" Worthen could paint! More than paint, he could draw. His paintings were actually just colored drawings, the colors reserved and drab. In his first lesson he made me sit for three hours drawing, with nothing but a lead pencil, a single egg. In the second lesson he moved the egg from the tabletop to the windowsill, into the direct sunlight, and made me spend three more hours with it. Sometimes I thought that I must be cackling or clucking in my sleep.

Well, I spent two years, three times a week, receiving assignments and criticisms from Spot Worthen. I never asked my father, or Henry Worthen, what tuition was being paid to the man, who always dressed and smelled as if he were penniless. On my own I did bright watercolors of the Little Rock parks and the Little Rock townscape and the view of the river from Spotiswode Worthen's studio, but my teacher did not appreciate these; he was scornful of "views." His studio and living quarters were in an ante-

50

bellum warehouse fronting the Arkansas River, down on Markham Street, half an hour's walk from my house. The north windows had a fine vista of the muddy river and the picturesque village of Argenta on the opposite shore, but it never was a subject for him. The human figure, he told me, contained heavenly horizons more sublime than any landscape. He parked me in front of endless plaster casts of torsos and elbows, noses and knees, ankles and navels.

Once I asked my sister Cyrilla to pose for me without her clothing, and she was willing, but her figure was so scrawny and limp that the result, when I showed it to my teacher, curled his lip in scorn. "Use a mirror," he suggested, and I followed his suggestion, in warm weather, spending many long hours at a dresser, studying and drawing the full front view of my own naked body. When I showed the drawings to Spot Worthen, I was surprised (and maybe a little pleased) to see that his aged, wan cheeks actually blushed.

"Good," he said. "Certainly good. Continue. But notice . . ." and he pointed out the various muscles I had missed or slighted.

He did not give me art history lessons as such, that is, no instruction in appreciation of the great artists of the past, but occasionally he talked about theory, and about the great masters (B.F.L., I came to call them: "before Fantin-Latour"). "Do you know why all of the great painters have been men?" he asked me once, and without giving me a chance to point out that Artemisia Gentileschi, Marietta Tintoretto, and Judith Leyster, to name only three, were female, he said, "Because only the male has a body which is charged with divine afflatus." Modesty prevented a sarcastic comment I could have made on that, and I kept silent as he went on to explain how the female body is a lovely and graceful subject, analogous to soft, slow music, but only the male body was truly heroic, capable of grand mordents and cadenzas. The great Michelangelo had a good reason for making even his nude females look masculine.

One day toward the end of my second year of study with Spotiswode Worthen, he impetuously swept his hand against the plaster cast I was drawing, knocking it to the floor, broken, and yelled, "Tate!" and summoned the black youth who sometimes came to the warehouse to clean it. He was a young man, perhaps not as old as I (I was twenty), tall, not dark-black but light-brown, and frightened, or clearly uneasy, in my presence. Here in the Ozarks, where there are virtually no Negroes, you would never understand how delicate the relationship between black men and white women must be. He took off his hat and held it in his hand as he bowed his head to Spot Worthen and waited for orders.

"Do you have a dollar on you?" Spot Worthen asked me.

"I think I may have a dollar," I declared.

"Give it to him, and he'll pose for you."

"I'm not certain I want him to pose for me," I said.

"Because he's a nigger? They make good models. Velázquez, Copley, Géricault, they all used niggers. Your Edmonia Lewis did a lot of niggers, although she made 'em look like burr-headed whites, but what can you do in white marble? Give him the dollar."

The epithet did not make me flinch; in Little Rock in those days everybody called them niggers; I myself had sometimes referred to Samuel as "our nigger." But except for Samuel, a loyal old family servant, I had never been in a room with a black man before, certainly not one, as this one was now doing, at Worthen's command, removing his clothing. Before Tate removed his trousers, however, Worthen whispered something into his ear and handed him a rag, a long strip of bedsheeting, and pointed toward the part of the studio that was Worthen's living quarters. Tate went in there and returned a minute later wearing nothing but the strip of cloth wrapped clumsily around his hips. Worthen made adjustments to it so that as much as possible of the pelvis was revealed without sacrifice of decency, then he commanded me, "Draw."

I drew. For a dollar the black youth posed for three hours, never seeming to tire. He was extremely muscular, and his taut skin glistened with sweat. I did a front view, a side view, a back view, and an "action" pose of him holding a broom overhead as if it were a sword. The next time I came to Worthen's I did details of the muscles of the latissimus dorsi, the rectus abdominis, the gluteus maximus. I devoted a whole afternoon, once, to his hands, getting the ligamentum carpi volare just right. I drew him asleep, or pretending to be. I drew him stretching and bending and twisting and throwing. I drew him, or tried to catch him, falling and leaping and running and jumping and kicking. I spent almost forty dollars on the Negro, and once when, accidentally, the loincloth slipped down without his notice or Worthen's (the old artist had taken to sleeping through these sessions), I drew also what it had concealed, fascinated with the structure, although my face was so hot my eyes watered until I could hardly see.

That one drawing was my undoing. I kept it in my portfolio in my studio at home, along with the hundreds of other sketches of the Negro. Occasionally my father climbed up to my studio, and he was the only other person permitted there. Once when he came up for a visit, I had a group of the drawings spread out on the floor and was reviewing them.

"Jesus Christ, Viridis, who is this nigger?" he asked.

"His name is Tate Coleman, and he is Spotiswode Worthen's janitor and occasional model."

"Model? You mean he stands around like this with his clothes off?"

"When he's asked to."

"With *you* watching him?"

"That's how I did these drawings, Daddy."

"*You* drew these pictures?" He began to pick them up, one by one, and then to drop them, as if they were contaminated. He took my portfolio and opened it and exclaimed, "How many times did you *do* it?" I had momentarily forgotten about the one improper drawing, or I would have sought to stop my father's ransacking of my portfolio. By the time I remembered, it was too late. He held the offending sketch at arm's length and emitted a long whistle with his pursed lips. Then he said, not to me but to himself, "Yep, they're *long*, all right." Then he asked me, "Did you have to rub it to get it to be that long?"

"Daddy!" I said.

He ripped the drawing in two. Then he ripped it in four. Then eight, and into tiny fragments. He threw his handfuls of torn paper into the air and they drifted down like snowflakes. "Why don't you give up this art foolishness and take up a nice hobby? Have you ever thought of riding? Would you like to have a horse?" I shook my head. "I'm getting you a gelding," he said, and he walked out.

To preserve all of the art I had completed up until that point—several portfolios and a number of canvases—I hid it in the attic. My father removed all the rest of the contents of my studio, locked it, and bought for a high price a chestnut Arabian gelding, which I named Géricault after a famous artist who painted horses, although the groom, servants, and everyone else called him Jericho. Spotiswode Worthen had to go to a hospital. I sneaked away from my riding lesson to visit him there. The old artist was very ill and could scarcely talk. I said I was sorry I'd had to discontinue my lessons with him. I had learned a lot, I said. I was very grateful. It had been a meaningful experience for me. Nothing that I had ever drawn had been as interesting as the body of Tate Coleman.

"That body," Spotiswode Worthen managed slowly to speak, "was found, with a large rock tied to the neck, in the river, downstream a ways."

I tried to lose myself in my riding: with all the fervor I had devoted to painting and drawing, I studied and practiced manège, a fancy word for fancy horsemanship. At a time when most women still rode sidesaddle in their long dresses, I raised eyebrows with my jodhpurs and English jumping saddle. I took Géricault for long rides in Pulaski Heights, west of Little Rock; I rode out as far as Pinnacle Mountain, and I rode back so fast and furious that passersby thought I was being pursued. Sometimes mounted policemen did pursue me, to see if I needed assistance or to find out why a woman was wearing pants in the city limits of Little Rock, but they never could catch me or stop me. I jumped ever-higher fences and walls and fallen tree trunks, anything that got in my way. It is a wonder I didn't break my neck. I took lessons in how to fall, and I had several falls, and more than once I was cut and bruised but never broke anything . . . except, eventually, one of Géricault's legs, broken so badly that he had to be shot.

The day after Géricault was shot, in August of 1908, I packed a trunk and took a train for Chicago. I had been gone for several days before my mother or sister or the one brother still at home, Henry, noticed that I was missing, and Cyrilla wrote to tell me how they expressed astonishment that Daddy had not only permitted me to leave but had wired a Chicago bank with funds sufficient to keep me there for a year. Was he mellowing in his middle age? Did he feel guilty for depriving me of my art? He wasn't simply letting me leave the nest, was he? How would they all do without me? How would Daddy do without me? He was saying he hoped that Cyrilla could learn to take my place, and nobody knew then, yet, just exactly what he meant, but Cyrilla knew, and she asked me in the letter if it was true that she was going to be expected to substitute for me in *that* regard as well. I told her I would not let him do that to her.

Two bronze lions flanked the entrance to the Chicago Art Institute, a huge new building in the popular Italian Renaissance style. I felt when I passed between the lions the same way the ancient Hittites and the Mycenaeans felt at their lion gates—that I was acquiring the animals' strength and energy, that I could do anything I wanted, that nothing was going to stop me. Thus I was prepared for the shock of the pictures I saw inside the museum. Remember, now, I had never seen art in the original before, except for a few paintings of his own that Spotiswode had shown me. There were no museums in Arkansas. The poor reproductions in black-and-white in the cheap art books I owned or could borrow had not prepared me for encountering the originals. Now I saw why Spotiswode had abhorred the Impressionists: they violated all the rules he had drilled into me. And the modern artists, more recent than the Impressionists, were even more extravagant. I stood a long time before an enormous tapestry-like park scene done all in tiny dots by an artist named Georges Seurat. But even his color was mild compared with that of another Frenchman by the name of Paul Gauguin, who, I was sad to discover, had died five years before. If only I could have studied with him instead of with Spotiswode! I spent a very long time standing in front of the paintings by Gauguin.

Finally I tore myself away from the museum and visited the classrooms and studios. The fall semester had not begun, but the rooms were ready, row upon row of easels like a factory of some sort, and the walls held examples of student work from the previous year. I examined these, finding the drawings and paintings staid and stodgy and amateurish compared with the art I had just seen in the museum. I noticed that each painting or drawing had a date and a circled number: 1, or 2, or 3, and I assumed, correctly as it turned out, that these numbers were the monthly ranking of each student's work, following the French academic teaching system. Would I ever achieve a No. 1 or even a No. 2? On a bulletin board I found a list of the names and numerical ranking of the student body. Nine hundred and thirty-seven aspiring artists! I noted the name of No. 937, Marybelle Curtis, and reflected that the poor girl must feel terrible. What if I myself became No. 938? No, I was too good, I was too confident, but I did not like the thought of all that competition.

Chicago was such a huge place. I had prepared myself to find it a hundred times bigger than Little Rock, but I had not known it would be so dense, and so dark, and so vertical, and so *flat*, and so windy, and so crowded, and so smoky, and so dark, and so noisy. I had trouble understanding the way people talked, and they seemed totally unable to understand what I was saying and asking. After a particularly exasperating attempt at communicating with a streetcar conductor, I said aloud, "I might as well be in France!"

That casual remark stunned me into long and serious reflection.

Those bold artists whose work was hanging at the Institute, Seurat and Gauguin, had been French. Spotiswode Worthen had told me that all of the great painters of the last hundred years had been French, without exception (only before Fantin-Latour, of course). I had read an article in one of Spotiswode's art magazines about an American woman with a French name, Miss Mary Cassatt, who was living in Paris, in her sixties, after having studied for years with the Impressionists, especially the one who could draw best, a man named Edgar Degas, now blind and in his seventies. Miss Cassatt was, like me, the daughter of a wealthy American banker. Would she be sympathetic to my story and situation if I could meet her and talk with her? Might she introduce me to Monsieur Degas?

I never enrolled at the Chicago Art Institute. I would never meet Mary Cassatt, let alone Edgar Degas, but I did put my trunk back on the train, after withdrawing all of the money my father had sent to the Chicago bank. I sent my father a telegram, which read: CHANGED MIND STOP GOING TO PARIS STOP YES GO AHEAD STOP YOU MAY HAVE CYRILLA STOP LOVE VIRIDIS.

The terrible guilt I should have felt for saying that was obliterated by the excitement of what I was about to do.

In New York I discovered that I would need a passport and would have to wait a few days for it, and I used the opportunity to visit the museums there, where I saw more and more of those Impressionists and the moderns. Some of the paintings had labels reading: ACQUIRED THROUGH THE GENEROSITY OF MISS MARY CASSATT, and I had a constant fantasy of what the generosity of Miss Mary Cassatt was going to do for my life.

That fantasy sustained me during a horrible ocean crossing. Can you imagine the ocean, Latha? Can you picture water in every direction, with waves of it rising up fifty or sixty feet? The boat I was on, a steamship called the *Lusitania*, the same one that would be sunk by a submarine seven years later during the Great War, was a huge craft of over thirty thousand tons, but even with that great size it was tossed on the waves like a toy. The sea was so rough that the crew themselves became frightened and convinced that we would sink. All the passengers were sick or scared to death or both. I began to believe that death at sea would be my punishment for letting my father have Cyrilla.

But the voyage itself seemed punishment enough, and lasted nearly a week. When Nail escaped the electric chair that first time, I already knew the feeling of survival, of being given another chance. And the elation of survival stayed with me during some of the disappointments that came soon afterward: when I arrived in Paris eager to meet Miss Mary Cassatt, I discovered that the American lady had returned to Philadelphia for an extended visit. I attempted on my own to visit Edgar Degas but was told that he was not receiving visitors.

They call Paris the City of Light, but it struck me from the beginning as the City of Dirt: grimy streets filled with grimy people rushing madly nowhere. If Chicago had intimidated me, Paris left me terrorstruck. You cannot imagine it. From the moment of my arrival in Chicago, I had been uncomfortable walking alone in the city; the feeling had increased in New York, and now, in Paris, it was almost unbearable. Men and women stared at me, or I thought they did, and made remarks among themselves, or I thought they did, understanding a few of their words, having not forgotten my home-tutoring in French. When I heard a man exclaim to his companion, "Tu as vu ces émeraudes?" I knew that he was referring only to the color of my eyes, but I was embarrassed.

My first days in Paris I tried to stay off the streets by retreating into the great museums, the Louvre and the Luxembourg, but the splendor of their masterpieces, my first sight of such incredible paintings by Botticelli and Titian and Poussin, gave me the firm conviction that I could never paint anything worthy of the canvas on which it would be painted.

Strange and huge and dirty as Paris was, I would not have remained there if I had not had a chance encounter with another American girl my own age, in October, named Marguerite Thompson, who was from Fresno, California, and was staying with her aunt in Paris. Like myself, Marguerite wanted to study art and intended to enroll at the École des Beaux-Arts. She and I discovered we had a common background, having grown up in small American cities with well-to-do fathers who had arranged for private tutors in French, and both of us had made copies of Gibson girls for friends in high school. But Marguerite had never drawn from the nude, not even the female nude, not even herself in private, and when the entrance examination for the École des Beaux-Arts required us to draw from the male nude (loinclothed, of course), Marguerite could scarcely hold her pencil steady and came close to fainting. I passed the examination with no difficulty, but Marguerite was required to enroll at the École de la Grande Chaumière instead, and she and I drifted apart. But not before

57

we had gone together to be introduced by Marguerite's aunt to an American woman named Miss Gertrude Stein, who lived on rue de Fleurus in a wonderful house with a friend, Miss Alice Toklas. Marguerite's aunt, Miss Adelaide Harris, herself a painter, had attended Christian Science Sunday school in San Francisco with Miss Stein, and they were old friends. During my brief chat with Miss Stein, who impressed me as the most emancipated woman I had ever met, I learned that she had a low opinion of the École des Beaux-Arts, and I myself was beginning to question how it was any better than the Chicago Art Institute. After a few weeks there, I transferred to the Académie Julian, where I was much happier. I remained there almost three years. Some of my classmates, as obscure then as I was, were destined to become celebrated.

In November I spent an entire Saturday and Sunday at the exhibition of the Salon d'Automne, where I saw for the first time the paintings of a group of yet little-known artists who were called derisively *fauves*, meaning "the wild ones." I learned at this exhibition the three qualities I wanted my own art to acquire: color, simplicity, and spontaneity. The Sunday I discovered the Fauves I also made the acquaintance of the girl who would become my best friend for the next several years, a French girl two years older than myself but appearing younger, called Coco. She has become recently very famous, but you would not recognize her name. In those years she was as much a nobody as I, although she knew some artists who were already on their way to reputation and money.

Coco was not enrolled at the Académie Julian but had attended the Académie Humbert and was now earning her living painting designs on porcelain. Her background was not at all like mine; Coco had never known her father, or even known who he was, and had until recently lived with her mother, a strange recluse who supported herself embroidering designs Coco drew for her. But Coco had quarreled with her mother and had recently moved into her own apartment in Auteuil in the western part of Paris. She needed a roommate to help with the rent, and I needed a companion in the lonely world of the big city. So perhaps we were destined for each other.

Coco and I, despite our differences in background, language (but I picked up French slang from Coco as fast as she spoke it), and temperament (I thought of myself as more serious and reserved than my flighty French friend), became very fond of each other. Coco, for all her lighthearted, capricious, even scatterbrained manner, was devoted to "modern" art, and to becoming a good painter with her own style, and she and I talked much about art. Auteuil is on the edge of the Bois de Boulogne, a great woodsy park, and there we took long walks together and talked about the differences between the Fauves and the more recent, geometrical painters called Cubists. I was delighted to discover that Auteuil had a famous steeplechase, where I could watch horses leaping hurdles as high as Géricault had done, and Coco and I went to the races together, although we couldn't afford to wager.

Coco had some friends she wanted me to meet: in particular, a Spanish painter by the name of Pablo, and a mistress of his who helped support him, named Fernande. I had never met a "mistress," and I was titillated by the idea.

But Coco herself was on her way to becoming a mistress to a dark-haired Pole she called Willy—which she pronounced Vee-lee—and she was quite eager to have me—whose name she pronounced Vee-ree-dee—meet him after he returned from traveling in Holland. Willy was twenty-eight (the same age that Nail Chism was when I first met him), and Coco said he "knew everybody" and wrote absolutely fabulous wild poetry. Coco had been introduced to him by their mutual friend Pablo.

Coco was wispy and tall, with an unusual oval face and dark hair, but I never thought she was especially pretty, and in fact she considered herself quite homely. But she aroused envy in me because she had such a boyfriend, whom she never tired of bragging about, and because she had just sold her first painting! I had never sold a painting and couldn't yet conceive of it. But Coco had, and she asked me to help her deliver the painting, and I recognized the address, because I had been there before: 27 rue de Fleurus. "Mademoiselle Gertrude Stein," I said. Coco asked, "You know her?" "We have met," I said, and indeed my compatriot Miss Stein received me cordially when I accompanied Coco to deliver the painting, which depicted Willy in the center flanked by Coco and their friends Pablo and Fernande. Miss Stein, it turned out, was interested in buying Coco's picture primarily because it portrayed Pablo, for whom she had an extravagant regard, and she showed me a brutal portrait of her that Pablo had done. Later Coco took me to see the Spaniard's squalid, cluttered studio in a building nicknamed The Wash-Boat at the top of the Butte Montmartre in order to show me an outrageous painting the Spaniard had recently finished. It showed a group of five misshapen prostitutes, and Coco claimed that she had posed for, or at least been the inspiration for, the second "lady" from the left, and I had to concede that at least that lady had a better face and figure than the other four, who were grotesque. I thought I was open-minded—or tried to be—but I thought that Pablo was not simply *fauve* but *fou*, and that this was the worst painting I had ever seen.

The painting that Coco had been working on for some time (and one of the important lessons I learned from Coco is that it's perfectly all right to spend months and months on one painting, even if it ends up looking as if it had been dashed off in one morning) was an expansion of the one she had sold to Gertrude Stein: it was a much larger canvas, and would show eight or nine people gathered around Willy. Two of these people were Gertrude Stein and her brother Leo. Coco had painted Miss Stein much more flatteringly than Pablo had done—perhaps in hopes that Miss Stein might want to buy the painting when it was finished, and would pay enough to keep her in clothes and food for the coming year. The painting already included portraits of Willy and an unflattering self-portrait of Coco, as well as Pablo and Fernande. Now Coco wanted me to pose so she could include me in the group scene, and she proceeded to paint me into the picture, the third figure from the left, beneath one of the extravagant flowered hats that Coco liked to dress me up in. It is a kind of paraphrase, not a copy but a restatement—of course without the grotesqueness—of Pablo's painting of the five prostitutes. There is even a pastoral landscape in the background, with the Pont de Passy, a bridge we liked to sketch. The painting makes me look prettier than I am. Recently I saw a photo of it an art magazine. That painting is done in the same style that later created the reputation Coco has: seductive and charming color, mostly pastels, pale blues and viridians, incomparable pinks, but essentially somewhat naïve, decorative, fashionable, transient, and without substance or depth. But that painting may be my only small claim to immortality. Each person has the enormous irises that became Coco's signature or trademark, and although my irises are bright-green, they do not convey any of my identity or personality. Coco's people never seemed to possess souls.

Coco finally introduced her Vee-lee to her Vee-ree-dee, and his first words to me (after bending low to give me the first hand-kiss I'd ever had) were "We've already met." When I looked puzzled, trying to remember where I'd met him, he gestured at the now-completed painting of Coco's and said, "That's you up there, my sweet one." I was surprised to see that Coco had flattered him somewhat in his central reigning position in the ensemble: he was actually fat—or, well, not *coarsely* fat, but fleshy, what people here would call pudgy, and not quite as dashing as Coco or her portrait of him had led me to expect. And the next thing he said to me, the first of many questions he would ask me without giving me a chance to answer them, was "Are you a virgin? No, you are not. And how do I know? Because of the shape of your forehead, there, and because of your fragrance. Ask Madonna if I have ever been wrong. Eh, Madonna? No, your forehead and your fragrance tell me that you long ago lost your virginity. Am I wrong?"

I had to shake my head, not because he was wrong or to tell him that he was not wrong but in wonder that he should know that. Often thereafter when looking at myself in the mirror I would pay particular attention to my forehead but was not able to tell what there was about it that gave away my secret.

Willy spent the night. Although I had my own room in the apartment, I could hear them, and I lay awake a long time, ashamed at myself for eavesdropping, shocked at Coco, disgusted by Willy, enthralled, transported, delighted, puzzled, dismayed, offended, and, I have to tell you, aroused, lustful, burning.

The next afternoon, after Willy had left, I had a brave impulse to ask Coco, "How many times did you and he . . . copulate?"

"Copulate?" said Coco, and laughed. "Oh, now, Veereedee, do you mean what Willy calls 'the game of navels' or do you mean 'midnight snack' or 'the ride' or 'the beast with two backs' or 'plucking the rose' or 'knitting wings' or 'the combat' or 'burying the pinecone' or 'yodeling' or something else? There are so many ways. We do them all. I don't keep tally. You say you are not a virgin. How do *you* do it?"

"Carefully," I said, remembering a joke I had heard about porcupines. Coco laughed, and we two girlfriends, uncomfortable talking about sexual matters, changed the subject.

But if girls are ill at ease discussing sex, just as I am at this moment with you, men are in their element, and I was always scandalized, or pretended to be, whenever Willy, Pablo, and their friend Max were telling dirty stories or making sexual commentary in our presence. Coco told me that she was glad for them when they became obscene, because it kept them from becoming violent, which is what happened whenever they talked about art.

Max was not an artist, just a clerk in a department store who wrote occasional strange poetry. Max was madly in love with Pablo, although he was not a homosexual. Pablo kept trying to get Max to take me to the opera. Max said he would if he had clothes to wear, but his clothing was terrible, threadbare and soiled. Pablo asked him why he didn't steal some decent clothes from the department store he worked in. Because his department didn't carry men's clothes. Why didn't he just take me boating? Or for a Sunday afternoon stroll up at La Grande Jatte? Because he wasn't fond of the out-of-doors. Why didn't he just take me to bed?

Nobody asked me what I would say if Max finally did ask to take me anywhere. I didn't think I would say yes. Max was, in addition to his awful attire, nearly bald, bespectacled, and shorter than I, which wasn't so bad, but he also had a chest covered with thick, curly black hair, which he exposed as often as he could, especially when he was doing his skit impersonating "the barefoot dancing girl," which was hilarious but scandalous. He was also a Jew. I had never known or seen a Jew before (the few in Little Rock were tavernkeepers or merchants I never traded with), but if all Jews were like Max, I was afraid that I might come to dislike all of them. He was loudmouthed, clownish, and crazy, with a malicious streak. When Willy, Pablo, and Max were sitting around scorching their enemies and arguing art, Max could become vocally more vicious than the other two. At these get-togethers, which usually took place at The Wash-Boat, or sometimes at Austen's, a bar in the rue d'Amsterdam they liked to frequent, the three men would become loud and vehement while we three women watched and listened, or Coco and I would chat and ignore Fernande, whom neither of us liked, and the feeling was mutual.

I developed a fondness for absinthe, which is a favorite French liqueur, green and bitter and tasting like licorice. But I had to be careful. I knew my mother was an alcoholic, and I didn't want to be like her. Willy and Coco were not heavy drinkers. Everyone had a bottle of wine at meals, and I had to be careful there too because I became genuinely fond of both white and red, but none of them drank heavily, except that about once a month Willy and Pablo and Max would decide to have one of their binges, which, oddly enough, did not make them more violent or misbehaving but, rather, excessively polite and courteous with one another and with us girls.

Willy slept at Coco's apartment about three times a week; Coco went to Willy's about once a week. Coco didn't like it at his place, she told me—they always had to make love in an armchair, because his bed was "sacred." Willy had many strange ideas, which Coco detailed for me.

Whenever Coco went to spend the night at Willy's and I was alone, I began to suffer from homesickness: not that my lonely nights in Little Rock had been a bit more enjoyable or even more comfortable than my lonely nights in Paris, but that being alone in Arkansas was a condition you took for granted, a natural state, whereas being alone in Paris was unnatural and hard to bear. I was even tempted to encourage Max. Sleeping with Max might be better than spending the night imagining what Coco and Willy were doing at that moment.

One Saturday night in the summer of 1909, I was having my usual reverie about Coco and Willy when there was a knock at the door, and I, wondering if it might be Max at last, opened it to find Willy. "Why, Willy!" I exclaimed. "I thought Coco was at *your* place."

"She is," he said. "May I come in?" Without waiting for a reply he entered the apartment, and as soon as I closed the door he embraced me passionately and attempted to kiss me.

I turned my head to one side to avoid his kiss and pushed against his large chest. "Willy! What are you doing?!"

"*Ô combien je t'aime!*" he breathed directly into my ear. "I adore you! I must have you! Meet my lips with yours!"

I stared into his eyes, which were hazel, and large, like Coco's, seeming even larger in contrast to his mouth, which was as tiny as a pimento. I permitted the pimento to mash against my mouth for a moment before I shoved against him again and asked, "Did you and Coco have another fight?"

"I haven't seen Madonna tonight," he explained. "I left her a note saying I had to go out for a while and would soon return and asking her to wait for me. I did that so that I could steal away to this place and be with you."

"That was a sneaky trick," I said. "Coco will be furious with you."

"You won't tell her," he said. "Come, let me recite for you a poem you have inspired." He unfolded a sheet a paper from one of his pockets and read it to me. The poem was called "*Lundi après mon lundi*," a play upon my name, Monday, and it was written as if he had composed it the next Monday after this weekend we had made love. He described our love-making as if it were a fait accompli and he were remembering it in graphic detail but with flattering sentiments: *Cette femme était si belle qu'elle me faisait peur* (That woman was so beautiful she frightened me) and *Elle balla mimant un rythme de l'existence* (As she danced she imitated a rhythm of existence) and *Qu'elle les dresse ses mains énamourées devant mon sexe* (Have her lift her lovesick hands before my sex), and so forth. I tried to remember if I had heard any of these lines before. I was touched that such a great poet—Pablo had called him the greatest poet of the epoch—would write an original poem for me . . . if it was original—even if the poem was less concerned with my specific identity as a person than with sex acts we had not yet performed. When he'd finished the poem, he looked with those hazel eyes longingly into my eyes and said, "Quickly, now, let us do it!"

I said French words which mean, crudely but honestly, "You just came here to fuck."

Willy was taken aback. But he was ready for it: "No, of course not," he said. "I came here because I need to have your opinions of Pablo's latest paintings, but I think we can talk more freely after we have put the nightingale in his cage."

I was ready for that: "I'd rather listen to the nightingale sing first."

"He is mute, for now. He wants only his cage. The cage is new, and he has never been there before, but he knows it is made of beautiful, warm red gold."

Willy stayed for two hours, longer than Coco should have had to wait for him, and when he saw that his finest blandishments would not work, he even tried solicitation of my intellect, a great effort on his part: "Well, if you can't open your legs, open your mind and tell me what you think of Pablo's pictures."

I was game. "I haven't seen his most recent things, what you call his Scientific Cubism. I did not like the *Demoiselles*."

"Hah! Nor did I. What did you find wanting in it, Mademoiselle Monday? The transformation of Negro sculpture? The mislocated physiognomies?"

"I think," I declared, "that Nature admires geometry but improves upon it in all Her creations. The artist should not return to geometry."

Willy stared at me, as if he had not been listening but now was ready to. "Would you mind repeating that?"

I then proceeded to elaborate on this idea—quite a firm conviction of mine, at the time and ever since—that geometry should not be emphasized at the expense of actual appearance. This was more than poor, lecherous Willy had bargained for; as he appeared to be dozing off, I produced an example that woke him up a bit: "It's as if I drew a skeleton of you and called it your portrait. Not that you wouldn't look better if you were more skeletal." I laughed teasingly.

But he only replied, petulantly, "You're saying I'm obese."

"No, I'm making a point."

"If I were thin, would you have sex with me?"

"No. You are Coco's."

"I am not hers! Nor anybody's! I'm mine! She doesn't own me, nor do I own her. We aren't even married."

" 'We are wed in all but fact,' she said you told her," I said.

He tried another tack. "You're an American," he said with contempt. "You Americans are all prudes, and you are probably frigid."

I had never heard that word in its sexual sense; I interpreted *glaciale* in the sense of unfeeling, which I was not, or reticent, which I unfortunately was, to my embarrassment. "You French," I said without reticence, and forgetting that he was not French but Slav, "are all libertines, and you are lecherous."

"We appreciate sex as we appreciate wine. Life without it is inconceivable."

"But not at every meal."

"Why not? You say you are not a virgin, my Viridis, and I believe you, but have you ever indulged to satiety? Have you ever even done it twice in one night? No, I think not. Sex is a thirst, and an appetite. Have you ever been satisfied? Are your *orgasmes* powerful?"

I had not heard of *orgasmes* and could not guess that what he was referring to was . . . what was that expression you used? "Get over the mountain"? Yes, I did not know that he was referring to getting over the mountain. I was not a virgin, no, not by a long shot, but *je n'avais jamais joui comme ça*, I had never been *satisfaite*, I had never been made to go over the mountain. Willy seemed to be waiting for an answer—this man who never wanted answers to his self-answering questions. I said nothing.

He took a different slant. "Show me your paintings. Let me look at your

65

art. If I cannot admire the beauty of your unadorned body, let me see your most intimate *croquis.*"

"All of my pictures," I told him, "are in my cabinet at the Académie Julian. I have nothing here."

He sighed, and seemed about to give up, but tried once more, one last ploy. "Are you ovulating and afraid you'll get pregnant? Very well, let me try *ta neuvième porte.*"

"My ninth door? What is that?"

"Don't be naïve. Count your openings. Which is ninth and last?" When I seemed puzzled, he guided me: "Start with your ears, two, your eyes, two, your nostrils, two, your mouth, one, downward."

"Oh," I said. "No," I said.

"*Ta douce rose.* You are still a virgin there, no? I will be gentle. I will take your rose very slowly and with the most delightful sensations. You will love it. You will become addicted to it, so that whenever I ask again, it will be mine, alone. You will even beg me to have it whenever I am able to stiffen my monument."

I laughed as an escape from embarrassment. I laughed at those words, *faire raidir mon monument*, such a conceited conceit. I drew a picture in my mind of his penis as a monument approaching my ninth door, and found it hilarious, and couldn't stop laughing. Willy's face began to grow very red, and he gave me a disdainful look and vanished.

I did not tell Coco of the visit, of course. Whenever I saw Willy after that, always in the company of Coco, I couldn't suppress a short, quiet giggle, like a spontaneous belch, or a short hike partway up the mountain, and he tried very hard to pretend that I did not exist. But I found myself in private, lonely moments imagining what it would be like if I allowed Willy's monument to enter my ninth door.

I ran out of money. The funds that my father had calculated would last me a year in Chicago did not last a year in Paris. I had put off writing home to ask for more. Now I had to. It was a difficult letter, and an apologetic one. I described the Académie Julian and my teachers there, particularly Monsieur Lévy, who was responsible for my having the rating of No. 3 in the school and who had encouraged me in resisting the temptation to become more *fauve*. I explained, or tried to explain, what Fauvism is, but then I realized that these pages were not going to make any impression whatsoever on my father, so I brought my letter quickly to its conclusion: that I was fulfilling myself, that I wanted very much to stay another year or so in Paris, that I hoped he would understand, and that I hoped he would send the money as expeditiously as possible.

I mailed the letter but realized that a month or more could pass before it reached him and brought his response back to me, and I could not borrow from my friends, who were no better off than I. I told Monsieur Lévy that I would have to drop out of the Académie Julian because I couldn't pay the tuition. He suggested that I try to sell some of my paintings, and he arranged with a friend, the director of a small gallery, to give me a showing. I selected, with the help of Coco and the advice of Pablo and Max (Willy abstaining), my best fifteen paintings, including portraits of my friends, views of the Bois de Boulogne, but chiefly interiors of intimate rooms, usually without figures, and Pablo lent me some frames that fit, for the duration of the show. The gallery could give me only one week, and it was not the best season, and I sold only one painting, my portrait of Pablo, to a person who, I suspected, was simply a patron of his.

The profit from that sale lasted scarcely two weeks, and I was not able to help Coco meet the month's rent on our *appartement* in Auteuil. The day I took down my show, the gallery had a last-minute visitor, my wealthy friend Marguerite Thompson. Marguerite admired the paintings although she did not want to buy one. The two of us had a Pernod together at a nearby café, and I learned that Marguerite had left the École de la Grande Chaumière, which had been too conservative for her, and was now at the École la Palette, where she was quickly becoming a little Fauve. Marguerite also wrote a weekly column for her hometown newspaper, the *Fresno Morning Republican*, a sort of "American in Paris" description of her experiences as an art student, and she wanted to use me and my show as the subject of this week's column, in which she intended to mention my "famous" friends: Willy, Coco, and especially Pablo.

"I didn't know they were so famous," I said.

"Close friends are never famous," Marguerite said, and took out her notebook and began to ask me questions about them.

"Do they pay you for writing the column?" I asked.

"Sure," said Marguerite. "Ten dollars a throw."

Without waiting to see if my father was going to answer my letter, I

67

wrote to the editor of the *Arkansas Gazette*, enclosing a sample of one of Marguerite's columns and asking if the *Gazette* might be interested in having me write something similar for them, on a weekly basis, or even daily, if they wanted it.

Waiting for a reply from the *Gazette* sustained me through a dark period of poverty that culminated in the arrival of this letter from home:

Dear Viridis—

Glad to hear from you at last. Wondered whatever had become of you. Sounds like you are doing okay. Always wanted to see Gay Paree myself but never could. Sounds like there is lots to see there and lots to do. Glad to know the teachers think you are doing okay.

Wish we could say the same but things are not going too hot here. Problems with your sister. The boys are all doing okay, Matthew got married in June, didn't know where to send you the invite. Your mother stays over to Hot Springs just about all the time. Doctors don't seem to know what to do, just keep her happy and reasonable sober.

Viridis, I am not dictating this to my secretary but writing it out myself. You should have known that Cyrilla could never match up to you. I don't know why I let you think that. She just plain could not take it, and I didn't know what to do. I guess I was desperate and tried too hard, and she couldn't take it, and tried to do away with herself. You don't want to hear the details, it would make you feel as awful as I did. I am going broke paying for her fancy treatments now on top of your mother's.

So if you think I've got loads of money laying around loose to keep you in high style in Gay Paree, you got another guess or two coming to you, girl. I think you better just catch the next boat home. I mean this. You do what I tell you, and come right on home. The enclosed draft on Credet Lyonnaize (sp) is to pay for your boat ticket, and your train ticket from NY to LR, and not for anything else, hear me?

Your poor old father really does love you and miss you something terrible and can't wait to hold you again and tell you many, many sweet things. See you soon.

C.J.M.

The days after that letter came are still a dream, or at least I remember them no better than we remember our dreams. Coco said that I spent many weeks just sitting in my room doing nothing except staring at my useless hands.

What saved me finally, or restored me, was my first real memory of those days: looking down at my useless hands and discovering that they contained a letter, which I vividly recall reading almost as if it were my salvation, a letter from Thomas Fletcher, the features editor of the *Arkansas Gazette*, who said that, yes, they would be interested in seeing a column I might wish to write, with a view toward regular publication (weekly, at best, not daily). I roused myself out of my fugue or funk, or whatever depression I was in, and wrote a column, which I titled "An Arkansawyer in Paris," trying to capture for the homefolks the sights and sounds and smells of Paris. My first column was devoted to the life of the streets: the quay along the Seine, with its many bookstalls where you could buy books and prints very cheap; the street musicians; a barrel organ pulled by a donkey; the strong, gray draught horses with their heavy carts; the colorful, picturesque caps the women wore, and the failure of the caps to cover the sadness in their eyes. For weeks after mailing it off to Thomas Fletcher, I feared that my column had captured the melancholy and suffering of Paris but not its gaiety. Yet finally Thomas Fletcher wrote back to say that the *Gazette* would be happy to use it and subsequent columns on a regular basis—although style or usage required them to change the title to "An Arkansan in Paris," and Thomas Fletcher was required to blue-pencil my references to Bohemian free love, drinking, and "abstract" art. The *Gazette* began to run my column weekly, and in Paris in those days it was possible, though difficult, to live on the $8.50 a week that the *Gazette* paid me.

Marguerite Thompson came into my life again, asking me if I wanted to join the American Women's Art Association of Paris and to show my work at the annual exhibition of the American Art Students' Club. I said yes, and took the opportunity to thank her for having suggested what was now my sole means of livelihood, my column for the *Gazette*. We two columnists exchanged notes and experiences. Marguerite was leaving Paris soon to travel in Bordeaux and perhaps Spain. Would I like to go with her? I couldn't afford it. Marguerite generously offered to pay my expenses. Why? "Because I like you," Marguerite said. "I like your work. You need to travel more, broaden your sense of landscape, get into the sunny South. Or are you afraid to leave your famous friends?"

No, I was all too eager to escape my famous friends, especially Willy, who could never take no for an answer and still attempted whenever he could to seduce me and, failing that, to insult me. As for Coco, our friendship was becoming strained, not by her suspicions (she suspected that Willy was unfaithful to her with every woman he knew . . . except me) but by our artistic differences: Coco's painting was becoming increasingly charming, sweet, fashionable, and, yes, *feminine*; she was pleased with its feminine daintiness and sought to capitalize on it; I thought her painting was becoming more superficial and losing substance in both subject and form, and I couldn't help telling her my reservations. In retaliation for my critical remarks on her feminine style, Coco called me an interior decorator who was all eye and no mind. Actually, her paintings and mine at that particular time were more similar than our arguments would have indicated, but we went our separate ways ideologically and, at last, geographically. I went with Marguerite to Bordeaux.

I never returned to Paris, except when passing through. With Marguerite I traveled to Burgos and Madrid during May and back to southern France for June; in July we traveled through Switzerland and to Germany (Nuremberg, Strasbourg, Heidelberg, and Munich). In August we rented a studio for six weeks in Bruges. Then we went to London for a while. I loved hearing English spoken again, and I decided to change the title of my column to "An Arkansawyer in London"—which became in Tom Fletcher's hands, of course, "An Arkansan in London." Tom had a cousin living there, a Little Rock man named John Gould Fletcher, who was becoming a well-known poet, or trying to, and when Marguerite decided to go back to Paris (to study at La Palette, where she would meet her future husband, the artist William Zorach), John Gould Fletcher helped me find a room off St. Martin's Lane, and Tom Fletcher raised my "salary" to ten dollars per column. I remained in London all that winter.

Before Marguerite returned to the United States and married Zorach, she invited me to rejoin her in the spring and summer of 1911, and we painted together in Avignon, Saint-Rémy, Arles, Les Baux, Martigues, and Marseilles. She and I shared a great love for the work of Vincent van Gogh and wished we had known him, and we tried to find the places he had painted in Arles, and we each painted our own versions of a little café in Arles that van Gogh had loved; neither of us imitated van Gogh, but we were inspired by him and felt a little of his passion. In those days not much was yet known or written about the life of van Gogh, who is very famous now, but I knew that he had been a very religious man who had remained a complete skeptic, and I knew that he had danced on the edge of insanity for a long time. I also knew that he had sold only one painting during his whole life, and although he had received slightly more for it than I had received for the portrait of Pablo, he had lived in wretched neglect and poverty. The painting I am proudest of having done during that period, which now hangs in the offices of the *Gazette*, is called *Olive Trees in Arles*, and it shows a quartet of low, twisting trees writhing and chanting in the southern sunshine against a background of mountains more like Cézanne's than van Gogh's. I did not use olive green in the picture but several shades of green that give the total effect of being olive: there are patterns of apple green, pea green, sea green, beryl, reseda, Kendal and Dartmouth greens, choiring together. The picture is suffused with a sense of hope, joy, and youth, although I wept the entire time I was painting it. Marguerite could not understand why I was crying my heart out while painting such a happy picture.

In October, Marguerite and her aunt and another friend prepared to sail on a voyage that would last seven months and take them to San Francisco by way of the Orient. Marguerite invited me to come, and assured me that I could make a good rail connection from Fresno to Little Rock—after, she hoped, serving as a bridesmaid at her wedding. I was homesick, and I said yes. We sailed from Venice, and I began to write for Tom Fletcher articles entitled "An Arkansawyer in Cairo," "An Arkansawyer in Alexandria," "An Arkansawyer in Palestine," "An Arkansawyer in Port Said," "An Arkansawyer in Calcutta," "An Arkansawyer in Mandalay," "An Arkansawyer in Hong Kong," and "An Arkansawyer in Yokohama." Needless to add, Tom Fletcher insisted each time on transforming me into an "Arkansan" before the columns saw print, but otherwise he ran most of them as I'd written them. He personally met my train when it arrived in Little Rock, because he alone had been wired from Fresno that I was coming home.

My father did not know, until he looked up from his desk in his private office at the bank one day and said, "Well, lookee who's here! You sure have gone all the way around the world, haven't you? Are you home to stay?"

From my purse I took a snub-nosed derringer I had been given by an art dealer in Los Angeles, and I let my father look into the barrel of it, and I said, "I'm home to stay, Daddy, but if you ever try to fuck me again, I'll kill you."

on

He did not know what to say. His eyes filled with tears. There was no mistaking the singing of the trees as their green boughs swayed, their limbs danced, their leaves rustled and trembled and quivered in quaver with their voices. A song of life.

"Well, Chism, you son of a bitch, what do you have to say?" the warden demanded.

"I," said Nail. It was all he could get out for a moment, as if he had said "aye." And at last he said the rest of it: "I'm right glad of that."

"You better be 'right glad,' you bastard," the warden commented. "Gabe, put the cuffs back on him. Take his stuff out of that death cell and throw him in with the others in the stockade. Let me know how he likes that."

The two guards took his arms once again and started to lead him out of Old Sparky's room. Fat Gabe was fit to be tied, he was so disappointed that Nail hadn't got it. Nail was going to be in real trouble with Fat Gabe.

"Wait, Mr. Burdell," said the lady from the newspaper, the one called Miss Monday. "Would it be possible for me to interview the prisoner before you return him to his cell?"

"Interview him?" said the warden. "What for?"

"Well," she said, "I'd just like to write up how it feels to escape death."

The warden snorted. "You jist heard him say he's 'right glad,' didn't you? What else could any man say?"

"Could I just ask him a few questions?" she requested.

The warden looked back and forth between the lady and Nail. "Okay," the warden said. "Here he is. Ask him."

"Do you mind?" she said. "He's not going to feel free to talk with everyone standing around like this."

"Well, I aint gon let y'all use the visit room," Burdell told her. "We don't let condemned men use the visit room."

"He isn't condemned anymore, is he?"

"He aint been pardoned, Miss Monday. He's only been reprieved."

The lady gestured at the witnesses' chairs, two rows of wooden folding chairs at one side of Old Sparky's room. "Couldn't we just sit here a few minutes?" she asked.

Again the warden needed time to make up his mind. His brains is real

73

slow, Nail reflected. "Well, okay, I guess," he said finally. "I'll have to leave Gabe here with y'all, and let me remind you, ma'am, this person is a convicted rapist and is dangerous. I ought to hang around too, but, hell, I'm late for my supper already."

"Mr. McChristian can handle it," the lady said, calling Fat Gabe by his proper name.

"*Mister* McChristian, huh?" the warden said, as if he'd never heard nobody call ole Gabe that before. "Well, *Mister* McChristian, you watch 'im, and if he tries any funny stuff you beat the everlastin sh— horse hockey out of him."

The warden and the others left the room. Nail sat down in the same chair he'd sat in to watch Skip get electrocuted, and Miss Monday sat in the same chair where she'd been sitting. Fat Gabe watched them as if they were getting ready to pull something funny. A sudden inspiration occurred to Nail: he could reach inside his jacket, take his blade, kill Fat Gabe with it, then take the woman hostage and break out of here. He would have to handle it carefully: right now Fat Gabe was far enough away to pull his gun beforehand. Nail would have to get him closer. But with these handcuffs back on his wrists, he wasn't sure that he could handle it, even if he got Fat Gabe close enough and moved fast enough. He hadn't even had a chance when he'd tried to reach his blade as Fat Gabe and Short Leg were putting him into the chair. They hadn't even given him enough time to—

"Hello."

The lady had spoken to him. He realized he wasn't paying her much attention. He looked at her. She had her notepad out, and a broken piece of charcoal pencil, which was all she had to write with, the same pencil she'd made that mark on his hand with before, the same pencil she'd used to draw that portrait of him that made him look so awful, the pencil now broken. "Howdy," he said.

"How *does* it feel?" she asked. "Or is that a stupid question? Were you all prepared to die?"

"No, ma'am," he answered her. "I'll never be prepared to die, until I'm real old and there aint nothin to live for no more."

She wrote this down, or tried to, the dull charcoal pencil making big clumsy letters, with few to a sheet before she had to turn the page over. Then she asked, "Did you really think it was going to happen? The exe-

74

cution, I mean. Did you still hope you might get a reprieve at the last minute?"

"Yeah, I guess," he admitted.

"Could you tell me what was going through your mind during those last minutes?" she asked, and added, "If it's not too hard."

"Well," he said. He thought. Both of them were looking not at each other but at Old Sparky sitting there forlorn and cheated but vengeful. He did not know quite how to say it, or even whether to try to tell her. Would she think he was nuts? Or just misunderstand? "I wasn't really thinkin," he said. "I was just listenin to the trees singin."

Her mouth fell open. She thinks I'm crazy, he said to himself, and cursed himself for having tried to tell her. She asked, very quietly, almost whispering, "What did you say?"

"Never mind," he said.

"No, tell me. Did you say—?"

"Forget it," he said. "I didn't know what I was sayin."

"You said," she said, "didn't you? that you were listening to the trees singing? Did you say that?"

"Maybe," he admitted. "I been feelin awful, tell you the truth, I don't know what I was sayin."

She laid a hand on his arm. "That's strange, because—"

"Don't touch the prisoner!" Fat Gabe hollered. "No con-tack allowed!"

She removed her hand and continued her sentence: "Because I was hearing the same thing. Trees. I heard trees singing. I swear." She laughed, and observed, "I didn't even know trees can sing."

A strange lady. He smiled at her and waited for her to ask something else.

"Can they?" she asked.

"Can who what?" he said.

"Trees. Sing."

"These were."

"What kind of song?"

"Want me to play it for ye on my harmonica?"

"Yes! Would you?"

"Fat Gabe, would you fetch my harmonica?" he asked, grinning so Fat Gabe would know he was just funning.

Fat Gabe snarled, "I'd like to shove that mouth organ up your— Listen,

Chism, why don't y'all jist shut up this love song and git your goddamn talkin finished?"

"Do you really have a harmonica?" the lady asked Nail.

"Yes'm, I do," he said.

"I hope—" she said. "I hope sometime I can have a chance to hear you play it." Then she held out her hand. "My name is Viridis Monday." He did not take her hand, and then she must have remembered that Fat Gabe had forbidden their touching, for she withdrew her hand.

"I reckon you know my name," he said. "Pleased to meet ye. And you know, don't ye? that I wouldn't be alive right this minute if you hadn't drew that pitcher."

She smiled. She had such a nice, pretty, clean smile, teeth real good and straight and white. She didn't use a whole lot of lip-rouge either, the way most women did these days. She said, "Mr. Chism, I'd like to help you. I'd like to do some investigating. I'm not really a reporter, I suppose you know. I'm just an illustrator. But I know how to do what reporters do, such as checking into facts. There's one fact I'd like to determine: whether or not you . . . you actually did what they said you did, to that thirteen-year-old girl."

Nobody had made any reference to Rindy in a long time, and at the mention of her Nail clenched his jaw, narrowed his eyes, and took an involuntary deep breath. "Lady," he said, "there's only three people on this earth who honestly and truly believe that I'm innocent. One of 'em is me, of course. The other'n is my mother. And the third one—" he paused, and gritted his teeth to pronounce her name: "is Miss Dorinda Whitter, the so-called victim."

"I would like," Miss Monday announced, "to talk to all three of you. Right now I'm talking to you. Why do you think the girl would have falsely accused you?"

"Now, that's a real long story," he said. "Fat Gabe aint et his supper either, and he aint gonna want to hang around and let me tell it to you. Right, Fat Gabe?"

"Boy," Fat Gabe snarled, "I've tole you before: you don't *never* ask me no questions. I do the askin, you hear me?"

"Yes, boss," Nail said, knowing that Fat Gabe was going to get real mean with him as soon as this lady left. Again he flirted with the notion

76

of killing Fat Gabe now and taking this lady hostage, but this lady, he decided, was too nice to have to be subjected to something like that.

"The first thing I'm going to do," Miss Monday declared, "is find out the status of your reprieve. If Governor Hays did it himself, on his own, it's probably got some political motive and is very temporary. If the Supreme Court made him do it, it might be permanent." She stood up and stuck her notepad into the pocket of her coat, then pulled the coat tighter around herself. The sun had gone down; the room was very cold now. But Nail, despite the thinness of his cotton jacket, did not suffer the cold. The kindness of this lady warmed him.

He stood up too. "Lady—" he began, but decided that wasn't polite enough. "Miss Monday, why are you doing this for me?"

Again that pretty smile. "I don't know what song the trees sang," she said. "But somehow it told me that the trees would be very sad if you were killed for something you didn't do."

"Thank you," he said. "I thank you kindly." And he reached out his handcuffs and shook hands with her.

"I said no con-tack, dammit!" Fat Gabe hollered, and moved closer.

They separated their hands. "I'd like to meet the trees," she said, with one last of those smiles.

"This time of year," he observed, "they're as bare as bare can be."

off

Fat Gabe and Short Leg beat him up. He shouldn't have talked back to them. They took him from the death room downstairs to his cell, that dark, dank, cold, tomb-like little space that had been his home for months, since the day in August they'd brought him to The Walls. The cell was in a sort of basement of the electric light and power building that held not just Old Sparky's room but the transformers and dynamos and generators and the rest of that stuff that charged up Old Sparky and all the lights in The Walls and even some of the freeworld neighborhood out beyond in southwest Little Rock, along the Hot Springs highway. Fat Gabe and Short Leg took him back down to that hole, and Fat Gabe said, "Get your stuff."

He didn't have much to get: his change of underwear, his comb (he wouldn't need it) and toothbrush, his harmonica, his 1914 calendar nearly all marked up, just twenty-nine days unmarked left to go, the Bible that Jimmie Mac had lent him and which he read for entertainment: the action stories of those old Israelites fighting the Moabites and Midianites and Ammonites and Philistines, and Old King Solomon's song, which didn't have much excitement in it but was real pretty, what the king said to that lady; that, and his copy of *Dr. Hood's Plain Talks and Common Sense Medical Advisor*, which somebody had left behind in the death cell, eight hundred and ninety-seven pages he'd already read three times, no stories but interesting topics like "Sexual Isolation," "Prostitution," "Prevention of Conception," "Diseases of Women," and "Unhappy Marriages," and hundreds of pictures he knew by heart now: vital organs, anatomy of men and women, diseases of the ear, eye, and throat. He thought of leaving it, but you never could tell when he might want to use the pages for the makes of a cigarette, not that he had any tobacco left, but you never could tell.

"I like it here," Nail observed. "Why've I gotta move to the stockade?"

Fat Gabe hit him with the back of his hand swung hard across his face. "That's *twice* this evenin you've ast me a question, Chism."

Short Leg, who wasn't as bad as Fat Gabe, had the kindness to explain: "You aint condemned anymore, at least not for right now. You caint stay in the death hole till you get another date set up with Old Sparky."

Nail wiped the blood from his mouth and turned to call good-bye and good luck to Ramsey, the quiet murderer who'd been moved into Skip's cell when Skip was killed. Ramsey did not answer. Then the two guards marched Nail up out of the electric light and power building, across the yard, and into the main building, to the stockade, which was just one huge room, a barracks with few windows covered with wire mesh as well as thick bars, in which three hundred men were crowded together. The beds were double-tiered, and, as Nail discovered, four men slept together in each bed. He had slept in the same bed with his brothers Waymon and Luther; he knew how to sleep with other men, but those had been his own kinfolks, not strangers. The blacks and the whites were separated: the three men he would have to sleep with were all, more or less, the same color as he. Those three were sitting on the edge of their double-bunk or standing around it, waiting to see who the new man would be, and they sized him up; he was taller than any of them.

"Don't I get any supper before bedtime?" Nail asked his guards before they abandoned him there.

Fat Gabe stood on tiptoe to hit him again, in the face, then slugged him in the stomach to bend him down to his own level, and backhanded him once more across the face, to knock him down. "That's *three* questions you've ast me, Chism. When will you know better?"

Short Leg removed his handcuffs. Nail wanted to take out his dagger and slash up both of them, especially Fat Gabe, but it wasn't the right moment yet. He had suffered worse beatings than this. He remained sitting on the floor, holding his arms around his knees.

"New boy, what's your name?" asked one of the three men at his double-bunk. He was a young man nearly as corpulent as Fat Gabe but not as muscular. Nail Chism told them his name. He learned theirs, or, rather, their nicknames, for each man in the prison was known only by his nickname, and his sentence, or "time." The fat one was called Toy, doing two years for stealing a bicycle. There was a thin one called Stardust, who did not look at Nail when he was introduced, who did not look at anything, who seemed to be staring at something impossibly far away. He had written bad checks and was doing three. The third one, doing five for safecracking, was a glowering, ugly, scarfaced man not as tall as Nail but more powerfully built, called, for a reason Nail never learned, Thirteen.

Nail's bunkmates understood his name to be Nails, and thenceforward everyone called him that; it stood him in good stead, because it suggested being tough as nails, mean as nails, hungry enough to eat nails. He got a chance to earn his nickname that first night: Thirteen tried to persuade Nail to let him put his penis in Nail's mouth; Nail declined rudely, and later, when they'd gone to bed and Thirteen was sleeping behind Nail, Thirteen tried to force himself into Nail's anus; Nail whipped around and hit him, and Thirteen fought back viciously. The two men slugged and whomped and whacked each other all over the barracks before the night guards came in with wooden clubs and knocked them both senseless.

When Nail regained consciousness in the short hours of the morning, he found he was on the cement floor between bunks. The floor smelled of piss, tobacco spit, and shit, and it was harder than nails, but at least he had it to himself. He rolled over and cradled his head on his arm and settled himself for sleep, but he became aware of the sounds: a general steady, grinding hum of many noses snoring in unison and counterpoint, punctuated by voices mumbling in nightmares or severe dreams; occasional grunts, snorts, creaking of bedframes; and, reminding him of bullfrogs croaking on the creekbank, a chorus of farts. He listened to this mixture of sounds for a long time until it became almost monotonous, no longer novel and interesting. He rolled over to cradle his head on the other arm. He found himself thinking, for a while, of Miss Monday. What had she said her first name was? Something he'd never heard before. Maris or Berdice or Vernice. She was a real looker, good for the eyes, classy and sniptious, spiffy and neat. In fact she was the spiffiest creature ever he'd seen. She was friendly too. And nice! Why, there'd been few women he'd ever known, his sister Irene for one, who were as nice. Had Berdice Monday really meant that about the trees? Or had she just been saying that to humor him? What call did she have to make him feel good? Anyway, he did feel real good, thinking of her, and it helped him fall asleep at last.

Hers was the first face he saw in deep sleep, that lovely smile, only this time it wasn't smiling but looking sad because he was sitting in Old Sparky waiting for Bobo to pull the switch. Only it wasn't really him, it couldn't be him, because there he sat beside Vernice Monday, that was sure enough him. Then who was this him sitting here in this electric chair? He looked at his strapped arms and saw they were black. He realized that this evening wasn't the evening of the day before, December 2nd, *his* day, but the evening of October 31st, time had gone all the way back to Halloween, more than a month before, and he was a black boy named Skipper Thomas,

80

who had been accused of killing his white lady that he worked for, although nobody'd ever seen him do it or had any evidence whatever and he'd worked for her long enough to know that it was her own nephew who'd done it so he'd get the money she left, but it was too late now, there was Mr. Burdell the warden with his hand in the air, and now he drops his hand, and I feels it! I feels the current coming up my legs and down from my head and meeting in my innards and there's Mr. Bobo with his dull dumb blank look like he's just absentmindedly broken off a limb from a bush, only it's not a limb it's the switch-handle, the switch-handle is down, the current is surging, my body is rumbling like a freight train, my head is shaking awful, I am biting my tongue nearly in two and trying to say to the trees, Save me, trees! Oh trees, save me! I'm not ready to die-ie-ie-ie! and I am trying hard to keep my heart still beating, my heart is pounding to keep from ever stopping, my heart will go on and on, although my head begins to hurt like no headache I've ever known, my legs are shot through with the pain of a thousand needles, my skin is all on fire, my stomach is boiling and about to come up through my gullet and into my mouth, I am in awful pain! and Mr. Bobo unbreaks the broken twig, he raises the switch-handle back up to where it was, and I know that I have lived! The current has not killed me, my heart beats strong, I am still alive, but the pain! The good God never intended for any of His mortal creatures to feel a pain as terrible as this, to burn like this. I look at Miss Maris Monday and her face is all stricken in what she knows must be my pain, and I look at Mr. Nail Chism sitting there beside her and he too has clenched his jaw and his eyes are stricken not because he knows this is what he too is going to have to endure come December but because he knows that no human being not even a worthless black nigger like me who shouldn't have been born in the first place ought to bear such hideous agony as this death that burns and tears and strips all of my flesh and soul except my heart which still beats strong and wants to live! and Mr. Nail Chism's eyes get wet and he yells, "Goddamn you, Bobo, turn up the juice and leave it on!" and sweet-faced lady Miss Berdis Monday puts her hand on his arm to calm him down. Mr. Bobo looks at Mr. Burdell the warden and Mr. Burdell nods his head once and Mr. Bobo pushes the switch-handle back down and once more I feels it! Once more I feels the divine almighty current charge like a thousand horses running through my veins and the violent fire burns away my pain for one long forever although my teeth are one by one jarred loose in my mouth and my eyeballs get rolled back inside my head so that I am blind and can no longer see the sweet but stunned face of Miss Vernice Monday and the sympathetic scowl of Mr. Nail Chism and I can't see nothing only the raging of the horses that trample upon my heart but still can't make it stop. The horses give up. The current stops. My eyes are blind, my nose is stopped by the stink of my burning skin, only my ears can hear the voice, it's no angel coming for to carry me home but that warden Mr. Burdell: "Is he dead?" No, I am not dead, but I have now abandoned God before He ever had a chance to abandon me: I have done went and quit Him for eternity because no God however powerful or wrathful could create the kind of pain that wracks me now: this kind of pain could only be the work of Satan; only the Devil Himself could be evil enough to create such unspeakable torture and punishment as this burning pain.

I spit out my fallen teeth to free my tongue, and I cry, "Mo juice! In de name ob de Debbil, mo juice!"

A hand was shaking Nail's shoulder, and he raised his head from the concrete floor. The first light of dawn was coming into the barracks, and the face peering into his own was that of the mute Stardust, who was not now mute: "Is it orange juice you're asking for? We don't have any."

Nail sat up and gave his head a toss to clear it. "What?" he said.

"You were screaming for juice," Stardust said. "We haven't even water to drink. If you are very thirsty, I will pee for you."

"Leave me alone," Nail said, and turned away and tried to sleep again.

The only advantage to being in the stockade instead of the death hole, he discovered later that day, was that in the stockade you were sometimes allowed to go to the visit room, a wooden shack built up against the high brick wall of The Walls, which had one door leading through the wall to an anteroom, beyond which was the outside world. The visit room was divided down the middle by a screen of heavy wire that nothing larger than a nail could pass through. A trusty-guard with a shotgun and a pair of holstered six-shooters guarded the room. Once a month you were allowed one visit to the visit room, for not more than fifteen minutes . . . if you had anyone who wanted to come and talk to you. Many of the men never had any visitors. If you were in the death hole, you were not allowed to go to the visit room; the only visitor who could come to the death hole was

Jimmie Mac the preacher, or your lawyer, if you had a good one, or, the day before your death, your mother or wife or sweetheart. Nail's mother had not been able to make the long trip from Stay More.

But Nail had a visitor his first day out of the death hole. Short Leg came and got him and escorted him to the visit room. It had been so long since he'd last seen his older brother that he hardly knew him.

"Waymon!" Nail said, and he wanted to ram his manacled hands through the wire screen so he could shake hands with old Waymon. "What're you doin here?"

Waymon grinned. "Came to take yore body home," he said. "You know them two ole mules, Spiff and Greeny, that you used to hire out from Ingledew's to take yore wool to Harrison? Wal, I've got 'em right out's yonder, hitched to a wagon with a coffin in it, purtiest piece of carpentry ye ever seen. Took me ten days to git to Little Rock, cold as it's been."

Nail couldn't help laughing, and when he laughed, so did Waymon. The guard looked at them as if they'd gone crazy. "I shore hate to disappoint you," Nail said, "and make you go home empty-handed."

"What have they done to ye?" Waymon asked. "Brother, you look lak somethin the cat drug in. Got a knot on yore bald haid the size of a baseball. And all them bruises! What did they beat ye up fer?"

"Askin too many questions," Nail said. "Leastways, I'm alive."

"Shit, I never liked to stand around through a funeral, nohow," Waymon said. "And it would've cost us forty dollars for yore headstone. Paw spent the last cent we had for that new lawyer, Cobb."

Nail did not find that funny. "That right? He oughtn't've done that."

"And mortgaged the farm besides."

"*Mortgaged?*" Nail was indignant. "Who put the mortgage on us?"

"John Ingledew," Waymon said. "The Jasper bank wouldn't even talk about it. But Ingledew's bank needed the business, I reckon, and he give Paw three hunderd dollars for the whole place, includin Maw's old eighty."

Nail's hands spread against the chain of the handcuffs as if he were trying to break it. "I'll kill that son of a bitch."

"Naw, Nail," Waymon said. "Ingledew's doin us a favor. All them Jasper folks is on the side of Sull and Duster Snow and them. Wasn't for John Ingledew, we couldn't never've got ye that new lawyer."

"How is Paw?" Nail wanted to know.

"Porely," Waymon said. "But not on account of this business. You know he's had that heart dropsy for some years. Doc Plowright says he ort to go up to the hospital up to Harrison."

"Why don't he?" Nail asked, and when Waymon did not answer but just hung his head, Nail asked, "Don't he have none of that three hunderd dollars left?"

Waymon tried to explain. It was complicated. That new lawyer they'd hired, Farrell Cobb of Little Rock, wasn't charging them the whole three hundred dollars for his appeal to the Supreme Court. Part of it was a "retainer," which, Waymon attempted to explain, was to make sure that Mr. Cobb would do everything he could, for as long as it took, to get Nail out. The agreement with Cobb stipulated that in the event of Nail's electrocution, Seth Chism would get a partial refund.

"Shit," Nail commented. "Paw'd be better off if I was fried, after all."

"Don't ye talk lak thet, Nail," Waymon pled. "Yore life is worth a whole lot more than three hunderd dollars."

"It aint worth more than our whole damn farm!" Nail said. Then he asked, "How's my sheep?"

Again Waymon hung his head. "Nail, I hate to tell ye. You know I hate to tell ye. What few of them sheep the drought didn't git, the dogs got."

"Ever last one of 'em?" Nail asked. "Didn't they leave me a lamb or two?"

Waymon shook his head.

"Well," Nail said, and pictured his pastures empty of their flocks. Right now there would be no grass: the last of the autumn grass would be gone, and the spring grass not started yet. He asked, "How's Maw?"

"Jist fine," Waymon said. "She wanted to come with me, but Paw wouldn't let her. She'll shore be glad to see that I'm bringin a empty box home."

"Irene? How's she been?" Nail asked of their sister.

Waymon gave his head a tilt and dip. "Lonesome, don't ye know? But she's a big help to Maw, and they keep each other company, I reckon."

"She don't see Sull no more?"

Waymon shook his head. "She aint been back to Jasper one time since yore trial."

They talked until their fifteen minutes were up. Waymon told him that he had accosted Sull Jerram on the square in Jasper and told him that he,

Waymon, intended to put him in his grave if Nail died in the chair. Waymon's parting words to his brother were "Well, you didn't die in the chair, but I'm a mind to put Sull in his grave anyhow, for what he done to ye."

Waymon was not the only visitor he had that day. Two more visitors came before dark. You were supposed to get only one visit a month, but these two didn't count, because they were the preacher and the lawyer. The preacher was Jimmie Mac, who said he just wanted to say he was real happy that Nail was still alive and he wondered if Nail had had time yet to make up his mind that the good Lord Himself had seen fit to spare him, and wasn't that enough to convince him that the good Lord really did exist and cared for him? Jimmie Mac was disappointed to learn that Nail had not followed his advice and spent his last hours in prayer, but he could understand how a feller might have other things on his mind at such a time. But now that the execution had been postponed, didn't Nail think he had some time to seek out the Lord and take it to Him in prayer and ask Him for His forgiveness and blessing and promise of salvation forevermore? Didn't Nail know that God loved him? Didn't Nail realize that God works in mysterious ways and we are not to question His wisdom but glory in His deeds? Had Nail read Hebrews the twelfth chapter and the verses three through thirteen, especially the sixth verse: "For whom the Lord loveth he chasteneth, and scourgeth every son whom he receiveth"? Didn't Nail wish to be a son of the Lord and endure the Father's chastisement? Couldn't Nail understand what a challenge it was to be chastened and punished and to survive whole and pure in the sight of God and reap the rewards of life everlasting and the fruits of righteousness?

"No," replied Nail.

"No which?" asked Jimmie Mac.

"No I don't have much use for that Lord," he said.

The lawyer came just before suppertime and wasn't required to use the visit room but was allowed to sit with Nail right in the mess hall. The lawyer was right at home here in The Walls and had been here many times before. "The missus is expecting me shortly or I'd break bread with you," he apologized, wedging himself in between Nail and the fat convict named Toy on the long bench. There were only two tables in the mess hall, but each of them was the length of the room; all of the white men sat at one table, all of the black men at the other. "No reflection on the quality of the food, you understand," Farrell Cobb remarked, lowering his voice conspiratorially. The food was the same Nail had for lunch and for breakfast, the same food they'd served him when he was in the death hole, the same food everybody got three times a day, seven days a week: one piece of cold cornbread, one small chunk of mostly fat probably from beef but hard to tell, one cup of something warm that Nail had never been able to determine was supposed to be taken for coffee or soup but that could be either, or neither. The butcher shops of Little Rock were swept of their scraps at the end of the business day, and the fatty scraps were served at the Arkansas State Penitentiary.

Farrell Cobb stared at Nail's plate, and his lips formed themselves into a suggestion of nausea. "In Mississippi," he whispered, "they don't get any meat whatsoever." He looked around to see if any of the other men crowded along the benches were listening, but none of them were paying any attention to him, having already noted his suit and tie, his heavy overcoat which protected him against this biting cold, and having either recognized him or stopped wondering what he was doing here; or having never cared to begin with. "Just beans or cowpeas," Cobb added, and added to that, "Well, I guess you'd not mind a serving of beans or some other vegetables too, but my experience is, the prisoners given a choice would always rather have a bit of fat meat than a bit of beans." Nail ate. "Now, here we are discussing the menu when we ought to be considering more important matters, such as those contusions and risings you've recently acquired. Can you hear me?" Farrell Cobb kept his voice low and his mouth close to Nail's ear. "If your beatings were provoked, all I can advise is to be very careful, to follow all the rules, to show proper respect for your keepers and superiors, to strive at all times to conform to the system, and to do nothing that might be construed as rebellious or aggravating. On the other hand, if you were beaten without provocation, that is indeed a sorry state of affairs, and one that I have protested time and time again, to little effect, I'm afraid, since, as you may have observed, it appears to be the routine in this institution, as everywhere else. I suppose we ought to condone a little corporal punishment in our efforts to wipe out capital punishment. But I know it hurts. I don't approve of the strap, let me tell you." Cobb's gaze wandered up and down the table, seeking out the men who had obviously been victims of the strap and had recent cuts, welts, stripes, or scars to show for it. Nail kept chewing and let his eyes follow

Cobb's. He had not received any strap yet himself, only the backs and fronts of hands, and wooden clubs, which were bad enough. They had better not try to use any strap on him. "Well now, here we are talking about the mistreatment of prisoners as if anything could be done about it, when that is not really what I'm here to talk about at all. What I came to say was to give you a little report on our little efforts to get you out of that little old hot squat." Cobb's chuckle was audible to the other men, who raised their eyes from their plates to see what humor was the cause of it. Cobb noted his audience, and appeared on the verge of repeating his clever term for Old Sparky in order to amuse them. But he did not. Instead, he asked Nail, "Well, what do you say?"

"What do I say?" Nail asked.

"Yes: what do you have to say?"

"I'm fine, I reckon. How about you?"

"No, I mean, aren't you going to say anything to me for what I did to get you a stay of execution?"

"Oh," Nail said. "Thank you. I appreciate it."

"You're welcome. Let me tell you, it wasn't easy. I was on the telephone all of Tuesday night and most of yesterday. Thank God and Alexander Graham Bell. I'll have you know I even placed through a telephone call to Fort Smith, to reach Judge Bourland, and that's what? a hundred and fifty miles of telephone wire. If that wire hadn't been there, you wouldn't be here right now. It was Judge Bourland who got the Supreme Court to agree to hear your appeal, and it was his special-delivery letter hand-delivered to Governor Hays at 4:50 P.M. yesterday, just ten minutes short of the time the governor was to quit for the day, that persuaded him to use his authority to stop the execution."

The gong clanged to signal the end of suppertime. The men stood as one, executed a right face—except Farrell Cobb, who turned the wrong way—and marched out in lockstep. Mr. Cobb got himself in line and attempted the lockstep in following after Nail, continuing to talk into his ear from behind but having to crane his neck to do so: "Judge Bourland said, and I quote him, that your defense was 'butchered.' Without naming names, he as much as called your James Thomas Duckworth a dolt and a bungling idiot who ought to be disbarred. I know that if we get the case to the full court when it meets again in January, we can convince them that Duckworth didn't take the proper steps for appeal, not to mention

87

that he made a perfect shambles of the trial itself." At the door to the barracks, which Farrell Cobb could not enter, he quickly asked, "Is there anything I can do for you? Anything you need?"

"You said you'd get me home for Christmas," Nail reminded him.

"Well, I am always an optimist," Cobb said. "In this profession you must be constantly hopeful and confident. What say let's shoot for Valentine's Day, at the latest?"

Later Fat Gabe came to his bunk, with Short Leg and two of the Negro trusties, whose job, he discovered, was restraint more than anything else. "Uh-oh," said Toy, and Stardust looked off into the next century, and Thirteen pretended he didn't exist.

Fat Gabe said to Nail, "Who told you to talk to that man?"

"He did most of the talkin," Nail replied.

"You think you're some kind of privileged person? You think just because you beat the chair you can have special treatment? You think you can have company at supper?"

"I didn't invite him," Nail pointed out. "He's a lawyer."

"You talkin back to me?" Fat Gabe yelled.

"Nope, I'm jist tellin ye who's who and who's what."

"That lawyer was Farrell Cobb, the biggest ass-licker in Pulaski County," Fat Gabe said.

"You may be right," Nail said.

"You sayin I'm not right?" Fat Gabe said.

"Naw, I said you may be right."

"That's what I thought you said, Chism. You think you're somebody important, don't you, just because you beat the chair? The chair couldn't kill you, but I've got a notion to do it. Take down your pants."

"Huh?" Nail said. "It's too cold."

"TAKE DOWN YOUR PANTS!" Fat Gabe yelled into his face. Nail did nothing. Fat Gabe looked at the two Negro trusties, each in turn. "What are you coons just standin there for? Take off his pants."

While one of the Negroes and Short Leg held him, the other Negro pulled off his pants and then ripped off his underwear. "Turn 'im around," Fat Gabe said, and they turned him to face the bunk and held his arms along the upper bunk. Nail could not see the instrument of punishment, but as soon as the first blow had fallen, he could picture it exactly: a strap of harness leather two and a half feet long by two and a half inches wide, attached to a wooden handle sixteen inches long, held in Fat Gabe's hand, and swung back as far as he could reach. The other convicts made way to give Fat Gabe swinging room. Nail's father Seth had tanned his hide, the last time, with a length of plow harness, when Nail was eleven years old and had refused to get up in the middle of the night to stoke the boiler in the still. Nail could still remember it, and he remembered counting the blows: ten in all, which had been enough to persuade him to obey his father the next time Seth asked him to do anything. I haven't disobeyed anybody, Nail thought now, except I wouldn't take down my pants like he asked me to, and I had a good reason for that: it's freezing in here. But he felt already the heat of his smarting buttocks warming his whole body. He wasn't cold anymore, just incredibly sore, and he counted the number of licks beyond ten: eleven and twelve and thirteen. You'd think Fat Gabe's arm would tire out, but it didn't. Something wet was trickling down the back of his legs, and he hoped it was shit but knew it was blood. Fourteen and fifteen and sixteen. As long as the blows had been falling on his skin it had been possible to bear them, but now each lash cut into wounded flesh and seared the raw underskin. Seventeen was an awful one unto itself. Eighteen was unbearable. Nineteen made him feel faint. Twenty . . .

He heard a voice say, "Turn him around," and the two blacks who were keeping him from reaching his dagger and murdering Fat Gabe turned him toward his assailant, who was wearing a look as if he were not tired but enjoying himself, and who swung back the strap aiming to lash Nail on his genitals.

He begged for the first time in his life. "No!"

But Fat Gabe hit him there, and it was much worse than being hit on his buttocks. Even the torturer seemed to retain a shred of fellow-feeling to realize how hideous the scourging must have felt, and he was not putting the full force of his swing into the blows but checking them so that they slapped against Nail's genitals without cutting, only stinging and bruising. Nail lost consciousness.

How much later he came to he couldn't tell, except that it was dark and there was a face close to his own, speaking to him. The voice was Toy's, and Toy had very bad teeth, which gave his breath a rancid stench, especially so close: they were lying side by side in the lower bunk. "They done that to me last week," said Toy. "It helps if you kind of draw your knees up towards your chest. Here, you can have my space to draw up your knees. Like that. It keeps your balls from killing you. Don't it? Do you feel some better that way?"

"Hush," Nail said. "Let me sleep. Thanks."

"You know what they strapped me for?" Toy went on. "At dinner once Stardust wouldn't eat his bread, sometimes he don't eat at all, and once when he left his bread like that I was real hungry so I took it and ate it. You know we aint supposed to touch nobody else's food 'ceptin our own?"

"Yeah, that's the rule," Nail said. "Let's be quiet now and go to sleep."

"One of them nigger waiters saw me grab it, and he reported me, and I got twenty lashes behind and ten in front." Toy sighed, and his sigh carried a full blast of fetor.

"Fat Gabe is the meanest feller on this earth," Nail remarked. "Now hush. Shh. Let me sleep."

"It wasn't Fat Gabe that put the strap to me. It was the warden," Toy said. "Mr. Burdell." And Toy went on talking. He seemed on the verge of telling Nail his whole life's story, and Nail began to crave some ventilation. Toy was born in Lonoke, Arkansas, and had been all the way to Memphis, a big town. He once went to a whorehouse in Memphis. He'd saved up his money from picking strawberries and wanted to find out what having two women simultaneously would be like. He picked out a light-haired one and a dark-haired one. Nail told himself that Toy must have had better teeth in those days, or no woman would have come near him. Toy began to tell what each of the women had done to him, or let him do to them.

" 'Scuse me," Nail interrupted suddenly. "I need to go out real bad." He climbed out of the bunk and painfully stood up, clutching his groin. He was not going out, of course, but he needed to find the pot, not just to get away from Toy; he was suddenly very sick in his bowels. If he didn't get to the pot soon, he'd mess his pants. The barracks had a couple of those enameled tin slop buckets: a white enamel one for white men, a black enamel one for black men. In the dark it was hard to tell them apart, but Nail didn't care. At least he had the decency to *use* the pot; most of the men thought that using the slop buckets was dandified, pretentious, effeminate: they preferred using the floor, and you had to be careful where you walked, especially if you were barefoot, as many of them were who couldn't afford shoes. Nail never took off his brogans, but still he could feel an occasional squish beneath his feet as he stumbled through the rows of bunks, feeling his way with his hands, and touching an arm or a foot here and there, and unwittingly waking a man or two, who cursed. He reached one of the pots, black or white, just in the nick of time. The pot smelled far worse than Toy's breath, and Nail poured into it a searing torrent of distress from his guts. He continued to squat there until long after the stabs and quakes had stopped tearing within him. He hoped that if he waited long enough, Toy would be asleep when he returned to the bunk.

But Toy suffered from insomnia and welcomed him back and resumed his long story of the Memphis brothel. Then he thought of an even better story: the time he found that nymphomaniac in the strawberry patch. He had to interrupt this story twice to allow Nail to stumble off into the darkness to the commode. Toy was still breathing his vile story when Nail managed at last to doze off.

The five o'clock gong woke him. Toy was still talking but had rolled onto his back and was telling his story to the ceiling, a tale of some De Valls Bluff girls who gang-raped a twelve-year-old Lonoke boy, not Toy but his cousin Virgil. At the fifth clang of the gong a guard yelled, "Rise and shine 'em, squad up and jump." When Nail tried to get out of bed, he knew he was not going to be able to rise or to shine, to squad up or even to eat, let alone to jump. He was sicker than a dog, and it wasn't any food he'd eaten that had done it either.

As Toy, Stardust, and Thirteen lined up and prepared to get into lock-step, Nail said to them, "Tell 'em I need a doctor."

Much later in the morning two Negro trusties, not the same two who had held him when Fat Gabe laid the strap on him, came and got him and dragged him upstairs to the attic. It wasn't a bare attic but had been fixed up into a kind of room. It had two windows, both of them rendered almost opaque by flyspecks. There were dirtdobber nests on the rafters. The black men put him on one of the two cots and left him there. He was too sick to get up and reconnoiter the surroundings, but from where he lay he could see the blurred shapes of black bars through each flyspeck-frosted windowpane. The whole room smelled foul in a new kind of foulness that was almost a relief from the smell of Toy's breath and the slop bucket because it was different: a smell of sickness and decay and, yes, something that Nail realized he'd never smelled before: death. The cot that Nail lay on had gray sheets that were ripped and stained but appeared to have been washed recently, while the other cot had sheets and blankets that were thick with dried blood and other discharges. The room was terribly cold yet not absolutely frigid; Nail realized that because it was in the building's attic it received some warmth rising up from the barracks below, what little body heat the three hundred men had generated. The extreme cold of the room would not ordinarily have bothered him, but now in this sickness he was weak and began to shiver uncontrollably. Nail had enough strength to reach the other cot and remove its bloody blanket and wrap himself in it.

Eventually a man came in, accompanied by two more of the black trusties. He was dressed like them, dressed like Nail, in clothing printed with wide gray stripes. He wore thick spectacles and did not look like a criminal. He stared down at Nail not with curiosity or kindness but with a kind of boredom, and he asked, "What do you need?"

"I need a doctor, I reckon," Nail said.

"You won't get one," the man said. "I used to be one. I'm the closest to one you'll find. Gode's my name. Now what do you need?"

"Something for my stomach," Nail said. "Or my bowels. Or both."

"Gaumed up or trots?"

"Trots."

"Wee-wawed any?"

"Wee-wawed?"

Doc Gode did a pantomime of vomiting. "Puked."

Nail shook his head and pointed at his mouth. "Not at this end."

The man was staring at the top of his shaved head. "You been in the death hole? Your head's peeled."

Nail nodded. "I cheated the old hot squat," he said, and smiled.

Doc Gode didn't smile back. He reached inside his pocket and took out a key. On the wall of the flyspeck room was a wooden cabinet, its two doors latched and padlocked. The man unlocked and opened the cabinet. The two shelves inside contained a blue bottle, a brown bottle, and two bottles in shades of green, as well as a roll of gauze and a few other items. From where he lay Nail could only read the label on the brown bottle: CARBOLIC ACID. The ex-doctor took down one of the green bottles, uncorked it, and handed it to Nail. "Take just two swallows of this," he commanded.

The label read: PAREGORIC. The name sounded sinister. "What does it do?" Nail asked.

"It will ease your guts," the man said. "Come on. Take two swigs and hand it back."

The stuff didn't taste too bad. After a second swallow Nail handed the green bottle back, and Doc Gode returned it to the cabinet. Before he could close the cabinet, Nail requested, "Could you take a look at my behind? I reckon I may need a bandage back there."

The man motioned for him to turn over, then pulled down the back of his pants, took a look, and said to the black trusties, "Hold 'im, boys." The two Negroes grabbed Nail's arms and gripped tightly, and soon Nail felt a burning on his butt worse than the licking he'd received, and he screamed.

When he got his voice back and could see through the tears in his eyes, he saw Doc Gode holding the unstoppered brown bottle, CARBOLIC ACID, and he said, "Ye gods! What was that for?"

"A little disinfectant," Doc Gode said. "It'll keep the germs out. But I can't waste any wrappings on that. Just don't sit on it for a week."

There was a commotion on the stairs, the door flew open with a crash, and two more of the black trusties came into the room, carrying the limp form of a middle-aged white convict, naked, his entire body flayed: flaps of his flesh were dangling loose, two-inch strips of skin hung from wounds that looked as if they had been scorched with a hot iron, and he was covered with blood.

The blacks dumped the body onto the other cot. One of them said, "Marse Gabe done really laid it on 'im." There was almost admiration in his voice, as well as awe. "Ole Marse Gabe done whupped de daylights out ob dis po buckra."

Doc Gode lifted the man's dangling arms and folded them over his chest. He opened one of the man's eyelids and looked closely at the unseeing eye. He felt the man's pulse. He turned his head and looked at Nail and asked disdainfully, "Now you see why I couldn't waste any bandages on you?" Doc Gode took down the roll of gauze from the cabinet and the bottle of carbolic acid. He gave Nail one more look. "You don't want to watch this."

Nail turned his head away. He listened but heard no sounds coming from the victim, and a good while later, when he stole a glance in that direction, he saw that the victim's worse wounds had been wrapped and taped, but many areas of his body were still raw and bloody.

Mr. Burdell came into the room. "What's goin on up here?" he demanded. "Y'all havin a party?" He saw Nail and said, "What're *you* doin here, Chism? Playin off?"

"Doc Gode's been treatin me for what ails me," Nail said.

The warden looked at the ex-doctor. "What's wrong with Chism?"

"Dysentery," said Doc Gode.

"No shit?" the warden said.

"Too much shit," Doc Gode said.

Nail couldn't help laughing, even though it was a serious matter if Doc Gode was truthful: Nail recalled reading about it in *Dr. Hood's Plain Talks and Common Sense Medical Advisor*. But Doc Gode too was chuckling a bit, and maybe he wasn't serious.

"What's so funny?" the warden demanded, but then he seemed to become smart enough to catch the joke, and he smirked and said, "Well, if you got any shit left in you, Chism, we will beat it out." The warden lost interest in Nail and began studying the other patient. "He don't look too good, does he?" Burdell said.

"Very weak pulse," Doc Gode said.

The other fellow looked done for, Nail observed. He couldn't recall ever having seen the man before; he was just one more convict among the hundreds; but Nail suddenly found himself inventing the man's life: he had a wife somewhere out in the country and a whole bunch of children; he had a mother still living, and some sisters and brothers; he had worked hard all of his life, toiling in the sun, until the day he got in trouble and was sent to the pen. Probably he was hoping he could get a Christmas pardon and be home with his family.

"Mr. Burdell, sir, could I say somethin?" Nail discovered himself requesting before he could have the sense to stop himself. The warden turned away from the dying man and looked at Nail. Burdell didn't say, Yes, go ahead, but he didn't say, No, keep your trap shut, so Nail went ahead and said what he had to say: "Sir, I know that Fat— I know that Mr. Gabriel McChristian is jist doin his job, and I know it aint a easy job either. But I jist wonder sometimes if you know, sir, how evil he is. *Evil.* This world is full of cussèd wickedness and cruelty, but when a feller gits a crazy pleasure out of causin awful pain to another human bein, he aint

94

jist wicked or cruel, he's evil, he's criminal, he's sick in the head. Don't that bother ye none, sir?"

The warden just stared at him. Then the warden and Doc Gode exchanged looks. The black trusties exchanged looks, and one of them rolled his eyes up into his head. Finally the warden prefaced whatever response he was going to make by saying severely, "Chism—" but then he seemed to change his mind and adopt a milder tone, although it was a strain on him. "Nail, I know we aint perfect, none of us," he said. "And ole Gabe is prob'ly the *least* perfect amongst us, shall we say? But evil? *Evil*, did you say?" The warden abandoned the effort to be polite. "Who the fuck are *you* to tell me about evil? You raped a kid, Chism. You grabbed a little girl and knocked her down and rammed your hot cock into her tiny little cunt! You tell me about evil! She begged you for mercy, and did you have any? Don't you talk to me about evil, you miserable son of a bitch! I'll show you what evil really is before you git your ass fried!" The warden whipped around and yelled at the trusties, "Git this bastard out to the yard!" As the trusties dragged Nail off his cot and toward the door, Burdell spoke up close to his face, shaking a long, trembling finger at the man dying on the other cot. "You know why he got beat? Huh? Because he was tryin to *escape*! I swear, Chism, when we git through with you, you're gonna try *real* hard to escape."

They took Nail out of the flyspeck room, out of the building, into the yard. It was a big yard, acres of empty ground between the building and the wall. They stood Nail up and told him to walk. But he couldn't walk. They picked him up again and kicked him and hit on him and told him to walk. He walked a bit. It began to snow. At first just feathers but then heavy flurries. His bare head and his shoulders became covered with flakes. And his back, when he fell. The rest of the day they kept picking him up and making him walk. The blacks complained to one another of the futility of it, the dumbness of it, the monotony of it, but they kept on with their job.

The man in the flyspeck room died. Before they hauled him off for burial, they placed his body on the floor at one end of the barracks. Warden Burdell made a short speech warning against attempted escape, and Fat Gabe and Short Leg moved among the men, clubbing one who protested that the dead man had never tried to escape. When Burdell's speech was finished, all three hundred of the men were lined up in slow lockstep, and each man, black and white, was required to bend down and shake hands with the corpse and say good-bye. Each man except Nail, who couldn't lift his head from his bunk.

Fat Gabe came to his bunk. "Can't move a finger, hey?" Fat Gabe asked, but Nail couldn't even talk. Fat Gabe moved his face close so that his words spattered Nail with flecks of spittle: "I got a mind to move a few fingers for you, boy. But not tonight. I'm gonna save you. I'm gonna save you till you're strong enough to 'preciate what I'm gonna do to you. You got to be able to move to 'preciate what I'm gonna do. Gonna let you *know* what evil is. Gonna make you *learn* what sick in the head is. Gonna do crimes on you that *spell out* what criminal is." Fat Gabe cleared his throat twice, hawked, and spat at Nail a faceful of phlegm.

Nail lost track of time. He couldn't remember having had anything to eat, he couldn't recall ever being able to get up and go with the others to the mess hall, but he didn't have any memory of anybody bringing him anything to eat. Probably he didn't eat at all, for a week or so. But he didn't have any memory of having to get up and go to the slop bucket either. Or use the floor. Strange, he didn't know thirst even. His bunkmates began to try their best to pretend he wasn't there. Toy said to him once, wonderingly, "Did you really truly rape a little girl?" All that Nail could manage was to mumble, "She wasn't little." And when it occurred to him to add, "And I didn't rape her neither," Toy had disappeared, and never spoke to him again after that. Another time, in the night, someone— he figured it was Thirteen—tried to insert a penis into his mouth. Nail had just enough strength to raise a hand to stop the action. The owner of the penis said, and it sounded like Thirteen, "You did it to that little girl, didn't you?"

Nail discovered that if he tried hard enough he could shut out entirely the Arkansas State Penitentiary in bitter December and make it into a hillside of Stay More in the middle of June with his sheep all around him. He could do anything he wanted to, with those sheep. They would gambol into square dances when he played the right tunes on his mouth organ. The fescue was cropped a bronze-green by their grazing, but the orchard grass was still like emerald, and behind the green meadow rose the turquoise mountain, and beyond it the blue-green hills, and beyond those the light smoky blue of faraway Reynolds Mountain. When the sheep finished their dancing, they would crawl up leaf-dappled under the green shade of

96

the big oaks at the edge of the meadow, and there they would kneel and nap, and Nail would nap with them, long in the summer afternoon, listening to the clear spring gurgle down the talus. When they woke up from their nap, they were whole and sound and sane and ready to play some more, and Nail would play his harmonica for them and feel almost well.

His bedclothes were often damp with blood and pus, and he couldn't understand why, because his wounds seemed to have scabbed over enough not to be bleeding. Eventually he was able to determine that the blood and pus were coming from his bedmate, who was now Stardust, and he didn't know if it was because they were flogging Stardust too; he tried not to listen when they were flogging somebody and the poor devil was screaming his head off. Stardust was not one to talk, anyway. But then Stardust began noticeably to take leave of his senses, as if he had not already left them long ago: he could be observed standing beside the bunk, moving his hands in the air as if building imaginary trees, root to bough, twig to trunk. That's all he did, when he was not crooning. He would stand for hours making trees until Fat Gabe would come and cut him down and dump him in beside Nail, where he would bleed and ooze. Finally Stardust and his few belongings were gathered up and taken away to the state hospital for the insane . . . which, I have good reason to know, was not a better place.

As soon as Stardust's spot was empty, they filled it with a new man, or a kid, rather, a boy maybe fifteen, sixteen at the most, whose hair reminded Nail of that woman's, what was her nice lady name who came and what was it she pretty girl had hair that same reddish sort of, Friday, Saturday, Sunday, Monday, yes her name was Monday, *that* lady, this boy his hair is like hers, red, he could pass for her kid brother only she was too nice a lady to have a kid brother to get hisself in trouble and thrown in the pen. This boy had stolen a horse. Nail listened, which was all he did these days and nights, when he wasn't running off to those sheep-cluttered hills in Stay More. The boy's name was Ernest something, but they were calling him Timbo Red because he came from Timbo, Arkansas, up in the hills of Stone County. Timbo Red talked more or less the same way that folks up home talked. Most of these fellers in here sounded like east Arkansas or downstate somewheres or probably outlanders from some other state, but Timbo Red sounded nearly just like Nail's kid brother Luther, and Nail took an interest in what he was doing and saying, and he took a special interest that first night when Thirteen tried to seduce the kid. Nail still couldn't talk very strong, but he had enough strength to raise himself up and say to Timbo Red, "Boy, don't ye let this here feller show ye his jemmison, or you'll hate it."

Thirteen turned on Nail. "My *what*?" he said.

"Keep yore pecker in yore pants, Thirteen," Nail said.

"Shit, mine is better than yours," Thirteen snarled. "You want to git him to yourself? I claimed him first. He's good ripe cherry punk, and I got him, and I aint gon let no man mess with my bride." He put his full palm over Nail's face and pushed down hard and mashed Nail's head down into the bunk. Then he resumed his seduction of Timbo Red, telling the kid that it wouldn't hurt a bit, not anywhere like the way the kid would get hurt if he didn't get his sweet ass out of those pants real damn fast.

Nail listened. He tried to tell if the kid was scared or eager or what. Some boys liked that kind of thing; there was a big old boy several bunks over who couldn't seem to get enough of it and would drop his pants for any feller who asked, and sometimes even went around asking them. Nail listened and thought he could hear Timbo Red asking to be let alone. The way Nail's mind ran away from him these days and wound up in that Stay More meadow faster than he could think, his mind was now beginning to believe that Timbo Red was Miss Friday or Miss Monday herself, asking old Thirteen to leave her be. Nail couldn't just lie here and let that nice lady be took against her wishes, or even took with her wishes by somebody foul like Thirteen. Now she seemed to be squealing. It wasn't a very happy sort of squeal. Nail's fingers were absently fooling with the collar of his jacket, and then slipping inside the jacket and fooling with the string around his neck. And then his fingers touched that steel. It was still there; he had almost forgotten about it in the what? weeks or days or months or whatever time had passed since he had intended to use it. He still had to remember not to roll over onto his stomach at night, or, if he did, to do it carefully so the razor-sharp dagger didn't cut his chest.

He took a deep breath and somehow got his legs up and under him so he could crouch and use what energy he had left to reach over and fall against Thirteen and pin him down and hold the dagger up to his eyes so he could get a good look at it, and then Nail said to him, "Thirteen, d'ye want to try out the edge of this and see how sharp it is? Or will you jist take my word for it?—it'll leave a gash from one of your ears to th'other'un in jist one swipe."

Thirteen scrambled away from the kid and away from Nail. "Where'd you git that shiv?" Thirteen asked.

"Been savin it fer ye," Nail said. "And I'll use it on ye if you touch her again."

" 'Her'?" Thirteen said. "You want 'her' for yourself, huh?"

"*Him*," Nail said, flustered. "He ast ye to leave him alone. I'm askin ye to leave him alone. Or die. You choose."

"Them guards catch you with that pigsticker, they gon make *you* die," Thirteen grumbled, but he didn't bother the kid for the rest of that night, and maybe not for the next few nights either, Nail couldn't tell how many nights went by, one after the other, without the kid being bothered.

One night Timbo Red just tapped Nail on the shoulder and said, "I thank ye, mister."

Timbo Red did not lose his virginity before Christmas, but he got the dose of the strap that Fat Gabe measured out to let anybody new know who was boss. Nail, listening, was not able to determine that it had been provoked. Probably not. Timbo Red seemed to be trying his best to get along with people; his lockstep was always right in line, and he tried to be well behaved and inconspicuous. Somewhere he had found a piece of white chalk, the same kind you write on blackboards with, and he would sit on the concrete floor drawing pictures on it. He could draw pretty fair. More than pretty fair, really. He could make an eagle that looked like an eagle and a black walnut tree that looked like a black walnut. The way he would sit and draw also reminded Nail of Miss Monday. Timbo Red's drawings got walked on, but he didn't care, and somebody always pissed on the drawings during the night and erased them that way, but Timbo Red would just start a fresh one the next morning. If Timbo Red ever did anything that might have provoked Fat Gabe, it must have had something to do with the way he was arting up the floor.

But more than likely, Fat Gabe just felt it was time to let the kid know what the strap felt like. Coming from a dirt farm in Stone County, Timbo Red probably knew the feel of harness leather on his hide the same way that Nail did, and he took the first ten lashes without even flinching. Fat Gabe was halfway through the second ten, and panting like a horse, before

Timbo Red gave any sign that he even noticed what was happening to his behind. But along about the fourteenth lick the boy started to weaken. He whimpered. At the nineteenth lick he was broken and sobbing. Fat Gabe didn't stop at twenty. Usually, twenty swings of the strap was all that Fat Gabe could manage at one time, but he was mad because the boy had tried to hold out on him like that, and he kept going. The boy kept sobbing like a child.

Nail didn't bring out his dagger, although he was tempted. Instead, he brought out his harmonica. He had never played it before where anybody could hear him. He had played it all the time when he was alone in the death hole, but not once since then, and he missed it. Now he wasn't even sure he could get the tune right, but from the first note he blew into it, he knew he could do a fair job. He played "O Little Town of Bethlehem." He played it loud, he played it lively, he played it with his tongue and lungs and heart. He played it loud enough to drown out Timbo Red's crying. He played it louder than the crack of Fat Gabe's strap.

Everyone listened. A few men tried to hum in tune. From several bunks away a good tenor voice picked up at: ". . . above thy deep and dreamless sleep, the silent stars go by . . ."

"Pack it up, Chism!" Fat Gabe hollered, and he stopped beating Timbo Red and started swinging at Nail, who scooted over to the far side of the bunk so Fat Gabe couldn't reach him without going around. Nail finished the carol and started playing "Deck the Halls."

One by one or in groups of several, the men of the hall joined in singing the words, and the blacks joined the chorus with: "Deck de haws wif baws ob holly!" One man at the end of the barracks climbed to an upper bunk and stood up and began to conduct the choir, waving his arms as if he'd once been a high-school band director. Everyone was singing.

Fat Gabe stopped beating on Timbo Red and shyly tried to sing, "Fa la la? La la? La la LAH LAH!"

Nail Chism played "Good King Wenceslaus." He played "It Came Upon the Midnight Clear." The three hundred voices singing, or trying to, drifted beyond the wall and reached the warden's house, the big two-story Victorian on the downslope to the highway. When the warden arrived at the barracks, Nail was playing "Silent Night," which was the last one that he knew. Mr. Burdell arrived in time to contribute "Sleep in heavenly peace," twice.

Then he smiled. No one had seen Mr. Burdell smile before. He said, "Well, gentlemen, it looks like you're already in the spirit of the season." He took from his pocket a letter, which he unfolded. "This year Governor Hays has seen fit to grant Christmas pardons to a total of thirty men. As follows." One by one the warden read the names, pausing after each to allow time for the men to whoop and holler and slap backs and carry on. Of course the two hundred and seventy men who were not pardoned were feeling low, and this included Nail, although he hadn't expected to hear his name on the list.

But his Christmas did not go unnoticed. Farrell Cobb came to visit, and stood beside Nail's bunk for a while, and gave him a present. "The missus fixed it," Cobb explained. "Hope you like fruitcake, although it's such a tiny one." Nail sampled a few bites, his first ever. Before the lawyer left, saying he hoped to bring good news from the state Supreme Court when he came again in January, he elaborately looked all around them to see if anybody was watching. Nobody was. Nobody cared what Cobb was doing there, or who he was speaking to. The nearest black trusties were shooting dice against the wall. "You can read, can't you?" Cobb asked, and when Nail nodded, the lawyer reached inside his coat and brought out an envelope and handed it to him. The lawyer put his finger to his lips and said "Shhh," and then he winked and departed.

Nail tried to sit up in his bunk to open the envelope. It contained several sheets of paper and something very small wrapped in tissue. Nail read the signature first and, thrilled, backed up and read each word with deliberate slowness.

December 22, 1914

Dear Mr. Chism,

They haven't let you see any of my previous letters, have they? I asked your attorney, Mr. T. Farrell Cobb, if it might be that the "authorities" are not allowing you to receive your mail. He said that it is a common practice for the warden and his assistants to open and read letters to check for contraband, inflammatory statements, scurrility, or information damaging to the morals and well-being of inmates. None of my previous letters to you contained any of these things.

Shortly after I last saw you, I attempted to visit you at the peniten-

101

tiary, but I was told that you are permitted to have only one visit per month, and that you had already had your December visit, so I will have to wait until January. I went straight home (I live here in Little Rock) and wrote to you.

Have you, I asked myself, chosen not to reply to my letters? That is possible, and you certainly have no obligation to respond. I did not ask you anything that required an answer, with the exception of my request for the whereabouts of your hometown, Staymore. I have, without any vanity, re-read the first drafts of my letters to you several times, in order to discover what they might have contained that could have accounted for your silence. I have not been able to determine anything possibly untoward or disagreeable in them. Thus, I like to think, and I *do not* like to think: they wouldn't let you have my letters.

So I am resorting to this expedient of asking Mr. Cobb to "smuggle" this letter to you. He said that he would. He seems a kind and well-meaning person, and I say this not to flatter him in case he is reading it too (Mr. Cobb, if you are reading it, please honor our agreement and deliver it as promised) but because there are so few decent, humane, compassionate men in this world. You are one yourself, Nail Chism, and you are rare, and that is the reason I have chosen to burden you with my attentions and devotion. If I have little else in the way of qualifications for existence, I have the ability— some would call it talent—to draw and paint the human likeness, and in the process to "read" the . . . whatever you wish to call it: soul, psyche, spirit, essence, of the subject, sitter, victim, poser, person. I am not bragging, and I do not boast that the finished work of art *conveys* this inner character of the person (or even that it is a "work of art," whatever that is), but I am sure of my knack for seeing it, and when I saw *your* spirit in those terrible moments that were presumed to be your last, there in that awful room with that hideous chair, I knew you, and I understood you, and I intuited you, and I appreciated you in a way that I have not been allowed to feel toward another human being.

Yes, I know you may be telling yourself: here is one more of those many lonely ladies who like to cultivate convicts, and who visit or correspond with prisoners, especially those condemned to die, and play upon the men's desperate need for sympathy in order to gratify their own wish for an imaginative relationship safe from entanglement, safe from physical contact, and above all safe from permanence. Some of these women see themselves as substitute mothers or nurses or sisters, and they think they are purely altruistic and they glory in their charity, while other women—widows, spinsters, the jilted and the frustrated—who have had unpleasant experiences with men who were free to touch them and free to hurt them, are craving a liaison which now permits them to have the upper hand, to be free to say no, free to manage and schedule every aspect of the association, and free to quit at any moment.

Please believe that I have never before written to a prisoner . . . or, for that matter, written a letter as long as this one to anybody. And please believe that my only interest in you is a deep certainty of your innocence, and a consuming desire to prove it.

When I first knew you, I was disposed to hate you. Do you remember our first meeting? We were both members of the "audience" at an execution. Before I was permitted to enter that room, I was lectured by Mr. Harris Burdell, the warden, who only with great reluctance had acceded to the request of my employer, Mr. Thomas Fletcher, managing editor of the *Arkansas Gazette*, that I be allowed to make a drawing of the condemned man, a young Negro. Mr. Burdell warned me that I would be sitting next to you, and he told me the crimes of which you had been accused and convicted and for which you had been sentenced to die. I suppose that Mr. Burdell was simply trying to frighten me, having failed to dissuade me from experiencing the horrors of the execution itself. But I was not afraid of you, because I despised you so intensely. The *Gazette* had carried a story of your original trial, and although the details had struck me as a ludicrous miscarriage of rustic backwoods justice, there was no mistaking the nature of the offense itself: a girl of only thirteen brutally abused and raped. Mr. Burdell personally checked my hair to make sure that I was not wearing a long hatpin with which I might stab your heart or put out your eyes. But I had not even seen you! When you were led into the room and given your seat beside me, I steeled myself to behold in your eyes the corruption and savagery which would have permitted you to commit such an abomination, and thus I was greatly surprised to detect such gentleness, such goodness, and such compassion as would preclude your hurting anyone, let alone a thirteen-year-old girl.

And you remember, I'm sure, how you inveighed against that butcher of an executioner, Mr. Irvin Bobo, when the first charge of electricity failed to remove the poor Negro from this world. You called upon God to damn Mr. Bobo, and although I had the feeling that you were spontaneously invoking God without any real belief in Him, you conveyed exactly the words that I would have spoken myself if I had not temporarily closed myself off from all feeling.

Often at night when I am trying to fall asleep I hear your voice shouting those words. And when you yourself sat down in the chair and the warden lifted his hand and Mr. Bobo placed his hand upon the switch, I said aloud, "Goddamn you, Bobo, turn up the juice and leave it on!"

But you were spared! Although you weren't pardoned or your sentence commuted, you were not murdered. I have learned as much as I can about the reprieve: I've talked to Mr. Cobb (hello again, Farrell!), I've talked to Judge J. V. Bourland and Judge Jesse Hart; I've even had a short audience with His Excellency George W. Hays Himself (although the governor, I regret to say, doesn't even seem to know who you are), and I know that you are still very much in peril of having another date set for the electrocution. I intend to do whatever I can to prevent this.

I have received permission from my employer, Thomas Fletcher (who is another of the rare breed of gentle and kind men), to investigate the case completely. As I told you, I'm not one of the *Gazette*'s regular reporters, only a member of the layout and design department, where I am usually found trying to enliven the margins of inner pages with my little sketches. But I have written for the *Gazette* in the past—the longest thing I ever wrote, before this letter, was an article, "An Arkansawyer in Calcutta," a place where I saw some of this world's most unkind and uncompassionate men. Mr. Fletcher has promised to free me from my usual duties long enough to permit me to finish my investigation.

Only these severe winter storms we've been having have prevented me from attempting to find and to visit Staymore. But when we get a thaw in January, I'm going to locate it . . . even if I can only reach it on horseback! (I should have said I have *two* talents: the other one is that I am a "cowgirl.")

I have three requests, if you will be so kind:

1. Where is Staymore? I have a map showing Newton County but cannot locate your town. Is it north of Jasper? What kind of roads lead to it?

2. What people should I talk to? Can you give me the names of any witnesses who can account for your whereabouts at the time of the crime? Also, any character witnesses. Who was your best friend?

3. Before I go, is there *anything* I can do for you? Is there anything you need? Will they allow me to send you a basket of fruit and some cookies? May I smuggle you a book or two? Do you enjoy reading? Any favorite authors? Are you well clothed? Do you need any personal articles? Please do not hesitate to respond to these requests, and do not think of the expense. Meanwhile please accept the enclosed trifle as a token, a talisman, a keepsake, a substitute for a *real* Yuletide. Merry Christmas, and many more.

Sincerely,
Viridis Monday

Nail Chism read this a second time before he opened his present. In due course he would come to know it by heart. He would unfold it and read it when no one else was looking (and no one else ever was), again and again, until its creases broke and it began to turn dirty and frayed. But for now he read it only twice, and then he picked open the tiny wad of tissue paper.

Inside was a gent's charm, the kind of chain ornament you hook on one end of your watch chain, if you have a watch, but Nail didn't. It was made of gold and must have cost her several dollars. But she must have had it special-made by some jeweler, because it didn't look like a store-boughten gent's charm. It was in the shape of a tree. Not a Christmas pine or a cedar, nor a hardwood you'd be able to recognize, but just a *tree* tree, no mistake. Nail turned it over. She'd had the trunk on the backside of the tree engraved in tiny letters: To N.C. FROM V.M. XMAS 14.

Even if he'd had a watch, and a watchpocket to put it in, he wouldn't have worn this on a chain for all the world to see. Instead, he attached it to the string around his neck that held his dagger, and wore them both hidden inside his shirt and jacket. It was the nicest Christmas present he'd ever gotten. He could hear that little tree singing to him.

And on Christmas afternoon the Salvation Army was permitted to come into the building and serve a soup that actually had some chicken in it, and with real biscuit besides. The men were required to sit through a long sermon before they were allowed to drink the soup, which was cold by then, but Nail was able to make it to the mess hall on his own legs, for the first time in weeks, and to drink his soup.

Afterward, as the men were waiting to leave the mess hall, required to keep lockstepping in place until the line could move again, Nail discovered that he was lifting and setting his feet right beside the standing figure of Mr. Harris Burdell, who was observing the Christmas festivities.

"Warden Burdell, sir," Nail managed to say, although his words were nearly drowned by the men tramping the floor with their feet. "I sure do 'preciate you lettin us men have a good Christmas dinner like this. I know I don't deserve it, and I know I don't deserve nothin on account of my misbehavior. But I jist want to thank you, sir. It is real good of you. And Merry Christmas to you, Mr. Burdell."

"Same to you, Chism," Burdell said, without smiling but without any rancor or malice in his voice.

"Sir, my brother told me that our ole mother is a-dyin, and he ast me could I jist send her a few last words. Sir, would there be any way I could git me some writin-paper and a pencil? Sir, I'd do jist anything if I could have me somethin to write a letter to my dyin mother."

The line was beginning to move. Nail looked pleadingly over his shoulder at Mr. Burdell, who did not seem to have heard him. But a few days later one of the blacks who waited on the table at dinner wordlessly placed beside Nail's plate a lead pencil and a penny tablet of lined paper, which, Nail counted, contained twenty sheets. He used a sheet dutifully to write a letter for Mr. Burdell to see, censor, and mail:

Dear Momma,

Waymon told me about you. I hope you are better. You know we are going to meet again in Heaven, where they are saving a special place for you. I'm sorry you did not get to see me again. Waymon said you were not able to come with him to Little Rock, and I under-

106

stand. You must try to take care of your self better. I wish there was something I could say to make you feel better but all I can say is I love you and do not worry about me. What happens to me is in the hands of some one far better than me. And I aim to see you, all bye and bye, and you can count on it. Please be happy.

Your son with love for ever,
Nail

His mother might puzzle just a little over that—*if* she got it—but he knew that Waymon would help her understand any of it that she couldn't, and he would explain the rest of it to her when he saw her, not in Heaven, which was a strange land to him, but in Stay More, one of these days.

Then he used several sheets of the penny tablet to write the following, which he did not give to Mr. Burdell to see, censor, and keep from mailing.

December 29–31, 1914

Dear Miss Monday,

How can I hope to answer? You write like the morning breeze soughing through the cedars, like a hive full of honey, like sun climb on the ridge, you write easy as breathing, like an angel's sigh, and I am dumb.

How can I hope to thank you? You give me more than a gift, far more than this tiny tree trophy I'm wearing now next to my lungs, far more than any fruit basket or book you want to bring me, even far more than the many hours you've done already spent talking to folks on my behalf. You give me hope, real hope, but that is not the greatest gift. You give me your "attentions and devotion," although you call them a burden and they aren't, but they are not the greatest gift either. You give me words nice as music singing where my merit hides, but they are not the gift which gladdens me greatly.

The gift which greatly humbles me beyond any speaking of thanks is that this world don't have very many women in it who are able to like themself enough so that they have so much left over they can give some to a man, and you are one of those, you give me some of that self-respect or self-liking that you have left over after you get done helping yourself to it.

I would beg you please don't misunderstand if I did not think you know what I mean without any insult or accusing you of pride or airs or vanity, which I don't mean at all. You are not just a uncommon kind woman, Viridis Monday, but a woman more uncommon than that: a *smart* kind woman. Not a woman who is kind because she is too dumb to know any better and goes around trusting everbody and being sweet and stupid and benevolent because there's not a thought in her head to keep her from thinking she ought to trust and be sweet. No, you have thought it all over. You have even thought about how much of that trust and sweetness you ought to spend on yourself before you go throwing it around to others less deserving.

And then you discovered you had enough to spare and you shared it with me. I can accept it from you with gladness and gratefulness because I know you can afford to spend it, which maybe you can't afford to do on a basket of fruit or a book, not to mention this solid gold gent's charm you gave me. You won't misunderstand this either: that I sure do appreciate the gent's charm, and I do know exactly why it's a tree, and why you asked them to make it like that, and I will still be wearing it to my grave or old age, whichever comes first, but it bothers me some that it cost you money that maybe you couldn't afford, the way you can afford to let me have some of that leftover self-respect.

You do not know me. I believe that you are blessed with some kind of ability to look a person in the eye before doing their picture and tell whether that person is good, bad, or not worth shooting. You make better pictures than I ever even drempt was possible to draw. I don't know you either but I know that you must have seen all kinds of eyes. Clear, squinty, keen, beady, bright, dim, smiling, pink, crossed, hawk, walled, dull, catty, goggled, popped, bug, glared, blinked, squinched, cataracted. Enough of all kinds to be able to look in their eye and tell what demons are afollowing them or what angels are aleading them.

But you don't know me or any of my life except what they said I done to that girl, which you know I didn't do. You don't even know how the way that I was raised and what I come to want to do with my life was such that I couldn't never even have thought about doing it to her. You don't know the hills of Stay More, and you don't know the Ingledews, Duckworths, Bournes, Whitters, Plowrights, Coes, Bullens, Murrisons, Dinsmores, Kimbers, and Swains, and only one Chism, me, and not much of me. Even if you did know ever last one of them, you'd just have the makings of a start on knowing somebody like Sull Jerram, who is waiting at the end of your investigation like a toad sitting on a rock all day long waiting for a butterfly to get within shot of his tongue.

But Sull Jerram is not real Stay More folks, though he was born there. The closest Judge Jerram ever come to being Stay More folks was somehow persuading my nice but not very bright sister Irene into marrying him. She's my half sister, actually. But I am not even going to start in trying to tell you about all these people. If you want to begin from scratch and try to get to know Stay More, in the dead of winter, or at any time, you would probably enjoy it, even if you never found a shred of proof that I didn't rape Dorinda Whitter.

She's not the one you should start with. She's the so-called victim, and many a time I have told myself that she couldn't be just playing off that way, that somebody actually must have done it to her. And I think maybe whoever done it to her done it just so the law would believe her when she got up and said what he told her to say.

There is another girl you ought to talk to first, if you are really of a mind to visit Stay More. Her name is Latha Bourne, and she is about the same age as Dorinda, and I reckon you could say they was best friends at one time, maybe still. But she is another one of them females who like yourself is able to be honest enough with herself to have some left over to be honest and kind and smart with other people. If you want to look into a pair of eyes, start with hers.

As for character witnesses, any man, woman or child in Stay More who ever knew me or just saw me out yonder in the pasture with my sheep will likely tell you whatever you need to know. But you should be sure and talk to the fellows that sit on Ingledew's store porch, except this time of year they won't be out there on the porch, they'll be inside sitting around his potbelly stove. And Willis Ingledew himself can tell you I was there on that porch that time they said she claimed it was done to her. I'm sorry to have to say, though, that there isn't one of those folks who could let me call them best friend.

I'm not too sure just what that is, tell you the honest truth. My brothers are both real good friends but they're brothers so maybe that don't count.

Right now I feel like you are my best friend.

On the back side of this sheet I've drawed a sort of map that ought to help you get from Jasper to Stay More (that is the way it is always spelled, not Staymore all one word the way you did it). All the roads thereabouts are hell on autos. But I have to tell you, Viridis Monday, I can't imagine a lady riding a horse into Stay More. Nobody there has ever heard tell of a cowgirl and their tongues are sure to wag out of their faces.

But come to think on it, let them wag. This time of year they don't have nothing to talk about anyhow. Just give each and ever one of those Stay More folks that smile of yours, which is I swear the nicest smile I ever saw on any creature except one of my late lamented sheep. Tell everbody I said hello, and give them all my love.

And to you, good lady, there are no words, except:

Your friend,
Nail

P.S. I really can't use anything myself I don't already have, but if you'd like to bring something the next time you come or send Mr. Cobb with it, there is a boy here who is a friend of mine and very good at drawing like you and even has hair like yours but he has nothing to draw with excepting a piece of chalk. If you could smuggle one of those drawing pencils like you use and that type of pad. We would appreciate it.

Then he just had to wait for a chance to get the letter out to her via Farrell Cobb. He did not have an envelope, but he kept the pages folded three times and pressed inside his copy of *Dr. Hood's Plain Talks and Common Sense Medical Advisor*, where he could get the letter out and slip it to Cobb the next time he showed up.

———

January came, a new year, 1915, without any observance or notice. The few men who had old calendars ripped them up, and the fewer men who had new calendars brought them out and began to mark off the days. The flyspeck room always had a waiting list of patients suffering frostbite from being sent off to work at the lumber yard or the brickyard or on the Rock Island railroad. Nail was able to walk around pretty well, although he'd lost forty pounds and wouldn't have known himself if he'd had a mirror to meet himself in, which he didn't, but he was not able to be sent out to work, even if it was permitted, which it wasn't. Convicts under sentence of death, according to law, could not be made to work, or even volunteer to work, and he was still under sentence of death although he wore stripes like the other men (condemned men, by the same law, could not be made to wear stripes since it was assumed they would never escape). He could tell by feel that his hair was growing back in; it was just as well he couldn't see that it was coming back in irregular patches of white and his usual old brownish blond.

He didn't have a calendar, but he was well enough and sane enough to keep count of the days, and to know that two weeks of January went by before he ever got a chance to "mail" his letter in care of his lawyer. Those two weeks were restless ones. The other men weren't speaking to him. If his harmonica at Christmas had temporarily thawed the chill of their hatred for a child-molester, it was just as temporary as the thaw in Fat Gabe's cold blood. Nobody spoke to Nail except Timbo Red.

The boy sensed that Nail was a fellow mountaineer, even without recognizing it in his voice. One morning while marking up the floor with his chalk as Nail watched him, Timbo Red looked up and said, "Do you 'member what a bar looks lak?"

"Why, shore," Nail said, a bit surprised that someone had spoken to him.

"Could ye draw one fer me?"

Nail laughed. He could see a bear as plain as if one were sitting on the edge of the bunk, but he couldn't draw a bear, or anything else. "Son, I can just barely draw my name," he said. "But why don't ye give it a try, and I'll tell ye what's right and what aint."

So Timbo Red commenced attempting to draw a bear from memory or imagination, and Nail would point out that the ears were a little off, or the nose was too flat, and the eyes looked a little more gentle than that, et cetera. Soon, between Nail's talking and Timbo's drawing, they had themselves a pretty fair bear.

Nail wanted to tell Timbo Red about Miss Monday. He wanted to tell the boy that he hoped to get him one of those drawing-sticks made of charcoal that real artists use, and something to draw on more permanent than a pissed-on floor. But he didn't want to count his chickens before they hatched, and he hadn't even been able to send the request off to the lady.

Nail and Timbo Red talked about other things. They talked about hunting and fishing, and which was the best gun for a squirrel and the best bait for a bass. Timbo Red had never seen a panther up close, and Nail described one and their habits and how to shoot one if you had to.

Sometimes, when they weren't talking about wildlife, Nail would tell the boy some of the old tall tales that he'd heard from the oldtimers: tales of kings and princesses and monsters, tales of trickery and daring and brave escape. Nail had never before been a storyteller, just a listener, and he was a little surprised to discover he had a talent for it. The boy made a rapt audience, especially for the stories about brave escape, and that helped.

Out of the blue one evening Timbo Red asked him, "Was the gal ye took willin, or didje really have to force her?"

Nail stared at the boy, not understanding the question for a long moment. Then he simply said, "There wasn't no gal."

Timbo Red, for one, believed him. He got Nail to tell him the history, to tell him about Dorinda Whitter and Judge Sull Jerram and the county sheriff and the moonshine business and all that. When Nail had finished the long story, Timbo Red declared, "I knew a gal lak thet wunst." Timbo Red talked about this old Stone County gal who was cut from the same bolt of gingham that Rindy was, and who got an innocent man in bad trouble, although he left the country before they could send him to the chair. "What's thet cheer like?" Timbo Red inquired, and wanted Nail to give him a complete description of Old Sparky. On the floor Timbo Red drew a chalk picture of Old Sparky that was amazing, considering he had never actually seen the chair himself. For some reason that drawing was allowed to remain for several days before it got pissed away.

One day Nail was telling Timbo Red the story of the king and his daughter Rhonda, who was beheaded by her father because she wouldn't let him seduce her. The climax of this awful tale was interrupted by the appearance of Farrell Cobb. Nail just looked up from watching the reactions of his listener to his tale and there was the lawyer standing there, unsmiling. Farrell Cobb himself looked like someone who'd just been required to behead his own daughter. He looked like a preacher at a funeral. Nail's heart took a jump and got caught in his throat.

"Bad news, huh?" Nail said.

Cobb nodded. "I regret to say," he obviously regretted to say, "that the state Supreme Court doesn't want to hear your appeal."

"What do you mean?" Nail asked. "Did they shut the door on ye?"

"Figuratively, yes. Literally, I was allowed to present my request to be heard. They gave me all of an hour. Most of them listened. Judge Bourland spoke to them also, on your behalf. Judge Hart asked some intelligent questions and seemed genuinely interested in our case, but the others . . ." Farrell Cobb raised his hands as if trying to lift an impossible weight off his shoulders. "I'm sorry. The general feeling seems to be that unless Circuit Judge Villines recommends commutation of his original sentence, that sentence must be carried out."

"But Villines is in cahoots with those fellers who did it!" Nail protested.

"Did what?" Cobb asked.

"Raped the girl and tried to pin it on me!"

"Why would Judge Villines want to do that?"

"That's a long story, and I'm surprised at ye that you haven't heard it."

But, as always, Farrell Cobb was not disposed to hang around for chitchat or complicated stories. He drew a piece of paper out of his pocket and said, "Sign this, please. It's a shot in the dark, a hundred-to-one chance, but it's all we can do. Do you understand what a habeas corpus is?" When Nail shook his head, the lawyer explained, "The writ might get you out of here and into a courtroom for a hearing. But as I say, probably not. And if not, your execution has been reset for April 20th."

Before Cobb could leave, Nail remembered Dr. Hood and got the book from under the bunk and took out the letter for Miss Monday. He looked around. Nobody was watching or paying any attention except Timbo Red, and he was a friend. "Mr. Cobb, could you deliver this for me?" Nail asked his lawyer. "Or someway get it to her? It's my answer to what she wrote."

Cobb grinned, winked conspiratorially, took the letter, and put it inside his coat. "I feel like Cupid," he remarked.

"Look," Nail said, "if they're gonna go ahead and electercute me in April, I don't guess there's anything she could do to stop them. So tell her that, would ye?"

"She already knows," Cobb said. "But I think she's still determined to save you. How, I don't know."

When Cobb had left, Timbo Red said to Nail, "Now I reckon I know why you carry that blade around yore neck. You aim to use it if they try to kill ye. Just hurtin ye aint enough, but if they try to kill ye, you'll take a few to Hell with ye."

For the rest of January, Nail waited to see if Cobb would come again with more news or another letter from Viridis Monday. He did not. Just as Viridis Monday had reread her earlier letters to Nail to determine why he hadn't answered them (when in fact he hadn't received them), Nail began to call up the words he had written to her and wonder if he had said anything that might have offended her or put her off. All he could find in his memory of his letter was that business about his sheep having a better smile than hers. Maybe that insulted her. But maybe she was planning to come see him instead of write to him again. Nail was owed a fifteen-minute trip to the visit room this month, and he kept hoping that Short Leg would come and take him there, but Short Leg did not.

Most of the men who were not taken out each day to work were transferred to the new prison farm at Tucker downstate, where conditions were supposed to be even worse than here, and there were afternoons when Nail had the barracks practically all to himself, because even Timbo Red was out somewhere working. The only ones besides Nail who didn't get sent out to work were those too sick or too frostbitten or too injured from floggings to be able to move. Nail wasn't sick anymore, but they wouldn't send him out, because of the law.

He never left the building until, late in the afternoon on January 30th, Short Leg came and got him. Nail's low spirits soared up, and he walked so briskly that Short Leg had to grab him at one point when he was heading toward the visit room and say, "Not that way, Chism. *This* way," and then led him into the power and light building where Old Sparky was. For one terrible moment Nail thought perhaps he'd misunderstood the lawyer and that Farrell Cobb hadn't said April 20th but January 30th, or maybe it was already April 20th and Nail hadn't been paying good attention.

But it was just that he was required to witness again. It was time for

Ramsey. Nail was the first witness to sit; and before the others came he had to sit a long time, expecting and hoping that any minute the door would open and in would walk Miss Monday to do her drawing of Ramsey. Nail looked at the window and calculated that sundown was maybe still half an hour off, and maybe Viridis Monday could come and sit beside him and they could talk for a while, and if no one was looking he'd even sneak her a peek at his tree-shaped gent's charm. He'd thank her again in a way he couldn't do in writing because he couldn't express himself that way. He'd thank her most for wanting to go to Stay More and meet folks and try to find someone who could help get him commuted. He'd tell her what had been on his mind these past few days: that when April 20th came around, he'd appreciate it if she would stay at home. He didn't want her coming to his execution, not even to yell at Bobo.

He didn't have to yell at Bobo this time. The other witnesses came, but Viridis Monday wasn't one of them. Burdell came. Fat Gabe came, bringing Ramsey, who was twisting and screaming at the top of his lungs and begging Jesus to save him. For a minute there Nail couldn't believe it was Ramsey, who had been so silent and withdrawn. But it was him, changed into a wild lunatic. At one point he broke loose from Fat Gabe and fell down at Mr. Burdell's feet and wrapped his arms around the warden's legs and begged and pled and said everything he could think of that might move him, but Mr. Burdell just motioned for Fat Gabe and Short Leg to get him back up and into the chair, and they did. Jimmie Mac tried to say the final prayer, but his words were drowned out by Ramsey trying to get people to believe that if he had just one more chance he'd be the best man the world ever knew since Jesus Himself.

Bobo seemed to be relieved to shut out that noise; he seemed to be pushing down a lever that would turn off all that screaming and pleading, and he left that lever down. He left it down too long, and the room filled up with the choking fumes of blackened flesh. One of the witnesses fainted and knocked over another one while he was falling. Another witness vomited all over himself and one of the others.

It was just as well Miss Monday hadn't been there.

———

February came. He imagined the buds were a-swelling. The trees were not going to sing for another month or more, but the buds swole up as if the trees were humming in practice and tune-up. The grimy windows of

115

the barracks seemed to be admitting more sunlight. Timbo Red took to drawing daffodils on the floor, not just stick figures with ball flowers stuck on them but real convincing daffodils that you could almost touch, that looked as if they were bright-yellow although they were black-and-white, that smelled like daffodils although they really smelled like piss.

The men who had "sweethearts" among the other men, the punks and queers, had a Valentine's party and exchanged modest gifts or sentiments. A lucky few men got to go to the visit room to see their real female sweethearts.

The powers of observation of men in prison take one of two directions: either they become oblivious to all but the most glaring sights around them, or they develop an ability to notice the most insignificant and inconspicuous little details. Nail one day noticed that Fat Gabe's belt had small notches cut along the upper edge, and he counted them, eighteen, and one day after another one of the beaten prisoners had passed away Nail counted again and there were nineteen notches.

One night in bed Timbo Red whispered into Nail's ear, "Sometimes I git so pruney and itchy I got a mind to go ahead and let Thirteen have me. Unless you want me. I druther it was you." Nail could not answer that, or respond, but later in the night, when it was clear the boy was not going to be able to sleep, Nail used his hand to get the boy over the mountain.

Often Nail asked himself why it was that he hadn't been returned to the death hole. If another date had been set for his delayed execution, April 20th, and he was once more condemned, then why wasn't he back in his old cell in the basement of the power and light? He preferred it there. It was dark and solitary and even scary, but he didn't have to put up with anybody except whoever was in the other cell, like Ramsey or Skip, who had been all right, for a couple of murderers. Sometimes he was tempted to request that Mr. Burdell return him to the death hole. Only two things kept him from it: one was he was genuinely fond of Timbo Red and wanted to keep an eye out for the boy and help him in whatever way he could, even if it meant what he had done that one night, which wasn't a queer thing to do but just handy and charitable, and the other reason was that in the death hole he'd never get to go to the visit room.

Not that he ever got summoned to the visit room. As February drew to its foreshortened close, he consciously prevented thoughts of the visit room from ever again torturing him. Some men in prison are capable of such self-control of their minds; they are able to put themselves to sleep at night or to resume sleep after springing awake in the middle of a nightmare by preventing their minds from thinking too much, or thinking about the wrong things. The visit room was a wrong thought, and Nail succeeded at last in abolishing it entirely from his consciousness.

Thus he was totally surprised one morning in late February when Short Leg came to his bunk, kicked his foot to draw his attention, and held out the handcuffs. "Visit room, Chism. There's a lady waiting to see you."

H e looked terrible. His hair was growing back in uneven patches, which were white as well as blond, reminding her of dustings of snow on the Stay More hillsides beneath the dark branches of trees. But his head was still splendid compared with his body, which looked starved and emaciated. He was smiling at her as if he'd never been happier in his life, but his body looked as if it had already died. She held out her hands to the screen that separated them, a screen so fine that she could not even get her fingertips through it to touch him. He put his hands up to hers, and although their hands did not touch, it was almost as if they were in contact. The guard motioned with the end of his shotgun barrel for them to remove their hands from the screen. Dropping her hands, she found her voice: "Hello, Nail." It did not cause her any discomfort to address him familiarly; she felt she knew him very well; indeed, she now knew many things about him that he probably did not know himself.

"Howdy, Miss M—" He started to address her formally but then asked, politely, as if making an important request, "What can I call ye?" And then suggested an answer: "Do you want me to call ye Viridis?" She nodded. "I've been lookin for ye," he said in a way that told her he had been counting the hours waiting for her.

"I've done a bit of traveling," she said. "I've been to your Stay More and back. It took me a while."

"On a horse?" he asked, grinning.

She nodded. "A mare, actually. Named Rosabone."

"You rode Rosabone all the way to Stay More?"

"No, we took the train as far as Clarksville."

" 'We'? Oh, you mean you and the mare?"

She nodded. He laughed. She declared, "Stay More is a beautiful place. A fabulous place."

"This time of year?" He raised his heavy eyebrows, which were the only good hair he had remaining on his head. "Swains Creek must be froze."

"Banty Creek is iced over, but not Swains Creek."

"You went up Banty Creek?"

"I went everywhere."

"Even my—even the Chism place?"

"Especially the Chism place."

"You met my momma?"

"I had some long talks with your mother."

"And Paw—how is he?"

"Middlin to fair."

Nail chuckled. " 'Middlin to fair,' huh? Who taught ye that?"

"Who does it sound like?"

"*Him*. Paw. You said it almost like he was standin right here."

"He wishes he were. He said to tell you, 'Boy, don't ye never fergit, yo're a Chism, and Chisms don't never quit.' "

Nail shook his head in wonder. "It's almost like you brought his voice with ye."

"I brought all their voices with me." She looked him closely in the eye, as near as the screen would permit. "And the voices of the trees too. In your front yard, looking out over the whole valley and the next valley over, there are two huge trees. Sockdolager old trees!"

" 'Sockdolager . . .' " Nail chuckled. "You didn't hear that one from Paw."

"No, from Willis Ingledew. But he wasn't talking about your trees. Nobody called your trees that, except the trees themselves."

Nail squinted his eyes intently. "They spoke to ye?"

She smiled. "In a manner of speaking. They don't use our language, of course. And you and I are both crazier than coots."

Laughing, he said, "Those trees are a walnut and a maple. I used to climb that walnut plumb nearly to the top, and I could see all the way to Jasper. And that old maple, the peckerwoods would ring it and make the awfulest racket while I was tryin to build play roads around the roots."

She saw him again at the age of nine, alone, building his play roads beneath the maple. Alone because, Nancy Nail Chism had told her, the nearest kid his own age, E. H. Ingledew (always called E. H.), now the village dentist (who'd sat Viridis in his chair while he answered her questions because that was the only way he could talk to anyone), lived a long way off and was from a better family that didn't "mix" with the Chisms.

A precious one of their fifteen allotted minutes escaped while Nail reminisced about the trees in his yard and Viridis again pictured him there. She was hoping he wouldn't ask about his brother Waymon so that she wouldn't have to tell him.

119

"Well," he said at length, "didje git to talk to Latha Bourne?"

"Oh, yes!" Viridis exclaimed. "You told me once there were only three people who really know you are innocent: yourself, your mother, and Dorinda. That's a very conservative estimate. Everyone in Stay More *believes* you are innocent, but Latha Bourne *knows* you are innocent. She's a remarkable young lady. She is, as you told me, honest and smart and kind. I'm very fond of Latha Bourne."

Nail shook his head. "What I could never figure is how come a nice girl like her become chummy with Rindy Whitter in the first place."

She looked at him. She did not know how to say this, but she tried: "Dorinda Whitter is not totally bad. She's not very intelligent, and what little sense she has is corrupted by her greed and selfishness, but she is not hopelessly malignant."

"Oh, so you talked to her too?"

"I talked to everyone, Nail."

"Everyone? That's an awful lot of people."

Their allotted time was running out. She opened her purse and took out the bundle of pages and peeled off the top sheet. "Let me read the beginning," she said, and read: " 'To His Excellency Governor George W. Hays. We, the undersigned, residents and voters of Newton County, Arkansas, do hereby solemnly petition Your Excellency to consider the sentence of death under which our friend, Nail Chism, has been placed, wrongly we feel. We each and severally believe him to be innocent of the crime of which he was charged, and we humbly entreat Your Excellency to wield your authority to pardon him, or at least to commute the sentence of death.' "

Viridis held up the many sheets so that Nail could see the signatures. "There are 2,806 names here, in all," she said. "Of course, many of them are just X's, but in each case where the person was unable to write his or her name, I have filled it in beside the X. See?" She held up page after page for his scrutiny.

Nail peered at the sheets as closely as the screen would allow. "I declare, you've got *ever*body on there!" he exclaimed. And she did, and she knew it: people from all over Newton County but particularly the Stay Morons: all the Ingledews, Duckworths, Plowrights, Swains, Coes, Chisms, Bullens, Bournes, Murrisons, Cluleys, Dinsmores, Kimbers . . . yes, even the Whitters. Of course all of the names were male; a voteless woman's name carried no weight with the governor. But there was one female name, and Viridis held her forefinger on it and said, "Now, here's an X, but beside it there's an attempt to spell out the name. Can you make out the letters?"

Nail slowly read and spoke each letter. "D," he said. "O, and R, and I, and N, and—" He stopped, he looked up at Viridis, and his eyes were questioning so that what he said next sounded almost like a question but was actually a statement, just whispered: "It's *her*."

Viridis nodded. "Now, listen, Nail. Our time is almost up. I'm going to go home and try to write you some of the things that I don't have time to tell you, and I'll get Farrell Cobb to bring you the letter within a week. There's so *much* I have to tell you about my trip to Stay More. I have to tell you about Judge Jerram . . ."

"Don't tell me you met him too?"

"I had some very unpleasant encounters with Judge Sull Jerram. I'll tell you about it. I've got so *many* things to tell you, but for now our time has run out."

"Hell," Nail said. "They ought to give us thirty minutes, on account of I didn't get any visit time during January. I'm owed twice as much, aren't I?"

"You certainly are," she said. "But I can have only half of it. I've talked to Mr. Fancher—the one you call Short Leg—and he says that you can have another fifteen minutes for the time you didn't have in January." She smiled. "But not with me. There's someone else here waiting to see you. I've got to go. I'll be your first visitor for March. Good-bye for now, Nail. Take care, and promise me you'll try to eat whatever they give you."

"Who—? What—? Hey!" Nail protested, but before he could say anything else, she got herself out of there. In the anteroom she gave a sigh both of relief at getting out on time, in fifteen minutes, and of disappointment at not having been able to talk to him more.

Then she turned to the bench where the girl was sitting. "All right, Dorinda," she said. "You be a good girl and get yourself on in there."

off

Off she had gone to Stay More, in the middle of the winter, and we had met. To me, at first, she had been simply that stranger-lady everybody was already talking about so much that the gossip reached me before she did. The first I had ever heard of Viridis Monday was Bertha Kimber telling my mother, "Ay-law, Fannie, they's a womarn a-stayin down to the Ingledew big house and done rid her mare plumb from Little Rock!"

But Viridis did not ride the mare all the way from Little Rock, which would have taken forever even if she and the horse both had not frozen to death. No, she put the mare on a train, and they rode the train for most of the way, and she rode the mare only the last sixty miles or so of the trip . . . but that is getting ahead of the story.

Tom Fletcher did not want her to do it. The *Gazette*'s managing editor tried not just once but on several occasions through December and January to dissuade Viridis from making the trip. When it became obvious to him that she would not be discouraged by the weather reports, deterred by horrendous descriptions of the Newton County terrain and roads (or lack of them), daunted by the obvious futility of the mission (Fletcher himself, he later confessed to her, had done some checking and sent a couple of seasoned statehouse reporters out to gather the facts and determine that Nail Chism was guilty, and that unless and until Arkansas joined the other states that had abolished the death penalty for rape there was not going to be any way to get the sentence commuted), diverted by a more interesting assignment (he offered to let her cover the legislature's debate on whether or not Arkansas would go totally dry)—only then did he attempt to kid her out of the "mission" by making it seem an adventure into terra incognita: She would need, he said, to hire some guides, and an interpreter, and a band of bearers. She would need an English-Ozarkian dictionary and phrasebook. She would have to get herself a raccoon coat and a coonskin cap and carry an elephant gun. As a joke, Tom Fletcher had the boys down in the pressroom print up a mock article, "Elephants in the Ozarks," which he left on her desk.

When it became clear to him (and he was a wise man as well as a practical joker) that nothing would stop her from going to Stay More, he called her to his desk and sat her down and apologized for having belittled her plan, and announced that he had given it some serious thought and decided not only to let her go but to take her himself. If she could just wait until early March when it warmed up a bit, he could get a few days off and borrow a Columbia touring car, which would get the two of them up there and back to Little Rock in no time. He had checked the route as far as Jasper, where, he knew, there was a fair hotel called the Buckhorn they could put up at. Separate rooms, of course, he added, and winked.

Viridis liked Tom Fletcher quite a lot, but she did not like the idea of waiting until March, or of having her own investigation paced and directed by her boss. If it was all the same to him, she said, she'd appreciate having her total independence.

When the time of her furlough from the *Gazette* approached, he called her to his desk again and laid out before her the timetables of the railroads. She could take the St. Louis & Iron Mountain train westbound as far as Van Buren, transfer there (after a night's layover at a fair hotel) to a St. Louis & San Francisco (or "Frisco") train, which would take her north to Fayetteville, or, rather, to Fayette Junction, the terminus of the Frisco's spur eastward to Pettigrew, where, after a night (at a fair hotel), she could hire a driver and buggy to take her over the mountains a day's ride (or a day and a half, at most) to Stay More. She ought to be able to make the whole trip, there and back, in a week.

Viridis thanked Tom Fletcher for his concern and his help, but she had already planned her itinerary, and her modus operandi. She intended to put her own Arabian mare aboard the Iron Mountain train, which she would ride only as far as Clarksville, then alight there and ride the mare northward for two days until she reached Stay More.

Tom Fletcher consulted his maps and tables. "But there aren't any fair hotels in that wilderness," he said. "And you're not going to camp out under the stars in this weather."

She smiled and told him she would manage, without any camping out. She was not taking a bedroll or any equipment other than a spare blanket for extra warmth if she needed it, and a heavy horse blanket for her mare. Her saddlebags—and she was using an American western saddle, not an English riding-saddle—would contain only her changes of clothing, one dress neatly folded, spare jodhpurs, extra shoes, her writing-pads, pencils, and her sketchbooks and drawing-supplies.

"Aren't you going to be armed?" Tom Fletcher asked, and when she showed him the derringer she kept in her purse, he laughed and said it might deter human molesters but wouldn't work against an elephant . . . or, okay, there weren't any of those, but there were real wolves, bears, and panthers. He persuaded her to accept the loan of a Smith & Wesson revolver, which, he said, would not kill wolves, bears, or panthers but would certainly intimidate them. Since, he warned, facility in the use of a revolver is not easily acquired, he offered to give her some lessons. "Let's climb into my Ford and drive over to Big Rock and shoot bottles."

That was their first "date." Emboldened, a day later he asked her to dinner. Tom Fletcher was a thirty-two-year-old bachelor possessed of a strong, handsome face despite overly bulging eyeballs, and, as we've noted, wisdom and humor. He was a first cousin of a Little Rock literary light, then living in England, named John Gould Fletcher, who would later acquire a reputation as one of the Imagist poets. At dinner, in the restaurant of the Capital Hotel, Tom made one last effort to talk Viridis out of her "quixotical quest." Failing, he declared, "I'm awfully fond of you, Very, and if anything happened to you, I'd kill myself."

Nothing, really, happened to her, except for a couple of scares. She had the time of her life. Even her horse seemed enlivened by the adventure. The mare, which she'd owned now for nearly a year, was a grandniece of Géricault, her jumping horse of old, and although Viridis did not jump her a lot, she was capable of it. Viridis had named her after a famous French woman painter of the last century who had specialized in horses, Rosa Bonheur, but Viridis had shortened this to the playful "Rosabone," to which the mare responded. Before her sudden interest in Nail Chism, Viridis spoke only to Rosabone. Tom Fletcher pointed out to her the similarity between "Rosabone" and "Rocinante," the wretched horse of Don Quixote.

Rosabone did not balk at being loaded onto a cattle car of the Iron Mountain train; it was an enclosed car, albeit an unheated one, and Viridis draped her liberally with a thick horse blanket. Then Viridis settled down in the passenger car to watch as the train maneuvered the Baring Cross bridge over the Arkansas River into Argenta. The stations they passed, or at which they briefly took on mail or an occasional passenger, on the way to Conway—Amboy, Marché, Wilder, Palarm, Mayflower, Gold Creek— were the same little jerkwaters and whistlestops she'd passed through twice every weekend during her semester's attendance at Conway Central College and Conservatory of Fine Arts, and the sight of those familiar, almost identical clusters of wooden false-fronted stores and the little railroad depots brought back to her the impoverishment of her collegiate experience. She had come so far since those days, and yet, going back again now, especially as the train pulled in and stopped for a while at Conway, within sight of her old campus, she felt as if she were recapturing something she had lost, or getting another opportunity to do something she had neglected, the first time around.

Conway had really been the limit of her penetration into the Arkansas hinterland, and now, as the train left it and gathered speed to the northwest and the uplands, which she could see already in the distance, she felt that she was going to explore some recesses of her native state that she had not known before. The train followed a generally westward course paralleling the Arkansas River and passing through towns, some of good size, that seemed to have been created by the railroad and had avenues flanking the tracks, and new business buildings: drugstores, hardware stores, furniture stores, even a small theater or two. Passing through Atkins, she had a clear view of the new brick façade of the J. M. Maus Company, a two-story block that was more like a Little Rock department store than a backwoods general emporium. To one side of the store the wagons of trappers were unloading their contents of furs, fox and possum skins, to be traded for merchandise. The people, especially the men, did not exhibit any pretense or cultivation in their appearance; they were an anticipation of the roughcast yeomen she would encounter in Newton County.

She rode into the sunset at Russellville, and thereafter the little stations the train passed were illuminated only by single lights over their depot signs: Ouita, Mill Creek, London, Scotia, Piney. There are so many little towns out there, she reflected, and so many little lives, all of them strange to me. There are two aspects of travel by rail that she was acutely aware of: one is the sense of "out-thereness," of all that lies on both sides of this passage; and the other is of this passage itself, this channel, this extended tube through which one is passed, with a beginning and an end.

She broke free in the middle. Halfway between Conway and Fort Smith, at Clarksville, she left this tube and entered the out-there. After a night at the St. James Hotel, where she sheltered Rosabone in the hotel's horse-barn, and after a good early breakfast of oats for the mare and oatmeal for

125

the rider, they struck out northward along a winding road pointing toward the mountains. The morning was very cold but clear, the air bracing. Viridis let Rosabone set her own pace, with an occasional run on the downslope of hills. Horse and rider had not gone more than a few miles, as far as Ludwig, before they encountered the first signs of astonishment in bystanders or other riders. The other riders were all male, and they had to look twice to see that she was not, and then, if there were two or more of them, they had to do a lot of talking among themselves about this exceptional circumstance of a lone woman in pants riding astraddle. Yard dogs who ordinarily would have chased a passing horse for a while ran out and took one sniff and gave her a tilted-head look. Women stood with their hands on their hips and their mouths open.

But there were not a lot of people. North of Harmony, which she reached at midmorning (and paused to admire the quaint stone church there), the fields gave way mostly to forests, with only an occasional farm before she reached the village of Ozone. How did she know, and later tell me, these names of towns—Ludwig, Harmony, Ozone? (There were no road signs in those days.) Because, in every village she passed, she stopped to ask someone, just to be sure she was on the right road to Newton County. In the case of the last place, she said, "Ozone? That's an unusual name. Is it because of the quality of the air?" The air there, as elsewhere in the Ozarks, was sweet and clear and heady. "Couldn't rightly tell ye, ma'am," the man said. "Hit's jist been called thet, fur back as I can recall."

When, shortly after dark, at the top of a steep climb up Moon Hull Mountain, she reached a village that had a hotel, or something resembling one, although the simple sign said only HOTELL, and inquired of the village's name, a man told her it was called Loafer's Glory. Which indeed was its name (I had been there once with my mother, who had an aunt living there; it was the farthest I'd ever been from home), but officially, as far as the United States Post Office Department was concerned, an institution that often made unfeeling mistakes, as I would come to learn to my sorrow, the place was named Fallsville, which it is still called on maps, at least those few maps which show it. There's nothing wrong with "Fallsville," and there was, as Viridis discovered the next morning, a pretty waterfall in the headwaters of the Mulberry River, but Loafer's Glory is a fine name for a town, almost as fine as Stay More. The Dixons, Bowens, Habbards, Rykers, Cowans, Durhams, and Sutherlands did as much loafing in their village as the folks in ours did of staying, which is to say, for as long as they could, until neither loafing nor staying was any longer possible or glorious.

Loafer's Glory is down in the southwest corner of Newton County, but Viridis didn't realize she had already reached the county of her destination. She still had a hard day's ride to go to reach Stay More. She and Rosabone needed a good night's rest, which the "Hotell," Sutherland's, provided. It was like no hotel she had been in before: two guest rooms upstairs sharing a common washstand, her room just large enough for an old-fashioned iron bedstead with a cornshuck mattress and a pair of light down quilts over it. The occupant of the other room was a traveling "drummer," or salesman, for a wholesale grocery outfit in Fayetteville. He tried to get friendly. He suggested to Viridis that they might get warmed up with a little peach brandy he had with him, but she declined, saying she'd had a hard ride today and expected a harder one tomorrow. She got up in the morning before he did and beat him to the washstand, and was finished with her breakfast before he came downstairs.

There is a Y in the main road at Loafer's Glory, and the left fork would have taken her into Madison County and toward Pettigrew, which Tom Fletcher had suggested as the terminus of her rail ride, but she took the right fork eastward toward Swain and Nail, a village named for the maternal grandfather of Viridis' obsession. She did not know this then, but she reached it in midafternoon, and, inquiring the distance and direction to Stay More (for it was here she would have to turn north again), was told that it was only six miles, but six rough, crooked, uphill miles, and she wouldn't be able to make it before dark.

She should have spent the night in Nail. Although the village had no hotel, or anything approximating one, any villager would have shown her hospitality and could probably have regaled her with stories about Jethro Nail, that maternal grandfather, from whom the hero of this story acquired a large measure of his sense of humor as well as his sense of injustice. But, so close to her destination, Viridis was eager to get on.

She would discover that Stay More had no hotel, or anything approximating one either . . . when she reached it. The reaching was hard. Of the whole journey from Clarksville, of her entire experience with bridle paths and trails and roads, those last six miles were the hardest. Indeed, that road from Nail to Stay More no longer exists today; it was the first

127

road to be given back to the forest when the Ozark National Forest was set up; the southern entrance to, or egress from, Stay More has been closed off ever since. You could almost say that Viridis found a place you can no longer get to. Or, at least, that she used a path that can no longer be traversed. Or even that both place and path existed only in the creation of her fancy at that specific circumstance of time.

There were stretches where she had to get down and lead Rosabone. Places where Rosabone stumbled in the snow. Places where Viridis, down and walking, stumbled in the snow. Rosabone was getting very tired. It was growing dark, the forest canopy was obscuring what sky light there was, and Rosabone could not understand why they weren't stopping if it was dark. Viridis tried to talk to her, but she was talking to herself, whistling in the dark, afraid. Once, as both she and Rosabone stood panting at the top of some defile they'd climbed, surrounded by huge boulders and enormous trees, she heard a noise, as of branches snapping, which caused her to fetch the revolver Tom Fletcher had lent her and make sure it was loaded, and to walk on for a while with the revolver in one hand and the mare's reins in the other. She emerged into a clearing, dimly lit but still with enough light for her to witness the sudden spectacle of a huge bird swooping down and seizing a rabbit. She could not tell what sort of bird it was—eagle, hawk, falcon—but she could clearly identify the big white rabbit, who, strangely, she thought, made no protest or sound of any sort as the talons of the raptor lifted it off the ground and carried it ever higher out across the treetops and over the valley.

She moved on until she could see that valley, then stood looking into it for a very long while, resting, letting Rosabone rest. The last strips of the sunlit sky sank beyond the westward mountains. The moon rose, and it was full, and every star was there. The northern slopes of hills that she faced still were covered with snow, against which the black trunks and branches of trees made a vast and intricate tracery. The snow, in this light, seemed more blue than white, and everything was silent and still. One by one, far down below, people here and there lit their kerosene lanterns, and the pinpoints of light scattered across the valley forewarned Viridis of the number of people she must encounter before her mission would be accomplished. The whole scene reminded her of a village land-scape at night as painted by van Gogh, although he had seen the moon and the stars far more passionately than she could now feel. "Well, Rosa-bone," Viridis said, as she remounted the mare, *that* is the end of our journey."

It was downhill from there on. When she reached the village, it was full dark, but the great moon and a few kerosene lanterns in windows gave some illumination to the buildings along Stay More's main street. Weeks after she had left Stay More, the next time the moon was full, I walked through the village one night attempting to see it as she had first laid eyes on it. Of course I knew each building, each house, and each store in a way that she did not: I recognized the dark, looming shape of Isaac Ingle-dew's gristmill, closed then because the Chism moonshining operation had used up all the cornmeal; another large building, whose triangular gable rose three floors up, I knew, pretending to be Viridis, would be one of my objectives: Willis Ingledew's General Store, where the men who would testify for Nail Chism congregated nearly every day, winter or summer; pretending to ride my horse on up the street, as she had, I passed between the two doctors' clinics, on my left old Doc Plowright's board-and-batten wooden shack with false front, he who had examined Rindy Whitter, and on my right across the street the new clinic of Plowright's only competition, young Doc Colvin Swain, a Stay More boy, just out of his training in St. Louis. The next building up from Doc Swain's was our principal business building, the ashlar stone Swains Creek Bank and Trust Company. I stood where Viridis had stopped her horse to stare at it, and then, as she had done, I let my eyes shift northward across the Right Prong Road (which she would take to get to my house as well as to the Chism place) to the only other general store on that stretch of main road, T. L. Jerram's, run by Sull's brother Tilbert. I must have stared at that one a little longer than she had, although then I couldn't even guess that one day I would own it and live there and have the post office in it, and that even at this present time my granddaughter Sharon would be living there still.

Viridis looked at what wouldn't become Latha Bourne's General Store and Post Office until June of 1932; there were lights of kerosene lanterns burning within the two wings of the store that were living quarters, and she was tempted to stop there first, just to ask for directions. It would have been ironic to ask Tilbert Jerram for help in the beginning of what would become her fight against his brother. But she did not. She turned

Rosabone around and began to ride slowly back down Main Street. There were lights burning at Doc Plowright's, but I don't blame her for having a sense, even then, that he wouldn't be very sociable. Across the road she could see through the window of Doc Swain's, where Colvin was sitting at a table peering through a microscope, and something about that—and the moonlit shingle hanging out front: C.U. Swain, M.D., Doctor of Human Medicine—convinced her that he was a very busy young man who wouldn't take kindly to an interruption. She only wanted to ask for directions.

Didn't dogs bark at her? When I attempted to retrace her movements through the village and the surrounding countryside, weeks later in the moonlight, pretending to be her, some of the dogs pretended I was her too, and although they knew me they barked at me. Doc Swain's great big old hound Galen nearly attacked me, and Doc Swain raised his head from the microscope and came outside and said, "Hush, Galen! Down, you dumb bawler! Oh, it's *you*, Latha. What are you doin out this time o' night?"

"Jist a-playin like I was *her*," I said, and he knew who I meant. "And I was jist wonderin, did dogs bark at her that first night? Galen must've."

"I reckon he did, but I never took no notice," Doc Swain said.

If there was anyone who heard the village dogs barking at her and thought to go see who or what the dogs were barking at, it was probably that old lady who lived two doors down from Doc Swain, in the big fine two-story house directly across the road from Willis Ingledew's store. This house had been built way back around the time of the War Between the States by old Jacob Ingledew, who died the year before I was born. He had been the founder of Stay More, he and his brother Noah, and right after that war he had served for a time as the governor of the whole state of Arkansas. Compared with Governor Hays, who wouldn't pardon Nail Chism, he . . . but I'm digressing. This lady had been a friend of his wife's when they lived in Little Rock at the governor's mansion, and when Sarah Ingledew came back to Stay More she brought her friend with her, to stay. In this year of 1915 both Jacob and Sarah had been in the Stay More cemetery for going on fifteen years, but this lady, who inherited the house, still lived on there, and would continue to do so until sometime in the early twenties (I wasn't living in Stay More the year of her death, so I don't remember). To tell the honest truth, I never knew her name. Older folks who had known Sarah Ingledew just called her Sarah's Friend, and in fact that's all that you'll find on her tombstóne. If she ever told Viridis her name, and she must have, it's not recorded.

But she came out on her front porch, wrapped in a thick afghan shawl, to see what the dogs were barking at . . . assuming the dogs were barking. That porch runs the whole length of the big house, and it has fancy jigsaw Gothic balusters running along the edge of it, hardly more than an arm's length from the road, and the lady stood up against that porch rail and looked at that moonlit figure on horseback. Viridis stopped and turned Rosabone toward the lady and said, in that genteel Little Rock/Paris voice of hers, "Good evening, madam. This is Stay More, is it not? I've just arrived in town, and I'd like directions for finding the Right Prong Road that goes to the Chism farm."

The lady smiled. "Which part of Little Rock are you from?" she asked.

Viridis was taken aback, to put it mildly, and her first thought was of some kind of conspiracy: somebody, maybe Nail himself, had gotten word to these people that Viridis was coming. But this woman was asking her *which part* of Little Rock she was from, as if there were divisions or distinctions, and—Viridis could not help noticing—this woman was not asking the question in the mode of expression or voice she would expect from a native of these parts.

"Why, the central part," Viridis answered. "Why?"

"Louisiana Street, Center, Spring, or Broadway?" the old woman asked.

"West of that," Viridis said. "Arch Street."

"I guessed as much. That's not exactly central. Well, as they say hereabouts, light down and hitch, rest your saddle. Come in and eat you some supper."

"I'm just trying to find the Chism place," Viridis said.

"You won't find it in the dark, or even this fine moonlight. Are they expecting you? They won't be able to give you a decent bed."

"I don't want to impose on you," Viridis said.

"Don't be ridiculous. I've room for your whole family, if you'd brought them with you. Well, maybe one of your brothers would have to sleep on the floor."

Viridis was delighted. She accepted the offer of hospitality and discovered that the woman had the whole large house to herself, eleven rooms, simply but tastefully furnished. Behind the house was a small stable, where Rosabone was housed comfortably for the night.

The woman had just been starting to prepare her own supper at the time Viridis arrived, and it was no trouble for her to make a double serving of everything: roast pork, boiled potatoes in their skins with chopped parsley, fresh garden kale (it survives January's freeze) cooked like spinach, and a light wheaten roll baked in a manner called Parker House. Viridis watched as these things came off of and out of a huge cast-iron and white enamel cookstove that gave off an additional fragrance of burning cedar logs, and of the sweet-potato pie they would have for dessert.

"Now," said the old lady, "if I can just remember where the governor left that bottle of Alsace wine. Excuse me." She disappeared upstairs, climbing the staircase with an agility that belied her years, more than eighty of them, Viridis guessed, and within a minute she returned, wiping the dust from, sure enough, a tall, narrow bottle of Gewürztraminer.

During the meal Viridis remarked, "You mentioned the governor. Were you speaking in the familiar sense of one's husband, father, superior, or employer?"

The old woman smiled with amusement. "He was not my husband, but he was my 'father,' you could say. He was definitely my superior, and certainly my employer." She paused to sip her wine, then added, "But Jacob Ingledew was also the governor."

"Of Arkansas?" Viridis asked.

"Don't the schools of Little Rock teach Arkansas history anymore?" the woman asked.

Viridis had actually taken mandatory Arkansas history in the eighth and ninth grades, but there had been so many governors and she couldn't remember their names. She asked, with a smile, "Which part of Little Rock are *you* from?"

"East of Main," the woman said. "Do you know the Pike mansion?"

"Of course!" Viridis replied. Her boss's cousins, the Fletchers, owned the mansion that had been built by Albert Pike. "Did you live there?"

"No," the woman said, smiling as if to excuse herself for misleading her guest, "but in the neighborhood, just a few doors to the east."

The conversation died for a few moments before Viridis decided to ask, "What are you doing in Stay More?"

"I'll be happy to tell you," the woman said. "But first you must tell me: what are *you* doing in Stay More?"

These two Little Rock ladies, the one eighty-six, the other sixty years younger, stayed up talking until bedtime, and even beyond, telling each other their stories and their reasons, very good ones, for being in Stay More. The old woman certainly knew about the trial and conviction of Nail Chism, although she did not know enough of the facts of the case to have any opinion on Nail's guilt or innocence. Summers she sat on her front porch and observed the men sitting on the storeporch across the way, and she knew which one was Nail, because he was taller than the others, younger than most of them, quieter, less inclined to joking although a quick audience for others' jokes, but of course she was in no position to say whether he had been there at his usual time on that particular afternoon, which was just one more June day in a passage of rare ones. Yes, she knew of the Whitters; they were the "dregs" of Stay More society, and Dorinda's oldest brother Ike had been the town's ruffian and rowdy until the day the lynch mob disposed of him. The woman showed Viridis a number of plugged-up bullet holes in the walls of her front rooms, souvenirs of a raging gun battle Ike Whitter and his cronies had fought with the lynch mob, who had commandeered her house and required her to cower in a back room, frightened out of her wits, while every pane of glass in her house was shattered. This had happened ten years before, but the old woman still trembled sometimes in recollection of it.

At breakfast the next morning (Viridis had slept wonderfully and warmly on a thick mattress stuffed with goose down, beneath several heirloom quilts, in a big walnut four-poster in the one of the three front rooms that had been Sarah Ingledew's) the gracious old woman, urging a second helping of bacon and eggs on Viridis, said, "You aren't intending to wear *those* today, are you?" and indicated Viridis' jodhpurs.

"I expect to do a good bit of riding," Viridis explained.

The woman shook her head. "You might do some riding, but you won't do any visiting if you wear those." And when breakfast was finished, she suggested they take their third cups of coffee back into Sarah's room. Viridis, the woman observed, was the same size that Sarah had been. The woman opened a walnut wardrobe, then took down a dress and held it against Viridis for a moment, replaced it, and took down another, until she had one that she considered "not too dressy but good enough." Viridis protested that she couldn't ride Rosabone in that dress. "You aren't going to ride Rosabone," the woman said, and then selected the shoes, which were twenty years out of style and unlike any that Viridis had ever worn.

And then the hat, or bonnet, rather. And a shawl. "And now the finishing touch, what Sarah called her thanky-poke," the woman said, giving Viridis a purse to carry, a purse larger and fancier than any she would ever have dared hold in Little Rock. The woman turned Viridis to look at herself in the mirror and commented, "I declare, if it weren't for your red hair, you *are* Sarah." Viridis felt a bit uncomfortable, not because of the fit of the clothes or their being twenty years out of fashion but because she felt she had no right to be wearing the clothing of the former first lady of Arkansas. She expected to do a lot of local traveling and interviewing today, and she didn't want to expose the clothes to dirt and dust and snow and mud.

The old woman dressed herself in attire that was also from an earlier era, the 1890s, and then she led Viridis out of the house, down the steps, and across the road to Willis Ingledew's General Store. The storekeeper (who was also postmaster of Stay More that year) was in his customary captain's chair facing the large potbellied stove whose stovepipe rose three floors straight up to the roof as the centerpiece surrounded by the balcony of the second floor, where the clothing and shoe departments were. There were a dozen other men sitting in chairs or on bulging wooden kegs within the radius of the stove's warmth. Two of these men faced each other across a cracker barrel atop which a checkerboard had been placed, but the men, Viridis noticed at once, were playing chess, not checkers.

One by one the men looked away from the stove or from the chess-players and took notice of the two ladies who had entered the store. One by one the men's jaws dropped open.

"How be ye, boys?" the old woman said. The response, she later explained with a light laugh to Viridis, was exceptional: it was customary for a man greeting a woman simply to touch the brim of his hat, or perhaps just to raise his hand in the direction of the brim, or, at the very most, to grasp the crown of the hat and gently raise it before setting it back down. Each one of these men whipped his hat entirely off his head and held it to his heart, and some of them even stood up. Holding their hats thus, they chorused, each and severally, "Howdy do, ladies," and "Fine mornin, ma'ams."

The storekeeper, Willis, standing up, was nearly as tall as Nail. "I'll be jimjohned," he exclaimed, looking at Viridis. "You shore guv me a turn. I thought fer a secont thar ye were Grammaw. Don't she put ye in mind

134

of Grammaw, Paw?" he said to one of the seated men, a very old man who simply nodded and didn't take his eyes off her.

"This here gal is Miss Verdus Monday," the old woman said, in a thick approximation of the local speech. "She hails from Little Rock, and come all the way here jist to see what she can see about Nail Chism's trouble. She thinks he's blameless. Don't ye, gal?"

Viridis had never before in her life been called upon to speak in front of a group, especially not a males-only enclave of general-store loungers. At first she could only nod in response to the question, but then she found enough voice to add, "Yes, and I hope all of you do too." She looked around at them, one by one. Each man was nodding his head.

"Willis, have ye still got that phaeton yore grampaw was so partial to?" the old woman asked the storekeeper, and when he nodded, she said, "We'd be obleeged to ye iffen ye'd hitch her up so's this gal could git up towards the Chism place."

"I'll carry ye myself, ma'am," Willis offered.

But the old woman said, "No need of that, Willis. Jist hitch it up to two of yore best hosses and bring it around."

As Willis exited through the rear of the store toward his livery barn, one of the others said to the women, "Don't ye gals be rushin off. Stay more and pull ye up some cheers or kaigs."

"Yeah," invited another man, "lift yore hats and rest yore wraps."

"She'll be back directly, I reckon," the old woman said. "Won't ye, gal?"

"I'd like to talk with each one of you about Nail," Viridis said.

"Shore thang," they spoke or grunted assent: "Any old time." "You bet." "Come back when ye can visit more."

Outside, the old woman indicated the phaeton that Willis was bringing into the road and asked Viridis, "Ever driven one of these? I'd go with you, but I think you'd feel more comfortable on your own, wouldn't you, now? Look, you turn right at Jerram's corner up there and you're on the Right Prong Road. Stay on it eastward without turning off to the left or right until you've reached the top of that mountain yonder. You'll see the Chisms' house on a cleared knoll set back from the road a ways on your left. Nancy Chism is going to be tickled to see you. So will they all. If I don't see you at bedtime, I'll know they talked you into staying. But come back when you can."

"I don't know how to thank you," Viridis admitted.

"You'll thank me enough with the pleasure of your company," the lady said.

Viridis drove the two-horse phaeton without any trouble, although she'd never driven one before. She drove in the direction she had ridden Rosabone the night before, up between the clinics of the two doctors, past the stone bank building, right at Jerram's store, which would become mine, right on the road I live on but not turning to the left on the Bournes' trail. I wasn't there anyway that morning. I was in school, across the creek, the other way. All oblivious to her driving the fine phaeton of Governor Ingledew right past my turnoff, I was standing at my desk reciting for Mr. Perry a poem from our reader, William Wordsworth's "Lucy Gray: Or, Solitude." It is about a lonesome young girl who gets sent on an errand in a winter storm and disappears, and it always brought a tear to my eye, especially when they traced her footprints in the snow as far as the middle of the bridge, and then no more.

> —Yet some maintain that to this day
> She is a living child;
> That you may see sweet Lucy Gray
> Upon the lonesome wild.
>
> O'er rough and smooth she trips along,
> And never looks behind;
> And sings a solitary song
> That whistles in the wind.

I never thought that "behind" could rhyme with "wind"; you'd have to change the way you say one or the other, and I didn't, as I read it, and Mr. Perry didn't correct me, and the way I pronounced "wind" was lost anyway beneath the sound of a sob from Dorinda, who then commenced another one of the crying jags she had all the time these days. As I said before, she no longer shared my desk; she had been moved, first down to where the third-graders sat, but then Mr. Perry had completely lost patience with her and had her sit over to one side of the first-graders, big enough to be their mother but too big to share a desk with any of them, so she was just sitting on the stool that Mr. Perry sometimes used for the dunce's corner and had to borrow from her when he needed to make somebody sit on it there, and of course there were jokes about her being our permanent dunce, with or without the corner. Whether or not she was dumb enough to be with the first-graders was questionable, but she certainly cried more than any of them ever did. The least little thing would set her off, and I should have known when I read "Lucy Gray" that it was going to give her a real fit of weeping. If only she knew that the lady who was going to save her soul was on her way up to the Chism place!

Up on the lilting mountain far above the village is a farmplace so old the trees still sing of it. There is a pretty trail rising from the village of Stay More to the farmplace; the trail meanders all over creation before it gets up there, and from places along it you can see forever across the hollers and the hills. The trees singing their fool heads off were a fat maple whose name I wish I knew and a gangling walnut I'd have to call a lady's name were I to dub it, neither of them with even a leftover brown leaf from last autumn, although their buds were swelling and the only green in sight, save the copse of cedars and the first sign of new grass, were the nests of mistletoe in the upper limbs of the maple, mistletoe a shade of green that you only see in winter, winter's green, which has a special song of its own. I wish Viridis could have heard these trees a-yodeling like crazy as she drove into sight of them, and maybe she did, for all I know. I don't know everything about this story.

I know how Nancy Nail Chism had been listening, not to her trees a-warbling but to the coffeepot a-rattling on the stove, sometime before: a sure sign that company was coming. While she was drying the breakfast dishes, she had dropped the towel, and that means a stranger will arrive very soon; she watched to see if she'd drop it a second time, which means the stranger will be hungry and need something to eat, but she didn't. Seth Chism had dropped his case knife while he was eating: that was proof the stranger coming would be a female; if he'd dropped his fork, it would have been a man on his way up the mountain. "Seth!" she'd said to him when he helped himself to some more of the elderberry jam even though he already had some on his plate; if you absent-mindedly help yourself to something you've already got on your plate, it means the stranger coming will be hungry for the same thing. While she'd drunk her own coffee, Nancy had paid close attention to the cup and noticed that coffee grounds were clinging to the sides of it, which was a sign that the visitor would

137

be bringing good news. Also, her left eye was itching; if her right eye had started itching, it would have meant that the visitor had bad news.

So even before Viridis drove into sight, Nancy knew this much about her: she was a woman, and she was coming to visit, and she would want some elderberry jam, and she would bring good news. Thus the only thing surprising when Viridis came driving up into the Chisms' yard was that she was driving old Jake Ingledew's phaeton and was wearing old Sarey Ingledew's visiting-clothes. Nancy's first thought was that the lady had the wrong house, but all those signs couldn't have been so far wrong. So Nancy went ahead and declared, "Howdy. We've been lookin fer ye."

Had Nail got word to them? Viridis wondered. She saw at once how Nail resembled his mother: Nancy had given him not just his eyes but his eyebrows, his long nose with its strongly shaped end, and his full mouth. Nancy was in good health, and it was almost like seeing Nail the way he ought to be.

"I'm Viridis Chism," she said, but then she put her hand to her mouth and corrected herself. "I mean, I'm Viridis Monday. You must be Nancy Chism."

"Yes'm, that's me," Nancy acknowledged.

"I've come from Little Rock to talk to you about your son Nail."

As Nancy told it later, the good news that she'd learned to expect when she'd seen the coffee grounds on the side of her cup was simply that Viridis Monday was *here*. Not that she brought word of any governor's pardon or Nail's escape or even that Nail was in good health, but that Viridis Monday was here to tell what she knew, to find out what she wanted to find out, to do what she wanted: to learn everything about Nail; to convince herself of what she already believed: there was no way Nail could have done what he'd been convicted of; and then to do what she intended to do: get everybody to sign a petition, which would go to the governor.

Viridis spent the whole day with the Chisms, not just Nancy but also Nail's father Seth, and his younger brother Luther, and Nail's older sister Irene, who had once been the wife of Sull Jerram and was, in fact, still married to him. Viridis would come back again later, several times, but this first day she would talk with the Chisms all day, or until time for school to let out, when she would come looking for me. Viridis listened to Nancy tell the whole story of Nail's life, such as it was, not very exciting or eventful or anything to brag about. In the whole house she had just a couple of photographs of Nail that she could show to Viridis, one taken by Eli Willard the year he first brought the camera to Stay More, and another one Nail had made up in Eureka Springs, the farthest he'd ever been from home until they took him off to Little Rock. The Eureka photograph was one of those trick pictures with props where you pose in front of a fake scene, and it showed Nail dressed in some Wild West costume with sheepskin chaps and a ten-gallon hat and a pair of six-shooters, standing in front of the Palace of Versailles, an incongruity that was lost on subject and photographer. But it was a good picture of Nail at the age of nineteen, handsome and sightly. Viridis asked if she could borrow the picture and have her newspaper make a copy of it, and she would return the original.

Spreading her elderberry jam on her biscuit, Viridis asked, "Did Nail ever have a girlfriend?"

Nancy Chism laughed a bit. "I have to tell ye a little story," she said, and she told about Nail's very first girlfriend, sort of. When the McCoys used to live at the next place down the road, the place where Waymon Chism lived now with his wife, there was a little girl named Dorothea Lea McCoy, about the same age as Nail, three, and sometimes when Mrs. McCoy came to visit with Nancy, she'd put "Dorthlee," as everybody called her, out in the yard to play with little Nail, under that maple tree that he thought was his own. Sometimes Dorthlee would get permission to walk up the road from her house to play with Nail under the maple even when her mother wasn't visiting Nancy. One day Dorthlee came running into the Chism house hollering, "Miz Chism, Nail's a-pickin yore flars!" and Nancy went out to discover that Nail was helping himself to the marigolds, making a bouquet. "Course I had to whup 'im fer it, for he knew better," Nancy explained to Viridis. Another time, later in the summer, Dorthlee again came running into the house, saying, "Miz Chism, Nail's a-pickin yore flars!" And once again Nancy found her son out in the flower garden, making a bouquet of zinnias. And once again she had to take the hairbrush to his backside.

Dorthlee's father decided to move to Oklahoma, where some of the good Indian lands were being opened to settlement, and the McCoys left Stay More. "Not too fur along after that," Nancy told Viridis, "in August I reckon it was, I happent to look out the winder and I seen little Nail out yonder there again in my flar gyarden. I snuck up behind 'im and susprised 'im." Nancy paused, wearing a great smile of fond reminiscence and wonder, and then she finished: "And Nail looked up at me, holdin this yere bouquet of flars, and he said, 'Miz Chism, Nail's a-pickin yore flars.' "

Viridis laughed, although a tear touched the edge of her eye, and said, "And you were so tickled you didn't punish him that time?"

"That's right. I jist busted out laughin. The funniest thing was, was the way he said it. He sounded jist exactly lak Dorthlee!"

Seth Chism too told some stories of his experience with the young Nail. One of these stories, he said, was famous all over Newton County: When Nail was just seven or eight, and hadn't yet started helping out at the still but knew where it was, he was playing out under his maple tree one day—he spent nearly all his time a-cootering around beneath that old maple out in the front yard—when a stranger rode up, a man on a big horse. Others who had seen the man said later that they couldn't tell whether or not the man was a government agent but it sure was a government horse. Anyway, he asked Nail where his daddy was, and Nail come right out and said, "Oh, Paw's down in the holler, makin whiskey." And the man asked, "Well, where's your mother?" and Nail said, "Maw's down there a-holpin him." "Sonny," said the man, "I'll give ye fifty cents if you'll tell me how to get to where your father and mother are at." Young Nail just held out his hand for the fifty cents, but the man said, "No. No. I'll give ye the money when I git back." Nail shook his head and continued holding out his hand. "You aint a-comin back," he said.

At noon Nancy Chism stepped on the porch to sound a dinner triangle, and the ringing of it brought Waymon Chism and his wife Faye up from the house below, and they all had dinner together. Nail's older brother, Viridis observed, didn't look much like him; he wasn't as tall, or as sinewy, and his eyes didn't have the quality that Nail's had, of seeming to understand everything at a glance with not simply intelligence but tolerance and quiet understanding. Like his parents and Irene and Luther, Waymon was eager to talk about Nail. Just a few more hours would pass before I would discover for myself what it was about Viridis Monday that could get Waymon Chism to open up and talk in a way that he wouldn't talk with strangers, let alone women: not just that he sensed she was there to help, or honestly intended to do everything she could to help; possibly she even had the *power* to help. In this regard she impressed Waymon in a way that Farrell Cobb had not.

But Viridis' presence in the Chism household almost started a family quarrel. If there was only one quality of Nail's that his brother Waymon possessed, it was a sense of outrage, a quick temper that bridled at injustice. The Chisms may have been lawbreakers, in that moonshining was illegal, but Seth Chism had taught his sons principles of honesty and justice from childhood. Seth had taught his boys never to start a fight but, if the other fellow started it, to finish it quickly to the other fellow's sorrow. Waymon Chism had told so many people that he intended to kill Sull Jerram if anything happened to Nail that word of this threat had reached Sull, and now Sull was threatening to kill Waymon first. This was understandable, but something nobody who knew Sull could understand was that Waymon intended to do the killing with his bare hands.

While Viridis was talking to Nancy Chism at the dinner table, she kept hearing mention of a gun in a conversation among Waymon, Seth, and Irene. She attempted to eavesdrop more closely, but every time she and Nancy stopped talking the others would hush.

It was Nancy who spoke up: "What's this here about a shootin arn?"

Irene started to speak, but Waymon shushed her. "No, Waymon," Irene blurted, "Maw oughta know it. Sull has got him one of these here automatic pistols, a Colt .45, and he carries it around with him. If Waymon don't keep away from him, Sull might jist use it on him."

"He'll have to draw it first," Waymon said. "He don't carry it in no hip-holster like the sherf does. If he started to pull that thang on me, I'd strangle him before he could git his finger to the right place on it."

"Son, you'd jist better git yoreself a arn," Seth said to Waymon, and the argument resumed as if Viridis were not listening to it. She sat and listened and tried to figure it out. Waymon refused to carry any weapon other than a pocketknife, which every man carried, not as a weapon but a tool, a utensil. Waymon wasn't planning to do any violence to Sull Jerram unless something happened to Nail, and now it looked as if maybe this lady Miss Monday could stop them from killing Nail.

But Waymon's parents and Irene were convinced that Sull Jerram intended to kill Waymon, not so much in actual self-defense as in prevention of Waymon's ever placing him in a position of having to defend himself. They tried to get Waymon to remember that the sheriff was on Sull's side, and in fact Sull's being county judge made him the sheriff's boss, even if they weren't such good buddies. But Waymon insisted he wasn't afraid of no sheriff neither.

After Waymon and Faye had gone home, Nancy and Irene put on their winter wraps and took Viridis out to look at the place. After a big midday dinner they needed a hike, and they walked all the way down into the holler where the big Chism still was perched beside the spring branch on a ledge beneath a bluff. It wasn't in operation at that time, but Nancy gave Viridis an explanation of how it worked, and Viridis wanted to know which part of the procedure Nail had been responsible for, and they showed her. Then Viridis wanted to see Nail's sheep pastures, and they took her to them, although they were bare of sheep and even of most grass, just patches of snow melting in the afternoon sun on the hillsides. Coming back to the house, they showed Viridis the maple tree at one corner of the front yard, its branches doing their best to wave at her because she couldn't quite hear its gentle singing. Viridis stood at the base of the tree and looked at the roots over which Nail had built highways for his toy wagons, and she could almost see his tin soldiers fighting on the parapets of the roots' knees.

Then Viridis was exposed awkwardly to her first experience of what we all of us take for granted: the traditional ritual of leave-taking and exchanging of polite, conventional invitations and counterinvitations.

Viridis said she had to find the Bourne place and talk with young Latha, as Nail had suggested.

Nancy looked properly stricken and said, "Don't be a-rushin off! Better take supper with us and stay all night."

Viridis was supposed to counter by asking Nancy to come and go home with her, but Viridis didn't know this. She just said she'd be back the next day, or soon, and she thanked Nancy for the hospitality and the generous heaping of Nail she'd served up. Nancy told her which turns to take to get to the Bourne place.

And here she came! I was just home from school and doing my chores, redding up the front porch with a broom, when here came that Ingledew phaeton (although I didn't know that's what it was; the last time the governor had driven it was before my time) a-turning into our yard. You could have swept me off the porch with a feather. Later, long after she'd gone, I would look at myself in the mirror with my lower jaw a-hanging open, just to see how awful I looked that way: she could probably see the bad teeth that E. H. Ingledew hadn't pulled yet. It's a wonder I had sense enough finally to close my mouth and answer her eventually, some time after she'd said, "You must be Latha."

Surely I had the sense to at least nod my head before I could find my voice? Maybe not. Maybe I couldn't even find my voice, because she went on and said, "My name is Viridis Monday, and I'm from Little Rock. I work for a newspaper. We're doing a story about Nail Chism of Stay More, who has been condemned to die in the electric chair, and I was told that you could give me some information that would help us."

Still I couldn't find my voice, except to say to Rouser, our dog, "Hush, Rouser! You jist hush!" His barking soon brought my father and mother and my sisters Barb and Mandy out of the house. Paw kicked old Rouser off the porch, and that shut him up. Momma said, and I could have died of mortification, "We caint buy nothin today, thank ye."

The lady smiled. She was the most beautiful lady I'd ever seen even a picture of, and she had the nicest smile I'd ever thought a body could have, and I've been practicing it ever since. "I'm not selling anything," she said, and then she repeated word for word what she'd just said to me, and she added, "Nail Chism suggested that I might talk with your daughter Latha about the circumstances of the case. He feels that she can tell me the truth."

"Wal, come on in and set by the far," Maw invited her, and we all went into the house, into the front room that was my parents' bedroom but also served as our parlor, so to speak, because you could sit on a divan as well as the bed, and the divan was up anent the fireplace. They gave her Paw's chair, and Paw had to sit on the divan with Momma, and all three of us girls sat side by side on the edge of the bed, with me in the middle, until Momma said, "Latha, why don't ye brew us up a pot of that coffee I save for the preacher?"

And I jumped up and started for the kitchen, but the lady said, "No, thank you, please, I've been drinking coffee all day up at the Chisms'."

"Oh," Momma said. "You've done talked to them, have ye?"

"Yes," Viridis said, and she was wondering how she could politely get me alone to herself, so she added, "and I'm trying to talk to as many people as I can while I'm in Stay More. I'd like to talk with each one of you, but I'd like to talk to you one at a time, if that's all right, and I want to start with Latha."

143

Paw gave Momma the elbow in her ribs, and a severe look. Mandy and Barb looked at each other like they'd just remembered it was Friday and they had something to do to get ready to go into Jasper tomorrow. Momma was the last to leave the room, and said, "But don't ye be a-rushin off, ma'am. Better jist take supper with us, and stay all night." By this time Viridis was beginning to understand that that was just what everybody said, all the time, whether they wanted you to or not.

The lady did stay to supper, but only because it was already getting cold on the table before she got done talking with me and she couldn't very well walk out and leave it to get even colder after they'd waited for us. We talked from right then, when my parents and sisters went out of the parlor and left us alone, until suppertime and then some past, before Viridis finally knew what to say the third or fourth time my mother asked her to spend the night, and even then she didn't know that you're supposed to counter it by saying, Come go home with me, so she just said, finally, that she was expected back by the old woman living in Jacob Ingledew's house, where she'd left her horse, and had to return this team and buggy to Willis Ingledew's livery. We were relieved, I guess, because we wouldn't have had anyplace for the lady to sleep, although I'd have been more than pleased to fix myself a pallet on the floor and let her have my place in the bed with Mandy and Barb. That's how much I loved her, by then.

But all of that didn't come until past dark. We still had an hour or so of daylight left. After the others left us alone in the parlor, Viridis looked at me and gave me that galuptious smile again and tried to hold me with her eyes. I was still too shy to look her in the eye at first, and I reckon I must have kept pawing the rug with my feet and trying to find something to do with my hands besides sit on them. I still hadn't said a word.

"Nail thinks you believe he's innocent," she said.

Finally I had to look her in the eye to let her know that I meant this: "I don't jist believe it. I *know* it." That was the first thing I ever said to Viridis Monday, I want it recorded here.

"You have nice eyes," she remarked. "He said you did."

I guess I blushed furiously. "You have better'uns," I declared.

Again that smile, and I must have tried to ape it without letting her see my bad teeth again. She reached out and put her hand lightly on my arm. "You know I'm here to save him," she said.

144

"Here?" was all I could think to say, as if it were here in this house that he was facing that electric chair.

"Here on earth," she said.

I was brave, and I said, "I'll tell you anything you want to know."

"Would you show me the playhouse?" she asked.

I had to think about that, I'm sorry to say. Looking back, I should have just nodded my head eagerly and said, "Come on!" But I couldn't quite yet bring myself to violate so easily a solemn oath, even if I didn't care a fig for the person I'd made the oath to. So I had to think about it, for a long moment, with the clock a-ticking away on the fireboard. Finally I said, "We swore we'd never tell anybody where it is."

"I understand," she said. And another long minute went by before she said, "Well, maybe you could just describe it to me."

I stood up. "No, I'll take ye. What I swore don't matter anymore. Not to me, it don't." I fetched my wrap and told Momma we'd be back in time for supper.

We weren't. It's a good brisk hike any time of year up the mountainside to the place where that old playhouse leans up against that old basso profundo oak tree. On that late-winter afternoon we had to walk around the snowy places, and she was being extra careful not to get the hem of her fancy dress in the mud. She talked a lot, telling me every little detail of how she'd come to stay with the old woman at Jacob Ingledew's and how the old woman had let her dress in Sarah's costume from twenty years before.

She seemed more impressed with that oak tree than with the playhouse, which was just a pile of lumber anyhow. She stood there looking up at the tree for the longest time. I told her it was a white oak tree. It was over a hundred feet high (I'd climbed it once as far as I could go and measured it with a ball of twine), and it must have been overlooked when they cut nearly every white oak in the county to make staves for whiskey barrels . . . not for Chism's Dew but shipped off to the big government distillers in far places like Kentucky. I'm not even sure that tree was on land that belonged to my father, but I knew I owned that tree as much as anybody did.

"Did you know," she said quietly, looking up at the great tree, "that Nail thinks trees can sing?"

I was surprised that she would say it like that, almost as if she didn't quite believe it herself. It wasn't till later that I learned she believed it just as fiercely as he did. I was also surprised at what I said myself then: "That makes two of us."

"Oh, do you believe it too?" she said, looking at me with delight, as if somehow all this business about singing trees were more important than the question of Nail's innocence. And then she asked, "Is this tree singing right now?"

I honestly couldn't have said that it was, at least I wasn't hearing anything, but I looked at her as if she were deaf, and said, "Don't you hear it?" I was just being playful, sort of teasing, but she looked startled and then began listening. When she perked up her ears like that, I did too.

We heard it.

Yes, the tree was intoning some sorrowful, deep spiritual, and there is no mistake that what we heard was the tree, but there was another sound in there besides. We listened, and even if the tree's keening had been our imaginations, because we *wanted* the tree to sing, that was not the main sound we heard. Because the tree was, I keep saying, a basso profundo, and this sound was more a mezzo-soprano, and it was coming not from the tree but from inside the playhouse.

I pushed aside the old discarded quilt that served as a doorflap for the playhouse, and I looked inside. There was Rindy, kneeling, head bowed, clutching against her bosom one of our oldest discarded dolls. She was swaying slowly to and fro, rocking the headless and mouldering dollbaby and crooning a sort of lullaby to it. She was wearing an old rag of a coat, a threadbare thing that couldn't be keeping her warm. Viridis followed me into the playhouse.

"Miss Monday," I said, making the introductions, "this here is Dorinda June Whitter."

———

Viridis Monday stayed a whole week in Stay More. Every night, sometimes before dark if she could manage it, she would return the team and buggy to Ingledew's Livery and then cross the road to Jacob Ingledew's house and sit up until bedtime talking to the old woman. That ancient dowager would serve a fortified wine from a Spanish town called Jerez. Usually Viridis reported in detail to the woman on what she had achieved during the day, and sometimes the woman would give her advice or at least make commentary on that day's events and accomplishments. It was the old woman who (out of her experience as social secretary to the state's first lady) drafted the wording of the petition to the governor, for Viridis to take with her on her rounds of interviewing the citizens of Stay More and some other places in Newton County, for their signatures or their X's. Surely, I thought, the woman herself would have been the first to sign the petition, but she was not, because, you have to remember, that was still four years before suffrage, four years before that June day when Congress would give women the right to vote or even to sign effective petitions. Except for Dorinda's, all of the signatures and X's on Viridis' petition were men's . . . including nine of the original twelve jurymen who had convicted Nail. If she could have found them, she would have had all twelve.

Viridis invited Dorinda and me to ride with her in the phaeton when she set off for Jasper to hunt up some of the jurymen. It was a Sunday, and sunny, the first really warm day we'd had that year, with the last of the patches of snow melting into the earth; a good day for a drive, without the road too muddy yet. Rindy and I both wore our best; hers was that same white Sears lawn dress she'd worn for the trial, which was out of season for February but all she had that would look good for going into the county seat on a Sunday. She was cheerful. I hadn't seen her so happy since this whole business had started back in June of the year before. Whatever burden of guilt had been mashing down on her was lifted by the confession she readily gave to Viridis, making a clean breast of it, exonerating poor Nail completely. She wouldn't yet give Viridis the details of just how Sull Jerram had put her up to it, but she was ready to swear that Nail had never even touched her. She was awfully sorry. She'd had no idea at all that they would take him off and put him in that electric chair and try to kill him. Why, she'd been led to believe the most they'd ever do to him was make him say he was sorry he threatened to sic the federal law on Sull and his courthouse pals.

The first to put his big John Hancock on Viridis' petition was Jim Tom Duckworth, who had been Nail's lawyer before they got rid of him in favor of that Farrell Cobb, and he didn't have any bitterness for having been dismissed and was a real gentleman about it: he not only signed the petition but wrote out an exact copy of it and put on his hat and coat and went off to get a whole bunch of signatures or X's himself. He was the one who gave Viridis the names and general addresses of the twelve jurymen. On her own it would have taken the whole week to find just those twelve, scattered as they were, but most of them lived in or near Jasper, and we spent that Sunday tracking them down. By the time Viridis had finished talking with two or three of them, the word had quickly spread and got ahead of us, and some of the jurymen we visited seemed to be expecting us. Some of them claimed they had been mistaken in the first place and had already done changed their minds long ago, and the few who hadn't, said that all they needed was to hear Rindy say that it weren't so, and here she was, to say it, if need be.

We got lost trying to find the jury's foreman, who lived on the Little Buffalo River up on the north edge of Jasper, and while we were driving around looking for his house we came across an Oldsmobile parked broadside blocking the road. Sitting behind the steering-wheel was Sheriff Duster Snow with three of his deputies there in the vehicle with him, all four men wearing their silver stars pinned to the outside of their overcoats. The sheriff asked Viridis who she was looking for, and she told him, and he said that that individual was not available. Those were his words. Then he asked did she mind if he had a look at that piece of paper she was carrying around. She showed the petition to him, and he studied it and looked as if he'd like to chew it up and swallow it. He kept throwing fierce looks at Rindy and me. Rindy watched me to see what sort of fierce look I was throwing back at him, and she did a fair job of imitating mine. Finally he passed the petition back to Viridis and bobbed his Adam's apple a few times and said, "Now lookee yere, ma'am, we caint allow no furriners a-comin in yere and a-stirrin up trouble." Viridis said she wasn't a foreigner but an American citizen, a native Arkansawyer. "You aint from Newton County," Sheriff Snow said, "and this yere aint none of yore business and hit's again the law to go stirrin up the jurymen such-a-way as this-all, and I don't aim to stand fer it. Now you better jist git yoreself on back to wherever ye came from, and stay out of this country, if ye know what's good fer ye."

Viridis simply took out her Eagle fountain pen and unscrewed the cap and held the pen out toward the automobile and said, "Would any of you gentlemen like to sign this petition?" and one of the deputies reached out to do it before Sheriff Snow slapped his hand away.

Later, when we found that lost jury foreman on the Little Buffalo, we got an idea of why the sheriff hadn't wanted us to find him: not only was he ready to sign the petition, but he wanted to make a confession of his own, that he had never been convinced of Nail's guilt, that he had tried to hang the jury but had voted with them only after the sheriff had threatened to run him out of the country if he didn't. Now, if Viridis would let him make a copy of that petition, he knew a good many fellows whose signatures he could obtain. He was still afraid of the sheriff, but he'd just as soon be run out of the country as have to go on the rest of his life feeling bad about sending an innocent man to that electric chair.

By the time we'd given up trying to locate one more of the jurymen, who'd gone off visiting relatives in Western Grove, it was getting so late in the afternoon that we knew we wouldn't make it back to Stay More before dark. And we'd be sure to freeze if we tried. So Viridis decided to spend the night at the Buckhorn Hotel, an old landmark in Jasper. Rindy and I would have to miss school Monday, but we didn't care; we'd never even dreamt of staying at the Buckhorn before, and we were so excited we couldn't sleep. Viridis had to entertain us past bedtime. She drew our pictures (I've still got mine, framed, one of my prized possessions), and she told us stories and descriptions of Paris and her trip around the world.

It was way past bedtime when a knock came at the door, and Viridis opened it, and there stood Judge Sull Jerram. He didn't have any of his henchmen or cronies with him. He just pointed past Viridis . . . at Rindy, who was sitting on the bed, and said, "I want to talk to her." Viridis said she was sorry but he hadn't even had the courtesy to introduce himself and she wasn't in the mood to entertain strangers at this late hour. Sull looked like she had spit in his face, and he said, "Lady, they tell me yo're from Little Rock. Okay, that's where that nuthouse is, aint it? That's whar she belongs. Rindy is rampin tetched in her haid, and ary fool thing she says to ye won't be but some lie-tale she jist imagined. Now send her out here before I come in thar and git her." But Viridis stood in the doorway and told him that if Dorinda was mentally unsound it would not be wise for her to talk with a man who was both mentally deficient and irascible. From where I sat I could tell that it took Sull a while to figure out those words, and then he got even more irascible. "I swear to God, lady, I'll make ye wush ye was never born! You don't know who yo're talkin to. You might be some big somebody down thar to Little Rock, but

149

this yere is Jasper, Newton County, by God, and I'm the by-God county jedge! Now, I got some words to say to Rindy aint nary bit of yore be- ness, and I aim to say 'em to her! Rindy! You thar now, Rindy! Gitch yore hide out chere!" Poor Dorinda was trembling something terrible and mak- ing little motions as if she were trying to obey him by getting up out of the bed, but she couldn't really move. Viridis told him to leave or she'd call the manager. "Call him, goddammit!" Sull hollered at the top of his voice. "He's a good friend of mine lak everbody else in this town! Call him and see what he does to ye! Snoopin meddler bitch!" Viridis put her hands up on his chest and gave him a shove that pushed him clean to the other side of the hall, and then she slammed the door and bolted it. She motioned for us to get back into the bed, and she took a step in our direction just in time to avoid the bullets that came blasting through the door. Sull fired three shots real quick that left three big holes in the door panel and broke the mirror on the dresser. Rindy screamed, and I guess I must have hollered myself. Viridis tilted the whole bed up on its side and got us down behind it, so it partly shielded us from the door. She crawled on her stomach to reach where she'd left her purse, and she opened that purse and took out her big six-shooter and cocked it and kept it pointed toward the door. But Sull didn't fire any more shots. Some other people in the hotel down the hall must have come out to see what was happening and were yelling at him, and then a man, it must have been the owner, was yelling at him, "Jedge! Jedge, have you done gone crazy?" I couldn't hear all the words out there in the hall, but finally the man said, "Git out of here, Jedge!" and repeated it a few times. Sull stepped back to the door, and his voice came through those bullet holes: "Rindy, now you lissen a me, gal! You jist keep yore trap shut, hear me? You keep that trap shut or I've got a bullet with yore name writ all over it!" Then it got quiet. After a while there was a knock and the manager asked if everything was okay. Viridis wouldn't open the door. She asked the manager to summon the constable. The manager said there wasn't no constable, just the sheriff. "Snow?" she said, and the manager called back through the door, "Yes ma'am. Want me to git him?" "Never mind," she said, and she straightened up the bed and turned off the lamp and we tried our best to sleep.

But of course none of us could sleep. By and by Viridis asked, "Do you know any good stories you could tell?" and I told the best ghost story I could remember, and that passed some time. "Rindy?" Viridis said. "Do you know any stories?"

For a minute I thought she might have already fallen asleep, but she hadn't. "Could I tell a real story?" she finally asked. "Not a tellin-story, no, not a windy, but the pure fack?" We didn't tell her she couldn't, so she did. "I'll tell you'uns how it come about that Sull Jerram ruint me."

From that night on, Dorinda and I were best friends again. We hardly had time to enjoy it, though, before Viridis took her off to Little Rock. Most people thought that Viridis took Dorinda to Little Rock as a kind of "living signature" on that petition to the governor. It looked to everybody as if all the governor would need in order to give Nail a full pardon would be a complete confession from Dorinda, in person. But a big part of the reason Viridis took her to Little Rock was to save her from Sull: Viridis was convinced that Sull would kill Dorinda to silence her if he had the chance.

When the word got around Stay More that we had spent the night at the Buckhorn and been fired upon by Sull, some people were of the mind that Viridis should have known better than to spend the night in Jasper, right in the hornet's nest, you might say. If it had been them, some people said, they would have groped in the dark on hands and knees to get back to Stay More rather than spend the night in Jasper. But the Chisms, at least, protested that Viridis had no idea what she was getting into and was smart to hole up in the Buckhorn instead of risking her neck and ours on the road after dark.

Waymon Chism was fit to be tied, and that's what they should have done to him. As soon as he heard what had happened, he disappeared. His wife Faye looked all over Stay More for him, and we heard from her how angry he was. Waymon didn't own a horse or other conveyance; remember, he'd had to rent those mules and that wagon from Willis Ingledew to go to Little Rock for Nail's body, which wasn't yet available. This time Willis said he hadn't rented any mule or horse, either one. He just disappeared, and later word came that he had been seen, on foot, walking into Jasper. It's an all-day hike if you leave early in the morning. He must have been too tired when he got there to do anything that would require physical strength, like wringing Sull's neck. Which was, apparently, what he intended to do. He had no gun. A cousin in Jasper who gave him a bed for the night said that he had tried to persuade Waymon to borrow his pistol. Waymon refused and set out from the cousin's house right after breakfast to walk the few blocks to Sull's house. The cousin stalked him, from a distance, to see what was up. It was worse than walking into the hornet's nest, except for one thing: the hornet was alone. He didn't have Waymon's sister sleeping with him anymore, he didn't have children, he didn't have an old mother to fight for her wayward son, and, best of all, he didn't have Sheriff Duster Snow and his deputies to be his bodyguards and sidekicks, not that early in the morning. All he had was his gun. And Waymon got to him before he could even remember which pocket he'd left it in, in the clothes he took off the night before. Waymon got to him before he could get dressed. Waymon got to him before he could get word to God. The cousin described it: "Ole Waymon jist kicked the door down and walked right on in thar. Purty soon he had drug that jedge out to the front porch, whar he commenced to toss him amongst the furniture and reduce it to kindlin and flinders. Shore, ole Sull fit him back, or tried to. Sull got in a couple of licks, one of 'em a lucky round-arm swing that knocked Waymon off the porch, but Waymon jist reached back up thar and grabbed Sull by his laig and flang him out into the yard, whar he really set in to clobberin the daylights outen that feller. I swear, I don't see how Sull ever got off the ground again. He was jist laid plumb out, purt nigh boggy and half-dead, while Waymon stood thar and guv him a leetle lecture, a sermon I couldn't hear on account of I was standin behind a tree too fur off, but Waymon hollered at him fer a good little bit, and Sull jist had to lay there and listen to it. Finally Waymon turned and stomped off. He was headin the opposite way from me, was the reason he couldn't hear me when I hollered. He'd done already got too fur off and guv Sull time to git up and dash in the house for his shootin-piece and come back out and run right up behind pore Waymon, when I hollered as loud as I could, but he was too fur off from me to hear me. I reckon he did hear me, but by the time he commenced to turn around, Sull had done already shot him in the back."

The bullet entered Waymon low in the backbone. Sull's second shot missed, and by then Waymon had turned and grabbed the automatic by the barrel and yanked it right out of Sull's hand and then hammered him atop his head with the butt of it, nearly fracturing Sull's skull. By the time the cousin reached them, they were both unconscious. He ran for a doctor. The doctor summoned another doctor. They tended to Sull first, because he was the county judge, the leading citizen of Jasper, well known to them both. After they had revived Sull, and Sull was busy telling his friend Sheriff Snow how he had shot Waymon in clear self-defense, the doctors decided to carry Waymon into one of the doctors' houses, where they operated. Between the two of them, after several hours of cutting and gouging, they managed to get the lead bullet out without completely ruining Waymon's spine. But they had to keep Waymon there in Jasper for the rest of the week and more.

Folks in Stay More were just about ready to declare war on Jasper. The Ingledews themselves were furious, and before you get an Ingledew riled up, you'd better have kinfolks two counties over who can keep you awhile. John Ingledew, our leading citizen, the same man who ten years before had assembled the lynch mob that took care of that desperado Ike Whitter, and who owned one of the two automobiles of Stay More (his brother Willis owned the other), was in favor of organizing the men of Stay More into an army, marching into Jasper, and taking control of the county government and law enforcement in a coup d'état. It was the time of year when most men didn't have anything to do anyway: too early to plow, nothing to raise except Cain, and the chess-players around the stove in Willis' store imagined they knew a way to capture the sheriff and checkmate the county judge.

One morning when Viridis was just a day short of one full week in Newton County, and had just about finished collecting all the signatures she could get for her petition, she was standing on the porch of the old woman's house, with her sketchbook held in one arm and her drawing-pencil in the other hand, making a picture of the scene of activity on the storeporch across the road: the men of Stay More assembling, each with his best firearm, rifle, or shotgun, and even a flintlock or two, and the storeporch filling up with men, their wagons parked in the road and the yard, or the horses and mules tethered to trees and the porch posts. I was watching Viridis make her drawing, amazed that she could "freeze" that bustling motion of all the men and animals. Dorinda and the old woman were with me, the three of us silently admiring the drawing that Viridis was making. Viridis stopped drawing when she heard the noise; we stopped looking at her drawing and turned our ears toward the north, and the men

153

around the storeporch stopped in their tracks too and listened. The noise grew to a roar, and we could see the cloud of February dust before we could see the vehicles coming into view, down the road from the north, with all the town's dogs chasing them: the first car was Sheriff Snow's Oldsmobile with deputies standing shoulder to shoulder on the running-board, followed by Sull Jerram's Ford so loaded that feet were hanging out the doors, followed by a third car bringing that circuit judge, Lincoln Villines, who had sentenced Nail to the chair. As soon as the first car came to a stop in the middle of the road in front of Willis Ingledew's store, all of the deputies jumped down and pointed their rifles and shotguns at the men of Stay More, who, we were told later, were kept from firing at the intruders only by the presence of us four females in the line of fire across the road.

The men of Stay More had to lay down their arms. Then the two judges, county and circuit, followed by the sheriff and his men, mounted the storeporch and took a commanding position in its center. Sull's head was so wrapped up with bandages that his hat would barely stay on. We four females stood on the old woman's porch and watched and waited. Sull looked around him as if he owned not just the store but the whole town, and then he held up his arms for silence and began to speak.

"Gentlemen," Judge Jerram said, "lend me yore ears. It's a right smart of pleasure fer me to come back home to Stay More on sech a fine mornin and see all you'unses once again. Sounds lak I'm a-startin one of my campaign sermons, don't it? I aint, though. No, friends, the 'lection aint till November, and I spect I'll be back here again afore then, but I shore do hope I don't never *have* to come back before campaign time in the fall." Judge Jerram paused and looked around to see if everybody got his meaning: that only two things would ever bring him to Stay More: one, campaigning for re-election, and two, restoring law and order. "Do I make myself real clear? You over there, John Ingledew, do you understand me? All you Ingledews! Now, I got jist as much respect for a Ingledew as I got for ary man, and I don't stand second to none when it comes to reverence and esteem for the Ingledews, but I am a-standin here to remind you that Stay More is still part of Newton County, and I am still in charge of Newton County!" Out of the corner of my eye I noticed that Viridis was drawing again, and I stopped watching Sull act big and started watching her sketch him: she was doing him in his most grandiloquent oratorical pose, with one hand pointed heavenward and the other to the turf of Stay More, and his face twisted into an unctuous parody of a country politician. He went on, "Do I make myself *real* clear? You can vote against me come autumn if you so desire, and I'll be out in the cold a year from now, but meantimes I have been elected to run this yere county and I aim to run this yere county, and these men . . ." (his hand indicated the sheriff and his deputies and even the circuit judge) ". . . these men are my duly sworn confederates and partners, and we have all got to work together and stand shoulder to shoulder and be in cohorts together! I will not brook no insurgence! Hear me? If ary man but raise ary finger to stand in my way, I will leave no stone unturned to flush him out! In the parlous state of affairs that this yere vale of tears has done come to, I stand here proud afore ye and I do solemnly tell ye: walk the strait and narrow path or I will bar the door! Now, does ary of you'unses *not* know what I'm a-sayin?"

Judge Jerram waited a long minute for anyone to answer his rhetorical question, but no one did. All of the Stay Morons just looked sad and beaten, or sad and sullen, one. Later the men around the stove in Willis' store remarked that Sull Jerram could have recited the Gettysburg address and it wouldn't have been any different; it wasn't what he said that mattered, or even how he said it, but the fact that he had come out here to Stay More with all those men behind him just to say something and let us know that he was still the boss.

When the speech was over, Sull Jerram and Sheriff Snow came walking right down into the crowd, through it, and across the road to where we were standing, and Sheriff Snow said to Rindy, "Now, little lady, you'd better jist come along with us." He and Sull and a deputy came up onto the porch of Jacob Ingledew's house.

Poor Rindy got herself behind Viridis and the old woman, as if they could protect her, and Viridis tried to. "Are you arresting her?" she asked. "What's the charge?"

Sheriff Snow attempted a smile. "No, ma'am, I wouldn't call it a arrest exactly. We'd jist lak to have us a little talk with her."

"If she's not under arrest, she's not required to go with you if she doesn't want to," Viridis said.

The sheriff exchanged looks with Sull, and Sull said, "Ma'am, you are re-quired to answer one question: how long are you stayin in this yere town?"

155

"I'm not required to answer anything for *you*, mister," she said to Sull.

"No?" he said. "I'll give ye a secont chance. You can answer this or face the consequences: *how long are you plannin to stay?*" Viridis just coldly looked him in the eye and did not answer. "Okay," he said to Sheriff Snow, "you kin arrest her."

"You're under arrest, ma'am," the sheriff said to Viridis.

"You can't do this," she said. "What are you arresting me for?"

"Obstructin justice," he said, and took her arm and tried to lead her down from the porch.

The old woman placed herself in front of the sheriff and slapped his face. "You had better arrest me too, Mister Snow," she said to him when he had recovered.

He held his sore jaw. "Who the heck are you?" he asked.

"If failure to answer questions is obstructing justice, then arrest me too," the old woman said.

"I jist might," the sheriff said. "You caint go around hittin on the high sherf of Newton County!"

"I can't?" the old woman said. She slapped him again, harder, on the other cheek.

For a second it looked as if Duster Snow might haul off and hit her back, but he got his emotions under control, at the expense of a beet-red face, and said, "All right, dammit, you're under arrest too." But Judge Lincoln Villines came up on the porch and whispered something into Sheriff Snow's ear. The sheriff looked at the old woman and then up at the porch ceiling over his head, and spoke as if addressing it: "So you live here in Governor Ingledew's house?"

Viridis still had her sketchbook open and was doing a trio of quick portraits: Sull, the sheriff, and Judge Villines, grouped together like a pack of rats, each of them rendered unflatteringly, almost in caricature. When I failed to suppress a giggle, Sull stepped around to take a look at what she was doing.

She had done him first, in a few quick lines that perfectly expressed the coarse bluster and bullying of the man, with those bandages around his head making him look like a clown, but perhaps he was too stupid to realize how unflattering the interpretation was, and his first response was cocky: "Hey! That's *me*!" But then he changed his tone and demanded,

156

"What are you drawin me fer?" Viridis ignored his question and went on finishing her quick sketches of the sheriff and the judge. Judge Villines seemed addled; he seemed to be aware that his portrait was being done, but he couldn't decide whether to protest or pose, though he inclined to the latter, trying to get his best profile into position and his nose tilted properly. Sheriff Snow had dropped his mouth open, and Viridis decided that he looked more characteristic that way, and she quickly redrew his face with a slack-jawed expression.

"Hey, yo're under arrest, ma'am," the sheriff reminded her. "You caint go makin pitchers of people when yo're arrested."

"Indeed, what air ye doing?" Judge Villines timidly inquired. And then he requested, "May I see?" She turned the sketchbook so he could see it. "Wal, I doggies!" he exclaimed. "That's shore a clever resemblance of ole Duster! Looks jist lak 'im. Don't it, boys? And I shore wush Mary Jane could see this yere one of me." He looked beseechingly at Viridis, and said, "I don't suppose you could be persuaded to part with it?"

"No," she said. "This is for the front page of the *Gazette*."

"The *Gazette*?!" the men said in unison, and Judge Villines wanted a clarification: "The *Arkansas Gazette*?"

Viridis nodded and resumed putting the finishing touches on Judge Villines, who was busy whispering in the ear of Judge Jerram.

Sull gave Villines a grudging look, as if the circuit judge had made an unpleasant suggestion, and then Sull glowered at Viridis and pretended politeness: "Did ye take the trouble to record my speech, ma'am, ye prob'ly wrote down that I didn't say nary a word about the Chism be-ness. I jist came out here peaceable to say hidy to my friends and cool down the ruckus. I don't have no personal involvement in the Chism be-ness."

Viridis made a sort of laugh and stopped drawing. She looked Sull in the eye. "Then maybe you'll explain why you shot Waymon Chism in the back."

All of the men tried to speak at once, but the sheriff's voice was loudest: "Goddammit, it was self *dee*-fense!"

Viridis ignored him and continued looking Sull in the eye. "Waymon Chism was shot *in the back*," she repeated herself, "by the same pistol that fired four shots at me in the Buckhorn Hotel."

"It was pervoked," the sheriff said lamely. "I mean, naw, *you* didn't pervoke him, and thar weren't no excuse for thet Buckhorn misbehavior, but Waymon Chism shore enough incited and aggervated and brung it on hisself."

Viridis turned and looked coldly at the sheriff, but she pointed her finger at Sull. "Why isn't this low-life coward in jail?" she demanded.

"Ma'am!" said the sheriff. "Watch who yo're talkin about! He's the county *jedge*! We aint about to put *him* in no jail!"

Sull said, "Duster, why don't we put *her* in jail like we was fixin to?"

"Now, now, boys," Judge Villines said. He was saying "boys" the same way everybody does in this part of the country, meaning any male even eighty or ninety, but I couldn't help feeling these "boys" weren't any older than me; they certainly weren't behaving any better than rowdy children. "Let's us not be rude to a representative of the *Arkansas Gazette*. Don't we want to show ourself in the best light and present a favorable front to the rest of the world? We caint go around arrestin gentlemen and ladies of the public press."

Sheriff Snow said, "We jist come over yere to git Rindy Whitter fer a little talk, Jedge. That's all we come over fer, but then this yere lady started makin trouble."

Judge Villines asked Viridis, "Couldn't these men simply have a few words with little Miss Whitter here, ma'am?"

"Not him." Viridis pointed at Sull again.

"Why, how *come*, ma'am? He's got a personal interest in this matter too."

"He certainly does!" Viridis said. I had the feeling she was losing her temper, and then, sure enough, she lost it. "He viciously tricked Dorinda Whitter into submitting herself to a sexual assault which he performed upon her himself, and he inflicted unspeakable pain upon her, and then forced her into blaming innocent Nail Chism for what he had done!" Not a word or utterance of reply was made to these words by anybody, not by the accused, not by the accused's confederates. The only sound to break the silence, finally, was a small, stifled sob from Rindy.

At last Judge Villines spoke up. "That's a very serious charge, ma'am, and it's totally unsubstantiated, and it's pint-blank hearsay, and I would be very careful before I'd go around sayin things like that."

"It will be said in the pages of the *Arkansas Gazette* as soon as I get back to Little Rock."

"Duster, you'd better th'ow her in jail!" Sull said. "It's too late to shut up Rindy. We better jist th'ow this bitch in jail and keep 'er thar!"

Judge Villines, such a mild man, lost his temper then. "Shut yore fool mouth, Sull! Aint you done made enough trouble already? Jist shut up, afore ye go and make it worse!"

"Yeah," said Sheriff Duster Snow. "Yeah, Sull, you heared the jedge. Let's us jist simmer down and shush it up."

There was a shuffling of feet as the men waited to see which of them would make the first move to leave. The old woman got the last word: "It will be so pleasant when all of you bastards have removed yourselves from my porch."

All the bastards got off the porch.

———

Viridis and Rindy left Stay More early the next morning. I was there to see them off. I hated it. My best friend, off and on, terribly off for the longest time but now back on again, going away to the big city, where I'd love to go someday, any day. We cried. "On't ye come wif me?" Rindy said. "Caint," I said. "Ess ast Miss Monday kin ye," she suggested. "No, there's not no room no way," I said. And there wasn't, atop that poor mare, Rosabone, who'd be loaded down a-carrying the two of them. Much, much later, when I learned all about the trip, I knew they had dismounted from Rosabone on the hills and ridden her only downhill and on the level places, and still she was a brave old mare to take them both plumb to Clarksville. Rindy had on a pair of one of her brothers' pants so she could ride astraddle behind Viridis, and Viridis had put back on those jodhpurs that she'd never had a chance to let anyone see her wearing except us.

Viridis and the old woman had a talk while Rindy and I were saying our good-byes. After I had said all I could to tell Rindy I hoped she would have a good time in Little Rock and how much I admired her and all, there was nothing more to say, so I listened to Viridis and the old woman. The old woman said she was sorry that Viridis had not received a more favorable impression of Stay More. Viridis assured her that the people of Stay More were just fine. The old woman said she hoped Viridis would want to come back. Viridis said there was no doubt whatsoever that she would be coming back. She wanted to come back in the spring, and in the summer, when all the shades of green would be in their glory and she

159

could paint them. The old woman said that any time Viridis wanted to come back she would be very welcome to stay here at this house.

Then Viridis turned to say good-bye to me. She shook my hand. I guess tears were running down my face. And I didn't cry easy. "Latha, I'll miss you," she said, and I knew she wasn't just being polite. "You were a wonderful help to me, and I'll never forget it. You be good to yourself, and I'll see you again in the spring."

"Miss Monday—" I tried to say, choked.

"Oh, please just call me Viridis, or Very," she said.

"Very . . . Viridis . . ." I tried, but it didn't sound natural or mannerly. "You are the nicest lady I've ever known."

One minute he is looking at the best girl on this earth, the next minute he is face to face with the worst one. Nail could not look at her. He looked at the guard for help, or some sign of fellow-feeling, but the guard, a white trusty called Bird, just looked bored and stupid, and had no idea that Nail's visitor was none other than the selfsame little trollop whose lies had put Nail in this hell.

She wasn't looking at him either. She had given him just a glance and then was watching the door behind him as if she were still waiting to see the person she was expecting to come in through that door. She didn't even know it was him. She don't even recognize what she's done to me, he realized. She just stood there uncertain and scared-looking, waiting for somebody who looked like what she remembered Nail Chism looked like, but that guy never showed up, so after a while her eyes came to rest on him long and careful, and then she just said one word, in hardly a whisper: "Nail?" He didn't nod his head or say anything to her. But she finally must have got it through her silly head that it was indeed him, because the next thing she did was to fall down on her knees and clasp her hands together as if she were praying to him. "Oh, Nail!" she wailed, the way some ladies at a revival holler, "Oh, God!"

He didn't say a word. He just looked down at her there on her knees. Somebody had spent some more money on some more clothes for her. She wasn't wearing that white thing she'd worn at the trial, that had made her look like her own idea of an angel. Now she had on a real nice wool coat, dark-green, and even a little hat on her head like she would wear to Sunday school, and a little purse in her hand, and fancy shoes that went up her legs. She even looked older than what she had been. Well, maybe she had done turned fourteen since that summer that seemed so many years ago. Nail realized that Viridis had brought her here, and that she had put her name on that petition, which meant that she was ready to admit that she had wrongly accused him.

"Nail, oh Nail, Nail, Nail," she said. "Please fergive me. Say you'll fergive me, please please oh *please*." The tears were running down her face and messing up the powder and rouge that somebody had put on her face.

He honestly did not know what to say, so he didn't say anything. Bird threw him a curious look as if he'd done something awful to the poor girl to make her get down on her knees and bawl her eyes out like that. He wanted to say to Bird, This here little old girl is the reason I'm in The Walls—now watch and hear her tell me she's sorry she done it. But he honestly did not know what to say.

"Oh, what have I *done* to you?" she squalled. And because he wasn't making any response to any of her words, she seemed to give up trying to talk to him and started in to talking to herself: "Oh, see what ye've done to him, you bad bad girl! Oh, look at his pore haid! You ort to be kilt yoreself, you big eejit! You ort to jist trade places with him!"

She kept on babbling to herself like that until finally Nail said, "Git up, Rindy." The sound of his voice at last seemed to jolt her back to the real world, and she looked at him as if he'd said something wonderful and nice to her, and she got one of those fancy shoes up under her and began to rise up.

She stood up, although she didn't stand straight. She was hunched in the back like she didn't have any right to hold her head up anymore. She stood bent over like that and said, "I done tole Very everthing the way it really was, that it was Sull and not you who done it."

"What did Sull do?" he asked.

"Ever last thing I tole in court that you had done, jist lak I tole it, on'y hit was him, not you."

"But you let him," Nail said.

She shook her head. "Naw. He tuck me. He tole me to play-like you was him, so's I'd know how it felt."

Nail slammed his hand against the screen separating them, as if he could knock it down. "The son of a bitch!" he said.

Bird waved his shotgun barrel. "Hey, watch it there, big fella."

Nail turned his back to Bird and Rindy so they could not see his anger. He walked toward the door leading out of the visit room but, on reaching it, turned and walked back to the screen, and said to her, "Did he hurt you?"

"Uh-huh, a lot," she said. "A whole lot."

"Then how come ye to . . . how could ye . . . Rindy, for godsakes, why did ye do a *favor* for him?"

She hung her head. "They paid me," she said.

"They?" he said. "They who?"

"The sherf and them," she said.

"How much?"

"They's sposed to of paid me thirty dollars but they never guv me but ten, and they said they'd give me the rest when you got . . . when they kilt ye in that burnin-cheer . . . but I said I didn't want 'em to do that. Nail, I believed to my soul that the onliest thing they'd ever do to ye was to make ye stop botherin 'em the way ye was, with the federal law and all. I had no idee atall they'd th'ow ye in prison, let alone try to put ye in the burnin-cheer."

"You sat there in that courtroom," he reminded her, "and you heared ole Link Villines sentence me to death."

"When he said that, I got the all-overs," she said. "I had the all-overs so bad I couldn't even think straight, let alone say nothin."

"You could've said somethin afore now."

"Sull would've kilt me," she said. "He tried. He tried to kill Very too."

"*What?*"

She used up a good chunk of her fifteen minutes to tell him the story of how Viridis had spent the night in the Buckhorn Hotel at Jasper when she was trying to find all the jurymen to sign her "position," and how Sull had come in the middle of the night to the Buckhorn and confronted her and fired at her through the door, and then how Viridis had kept Sull and the sheriff and them from getting to Rindy that morning the men of Stay More were about to invade Jasper. Rindy talked so fast Nail couldn't follow her and get it all straight. Now Rindy was going on about how Sull had tried to catch them as they were leaving Newton County and had followed them in his car up around Loafer's Glory, and they had had to ride Very's mare off into the woods to get away from him, and he had abandoned his car and come on foot after them and got close enough at one point to shoot up all the ammunition that his automatic would hold, and Very had fired back at him with a six-shooter she had, and maybe hit him, they couldn't tell, but they had got away from him, deeper into the woods, and lost, and when they got back on the main road to Clarksville they never saw any more of him.

Then she was silent. "Go on with yore knittin," he told her.

163

"That's all," she said. "That was day afore yestiddy. Then we come on down yere to Little Rock. Aint it a big place? Aint this town a sight on airth?"

"I don't rightly know," he admitted. "I aint seen much of it."

"You ort to see this yere big house where Very lives at," she said, and held her hands high over her head. "It's the beatenest house ever I seed. That's whar I'm a-stayin. Today we're gonna go out to the state capitol buildin and see the governor! We're gonna give that governor Very's position with all them names on it!" Rindy began to smile for the first time. "I'm gonna stand up thar in front of the governor and swaller my teeth and tell 'im it was all a big mistake. Then you jist wait and see if you aint out of yere in two shakes of a dead lamb's tail, I bet ye!"

"I hope that governor believes ye," he said.

"Oh, Very says he's *got* to believe me! I'm gonna tell him the *truth*, jist edzackly lak it was."

For the first time he was able to soften his tone. "That's fine spoke. I 'preciate that, Rindy. I shore do."

"And when you git out and come back up home, I hope ye won't be mad at me no more. I'll do anything you want me to do iffen ye'll fergive me."

"All I want ye to do is stay away from that Sull. He aint a bit o' good fer ye."

"Don't I know it? I shore learnt my lesson. He's the meanest feller on this airth. What he done to Waymon—" Rindy put both hands over her mouth.

Nail put both hands on the screen, in defiance of Bird. "Yeah? What was you about to say?"

"I aint sposed to mention Waymon."

"Rindy. Look at me. What did Sull do to Waymon? Tell me."

She whispered, "He shot him in the back."

"Naw! When was this? He aint dead, is he?"

Bird said, "Big boy, take your hands off that screen. Your time is up anyhow. Better get on back to your roost. Here comes Short Leg."

"Listen," Nail said to Bird and raised his manacled wrists to gesture toward the anteroom, "could you get that lady to come back in here for just a second? I got to ast her something."

"Sorry. You caint chaw your tobacco twice. Here's Short Leg."

"Rindy! Waymon's not kilt, is he? Don't tell me he's kilt!"

164

"No, Nail, he's still alive," she said.

"Goddammit! Jist let me git out of here!" Short Leg took his arm and led him toward the door. "Rindy, you make that governor let me out of here!" he called to her from the door.

"I will," she said.

off

For the longest time he heard nothing from the outside world. He became painfully aware of this fact of prison life: if you expect nothing, you'll be satisfied, but if you're waiting for something, even death, time will drag, each day will last a week, and if you take a minute to wonder when you're going to get what you're expecting, the minute will become an hour.

Could it be possible, as his calendar told him, that here it was March already and that weeks had gone by since Viridis and Rindy had made their visits to him and to the governor? Or had he just imagined both of those females and their visits? No, he had at least some proof of it, in the form of the sketchbook that Timbo Red was now filling up with drawings: Viridis had brought it for him, not exactly smuggling it in, as he had suggested, but openly giving it to Mr. Burdell and telling him that it was a gift from the employees of the *Arkansas Gazette* for Timbo Red, a talented young artist, and Burdell had let the boy have it, and Timbo Red was beside himself with joy. Nail would have been very happy for the kid too, except that it was really hard to be happy about somebody else's good fortune when your own luck was running so bad. He couldn't understand it. He spent all his time watching for the appearance of Farrell Cobb and an expected letter from Viridis. After a few weeks he even got up his nerve and asked the warden, "Mr. Burdell, sir, you aint happen to have heard anything about maybe Mr. Cobb is sick or anything like that?" and Mr. Burdell had just looked at him and grinned and shrugged his shoulders.

It was enough to drive a fellow crazy, if he wasn't already. Nail had two things that kept him from going over the brink: his tree charm, which he would finger in moments of intense anxiety, and the one December letter from Viridis, by now reduced almost to shreds; but no matter if it did eventually disintegrate, he knew it by heart. He almost knew by heart what the next letter would say, if it ever came—or at least what he would want it to say, and exactly how he would want her to say it: that she was setting him free.

In his restlessness he began to get the first exercise he'd had since they threw him in The Walls. He began to pace. Sometimes he couldn't just lie on his bed or sit on the edge of it talking to Timbo Red and watching him fill up his sketchbook. Often it was hard to watch Timbo Red's sketches, because the boy began to draw increasingly from his memory of the scenes of his youth that were pleasant: the creeks and forests and pastures of Stone County—woodland scenes and meadow scenes and deer at gloaming, tranquil pools and soaring crags and sunsets on the ridges. The kid sure could draw. You could almost *be* there, the scenes were so real, but they only made Nail's eagerness to get home even worse, and after watching Timbo Red draw for a little while, he had to get up and start walking. He walked up and down the rows of the bunks, the whole length of the barracks, several times and back. In the beginning of his hikes he made the mistake of wandering into the rows of the bunks where the blacks lived, and they stopped what they were doing or saying and watched him pass, and one of them reached out and stopped him and said, "Wat baw, you know way you is at?" and he confessed, "I reckon I don't," and got himself out of that neighborhood and back among the whites, who paid him no more notice than to the several other compulsive ambulators.

All of this walking increased his appetite, and he began to do what Viridis had advised him: eat whatever they gave him. He ate whatever was on his plate and watched for chances to filch crumbs of cornbread from anybody else's plate. He even regained a couple of pounds, at the risk of getting caught violating a main rule: don't ever eat anybody else's food. He began to sit next to men whose appetites he knew were poor: the old, the sick, the apathetic. He became adept at sliding his hand beneath the edge of the table and up over the edge to snatch any morsel remaining.

He walked and he ate and he regained some of his health. Then Fat Gabe caught him stealing food. Not Fat Gabe himself but one of the black trusties whose job it was to stool to him. But instead of giving Nail a dose of the strap, Fat Gabe did a strange thing: at the next breakfast he brought him an egg, the first egg Nail had seen since he'd been in The Walls, the first protein since Christmas. It was hard-boiled, not pan-fried the way his mother used to fix him a half dozen of each morning, but it was a genuine egg. He knew better than to ask any questions of Fat Gabe, so he didn't ask him what it was for, or what he had done to deserve it. He just ate it. At dinner Fat Gabe brought him an extra plate of cornbread and beef fat. He ate it. And at supper Fat Gabe did the same, or, rather, he began to have the trusty who waited on the table make sure that Nail got a second helping. This continued daily.

Nail wondered if Fat Gabe was getting soft. Or religious. Or just tired of being mean and evil. But no, if anything, Fat Gabe was growing even more vicious in his treatment of other men: he now had twenty-one notches on his belt, and he seemed to be getting so much exercise and muscular development from his daily floggings that he could administer up to forty lashes before beginning to tire. The two trusties who were required to sit on the victim's head and feet and hold him down often were exhausted from their efforts before Fat Gabe began to tire. And Fat Gabe was always seeking to refine the severity of his methods: he now had a long leather strap that had brass brads embedded in the tip to impart an extra fillip of pain and laceration. Then Fat Gabe discovered that boring a number of penny-sized round holes in the strap would not only reduce air resistance and make the strap faster and harder but also leave blisters and welts. No, Fat Gabe was becoming anything but soft. As an ultimate infliction of pain, certain to fill the barracks with endless screams, he sponged salt water into the wounds. Eventually Doc Gode was required by Fat Gabe to sit and take the victim's pulse and keep the torturer informed of the floggee's heart rate, in order to determine the maximum number of lashes—thirty-five or forty—that could be tolerated in one day. After forty lashes drenched with salt water, most men faced the prospect of three weeks upstairs in the flyspeck room recuperating or dying under Doc Gode's supervision. Every week Fat Gabe put another notch on his belt.

Nail considered the possibility that Fat Gabe was giving him extra food only because he had received orders from above—perhaps the governor himself had been influenced by Viridis (and Rindy too). But Nail usually ate his extra ration without reflecting on it: you don't look a gift horse in the mouth.

Most of the other men did not resent Nail for his extra food. As one of them put it, "A double helping of shit is *still* shit." But a few, especially those who had been sent out of The Walls all day to do hard work at the lumberyard or the brick kiln or on the railroad and had ravenous appetites when they returned, begrudged Nail his double servings of food because he was never even sent out of The Walls to work. One of these observed, at the table in the hearing of anybody watching Nail start on his second plate, including Fat Gabe's stoolie, "Nails is just gettin fattened up for the slaughter." And the men nodded their heads and chuckled or grinned.

Timbo Red too began to suspect that Fat Gabe was giving Nail extra food only because "he's tryin to git ye back in shape so's he kin destroy ye." Nail considered this and remembered the threat that Fat Gabe had made to him before Christmas: "I'm gonna save ya till you're strong enough to 'preciate what I'm gonna do to you." It had been noticed that Fat Gabe never administered the strap or any of his other tortures to ailing men, weak men, men too frail to fight back. He seemed to have a fondness for flogging men who were much stronger than he himself could ever aspire to be. Nail noticed that the most recent deaths from the brass-bradded lash and brine-soaked sponge had been men who were notably muscular, hale, and, at least until their punishment, indomitable. Nail decided he had better not give the appearance of becoming *too* healthy.

More men tried to escape. The coming of springtime always makes prisoners want to get out, to go home and do their plowing and planting, or at least to get out where they can watch the world wake up to the new season. The rising of the sap probably accounted as well for Fat Gabe's increased energy, and the severity of his scourge was another motive for attempts at escape. In the few years since the old state penitentiary had been torn down to give its hill to the new state capitol, and the high, thick barrier of brick on a hill outside of town had been stacked into the rectangle called The Walls, there had been only two or three successful escapes, and of those, only one was still at large, a murderer named McCabe, whose method of escape was kept a secret from both the public and the prison population. Every man inside wanted to become the second at-large escapee. They schemed and plotted, and conjectured about McCabe's possible modus operandi, and they tried to acquire lengths of rope, or to fashion rope out of stripped bedclothes, or to make primitive ladders. The few who managed to scale the wall without getting shot by the trusties manning the four towers at the corners of the The Walls made it as far as the swampy thickets to the south, where, within a few hours at most, bloodhounds tracked and caught them. A shed right behind Warden Burdell's house had six bloodhounds penned up and ready to go. According to rumor, the one man who had eluded the bloodhounds had disguised his scent by smearing mustard oil on his feet. But none of the rumors told how he had acquired the mustard oil in the first place.

Strong men who attempted escape that month of March were the especial targets of Fat Gabe's flagellations. He did not need to fabricate an excuse to whip them; attempted escape was a felony, and, to discourage others

169

from making the attempt, the flogging was made as visible and audible as possible: everybody had to gather in a thick circle around the inverted wheelbarrow over which the body of the man would be held by three trusties while Doc Gode took the man's pulse and a fifth trusty sponged salt water into the wounds that Fat Gabe steadily inflicted, to a total of one hundred and sixty, if the victim could bear the maximum of forty per day and live through four days of it. No inmate forced to stand and watch that performance through four days would give a *lot* of thought to attempting escape himself, but it was still an option preferable to death in the flyspeck room.

Fat Gabe not only kept feeding Nail all he could eat, he also began to let him outside the building. The warm weather made it necessary to open the windows and get as much air as possible into the barracks, and to get as many men as possible out into the Yard. The Yard was only a yard: merely all of the empty space between the brick buildings and the brick walls, a few acres of what had once been grass but was now mostly mud and sand, with just a smear of green here and there. Fifty men at a time, guarded by a shotgun trusty, would be allowed to go out into the Yard for an hour and walk, jump, run, waddle, or crawl—anything except stand and congregate and talk. Nail took advantage of being let out into the Yard to study the walls very carefully, to memorize the length and height and even the brick patterns of every section. He observed that the brick building of the engine room, which also contained Old Sparky and the death cells, was much closer to the wall than the main barracks. He noticed that at one place along the wall a corner of the engine building's roof obscured the view from the tower. Why, he asked himself, was he making all these observations if Viridis and Rindy were going to make the governor let him go? The answer, he told himself, was that week by week his chance of a pardon appeared slimmer and slimmer.

The month of March was marching on and he hadn't had his March trip to the visit room. Surely Viridis had at least *tried* to visit him. Once when Fat Gabe and Short Leg were making their rounds, Nail forgot that he was never supposed to question them. "Short Leg," he asked, "you don't reckon anybody came to see me at the visit room that you didn't tell me about, did they?"

Short Leg exchanged glances with Fat Gabe, the two of them astounded that an experienced convict would violate the cardinal rule against asking them questions. Short Leg didn't know whether to hit Nail or not, but when he raised his hand, Fat Gabe said, "He aint ready yet," and then he even smiled almost friendly-like at Nail and said, "We'll let that one go, Chism. Just watch it."

After the two sergeant-guards had moved on, Timbo Red exclaimed to Nail, "I tole ye, didn't I? They're jist a-waitin till ye git to lookin real peart afore they light into ye."

But just a day later, as if Nail's question had produced *some* result, he was summoned by Short Leg for a trip to the visit room.

It wasn't Viridis. It was Farrell Cobb. Nail complained, "I thought you generally came into the barracks to see me. Now you're using up my visit room time."

Cobb whispered, "They're shaking down everyone they admit to the compound." He patted his breast. "I didn't want them to find what I'm carrying."

"A gun?" Nail said.

Cobb laughed. Nail had never heard him laugh, nor suspected that he was capable of it. "No. A very thick letter. Pages and pages."

Nail felt stifling frustration. He swore. He glanced all over the edges of the screen separating him from Cobb, as if there might be some opening the letter could be slipped through. He studied the trusty, Bird, who was just standing there looking bored and blank. He inclined his head toward Bird and whispered to Cobb, "I don't suppose you could bribe him to let me have it."

Cobb shook his head. "I wouldn't want to try."

"Well, shit," Nail muttered. Then he asked, "Did you read it? I reckon you could just tell me most of it."

Cobb cleared his throat. Of course he didn't want to admit that he had read the letter. "I skimmed most of it," he said. "There isn't much news that I couldn't tell you myself. There's a very long account of her trip to your hometown and her meetings with the various figures involved in the case, such as Judge Sewell Jerram and the sheriff, et cetera. There's a long account of her attempts to see the governor. An unfortunate business. A truly lamentable state of affairs. She and the child, Dorinda Whitter, tried for a week to get an audience with Governor Hays. They sat in his waiting-room for three whole days. Yes, three days, and I was there with them part of the third day, when I finally demanded of the governor's assistant that we get admitted to his private office. Most regrettably, Viridis Monday was very angry by that time and her mood kept her from presenting her case effectively to the governor, toward whom she was openly hostile. In this letter . . ." (again Cobb patted his breast, where Nail could see a bulge beneath his suit coat) ". . . she gives reasons for her anger at the governor which are unjustified, I think. She even went so far as to tell the governor that he was responsible for Dorinda Whitter, that he would have to make the child his own ward, a preposterous suggestion, if I may say so, and I did say so."

"Go on," Nail said. "So you're tellin me the governor didn't buy none of it? No pardon, huh?"

"Not necessarily on account of Miss Monday's rudeness. The governor feels strongly that the whole business would have to go through strictly legal channels, the case would have to be referred back to a lower court, you would need to be retried if that could even be considered acceptable by the court, you would have to follow established procedures, you couldn't just impose upon the governor's charity."

"Didn't that governor believe what Rindy told him?"

"I'm afraid the child didn't get a chance to tell him her story. The governor insisted that she would have to tell it to a court, not to him."

"But didn't he even take a gander at that petition with all those names that Viridis had got signed for him?"

"He said he was most curious to know if the petition contained the names of Prosecuting Attorney Thurl B. Bean and Circuit Judge Lincoln Villines. It does not, of course. The governor is of the opinion that Judge Villines must recommend leniency to him, or at least recommend a retrial, and Judge Villines will not. I might add that Judge Villines is, it would appear, an old friend of the governor's."

"It would appear," Nail echoed. He asked, rhetorically and futilely, "What kind of governor is that man anyhow?"

"For now, the only one we have, alas," Farrell Cobb said, the closest he ever came to expressing any sentiment against the governor.

"So what's the next step?" Nail asked.

"Next step?"

"Yeah, how long does it take to get another trial, or whatever?"

Farrell Cobb shook his head. "You don't understand," he said. "The governor was our last resort."

172

"But didn't ye jist say something about the governor hisself says that the case has to go back to a lower court and git retried?"

"Only if Judge Villines recommends it, and he does not."

"Well, fuck Link Villines! If a judge does something wrong, he aint likely to ask somebody else to come along and tell him how bad he done. Of course he don't want a retrial!"

"That's the way the law works," Farrell Cobb said.

Nail stared at him in disbelief. "If that's the way the law works, you ought to be ashamed to call yourself a lawyer."

Farrell Cobb reddened. Testily he said, "Insults won't work with me."

"Then what in hell *will* work with you? Tell me that! What have I got to do or say to get some *help* from you?"

"Mr. Chism, I've given you quite a lot of help," the lawyer said coldly. "I've gone to some extraordinary lengths to appeal your case. In fact, I think it's safe to say I've worked harder on this case than any in my career."

"But I'm still going to the chair," Nail said.

Farrell Cobb did not deny it. But he didn't exactly concede it. After a while he just gave his head a slow shake and said, "Quite conceivably."

Nail gestured toward Cobb's breast, where the precious thick letter was. "Did she give me any hope?" he asked.

Cobb reached for the envelope as if to verify an answer but thought better of it and stuck his hand into his outside coat pocket instead. "As I seem to recall her saying, she said you should not give up. She said something about attempting to attract national publicity to your case."

"What does that mean?" Nail wanted to know.

"The big newspapers and magazines in the East might take an interest in you, and if there were sufficient national publicity, it could pressure the governor into reconsidering."

Nail thought about that. Bird announced that the fifteen minutes were up. Nail said, "Jist one more question. The national publicity would have to come before April 20th, right?"

"One would hope," Farrell Cobb said.

April came. Nail worked on his letter to Viridis. He wrote it and rewrote it, trying to get each sentence perfect in his mind before committing it to paper. Paper was scarce; he had only a few sheets left from the penny pad Warden Burdell had given him at Christmas. As a last favor Farrell Cobb had agreed to come back to the penitentiary when he could safely come into the barracks and take the letter out. Nail hoped that Viridis might come to the visit room even before then, but, as he told her in the letter, he didn't blame her for not coming: it was too painful, for both of them, to realize they couldn't say anything in just fifteen minutes. He told Viridis he wanted to remember her as he had last seen her: happy, beaming, exhilarated from her trip to Stay More, optimistic, bearing the secret of having brought his accuser to apologize. He said how profoundly grateful he was to Viridis for whatever she had done to persuade Dorinda not only to admit her wrongdoing but to come to him and tell him to his face. Even if he was executed, he would know that there was no greater proof of his innocence than a confession from Rindy herself. He said he was sorry that the governor had not heard Rindy say it. He said the only times lately when he got really angry, mad enough to fight Fat Gabe himself, was when he thought about the injustice of that governor making Viridis sit in the waiting-room for three days before letting her talk to him. He didn't blame her for getting rude to the governor. If it had been him, he would have been more than rude: he would have clobbered that governor. He confessed he spent a lot of time thinking about killing the governor.

Then he wrote:

I reckon you know that if they try to electercute me I aim to kill as many as I can beforehand and I reckon you also know how I aim to do it. But I have been thinking (which of course is what we all of us do too much of around this place) and have decided that if I'm going to die in that way, I might as well make one honest attempt at getting out of here before they even put me back in the death hole, which it don't look like they plan to do until the week before the electercution date. Before they put me back in the death hole, I think I know a pretty good way to break out of here, and I can do it all by myself if you could find some way to do just one thing for me. I need a little bit of mustard oil, just enough of it to smear on my feet to throw the dogs off my scent when I light out for the country. If there was some way you could smuggle me just a tiny bottle of that mustard oil.

But if you can't, and I have to go sit down in the chair on the 20th, I want you to promise me that you won't come and watch. I couldn't stand that. I sure would like to see you again before I close my eyes for the last time, and to tell the honest truth I'd like to still see nothing else except your beautiful face behind my closed eyes for eternity, but I don't want that to be the last thing I see before I close my eyes, I want to imagine it, I want to create you, I want to be able to take your face with me to eternity because I made it up all by myself.

There is one more request, if you can bear one. Then I won't bother you with any more of them. When I am gone I hope you will take the trouble that you would ordinarily spend on grief and instead do whatever you can for this boy, Timbo Red. He will make a great artist one of these days. Not nearly as good a one as you, but a great one, still, if he gets the chance and maybe some lessons and enough of those drawing materials. He ought to get out of here on parole before too very long. The only thing he ever done wrong was steal a horse, and they can't keep him long for that. If you could watch out for him when he gets out, I'm going to tell him a lot of things that I wanted to tell you so that he can go on for a long time telling you those things almost like I was still around to do it myself, and if you want to, you can pretend his voice is mine, just the same way you brought all of those Stay More voices with you so I could hear them.

If you was with me right now, you would be laughing because what I'm thinking about is, wouldn't it be funny if you was to introduce old Timbo Red to Rindy and they become good friends? Live happy ever after, and all that?

On second thought, maybe it ain't funny. But *you*, dear Viridis, please live happy ever after. Get me that mustard oil if you can. If you can't, don't let it bother you none. You done your best, you done more than any woman or man either could ever have done, and I and the trees will love you for it for ever more.

Then he could only wait and watch for Cobb, to smuggle this letter out. Every day that passed was a day lost he'd need to work out some way to get that mustard oil; he had the rest of it pretty well planned: getting over the wall at the right time in the right way. He didn't even tell Timbo Red of his plan, although he considered that the kid himself might need to escape sometime. But he did tell Timbo Red, day after day when they could talk, about Viridis Monday. Timbo Red had to admit he'd never known any female anything like her, and not because Nail was bragging on her or making her out to be better than she was; he was telling Timbo Red exactly everything that Viridis had done that he knew about, and just what she looked like. Of course he didn't tell Timbo Red to expect that Viridis was going to take care of him when he got out of the pen, but Nail was setting him up for it so he wouldn't be absolutely flabbergasted when it happened. But he did tell Timbo Red he hoped the boy would meet up with her if anything ever happened to Nail that he wasn't alive anymore, because then there were a few things he wanted Timbo Red to tell her, if he could remember them.

Timbo Red could remember them all. He could especially remember the directions to a few spots west of Stay More where you could look down into the valley and paint the most wonderful pictures of it. Timbo Red allowed as how he himself would sort of like to go and see some views like that, and even paint them, if he ever got aholt of some paints and learned how to use them.

"You'll git ye some paints, son," Nail told him. "Jist take my word fer it."

One evening at supper Nail was working on his second helping of cowpeas and cornbread when somebody crowded in to sit beside him on the bench, and even before he turned to see the face, he recognized the smell: the barbershop talcum powder of Attorney Farrell Cobb. Nail was both elated and irritated. He didn't have any more use for Cobb, except as a messenger, but that was essential. Cobb shook hands with him, which he hadn't done before, and Nail instantly detected something in their pressing palms. "A letter from her," Cobb whispered. "All folded up into a wad. Hide it. Enjoy it later."

As their hands came apart, Nail withdrew his with the precious wad in it and tucked it into his waistband, then took from the other side of the band his letter for Viridis. It was not wadded up, but there were only four pages, folded three times. He kept it under the table and placed it on Cobb's leg. "Kindly get that to her."

"Wait. No. I can't," Cobb protested, feeling the letter.

"Just stick it in your pocket," Nail insisted.

"No, really, they'd—" Cobb said, darting a glance around the room. "Sshh! They're watching us!"

Nail looked around. Fat Gabe and Short Leg were over at the end of the mess hall, but they weren't watching. The only one watching was the mess trusty, a black man. But he was watching the two of them intently, and he could clearly see Nail's hand on Cobb's leg.

"Take it, quick!" Nail said.

"No, take it back!" Cobb said. "Move your hand!"

The black trusty yelled, "GIT DE WADDEN!" Fat Gabe and Short Leg came over. The black trusty said to them, "Dem two done passed some paper," and pointed at Cobb. "Marse Buddell he say to watch dat man. Git de wadden."

Nail had taken back his letter and thrust it back into his pants band but in doing so had jarred loose the wad of Viridis' letter so that it fell down into his trouser leg. Fat Gabe said, "On your feet, Chism!" and as Nail stood up he felt the wad of Viridis' letter slide down his leg to the floor. Without looking down, he covered it with his shoe. Fat Gabe held out his hand, and said, "Whatcha got there? Le's have it!"

Nail held out his empty hands. "I aint got nothin."

Fat Gabe looked at Farrell Cobb and demanded, "He hand something to you?"

"Well . . . no, he . . . I don't have anything," Cobb said.

"Search 'im," Fat Gabe told Short Leg, who reached inside Farrell Cobb's suit coat and searched his pockets and then the pockets of his trousers.

"He's clean," Short Leg announced.

"Search Chism," Fat Gabe said. Nail wondered, Am I gonna have to use my knife before it's time? He hoped Short Leg wouldn't find his knife. But Short Leg went immediately to his trousers and, knowing that no convict's trousers ever had pockets, felt inside the waistband and brought out the letter. "Well, well," Fat Gabe said, snatching the letter out of Short Leg's hand and holding it up high. "What have we here?" He turned to Farrell Cobb and waved the letter under his nose. "He try to pass this to you? Or did you give it to him?"

"Well, not exactly," Cobb said.

"What do you mean, Mister Cobb?" Fat Gabe demanded. "Is this yours or his?"

"It isn't mine, I assure you," Cobb said. "I've never seen it before."

"Get the fuck out of here, Cobb," Fat Gabe said. Cobb hastily departed, and Fat Gabe said to Short Leg, "Get the boss."

Warden Burdell was summoned, and came, and Fat Gabe handed him the letter. The warden took out his spectacles and put them on. He unfolded the sheets, giving Nail a glance to indicate he recognized the writing-paper as the same he had given Nail to write his mother at Christmastime. He read the letter, grinning. Nail stood helpless, the sole of his shoe pressing down on the wad of Viridis' letter. Would he ever get a chance to read it? Finally the warden looked up and said to Nail, "So this was intended for Miss Monday of the *Gazette*, huh? As I suspected, she's sweet on you. Right?" Nail did not answer. The warden flapped the letter. "You say here that you'd like to kill the governor. Is that true?" Nail would not answer. "Answer me, or do you need Gabe to give you some persuasion?" Nail gave a semblance of a nod. "And it says here you're planning to kill a few of us before we electrocute you. You want to tell me how you're planning to do that?" Nail could not answer. The warden removed his spectacles and looked at Fat Gabe and Short Leg and said to them, "Maybe he thinks he can do it with his bare hands!" and both of the sergeant-guards laughed. "If you're so impatient to give it a try, Chism, your date with Old Sparky is right around the corner. I think we'd better put you back in the death hole to wait for it. But first . . ." (the warden inclined his head in the direction of Fat Gabe) ". . . first I believe my assistant here, ole Gabe, would like to inflict an appropriate punishment for your stupid attempt to smuggle this letter out of here. Is that right, Gabe?"

"Just let me get my hide," Fat Gabe said. "We'll do it right here in the mess hall."

"Very good. Everybody can watch," the warden said. "Except me. I wouldn't have much fun watching you get strapped, Chism. But I expect I'll have some pleasure watching you fry. Unless you find some mustard oil." Before walking away, the warden shook his head and said again, "Mustard oil!" and snorted a laugh.

Inmates hate to have to watch a flogging right after supper; several of them are sure to puke. The wheelbarrow was not brought in as a rack for Nail's body; he was just spread out right there face down on the dining table, with three trusties holding his arms and legs, while Doc Gode got ready to take his pulse.

There were three things Nail saw, in succession, before the blows started: first, the wad of Viridis' letter, still there on the floor, nobody noticing it or thinking anything of it, or at least not bending down to pick it up and find out what it was; second, the face of Timbo Red, who was looking at him with mingled terror and fierce indignation, whose sixteen-year-old eyes were already beginning to acquire some of the keen look of having seen too much of this world and having tried without success to make sense of it; and third, as Nail shut his eyes, that face with its caressing green eyes and frame of fire-red hair, that face he would always see whenever he shut his eyes until the very last time he shut them. He tried to fix that face in the darkness as the brass-studded lash opened up the skin of his ass. And when they sponged salt water into the wounds, he did not scream. He bit his tongue and gritted his teeth and hoped that maybe he would faint before the pain got too bad. The only sound he could hear at first, other than the loud slapping of the leather against his skin, was the heavy breathing of Fat Gabe exerting himself as he had never done before, almost as if he'd found a woman who was his match in bed and needed every bit of breath and thrust he could give her. And then Nail heard a man retching and heaving up his supper. And then another. Nail's own double-supper had risen in his craw and was threatening to choke him. Better to drown in his own vomit than be beaten to death. But he held it down, as he held back his screams that were begging him to let them beg.

He was not counting the blows. It was somewhere past thirty, but he wasn't counting. He was thinking how sad it was that Viridis would never see that last letter he wrote to her. No chance the warden would let her have it.

Fat Gabe seemed to be getting a bit frustrated. "Goddamn you, Chism, if you die, it's gonna be *me* who does it, not Ole Sparky." Nail made no response. There was a longer interval before the next blow, and when it fell Nail knew why: Fat Gabe must have hauled off and reared back as far as he could with that strap before giving it all he had. And all he had was not enough to bring a scream out of Nail, only a groan. And Fat Gabe cursed the trusty: "Nigger, goddamn you, *squeeze* some of that salt in there!"

Suddenly Nail felt someone tearing at his chest. He opened his eyes to see Timbo Red, who said, "Let me have that knife!" and grabbed the string

179

inside Nail's shirt and pulled it out, and tore the knife off it, tearing off too the gent's tree charm, which flew out and landed on the floor not far from the wad of Viridis' letter.

"No!" Nail hollered at Timbo Red, but before anyone could lay a hand on the kid he had stuck the knife into Fat Gabe's belly and pulled upward with all his might, tearing right up through the middle of his guts. Fat Gabe screamed and dropped the strap and clutched himself in the middle, and Timbo Red slashed the knife across Fat Gabe's throat, from ear to ear. Short Leg had his gun out, but before he could fire it, Timbo Red had plunged the knife into Fat Gabe's chest.

The trusties holding Nail had let go of him, and he too was up and watching as Short Leg, instead of shooting Timbo Red, decided to cock him over the head with the butt of his gun, and knocked the boy unconscious to the floor, right beside the wad and the tree charm. Nail sprang down beside him, and, while making sure the boy was okay, or at least pretending to care for him, he palmed the wad and the tree charm. A moment later, while everyone was watching Fat Gabe roll and toss and buck, Nail concealed his treasures by thrusting his hand down into his pants and tucking the wad up under the space behind his testicles and then hiding the tree charm in his anus.

In the confusion that followed, nobody paid much attention to Nail for several minutes. All of the trusties were there, including the armed ones. All of the half-trusties, or do-pops, came running, and everybody crowded into a circle about Fat Gabe, who was flopping and coughing up blood, his guts spilled onto the floor. Short Leg was waving his pistol as if somebody else might try to do something, and Timbo Red lay sprawled on his back, his eyes closed but almost a trace of a smile on his mouth. Fat Gabe, with his last bit of strength, pulled the knife blade out of his breast and held it as if to plunge it into Timbo Red. At that instant Warden Burdell came running in and yelled, "Christ, Gabe, what in *hell* is a-gorn on here?"

Fat Gabe's eyes clouded over, and he echoed one of the words as if he were already on his way there: "Hell." Then he collapsed and was dead.

———

Down in the death hole later that night, Nail lay on his side in the old, familiar, mouldy cot that had been his bed so many months in the autumn. It was almost good to be back. He was careful how he lay, because of the wounds in his buttocks, which still bled. It was absolutely dark, and he would have to wait until morning before attempting to read Viridis' letter, which was still in a wad tucked snugly into his groin behind his testicles. For now, he was watching again and again that scene in the mess hall, particularly those precious seconds when he had failed to prevent Timbo Red from taking his knife and killing Fat Gabe with it. If only he had acted quicker. The boy should have known that Fat Gabe wasn't killing Nail, that Nail would survive it, that it wasn't worth risking his own life to kill Fat Gabe. The boy had practically committed suicide. There was no way now they would ever let him go. If they didn't electrocute him, they'd keep him in The Walls for the rest of his life or, worse, send him off to Tucker Farm, where the hardcases would rape him to death. Nail was tremendously moved and beholden that Timbo Red would have done something like that for him, would have liked him so much that he would act impulsively to protect or save him, but he was sorrowful beyond all imagining that it had actually happened, and there was no taking it back. The sheriff of Pulaski County had come out to The Walls to arrest Timbo Red and take him off to the county jail, because that's the way the law worked, and the sheriff and some other men had taken Nail into Warden Burdell's office and questioned him for an hour, trying to find out if Timbo Red was Nail's "punk" and if the boy might have done it because he was in love with Nail. Finally Nail had lost his temper and demanded to know why that sheriff had never come out and arrested Fat Gabe for all the murders he'd committed on the inmates. That question had shut up the whole room for a long moment, and then Short Leg had taken Nail down here to his old home in the death hole. Before the heavy iron door clanged shut on him, Short Leg had remarked, "I'm just afraid that whoever the boss gets to replace ole Fat Gabe is going to be a meaner feller than he ever was." Nail had thought about that for a while, trying to determine if it meant that Short Leg had approved or disapproved of Fat Gabe's ways.

Before bringing him down to the death hole, Short Leg had let him pick up his stuff: his two books, the Bible and Dr. Hood, and his harmonica, which he hadn't played since that one time around Christmas. Now he raised it to his mouth, cupped his hands around it, and let his breath escape slowly onto the holes and reeds, and then he made one hand tremble to shiver the sound. The hand trembled pretty well all by itself without his willing it. He was still shook up. He drew in his breath slowly, changing the notes of the sound, making them more mournful, and he discovered he was playing a very slow and elegiac version of "The Battle Hymn of the Republic." *Mine. Eyes. Have. Seen. The. Glory. Of. The. Coming. Of. The. Lord!* The confines of the dank cell gave a special resonance to the haunting voice of the Hohner, so that the hymn was not one of praise but of loneliness, sadness, yearning. *He is trampling out the vintage where the grapes of wrath are stored!* The measured cadence of the poignant notes was molded by his hands, his lungs, and his lips into an expression of nostalgia and regret. *He hath loosed the fatal lightning of His terrible swift sword!* Nail made love to the instrument the way he'd sometimes had fancies of kissing Viridis. *His! Truth! Is! Marching! ON!* He stopped and took his lips away from the harmonica and said aloud to himself, "On?" and then he asked also, "Truth?" and he just lay there in dazed thought for a long time before he could again raise the instrument to his mouth. Then he played a few old ballads. He played a couple of his favorite love songs, "On Top of Old Smoky" and "Down in the Valley," the latter filled with the sound of the wind blowing through the valley, the loneliness of jail, the hope of knowing and seeing love. And then, to test the harmonica's range of perky and jolly tunes, he played "The Old Chisholm Trail." That was about an old cattle-driving road running from Kansas to South Texas, which, his daddy had told him, had been named for a kinsman, Jesse Chisholm, who didn't know how to spell his last name. It runs on through twenty-three verses, with the chorus of *Come-a-ti-yi-yippy* after each one, but twenty repetitions was all he could tolerate before he grew very sleepy and quit.

"Dat sho am sweet," a voice said, and Nail realized that the other death cell was occupied. They introduced themselves. His companion was Percy James, called Fleas, or Fleece, Nail would never be sure which. Fleas had carved up his wife with a razor while drunk at Christmas, believing she had been unfaithful to him. He was scheduled to sit on Old Sparky in just a few more days, he wasn't sure whether it was Tuesday or Wednesday. He wasn't too scared; an uncle of his had also had an appointment with Old Sparky, and, oddly enough, for the same offense. Nail and Fleas got acquainted until both of them grew sleepy.

Before falling asleep, Nail focused his mind away from the gashes on his buttocks to a spot nearer the front, that fleshy little mound where the skin of his scrotum joined his crotch, wherein the paper wad was nestled, which, both then and moments later in sleep, he imagined was the gentle thumb of Viridis.

182

The only light the death cells ever got was a wedge of early-morning sun that hit a small basement window and bathed the interior of the cells for an hour or so in a glow that in autumn and winter had seemed cold and menacing but now, in spring, was warm and promising, and lit the floor as well as the wall. Nail sat in that light and ate all of the hunk of rock-hard cornbread they gave him for breakfast. And drank his tin cup of water. He remembered his neighbor and called out, "Good mornin to ye, Mr. James." There came in reply a chuckle, followed by: "Moanin to you, Nails. Aint no wat man eber call me mistah befo."

Then Nail reached down to where the thumb still touched, and took out and gently unfolded the wad. He unfolded it once, twice, thrice, a dozen times: it was a sheet of ordinary white writing-paper, now turned grayish by the tiny pencil markings written in a fine hand with a fine point all over it, on both sides. He had to hold the paper very close to tell one line from another, and he had to squint to tell one word from another, and he had to reread to tell one letter from another. There were no margins. To save space, she had omitted the date and the greeting and the closing and their names, but these were not necessary.

This must be a poor substitute for at least fifty pages I have written you since my last letter. Nice Mr. Cobb says that he will try to get this to you if I am able to abbreviate it to only one page, and I must ask myself which of those thousands of words that I wrote at more leisure I need most to say here. I feel like writing in quick, three-word sentences: "All is well. Please be happy. You will live. Don't give up. *Gardez la foi.* We shall prevail. Truth will out. Justice will triumph. I love you." There, but don't you see how I can't say *that* in only three words? Yet I can't say it in one page either. Please believe I tried several times to visit you, but each time I was told that you were being punished for stealing food and were not allowed to have visitors. The last time I made an attempt, the guard, Gabriel McChristian, said he would let me see you if I would "step out" with him, which, I gathered, meant meeting him somewhere outside The Walls for some illicit purpose. I considered exposing his despicable bribe to the authorities, but these days I have very little faith in any authorities, as you can imagine, after my experience with the governor, which, I am the first to admit, I bungled by stupidly permitting myself to become irritated and indignant with "His Excellency." But he is such a mean-spirited, small-minded little politician, probably the worst governor that Arkansas has ever had. Your dear friend and mine, young Latha Bourne, went to great trouble to collect the signatures of nearly 2,000 Newton County women to add to my petition of registered voting males, with a wonderful letter (she sent me a copy) in which she beseeched His Excellency for clemency and reminded him, "None of us females can vote, Governor, but we can sure influence the men who do." As far as I know, Gov. Hays didn't read her letter or give her petition any more of his precious attention than he gave mine. But if he and the people of Arkansas are blind and deaf to the hideous injustice of your wrongful conviction and punishment, perhaps Americans in general will not be. I am trying very hard to find a publisher for one or more of several articles I've written about the case. So far, I've placed one in the *Houston Chronicle* and one in the *St. Louis Post-Dispatch*, which isn't much of an accomplishment, but at least it means that there are some editors who are interested in you, which is more than can be said, unfortunately, for the editors of Little Rock, including my former boss, Mr. Thomas Fletcher, to whom, I'm both sorry and happy to say, I've submitted my resignation. I am very hopeful that Associated Press, a national news service, will accept the best of my articles so that it will appear all over the country. Now, if you are interested in Dorinda, the pitiful origin of this whole mess, she is reasonably happy living here at my father's house and attempting to attend Fort Steele Elementary School, where, I am told, she is having problems with reading and comprehension as well as "ability to get along with others," but is making progress. She sends you her best wishes, her continuing (that is, lifelong) regrets, and her "bedtime prayers." Sometimes I feel inclined to prayer myself. You are right, I don't know you and I never asked you where you stand in regard to a Supreme Being, but I learned enough about you on my trip to Stay More to have the impression that you are not exactly a praying man yourself. If there is a God, He (or She) would at least have allowed Governor Hays to *listen* to Dorinda's story, but he (and He) would not. I don't believe in Governor Hays, either. I believe in you, Nail. I believe that men as good and as brave and as strong and as passionate as yourself are the highest manifestation of life on this earth . . . next to, of course, trees. If we were trees, if we were all rooted, and still, and swaying gently in the spring breeze, would we be happy? Perhaps, but we could still be cut down. Nobody is going to cut you down, my dearest. Not as long as I am still standing.

"Nails, mah fren, does I heah yo weepin? Do de sadnesses got you too? It aint no hep to cry. We got to be brabe, man. We got to face de music. You dry yo eyes now, heah me?"

Nail was not aware that he had made a sound, but he saw that a drop of water had fallen on Viridis' letter, and it wasn't sweat. He was almost glad that the letter he'd written for Cobb to smuggle out to her, that was probably right now on the warden's desk, would never reach her, because it was such paltry, numb, ignorant nonsense compared with her letter. The only thing he'd said that came anywhere near equaling the beauty of her letter was when he almost came as close as she had to coming right out and saying "I love you." How had he put it, or sneaked around not coming right out and putting it? Yes: he had written, "And I and the trees will love you for it for ever more," which wasn't the same as saying "I love you" or even saying "Me and the trees too love you" but just saying "We will" as if it hadn't happened already but was likely to happen if we just all got a chance to last forevermore. Thinking of trees, he remembered the tree charm and remembered where he had hidden it, and he fished it out and cleaned it off and hid it inside Dr. Hood. To take advantage of the morning light, he read for a while in Dr. Hood, which was written as if a real medical doctor were having a series of informal but educational chats with one of his patients. Nail received advice on what to do while his wife was delivering the baby. He happened to read, "In the event of prolonged labor, the ingestion of a small quantity of mustard oil will increase peristaltic movements of the stomach and possibly advance the contractions of the womb." Nail wondered who was supposed to drink the mustard oil, himself or his wife? Probably her. He flipped over to the section on *Pharmacopoeia* and read: "Oil of mustard—an ester of isothiocyanic acid useful as a rubefacient, counterirritant, emetic, *and to disguise one's scent from bloodhounds while escaping from the penitentiary.*" Nail gave his head a brisk shake and reread the definition and found the last part of it missing on the second reading, and told himself that he was beginning to go stir crazy . . . if he had not already been for quite some time now. It scarcely mattered that Viridis would never read his request for mustard oil; he couldn't use it now if he had a gallon of it. He would stay in this hole until . . . but, goddammit, it *did* matter that she would never read his request not to attend his execution. Somehow he had to get word to her that he did not want her to do that.

"How you doin there, Fleece Boy? Have you prepared yourself to meet your Maker?" Nail heard a familiar voice he hadn't had to listen to for quite some time.

"Yassuh, Reberen McPhee, I sho has. De Lawd say He gwine take me in His ahms and He aint gwine let dat ole sizzle chair hut me one bit."

"Well, that's good, Fleece, I'm real proud to hear that. How 'bout I read you some scripture this mornin?"

"I sholy 'preciate iffin you did, Reberen."

Nail listened to Jimmie Mac visit with Fleas for most of an hour, thinking that his turn would have to come next and he would have to give up the last of the morning sunlight to McPhee, when he'd rather use it to read to himself a couple of those nice love songs that Solomon wrote, especially that one about how beautiful the lady's feet were with shoes on them.

"Good to see you back again, Brother Chism. I mean, now, I don't mean it's good that you're back in the death hole, I just mean it's almost like a kind of homecoming. Right? In my experience I've known a number of men to actually prefer being down here to being up there. Up there they've got problems you don't have down here. Down here too it's kind of quiet and peaceful, don't you think? Up there it can get anything but. Now, I don't suppose you've had any revelations or second thoughts that might make it easier for me to get you ready to meet the Lord?"

It took Nail a little while to determine that this was a question, not a simple observation of reality, and at length he said, "Well, Preacher, I'll tell ye. I've done some thinkin, and I believe I can see God. Yessir, I can see the face of God as plain as I can see you a-standin there, and the wonderful thing is, Reverend, that God is a her, I mean She's a Woman. Did you know that?"

"I'm sorry?"

"Yessir, you are, because what I'm tellin you is, and you'd better believe it, is that here all along folks have been under the mistook impression that

God is a man, and a father. But She's not. No, I'm tellin you, She's a female, and a mother. She's the best mother ever there was."

Jimmie Mac did not say anything. He seemed to be searching his memory to see if he had ever encountered anybody who had ever said anything like this and, if so, what he had said in reply. But after searching corners of his memory he had forgotten he had, he couldn't find anything. Finally he said, "Well, Brother Chism, that's very interesting. But you're wrong. The Good Book tells us through and through that He's a him, and a man, and He took the form of a man when He became the Son of Man and died on the cross for our sins. They never hung no *female* up on a cross."

"Yeah, poor Jesus was a man all right, just like me, but God was his mother, not his father."

"That's blasphemy, Brother Chism. It hurts me to hear a man talk sacrilegious."

"You don't have to listen," Nail pointed out to him.

"Are you saying I'm not welcome here in your time of torment and travail?"

"You're welcome to hear me help you get straight about the sex of God."

Jimmie Mac did not come again, or, rather, he did not stop by Nail's cell when he came to visit Fleas, and that didn't last much longer, because Fleas was taken up to see Old Sparky on April 14th. It seemed as if all they were waiting for was somebody strong enough to take him up there. Sure enough, as Short Leg had feared, Fat Gabe's replacement wasn't a bit of improvement on him. For one thing, he was just as fat. His name was Gillespie Gorham, and from the beginning Nail thought of him as Fat Gill, but the first time he called him that, Fat Gill smashed him in the face and broke one of his teeth. Fat Gill did not slap, forehanded or backhanded, the way that Fat Gabe had done. He simply made a fist right alongside his cheek, then rammed it straight into the victim's face. "Call me fat once more," he invited. Nail did not.

Apart from his own execution, Nail had two things to expect: one, he would probably be required to witness Fleas' electrocution, and two, Viridis might be there too and he could sit next to her. And sure enough, when Fat Gill and Short Leg came to get Fleas before sundown on April 14th, the guards first handcuffed Nail and took him upstairs, then came back for Fleas, who had to be practically carried, he was fighting and screaming so much. Nail took his usual seat in the witness area and waited for Viridis as the other witnesses came. The guards managed to strap Fleas into the chair, but they wouldn't gag him, which was what he needed most; he was drowning out both Jimmie Mac's attempt to say "Our Father Who art in Heaven" and Nail's attempt to correct him: "Our *Mother* Who art in Heaven . . ." Viridis never came. Was Fleas' picture not worth putting in the paper? But then Nail remembered that Viridis had resigned from the paper. Maybe she'd tried to come and they wouldn't let her in.

Right before the end, Fleas, who was a very dark colored man of about thirty, seemed to recognize Nail. He stopped begging for life and looked Nail right in the eye and said, "Aint you Nails? I never seed you befo. You Nails, aint you?" Nail nodded. "Nails, could you play on yo mouf foggan fo me? Could you play 'Swing Low, Sweet Chariot'?"

"Shut up, nigger," Warden Burdell said. "You got any last words?"

"I'se sayin 'em," Fleas said. "I'se askin Nails to play on his mouf foggan fo me."

"He aint got his mouth organ, nigger. Sorry." Warden Burdell raised his hand and dropped it, and Bobo shoved down the switch, and the light dimmed and the dynamo hummed and Nail watched very carefully every twitch and jerk of Fleas' body so he would know exactly what to expect of his own body in six more days. When Bobo brought the switch back up a while later, Warden Burdell motioned Doc Gode to see if the victim was still alive. Doc Gode took a stethoscope and put it up against the black man's hot chest, but before he could listen, all of them heard these words crooning from the black man's mouth: ". . . Comin fo to cah me home! Swe hing low, swe heet chah ott!" Warden Burdell shot his finger at Bobo, and Bobo turned the juice on again and left it on.

As the witnesses were leaving, the warden said matter-of-factly to Nail, "You're next."

"Yeah," Nail said. He raised his voice so Bobo could hear. "And when you turn that thing on, don't turn it off until I'm black as Fleas."

"Still think you can take a few of us with you?" the warden asked.

Nail knew he could not, and back in the death hole he thought about that. They never brought him any knife, fork, or spoon to eat with. All he got was cornbread, and the fat meat he had to eat with his fingers, and if there were any cowpeas, they came in a cup he had to hand back. It was doubly unfortunate that Timbo Red's impulsive gesture had not only doomed the boy but also deprived Nail of the weapon he had intended to take to the chair with him. All the thought that Nail had put into preparing for his last minutes would have to be revised. At least, if it was any consolation, he knew now that Viridis would not be there, not because he'd asked her to stay home but because they wouldn't let her in. So it would just be him and his eight or nine male witnesses, Fat Gill and Short Leg, the warden, and Bobo. And Jimmie Mac. Nail realized that in order to have any hope at all, he had better try to get on the good side of Jimmie Mac and change God's sex back to male.

But Jimmie Mac never came again until his presence was required for the execution. And God remained a woman, an unseen one but a kind one, Who sent to Nail a small blessing in the form of the companionship of Timbo Red for Nail's last days. Sure, it was a mixed blessing: it meant that Timbo Red had been convicted of the first-degree murder of Fat Gabe and was going to be executed for it (in those days the killing of a police officer or "correctional" officer was considered the worst of all crimes). Almost as soon as Fleas was moved out of his death cell, Timbo Red was moved into it. But the man and the boy were neighbors for two nights before either discovered the other's presence. One morning Nail listened to the familiar sound for a long time before he finally recognized it for what it was: the skritch-skritch of a charcoal pencil on a piece of paper. Nail's voice was first: "So they let you keep your pitcher pad?"

"Nails? That you in thar, Nails?"

"Yep."

"Nails, I shore am sorry I tuck yore knife lak that. Reckon now ye caint use it fer what ye aimed to, kin ye?"

"Reckon not, Tim. But that's okay. I'm jist sorry I had the damn thing in the first place. If I hadn't of had it, you wouldn't be in the death hole."

"Shit. That thar Fat Gabe would of kilt ye."

"Noo, son, he weren't quite ready to do that, jist yet. You shouldn't of done what ye done, Tim. I shore 'preciate it, but they weren't no call fer ye to butt in lak thet."

Timbo Red was silent, thinking about that, and then he said, "Do ye know what? Tim aint my name. But it aint Timbo Red neither. That's jist what they call me."

"Shore," Nail said. "My name aint Nails neither. It's jist plain ole Nail. No Nails. It's a ole fambly name."

"What I figgered. They was some folks name of Nail up whar I come from."

"What is yore name, son? I don't recollect."

"Hit's Ernest. Ernest Bodenhammer. But with a name lak thet, you mize well jist call me Tim."

"Naw, I'll call ye Ernest, if ye want."

"And I'll call ye Nail."

In the death hole Nail Chism and Ernest Bodenhammer became more closely acquainted than they had during the months together upstairs in the barracks. Down here they had privacy. There was no one to hear them. A trusty came three times a day to bring the cornbread and cowpeas, and about once a day Short Leg or Fat Gill would come down and look in to see if they were both still alive and hadn't chewed through their bars.

They talked all the time except during the morning sunlight, which Ernest took advantage of to draw, and Nail to read; during all of the darker hours they talked, and before the 20th rolled around they knew almost everything about each other that was worth knowing. It wasn't until late the first night of their discovery of each other that their stream of conversation temporarily ran dry, and Nail volunteered to play a few tunes on his harmonica. He asked if Ernest had any favorites, and at Ernest's request he played "Fire on the Mountain," "Hell Tore Loose in Georgia," and "Big-Eared Mule."

It was while he was playing the last tune that Ernest interrupted him: "Hey, Nail! What's that there mouth organ made out of?"

Nail stopped playing. "Made out of?"

"Yeah. Aint it got some *metal* in her?"

Nail studied the Hohner. "Why, yes, matter of fact, she's nearly all metal, except for the board."

"Any *plates* of metal in her?"

"Yeah, she's got a couple plates."

"I got a idee," Ernest said. "Couldn't ye tear her apart and make ye a knife out of one of them plates?"

Nail reflected. "Hell, I could make *two* knifes with her, but I aint about to. Wouldn't be no use as a mouth organ anymore."

"Which'd ye ruther, yore life or yore music?"

"Ernest, you've mistook the idee. If I had me a knife, I couldn't save myself, I'd jist kill a good few of the others before they threw the switch on me."

"That's better'n nothin, aint it?"

"I used to think so. I aint so sure anymore."

But before he could fall asleep that night, Nail spent a good bit of time holding the Hohner in one hand, fingering it and thinking. He'd sure hate to tear it up, but it wasn't going to be any use to him anyway in three more days. Was that enough time to take one of the metal plates and sharpen it along the cement floor? Even if it was, the resulting weapon wouldn't be as firm or as dangerous as the knife he'd had before.

The next morning after breakfast, while Ernest was doing his drawing, Nail asked, "What are ye makin a pitcher of this mornin?"

"Ole Sparky," Ernest said.

"I didn't know you'd ever seen it," Nail said.

"I aint. I'm jist imaginin what it looks lak. But I may need yore help. Remember how you told me afore, when I tried to draw it with chalk on the floor? What are ye readin this mornin?"

"I aint readin," Nail declared. "I'm a-takin my harmonica apart."

All day and all night while they talked, Nail sharpened one of the metal plates against the cement floor. He was impatient and did not do it quietly, but their voices covered the sound of the scraping. "Tell me what's it lak raisin sheep," Ernest requested, and Nail instructed the boy on the art and science of sheep-raising. He began with the land itself: it was necessary to have well-drained pastures, because sheep cannot bear damp. Old, permanent meadows were better than artificial meadows because if Nature is left alone, She'll give you a greater variety of grasses. The best pastures face south but have a border of trees to shade the sheep during the hottest part of the day. The shade should be green, or purple-green, dark and dry and cool.

The next day, which by his reckoning was April 18th (he didn't have a calendar now, just a good sense of time), he had the dagger-like shape pretty well defined, and began honing the edge of it on the sole of his shoe as he told the boy about breeding sheep: the proper selection of the ram, picking him out not because he's biggest or heaviest but because he has good fleece and a good shape; the bringing together of the ram and the ewe; the proper time and place for the mating.

Ernest asked questions. "How big a peter does a ram have on him?"

Nail laughed. "Didn't you never see any sheep up around Timbo?"

"They don't raise 'em up thataway, that I ever heared tell. Is a ram's peter much bigger than a man's?"

"Not bigger'n yours," Nail assured him.

"Do tell?" Ernest became thoughtful and silent, but at length he lowered his voice and asked, "Did ye ever hanker to mount a yo?"

It was Nail's turn to be silent before he said, "Wal, shore. I reckon any feller would."

"But didje ever do it?" Ernest asked, and waited. He waited a good while before changing the subject. "Nail, you aint never been married, have ye?"

Nail cleared his throat. "No, I guess not."

"Didje ever have a womarn?"

Nail pondered. He said, "Yeah. I did."

"Tell me what it's lak."

"You never did?"

"I got real close one time, but she changed her mind. Was the one ye had willin?"

"She was willin." Nail remembered, and smiled. "Matter of fact, it was her idee."

"Tell me all about it so's I can draw a pitcher."

"You want a pitcher of 'em *doin* it?"

"Yeah, tell me how she set or laid down or whar she put her knees and her hands, and all lak thet. Tell me how you got down or knelt, and all. Did ye have yore clothes on?"

So Nail talked and described and narrated, and he heard Ernest's charcoal pencil going skritch-skritch. Ernest occasionally interrupted with questions. Was it dark? How far off was that coal oil lamp? What kind of covers was under them? Did they pull any covers over them? What color was her hair? Could you tell if the hair down there was the same color, or lighter? Ernest had a hundred questions before they were both finished.

"I wish I could see yore pitcher," Nail remarked.

"It aint my best one," Ernest reflected. "But it'll do. Looks jist lak ye. Or jist lak I remember ye. Have you changed any since I seen you last?"

"A mite older, is all."

And sometime in the night, Nail, insomnia filling his head with thoughts

192

of the day after tomorrow, listened to Ernest making love to his imagination and to himself. It went on awhile. Nail reflected that there was at least a ghost of a chance that the boy might get his execution stayed. He was only sixteen, and maybe that governor would take pity and commute Ernest in a way he couldn't for a grown-up convicted rapist like Nail. Ernest was real smart, and if he got commuted to life and got sent to Tucker, he might be smart enough to escape someday and maybe become a sheep farmer in some faraway place where he and Rindy could live happy ever after. Nail told himself to go ahead and finish telling Ernest all the things he wanted him to tell Viridis, just in case he ever got the chance.

On the 19th, the day before his scheduled execution, he did. Ernest listened carefully, remembering it all, for a long time before he interrupted: "What makes ye think I'll ever git the chance to tell her any of this? Ole Sparky's gonna cup my butt on the first day of May."

Nail was putting the last honing on his blade. He tested it with his thumb. "You jist never know," he said. He began cutting the cuff of his trousers to unravel thread for a string to hang the blade around his neck. He heard a noise and quickly hid the blade under his bedcover. Fat Gill and Short Leg came to his cell, along with a white trusty whom Nail recognized as the convict barber, carrying a pair of shears, a shaving mug, and a strop. Fat Gill handed the razor to the barber after first handcuffing Nail and warning him to sit absolutely still. With the shears the barber clipped off as much of Nail's regrown hair as he could; Nail reflected that this was the time of year he ought to be shearing his own sheep, if he still had any; he watched the hair fall into his lap and onto the floor, short shocks of white mixed with blond. Then the barber soaped Nail's head and shaved his skull. He worked rapidly and not very carefully; Nail felt himself get nicked twice and felt the blood trickling behind his ears.

"Want a mirror?" Fat Gill asked when the barber was finished.

Nail raised the middle finger of his manacled hand and held it stiffly upright for Fat Gill to sneer at.

When they were gone, Ernest's voice came: "What did they do to ye?"

"Shaved my head," Nail said.

"What'd they do thet fer?"

Nail realized the boy didn't have much of a conception of how the electrocution process worked, and he debated with himself whether to explain it. Would it help Ernest get ready? Or would it just make him

193

more scared than he was already, although he tried so hard to seem not to be? A thought suddenly occurred to Nail: tomorrow when they took Nail upstairs, they would take Ernest too, as a witness, and Nail's would be the first execution that the boy would see. He also realized that if Fat Gill and Short Leg were able to restrain Nail so that he couldn't reach his knife, Ernest would reach it and do to Fat Gill and the other men exactly what he had done to Fat Gabe. Nail didn't want that. Since they were going to kill the kid in Old Sparky anyway, Ernest would probably figure it made no difference if he died trying to help Nail take as many with them as they could. Nail could not allow that.

"Son," Nail said to Ernest, "I'm gonna tell ye exactly what they're gonna make you watch at sundown tomorrow. I want ye to know jist what you'll see, includin how I'm gonna kill a few of 'em first, specially Warden Burdell and that executioner, a son of a bitch named Bobo. But before I tell ye, I want ye to promise me one thing: you'll jist sit there and not lift a finger to help or git in the way or git yoreself in any more trouble than you already got. Will ye promise?"

on

$\mathbf{B}$ut Ernest Bodenhammer was not allowed to witness the execution of Nail Chism. Tom Fletcher told her later that the warden had wanted to include Ernest because it was customary to have a condemned man watch all of the electrocutions in order to give him a clear foretaste of his own, but that the warden had made an exception this time because in view of the way Ernest had killed Gabriel McChristian over Nail, the young man might very well create a disturbance during the execution. And besides, the warden pointed out to Tom, there wasn't really any room: the witness area was filled. All twelve of the chairs were taken up by reporters. Warden Harris Burdell had even had to turn away a few latecomers, including Viridis herself, who was late not because it had taken her that long to persuade Tom Fletcher to give her a press card, nor because she had needed more time to steel herself, but because she'd attempted unsuccessfully to convince Warden Burdell that she wanted to attend as a bonafide journalist, not as the condemned man's "sweetheart," as the warden insisted on referring to her. He had refused to admit her, but he had used as his excuse the crowded presence of reporters from, in addition to the *Arkansas Gazette* and its rival the *Arkansas Democrat*, the *Houston Chronicle*, the *Post-Dispatch* and the *Globe-Democrat* (both of St. Louis), the *Memphis Commercial Appeal*, the *New Orleans Times-Picayune*, the *Kansas City Star*, Associated Press, and, the farthest that any reporter had journeyed, the *Atlanta Constitution*. She had hoped to get at least one representative from the East, but the *Washington Star*'s man had missed his train connection and the *Philadelphia Inquirer* had decided at the last moment that there were bigger stories in Pennsylvania.

Tom Fletcher himself had represented the *Arkansas Gazette*, and afterward came to his car, where Viridis had been required to wait, and told her about it. The deathroom "crew," he said, had been caught completely by surprise. Warden Burdell had no inkling until the first reporter, from the *Times-Picayune*, arrived at his office just an hour before the execution was to take place, and requested an interview with the condemned man. Warden Burdell had to explain to him, and to the next eight reporters who knocked at his door, that condemned men were not allowed to speak to anyone other than the minister and the warden himself on the day of execution. It was tradition, if not ironclad rule. So some of the reporters had to content themselves with interviewing Warden Burdell, asking him such challenging questions that he replied to each with "I'm only the warden, doing my duty. I didn't sentence Chism to death, and it aint my business to pardon him."

Other reporters cornered the executioner, Mr. Irvin Bobo, age forty-two, who closely resembled the movie actor Charles Chaplin and whose breath reeked of liquor, and attempted to ask him questions. He was not able to invent a stock reply as the warden had, but he was quoted as saying, "I aint gonna kill no more white men after this one. I'm only good at killing niggers. If they want to kill any more white men, they'll have to get somebody else."

Reporters managed to locate two of the guards, James Fancher and Gillespie Gorham, and asked them several questions. Their boss had been able to give them only a few moments' warning, telling them to put on their neckties and comb their hair and not say anything stupid. Gillespie Gorham, thirty-one, a rather corpulent man, formerly a patrolman with the Little Rock police, solved the problem by repeatedly answering questions with "I don't know nothin." James Fancher, thirty-seven, who appeared crippled, one leg shorter than the other, was willing to talk and even to describe the condemned man's last hours, which had been spent in conversation with another condemned man (or youth) in an adjoining cell.

The reporters had then converged upon the minister, the Reverend James S. McPhee, fifty-two, who explained that he was not affiliated with any particular church and considered himself nondenominational although he was partial to the Baptists. He was a full-time employee of the St. Louis & Iron Mountain Railway, working as a conductor on the Texarkana run, but some years earlier he had received "the call" to make sure that all condemned men, black and white alike, had the final peace of knowing that God loved them and was willing to forgive them their crimes if they confessed and acknowledged Jesus Christ as their Saviour. No, this Nail Chism fellow had not confessed anything. He was an atheist. Well, not exactly an atheist, because he did finally profess some sort of belief in God, but he held the heretical notion that God was a woman. Reverend McPhee had accompanied Nail Chism on his previous "last mile" to the electric chair, and he had accompanied a total of thirteen men, all but two of them of the colored race, on their last mile to the electric chair since its invention, and he had never seen any condemned man approach the chair as coldly as Nail Chism did, which, Reverend McPhee believed, was probably a sign of guilt: Chism knew he deserved what he was getting. And yes, *this* time the minister hoped the execution would be carried out.

When Tom Fletcher arrived to take his seat in the witnesses' area, he noticed that all the other men had their press cards stuck in the hatbands of their felt fedoras, and he had to search for a while through his wallet to find his press card, which he hadn't flashed, let alone worn, for some years. He put it in his hat and took his seat in the back row of the folding chairs.

Eventually an iron door creaked open, and guards Gorham and Fancher entered with the prisoner, followed by Reverend McPhee. There was an audible collective gasp among the hardened journalists at the sight of the condemned man, although Tom Fletcher's first thought, he confessed to Viridis, was this: what could possibly have attracted Very to this fellow? Chism's wrists were held together very low, over his groin, as if protecting his private parts. A very tall man, his shoulders were somewhat stooped, probably the result, Tom decided, of long confinement in a bent position, although it appeared that the weight of the handcuffs on his wrists was pulling down his arms and his shoulders.

Chism looked at the witnesses and moved his eyes from one face to the next, as if he were looking for somebody. "*You*, probably," Tom said. His blue eyes, Tom noted, were his only handsome feature, contradicting the gangling frame, the bald, bony skull, the battered face, and the missing teeth . . . although this last did not become apparent until, after searching the reporters' faces, he smiled. "Why he smiled, I don't know. Was he glad you *weren't* there?"

The warden spoke to the prisoner. "Well, Chism, you've sure got twelve of 'em this time. Count 'em. They're all big-time, big-city newspapermen. Look at 'em. You're a celebrity, Chism!"

It was clear to Tom Fletcher that the warden was enjoying the scene and would probably milk it for all it was worth. The warden even faced the reporters and "presented" Chism to them, holding his hand out, palm up, beneath Chism's waist and making a little bow toward the reporters, like a circus ringmaster presenting his star performer. Tom said he wouldn't have been surprised if Chism had begun doing some tricks at that moment . . . but the trick came later.

The strange thing then, Tom said, was that the *Atlanta Constitution*'s man began clapping his hands. Tom knew him, and had tossed down a drink with him earlier that afternoon, but the man wasn't intoxicated. Maybe his applause was prompted by the warden's ridiculous bow. In any case, one by one the other reporters dropped their notebooks into their laps and began clapping too. Tom joined in, telling himself that he was clapping for probably the same reason the rest of them were: that they admired him as a man, knowing he was innocent and was coming to this end bravely, without fear or cowardice or hysterics. The warden seemed stunned at this continuing outburst of applause until finally he himself began clapping. So did one of the guards. The only people in the room who did not were the minister and the executioner, who looked embarrassed, as if they knew they ought to clap but didn't know how.

Chism did not bow. Tom wouldn't have been surprised if he had. Tom *was* surprised at what Chism did do: he spoke to them. "I thank ye," he said. "I thank ye kindly. I hope you fellers will git a good story for yore papers. I hope—"

"Shut up, Chism," Warden Burdell said. "You aint supposed to talk to them."

"Let 'im talk!" yelled the man from the *Chronicle*, and the others said, "Yeah, Warden, let him talk."

"Well, okay," said Burdell. "He's allowed some last words anyhow. Say your last words to them if you want, Chism."

And Nail Chism continued. "I hope that while you're here you'll trouble yoreselves to find out a few things about a boy name of Ernest Bodenhammer, who's not but sixteen years old and is downstairs waitin to die in that chair hisself. He's just a ole Ozarks country boy, like me, but he's got a talent I couldn't never hope to have: he can draw like a angel, although there's only one angel I ever saw do a drawing, and she aint here today, I'm glad to see."

The warden spoke. "Well now, that's enough now, Chism now."

"Let him talk!" everybody else said, and the warden shrugged his shoulders and fished out his timepiece.

"The other convicts call him Timbo Red," Nail Chism went on, "because

198

we've all got nicknames, like it would be bad for a feller to go by his real name. I reckon we figger a man's real name was what got him into trouble, and as long as he's got a play-like name he can pretend he's innocent. Now, you boys know that I don't have to pretend I'm innocent. But it's Timbo Red, or Ernest Bodenhammer, that I want to tell ye about, and I hope you'll write up his story. He aint innocent of killing a guard, because he really did kill that guard, name of Fat Gabe McChristian, who murdered more men than that electric chair ever done."

"Now that's enough, Chism," Warden Burdell insisted, and said to the witnesses, "I'm very sorry, gentlemen, but if you gave him a chance he'd talk to you from now until midnight."

The *Commercial Appeal*'s man stood up from his chair and declared, "We've got until midnight, then. Let him talk."

The warden held up his pocket watch and turned the face toward them. "He has to be executed at sundown, and it's nearly time."

The man from the *St. Louis Post-Dispatch* stood up and pretended to read from his notes: " 'Warden Harris Burdell refused a legitimate request from the press to allow the condemned man a minute to finish a thought-provoking statement.' "

"All right, dammit," Burdell said. "But watch your tongue, Chism. Watch what you say and don't go spreadin a pack of lies."

"It aint no lie that Ernest Bodenhammer does not deserve to die for puttin an end to the life of that murderin son of a bitch Fat Gabe McChristian!" Nail said, with the only flare-up of emotion they were to witness. Then, more calmly, he resumed, "Now, maybe you fellers think that this don't make no difference, but I just hope you can get a chance to see some of his pitchers that he drew, and then tell Miss Viridis Monday that I hope she will do what she can for him, and I shore appreciate what she done for me."

There was a silence then. The reporters waited for him to continue, but he did not. Warden Burdell asked him, "Was them your last words, Chism?"

"No," he said. "It's these: *tell her that I and the trees will love her forevermore.*"

"Okay, boys, strap him in," Warden Burdell said to the two guards, and they took him to the electric chair and made him sit down, and the guard named Gorham unlocked his handcuffs while the guard named

Fancher secured one of his arms with an old black strap of leather that seemed to have been cut from mule harness. Chism made a brief move as if to struggle, but the warden himself nervously helped them hold him until the strapping of his arms, and then his legs, was completed. The warden whispered to the condemned man something that the reporters could not hear. Then he looked at the executioner and asked, "Ready, Bobo?"

Mr. Irvin Bobo, despite his intoxication, was lucid enough to point out something to the warden: "You aint put the cap on him yet, boss."

"Oh," said Burdell. "Right." He motioned to the guard with the short leg to set the metal cap atop the head of the condemned man and strap it in place beneath his chin. "There, now." Tom Fletcher experienced a sympathetic shiver as the steel cap touched the man's shaved head. The warden and the guards stepped away from the chair. Mr. Bobo raised a hand to hold the switch-handle.

The man from the *St. Louis Post-Dispatch* stood up again and began to read: " 'The State of Arkansas last night put to death in its electric chair an innocent man, Nail Chism, twenty-seven. He had been tried and convicted of assaulting a young white woman who later confessed that he was wrongly convicted on her testimony. Appeals to Governor George W. Hays failed to gain a pardon or even to stay the execution. Last-minute appeals were made by a delegation of newspapermen directly to the warden of the state penitentiary, Harris Burdell, but Mr. Burdell remained unconvinced that the unfavorable publicity resulting would probably cost him his job . . .' "

"Awright, goddammit!" Burdell yelled, and grew very red in the face and stood in front of the press gallery with his hands on his hips and said, "You guys are makin it very difficult for me to exercise my sworn duties! Time and time again I've told you that I don't have any power whatsoever to stop this execution, and I'm not goin to stop it!" He turned and gestured. "Bobo, put your hand back on that switch!" The warden pointed his trembling finger at the condemned man. "Y'all keep talkin about him bein so innocent! Let me just show you gentlemen how innocent he is! That business he kept yappin about, about his punk pal Timbo Red Bodenhammer killin one of my men, was on account of a letter he tried to smuggle out of my prison, tryin to get it out to that same sweetheart of his he keeps

talkin about, Miss Viridis Monday, in which he told her, and I quote!"
The warden fished into each of his coat pockets before he found the letter
he was looking for, then began to read from it, first fumbling with his
spectacles to get them into place. " 'I reckon you know that if they try to
electercute'—that's *sic*, gentlemen, *sic*—'electercute me I aim to kill as
many as I can beforehand and I reckon you also know how I aim to do it.'
Now, gentlemen, we managed to intercept this threatening letter, at the
sacrifice of the life of my best guard, and I have been careful to keep a
close watch on this man Chism and attempt to determine just how he
intended to kill as many of us as he could. That means you too, gentlemen.
He intended to kill as many of you as he could. And how did he intend
to do it?"

The warden let his rhetorical question hang in the air defiantly for a
long moment. Several of the reporters were attempting to write down the
warden's words as fast as he spoke, and he was speaking very fast: "I'll
tell you how! We discovered that the past several days he has been sharp-
enin a piece of metal in his cell, a plate of steel, this long, taken out of a
mouth organ, a big harmonica. His young punk Timbo Red killed my good
man McChristian with a previous dagger that Chism had been wearin on
a string around his neck for quite some time, probably since the last time
we tried to electrocute him. So we suspected that Chism might try to make
himself another dagger. Unbeknownst to him, and to his punk pal Bodenhammer, we've been spyin on 'em this past week. Nail Chism went and
sharpened a piece of metal into a dagger, which he then tied to a string
around his neck, intending at the last moment to get that dagger out and
kill me and *you* and as many of us as he could! Now, is that man *innocent*?"

It was so quiet in the room that you could hear the electric dynamo
hum. At least, Tom Fletcher thought it was the dynamo, but he wasn't
so sure.

Nobody answered the warden, who looked defiantly around him as if
expecting an answer. "We all knew what was coming next," Tom said.
Warden Burdell moved toward Chism, saying, "Fortunately, we got him
strapped into the chair before he could get his knife out and use it on us.
But let's have a look at it and see how lethal it is!"

With a flourish the warden reached out and grabbed Nail Chism by the
collar of his shirt and literally ripped the shirt completely away, exposing

Nail Chism's bare chest and the string around his neck. But there was no dagger on the string—just some kind of small medallion, or ornament, which looked like a watch fob in the form of a . . . perhaps of a tree.

And what he had thought was the hum of the dynamo, Tom Fletcher decided, wonderingly, was some peculiar kind of remote, faraway singing, as if a choir were down the hill outside The Walls, or, no, not down the hill but somewhere up in the trees.

The gentleman from the *St. Louis Post-Dispatch* stood up for a third time and finished reading his story: " 'A display of last-minute theatrics by the overwrought warden failed to convince the members of the press that the innocent man was in fact a desperate cutthroat. The warden seemed completely dumbfounded when the dagger he intended to reveal failed to materialize. He looked unbelievingly at Nail Chism's bare chest, then even looked behind Mr. Chism, as if the missing dagger might be hanging down his back. Then the warden looked at the reporters in consternation. Most of those present were laughing at him. Apparently, laughter would militate against any order for the execution to be carried out, and it was not. The flustered warden fled from the room, declaring, as his last words, that he wanted to talk to the governor.' "

off

Off they trooped to the Monday house on Arch Street and had a party. She had planned it well in advance—planned it twice, in two different ways: If the execution took place, they would bring the body here, and she would wash it and dress it in a suit of her father's clothes and prepare it for burial in a plot she'd bought in Mt. Holly Cemetery, just a few blocks down the street. If the execution did not take place, and it did not, the men responsible for preventing it would come here to this house to celebrate, to see the suit of her father's clothes draped over the sofa and hear her explanation of it, and to put that into their stories if they wished. Wasn't that the sort of "local color" they sought?

She had even ordered the champagne, and had a case of it on ice in the kitchen. Call her overconfident. Or at least say that she was so very hopeful and faithful that she had not even paused to consider how to dispose of the champagne if it were not usable. Give it away? Pour it down the sink? Probably after the funeral she would have consumed several bottles of it quickly all by herself, hoping it would kill her, but it is important, gentlemen, to put into your stories that she had not even given a thought to what she would do with the champagne. As it turned out, very happily, she gave it to you, all you could drink.

And they drank past midnight. Only one of them, the *Globe-Democrat*, was a teetotaler and did not come to the party until it was almost over, when he arrived to report that he had kept watch at the penitentiary until all the lights were out, the warden returned from an unsuccessful attempt to see the governor, and James Fancher informed him, the reporter, for a five-dollar consideration, that the condemned man was safely back in his cell, where he and the young man in the adjoining cell held their own celebration until Mr. Fancher made them shut up.

Cyril Monday, her father, was both proud and uncomfortable to have so many journalists in his parlor and his kitchen and, the night being fair, out on his front porch, where, journalists being what they are, they smoked cigars and swilled champagne and kept the neighbors awake. Her father's occupation had required him to deal with many kinds of men, but he had little experience with journalists, certainly not a dozen of them at once. They were polite and respectful to him. One of them, the *Commercial*

Appeal, interviewed him at length over a bottle of the Mumm's, asking him such questions as: What did you notice in the childhood of your daughter that would have turned her into a crusader and heroine?

Some of these men, after several glasses of champagne, became excessively gallant and even romantic toward her, and before the evening was over she would receive, and decline, a proposal of marriage from the *Houston Chronicle*. Flattery flowed like the champagne. Tom Fletcher told her he'd never seen her more "radiant," and he called her "ebullient" and told her she was "tingling." No one had ever used those adjectives on her before.

At the request of the *Post-Dispatch* she went upstairs to Dorinda, told her to put on her best dress, then led her downstairs and presented her to the newsmen. One of them offered Dorinda a glass of champagne, which the girl sampled but did not finish. Several of the reporters stimulated the girl into conversation, and before long Dorinda was talking and talking.

When the *Kansas City Star*, who also happened to be the newspaper's art critic, asked to look at some of Viridis' paintings, she took him upstairs to her studio for a while, and he was quite impressed, or pretended to be. He asked her for her opinion of Ernest Bodenhammer's work, and she said that she was still looking forward to seeing the young man's drawings. The *Star* suggested that they go together to the penitentiary the next day to interview young Bodenhammer and see his work.

The man from Associated Press wanted to talk with her about Governor Hays. Was it true, he asked, that the governor considered black people a primitive race of subhumans? Yes, she said. Was it also true that the governor's primary objective in office was to build up a loyal political machine? Quite true, she said. Was Governor Hays using the prohibition issue as a football and playing quarterback simultaneously for both teams? She did not understand football, but yes, the governor had succeeded in making Arkansas almost totally dry while pretending to be sympathetic to the wets.

Her mother and her sister Cyrilla did not join the party, although both she and her father invited them to come downstairs. Cyrilla declined her sister's invitation with "Tonight belongs to you," and would not leave her room; later, however, Viridis looked in and saw the *Atlanta Constitution* sitting with her and offering her some champagne.

Only one of the reporters, the *Times-Picayune*, actually broached the possibility that Viridis' great effort to save Nail Chism was motivated by anything other than her humanitarian zeal. "Honey, let me ask you a question," he said to her in the kitchen while she was refilling the bowl of shelled nuts. "If they let Chism out of there tomorrow, would you run away with him?"

She paused, and gave a laugh to cover up the discomfort the question caused her. "It's very unlikely they'll let him out of there tomorrow," she said.

"But if they did," the *Times-Picayune* persisted.

"Oh, sure," she said with irony. "I've always wanted to be a shepherdess."

"No fooling?"

She looked him in the eye. "There are worse things to do with your life."

Tom Fletcher was the last to leave. Each of the newsmen, before leaving, thanked her not just for the party but for having invited them to Little Rock. She thanked each of them for having demonstrated the power of the Fourth Estate not simply to report events but to exert an influence on them. Then she was left to deal with Tom. She had drunk too much champagne. And, clearly, so too had he. She was still miffed at him, his earlier abandonment of her project, his refusal to let her or any of the *Gazette*'s other reporters spend any more time on what he had called "a lost cause," and now his Johnny-come-lately enthusiasm and interloping after she had gone to such great lengths to attract the out-of-state journalists to Little Rock. Some of his remarks this evening had clearly betrayed his envy of the larger newspapers represented here. And he had also said things to indicate he still considered Nail Chism an ignorant, grubby peasant. She had overheard him asking Dorinda, "But aren't you glad it wasn't *him*?" She had not heard Dorinda's reply.

Now Tom, tipsy and hanging back until the others were gone and her family had gone to bed, began to hint that he'd like to stay the night. She was too tired and too intoxicated to care, really, and her room was private enough, with its own entrance (or, rather, exit), for Tom to escape in the morning without anyone else in the house knowing about it. But she couldn't let him. She was still sufficiently sober to be faithful, with the same faithfulness that had saved a man from death tonight. She turned Tom away.

"You're in love with him, aren't you?" he said peevishly but unbelievingly, as he retreated.

She stared at him. She knew he would think less of her if she confessed, but perhaps it was time he began to think less of her. She confessed, "Maybe I am."

She was still nursing a hangover the next afternoon when the *Kansas City Star* arrived in a taxicab to take her out to the penitentiary, where he intended to demand an interview with Ernest Bodenhammer. She was all excited, riding out there; maybe she'd get to see Nail too. Maybe Burdell would be so intimidated and submissive as a result of last night's incident that he would permit her to visit Nail without the intervening screen of the visitors' room.

But Burdell wasn't there. His office was occupied by the new sergeant, a mere guard, Gillespie Gorham, who impressed Viridis as more repulsive than the guard he had replaced. No, he wasn't taking Burdell's office permanently, he was just holding down the fort until the new warden came up from Tucker. Yes, Burdell had been fired. No, the governor couldn't fire him, but the prison board could, and the governor had appointed the prison board. Until the new warden, Superintendent T. D. Yeager of Tucker Farm, arrived to take over, probably by the end of this week, Sergeant Gorham was not going to let nobody do nothing. So for them to even ask to see Ernest Bodenhammer or his "scribbles" was out of the question. The *Kansas City Star* had to catch a train for home, and said he hoped Viridis would let him arrange a show of her work in a good K.C. gallery.

The *Arkansas Democrat*, an evening paper, scooped the *Gazette* with the front-page story under the headline GOVERNOR 'FURIOUS' AT PRESS OVER CHISM INCIDENT; FIRES WARDEN and the subhead CALLS OUTSIDE JOURNALISTS 'MEDDLERS'; THREATENS TO 'THROW THE SWITCH MYSELF.' The *Democrat* gave a full report of the scene at the aborted execution, including the condemned man's moving appeal, not for himself but for his fellow convict, "less than of age" Ernest Bodenhammer, and his accusation that Bodenhammer's victim, the guard McChristian, had murdered numerous inmates. The reporter, to Viridis' embarrassment, quoted the condemned man's intended-to-be-last words, "Tell her that I and the trees will love her forevermore," and identified "her" as "Little Rock reporter-illustrator

Viridis Monday, 26, daughter of banker Cyril J. Monday," but was not able to identify the reference to trees.

Tom Fletcher invited her to the *Gazette* to watch what was coming in on the wires. Associated Press did not use those quotations or identifications but carried an abbreviated narrative of the drama in the death room, which, to Viridis' delight, was running nationwide, including the huge newspapers on both coasts. And the *St. Louis Post-Dispatch*, proud that one of its own reporters had been instrumental in stopping the execution, gave an entire page of detailed coverage, in addition to an editorial commending Viridis for her "dedication and bravery in the face of a politician's cronyism and malevolence."

Tom Fletcher shook his head and said, "Don't be surprised if you hear from the governor." So she was not surprised when she did, except by her treatment: she was not called to the capitol to wait for hours in His Excellency's marble-walled, marble-floored, marble-ceilinged anteroom and then to stand on the carpet in front of his huge desk and listen to his rantings. No, he invited her to dinner at the governor's mansion, which, although the governor belittled it as "just an old-fashioned big old pile of dark-red bricks," was one of the city's finer homes. The governor himself met her at the door and shook her hand with both of his, and introduced her to his wife Ida and his sons Grady and Bill, eighteen and ten years respectively. The five of them sat down evenly spaced around a dining-table that could seat thirty, lit by candles, and attended by eight black waiters. Later Viridis could not even remember what the food had been; it had not been outstanding, nor had the wine, a sweet red that would have been all right with the dessert. The governor and his family ate very rapidly, scarcely pausing between bites to make conversation about insignificant things: as near as she could recall, they had talked about the latest improved passenger cars on railroads and the opening of the new movie theater at Eighth and Main, the Crystal, where they were showing a gripping oriental mystery story, *Bombay Buddha*; everyone had seen it except poor Billy, whose mother wouldn't let him. They argued about whether or not the movie was dangerous for a ten-year-old boy. When they finally asked Viridis her opinion, she replied that she couldn't say, since she hadn't seen it herself.

Trying to be nice, she noted that young Grady was not much older than

Ernest Bodenhammer and would perhaps be interested in meeting the boy and seeing his artwork. "Artwork?" Grady asked, with a belligerent frown, and then: "Who's Ernest Bodenhammer?"

"A convict," the governor told his son. "Miss Monday, you see, makes a hobby of convicts."

"Oh," said Grady. "Why does he do *artwork*?"

"A hobby," Viridis said.

As soon as the dinner was finished, the governor dismissed his family and moved from his chair at the head of the table to sit next to Viridis at the side. "Now," he said, when they were alone, and only one waiter remained, to bring them some peach brandy. "Now, I want us to be friends. I have been thinking a lot about the last time we got together, and I think I owe you more than just an apology for my rudeness. I want you to understand that I was preoccupied with the Hot Springs business. Have you been keeping up with this matter of legalized gambling?"

She shook her head. "I've been preoccupied myself."

The governor laughed. "You certainly have! Trying to save that moonshiner must have been a full-time occupation for you! But anyway, some of my best friends want to legalize pari-mutuel betting at the racetrack over at Hot Springs. Would *you* want me to let them do a thing like that?"

"They've been doing that at Longchamp for centuries," she said.

"Where is Lone John?"

"*Longchamp*," she pronounced it more carefully. "In Paris. A racetrack in the Bois de Boulogne."

"You've been to Paris?"

"I lived there for four years."

"My, my," the governor said. "Well now, I'll be." He didn't say what he would be. "And your father gave you his blessing?"

"He didn't stop me."

"Well, that's amazing. But you know, I'm all in favor of taking the reins and bridle off of womenfolk and letting them run free. During my administration the lot of the fair sex has improved one hundred percent. I've reduced the women's working hours to a nine-hour maximum for a maximum of six days of week; that's only fifty-four hours a week. And my legislature has given you the right to enter into contracts and to own property in your own names."

"We're grateful, I'm sure."

"And one of these days soon we're going to submit to the voters a women's-suffrage amendment and see if we can't get you ladies a bigger voice, at least in the local polls."

"The fair sex will be your slaves."

"I'm only acting on my sense of what I think the people want. I very strongly believe, Miss Monday, that the State is the sum total of the will of the people. And now, that is why I must give my full support to capital punishment, however barbarous it may seem. Personally, I do not condone capital punishment. No, I do not. At best, it is a relic of mankind's slow, painful rise out of the Dark Ages. But if the State did not take upon itself the awesome responsibility for executing murderers and rapists, the people themselves would resort to mob violence and lynching."

"Did you know, Governor, that Arkansas is one of the very few states that still punish rape with the death penalty?"

"Of course I know it! You mean, still punishes *white* men with death. Every state still executes nigras for rape. Young lady, don't try to tell *me* about Arkansas in relation to the other states. That's the main reason I wanted to see you. This past week the state of Arkansas has become the butt of national derision and even contempt because of this Chism business. Just at a time in our history when we're making some progress toward correcting the country's notion that Arkansas is nothing but a barnyard full of rustic buffoons, along comes this moonshining rapist out of the Ozarks and sets us all back into ridicule!"

"Pardon me, sir, but I don't believe it's Nail Chism they're ridiculing. They have focused their scorn on a chief executive who refuses to listen to overwhelming evidence that Nail Chism is innocent."

The governor slammed his palm down on the table so forcefully that both their glasses of brandy toppled over. A black waiter hastened to handle the problem, which the governor ignored. "WHAT EVIDENCE?" he thundered. "The babble of the victim? The poor, frightened, illiterate backwoods child, driven out of her senses by a vicious assault and the most despicable rape and sexual perversion I've ever heard about in my long legal career, trying pathetically to undo this hideous act simply by recanting her testimony? *Please*, Miss Monday! It's perfectly obvious that that pathetic waif you went to such pains to recruit to your cause is not of sound mind and not capable of testifying for or against *anybody*."

"Governor, if you would let her talk to you for five minutes, you wouldn't say that."

The governor softened his voice. "Let me tell you a little story, Miss Monday. Not so very long ago my wife Ida and I received here at our house late one afternoon a Mrs. Ramsey, who had her little boy with her. It was not long until sundown, when the woman's husband was scheduled to die in the electric chair at the state penitentiary. The woman wanted me to listen to her little boy, and wanted my wife to listen too. The boy gave the most touching speech about how he loved his daddy and what a good man his daddy was. Ida, who gave him a piece of bread and butter and a glass of milk, had tears running down her face, and she looked at me with such reproach as I had never seen from her before, and she asked, 'George, doesn't this little boy move you at all?' and I said, 'Yes, Ida, but his father moves me much more, because the man committed such a cold-blooded, brutal murder, with no extenuating circumstances whatsoever, that I still seethe to think of it.' And at sundown they electrocuted Ramsey, the first white man I have refused to save from the electric chair. Nail Chism is the second. Let me finish. You think that I am deaf to the entreaties of good people, as my wife thought I was deaf to the little boy. But I tell you what I told her: that it devolves upon me as governor to investigate meticulously every last one of these crimes. I do not take death lightly. I will not allow a citizen of the state of Arkansas to die for *any* reason, unless and until I have satisfied myself that that man—and notice, dear girl, that I say 'man,' because I have never allowed the fair sex to be executed, and I will never permit it as long as I live—that that man is guilty beyond any shadow of doubt!"

"But the shadows of doubt are all around Nail Chism," she said.

The governor sighed and passed his hand across his eyes. "Are you aware," he asked, "that for seven years before becoming governor, I was a circuit judge myself? I know the burdens that Lincoln Villines faced, and I know how carefully he had to proceed in that lower court. But before I became a circuit judge, I was a farmer. I grew up on an impoverished farm in the scrub of Ouachita County, and until I was the age of Nail Chism, I was, like him, a simple farmer. Although I did not resort to the illegal manufacture of liquor to supplement my modest income, I saved my money to finance a legal education at Washington and Lee University

210

in Virginia. No, I have not been to Paris, but I have been to Virginia, a civilized place, the home of such men as George Mason and Thomas Jefferson, men who, despite their ownership of slaves, opposed slavery and favored abolition, but who believed, as I believe, that abolition can only be accomplished very slowly and gradually, not all at once, as we learned to our regret. It is the same with capital punishment."

The governor pointed out the lone black waiter who was still blotting up the brandy, and George W. Hays began to talk about him as if the man could not hear. "Do you think this man is ready for complete freedom? Do you think he is capable of making the wise decisions that are required by the responsibilities of citizenship? This particular individual, I happen to know, is not the low-grade type of nigra who crowds our penitentiary and our charitable institutions, but he is still quite primitive and in a childish stage of progress, not yet intelligent enough to hold public office or aspire to one of the professions, or . . ."

Viridis discovered that she was not paying close attention; her mind was wandering, and her gaze was straying from the governor's face—he looked so much like an older version of Tom Fletcher, with his protruding eyeballs and thick lips—to the wallpaper, and to her own hands in her lap. The governor seemed to have arrived at the notion that there was some connection between the plight of Nail Chism and what the governor called "the most serious problem of the nigra question." At least he did not say "nigger," as so many did. If Viridis tried very hard, and did not drink any more peach brandy, she could focus on his words and detect that he was now discussing the achievement of his administration in separating the white and colored convicts. One of his first acts as governor was the purchase of the Tucker plantation to serve as a "white-convict farm," wherein the exclusively white inmates could pursue their agricultural labors free from any contact with "culluds." This, the governor attempted to explain to her, was in keeping with his "concept of the age, and well-advanced civilization."

She interrupted. "And how would the execution of Nail Chism fit into a well-advanced civilization?"

"It would manifest the sentiment of the community that the community will not tolerate the violation of the sexual sanctity of the fair sex!"

"But the community," Viridis pointed out, "that is, Nail Chism's com-

211

munity, has given you petitions signed by four thousand people, more than half the population of Newton County, who do not believe that he violated the sexual sanctity of anyone."

The governor was fiddling with the silverware. He picked up a dinner knife and held it as if to stab her with it and said, "Miss Monday, if I were to murder you right now, and later fifty thousand residents of Pulaski County signed a petition that I had not done it, would that make me innocent of the crime?" The governor did not wait for her answer. "No: petitions never exonerate, they only beg, and I will not lend an ear to beggary."

"Nor will you lend an ear to *anyone's* protestation that Nail Chism is innocent."

The governor sighed again and leaned back in his chair and regarded her for a few moments before saying, "Let me ask you. You seem so convinced of the man's absolute guiltlessness. Would *you* want to find yourself alone with him in that child's playhouse, or wherever it was he raped her?"

"I would feel perfectly safe with Nail Chism."

The governor snorted in disbelief. "You would? I'm going to call your bluff, young lady. What if I threatened to throw you into his cage?"

"Do you mean put me alone into his cell?" she asked.

"Not just that," he said. "The man is occupying the so-called death hole down in the dungeon of the powerhouse out at the pen. It's like solitary confinement. And it's very *dark* most of the time, Miss Monday. Very dark and scary. Would you want to be locked in there with him?"

"For how long?"

"Long enough for you to beg to be let out. Long enough for you to realize just how 'innocent' he is. Long enough for you to cease and desist this humiliating campaign to save him from the chair."

"Are you saying that if I shouted, somebody would come and rescue me?"

The governor chuckled. "Not quickly. Not *too* quickly," he said, and let the implication sink in. "When Nail Chism tries to harm you, it will take a while for you to summon the guards. We hope. Yes, I am going to call your bluff, Miss Monday, and I am going to have you locked up with that man."

"When?"

"I'll talk to Warden Yeager in the morning, and—I think it probably begins to get very dark in the death hole about the middle of the afternoon. Can you go to Warden Yeager's office at three P.M.?"

"Yes."

The governor was startled by the quickness of her reply. "Are you absolutely sure you want to go through with this?"

"Are you sure you would let me?"

"You bet I am. I just want you to promise me that as soon as we let you out of there, you'll leave us alone. I would even be willing to wager that you'll be so changed in your opinion of that hillbilly pervert that you'll gladly attend his execution, which I intend to carry out at the earliest opportunity, if I have to pull the switch myself."

Viridis stood up. "Three P.M. Warden Yeager's office," she said, taking her leave.

At the door he said, "You won't need your nightgown or your toothbrush. Good night, Miss Monday."

She did not sleep that night. Her insomnia made her confront the question: what if she had been deluded about Nail? What if he actually was a rapist? She even imagined a scene in which he confessed that he had raped Dorinda and that he couldn't help himself. She anticipated that he was only an apparition of the man she had loved: he smelled abominable and the cell was the filthiest place she'd ever been. Such sleeplessness forced her eventually to picture (or did she actually sleep, and dream?) the act of love they tried to make, and it was not good at all.

In the morning, as she dressed and got herself ready for the day, and then as she baked three dozen cookies (oatmeal, chocolate, and pecan) to take with her, she told herself that the dream, or the conscious fantasy if that's what it had been, was just an attempt to consider, and dismiss, the worst contingencies. It would not be like that, at all. She and Nail would not even consider sex. It would defeat their purpose. They would talk, and talk, and talk, and possibly hold hands, maybe even, yes! they would kiss, although Nail himself would be very self-conscious and ill at ease because of his appearance (but it will be dark, remember?) and the fact that they hadn't let him take a bath in ages. She would do a good job of ignoring the unsavory atmosphere.

She told no one where she was going. She told her mother that she wouldn't be home for supper and might be gone overnight. At 2:30 P.M.

she telephoned for a taxicab and rode it to the penitentiary. She was met at the visitors' room by the sergeant with the short leg, Mr. Fancher, who escorted her out of the room across the outside length of the wall to another door, the one she had used several times before. It was a heavy, arched wooden door upon which Mr. Fancher rapped the familiar trite code, the beats of "Shave and a haircut, two bits." A trusty opened it and admitted them to the fenced corridor leading across the Yard to the powerhouse and the main building. In the upper windows of the main building, open to the late-April air, men whistled and howled, "Hey, babe!" and, "Up here, sweetie!" and, "Sugar, come and git it!"

Mr. Fancher escorted her to the warden's office. The new warden, Travis Don Yeager, met her at his door and invited her in. He was about fifty, and her first impression of him was slightly more favorable than that of Harris Burdell: he seemed cut from the same mold, and she guessed that he, like Burdell, must have spent countless hours in front of a mirror practicing a look of fierce determination and strength. But he tried to be polite, at first. "Welcome to the Arkansas State Penitentiary, Miss Monday!"

"I've been here before," she said.

"Yeah. Right. I didn't think." He made a mouth that might have been intended as a smile but came out as a smirk. "We oughta send you up to Jacksonville hee hee, our state farm for women hee hee, but we understand you prefer the company of males hee hee. I see you didn't bring your suitcase hee hee."

"I don't expect to stay long," she said.

"You gonna sleep in that dress hee hee?"

"If I sleep."

"Hee hee! Baby, you got the right idea. *If* you sleep, that's right, *if* you sleep hee hee. Well, are you all ready to go down and meet your roommate hee hee?"

"I've met him."

"You have? Well, that's nice. Did he tell you what he's gonna do to you? Aint you just a little bit scared hee hee?"

"No."

"Man's a convicted rapist. Did a job so awful on a little girl they gave him the chair, only the second white man ever to get the chair in history hee hee."

"I'm familiar with all the facts of the case," she said. "I'm ready to go."

"*Are* you now? Real *eager* and rarin to go? Hot to trot hee hee. You got it bad, sister."

"If you don't mind."

"Don't mind what?"

"I didn't come here to listen to your jokes. I came to see Nail Chism."

He dropped his light tone. "Sit down, lady," the warden ordered her, gesturing to a chair.

"Why? Do I have to submit to an interview or make out an application?"

"SIT *DOWN*, Miss Monday," he commanded, and put a hand on her shoulder and made her sit. Then he went around behind his desk and sat down. He studied her for a moment, and when he spoke again there was a remnant of the original politeness. "You honestly amaze me. You really came in here expectin us to let you move in with that rapist. You really truly meant to go through with it."

"What are you telling me?" she demanded. "Aren't you going to let me do it?"

"Do you think I'm crazy, girl?"

"I don't care whether *you* are crazy or not. The governor told me I could do it. In fact, it was his suggestion."

"Yeah, but he never thought you would. He told me to see if you showed up, he said he'd bet me that you wouldn't show up, but if you did, to find out if you really wanted to do it. You honestly want to do it, don't you?" The warden began shaking his head slowly back and forth as if he still couldn't believe it. "Maybe you're the crazy one hee hee. Don't you know you'd never get out of there alive? That man's got a dagger hidden somewhere down in his cell, and he'd slash your throat as soon as he got finished rapin you hee hee."

"I'll take the chance," she said. "Isn't that what this is supposed to be about? Taking the chance? Proving to all of you that he won't rape me, he won't kill me?"

The warden shook his head. "Too much of a risk. Maybe you're right. But if you was wrong, and anything happened to you, the newspapers would really haul us over the coals, and your family would sue the state of Arkansas."

She could only repeat, feebly, "The governor told me I could do it."

"You still don't get it, do you? He was just testin you, ma'am. The

215

governor told me not to let you under no circumstances get nowhere near that rapist."

"Couldn't I just visit with him awhile, under supervision? Couldn't I just give him these cookies?" She held up the paper sack containing three dozen oatmeal, chocolate, and pecan cookies.

The warden glanced at the sack. He said, "You're just another one of them women that latch on to convicts and make boyfriends out of them, like they're toys or cuddly bears or something. All of you ladies are crazy. You think you can turn them into nice little boys, and you're mistaken. You think you can save their souls or mend their manners or something, and you're wrong, and it's gonna kill you to find out how wrong you are. I been workin in prisons since I was a kid, and you wouldn't believe the number of broken hearts I've seen you ladies get." Again he slipped into his politeness and softly said, "I'm not gonna let nobody break *your* heart, darlin hee hee."

"Could I please see him for a while in the visitors' room?"

As if reading from a book, he said, "Condemned inmates of the death cells may not be transmitted to the visiting quarters."

"Then couldn't you, as a consolation for disappointing me, take me down to the death hole and let me talk to him through his bars?"

"It's awful down there, ma'am. I wouldn't want to go down there myself."

"I can stand it."

"Sorry. It's against the rules. We do everything by the rules here."

"May I use your telephone?"

"Help yourself. What for?"

"I'm going to tell the governor that you won't even let me see Nail Chism after tricking me into thinking I could get into his cell."

"Well, durn, *I* never tricked you. How long did you want to stay down in the death hole?"

"As long as you'll let me."

"Well, the visit rules say fifteen minutes in the visit room. Would fifteen minutes down there suit you?"

"Not as much as staying all night, but it'll do."

"You can't take them cookies. The prisoners have a strict diet hee hee. Leave them and your handbag here in my office." The warden summoned the guard, James Fancher, and asked him, "Hey, Jim, is that electric light

bulb wired up down in the death hole yet?" The guard shook his head.
"Well, you go get Gill, and you boys take a lantern and show this lady
down there, for fifteen minutes, and let her talk to Chism. Watch 'em,
and don't you let her touch him nor give him nothing nor do anything 'cept
talk."

So Viridis got to see Nail. Indeed, as the warden had said, it was an
awful place. Couldn't they at least keep it reasonably clean? Did there
have to be earth clinging to the walls? Weren't there any windows or holes
that could be opened for a little ventilation? The oppressive darkness and
dankness and cramping were accentuated by the feeble glow from the one
smoking kerosene lantern that Fancher carried, holding it down at his
side, not raising it, so that the light came up from below and gave Nail's
face a ghostly and sinister cast. Guards Fancher and Gorham flanked her
closely, standing a little behind her as if they were holding her back, and
they would not go away.

"Strike me blind," Nail said softly. "Don't this beat all? How did ye do
it?"

"I've got a *little* influence with the governor."

"You sure must. You must almost have as much influence with him as
you had with all them newspaper fellers. It was you, wasn't it, who got
them to come to my fryin party?"

"I suggested it," she said. "And it worked. It saved you, for the time
being, but I'm afraid I don't have a *lot* of influence with our governor."
She told him of her invitation to the governor's mansion the night before,
what they had talked about, and the governor's "calling her bluff" by
pretending to arrange for her to be locked in with Nail.

Nail was speechless. "Gosh" was all he could finally say.

"But they'll only let me see you for a little while."

"Fifteen minutes," said Gillespie Gorham. "Nope. There's only about
ten minutes left."

"That was a mean thing for them to do, to rue back on ye like that,"
Nail said severely. "Did you really want to come and stay with me?"

"Of course! I was dying to!"

"Gosh," he said again. He reflected, "I would've sure enjoyed that. Yes,
that would've been the best time of my life. But it's terrible messy and
stinky down here. No place you could even sit down without ruinin your
dress."

"I don't care," she said. "If I could just *be* with you . . ."

Nail slammed himself on the brow. "I aint introduced ye to my pal." He pointed at the wall. "Timbo Red . . . Ernest Bodenhammer is right in there." He called out, "Ernest! Here is Viridis!"

"Howdy, ma'am," said a voice from the darkness.

Viridis turned and tried to move toward the adjoining cell, but Gillespie Gorham blocked her way. "You're just supposed to visit Chism. The other one aint none of your business."

"Couldn't I say hello?" she asked.

"Say hello," Gillespie Gorham told her, but would not move to let her nearer the boy's cell.

She called out, "I'm pleased to meet you, Ernest. Nail has told me so much about you."

The young man called back, in a voice so much like those she had heard in Newton County, "He's shore told me a lot about you too."

"I want to see your drawings," she said.

"Aw, they aint much," Ernest protested.

Nail said, "Ernest, give her your drawings." And to her: "I reckon you couldn't see 'em too good in the dark, though. He's done filled up that pad you gave him, front and back every page. It's time he got him another pad, if you could manage it."

"Certainly, I'll get him one," Viridis said.

"Heck," Ernest said, "I'm due to sit on Ole Sparky myself in just a few more days. I wouldn't have time to use up a whole new pad."

"Could I borrow the one you've finished?" she asked him. "To look at in good light?" She wished she could see at least the outline of his form in the dark, but she saw nothing of him.

His voice said, "Wal, yeah, I reckon, but they shore aint nothin to brag about."

At the edge of the sphere of feeble light from the lantern she saw the sudden protrusion of a square thickness that she recognized as the corner of the drawing pad being offered to her. She reached for it, but Sergeant Gorham stayed her hand. "You aint supposed to touch nothing," he told her.

"It's only a sketchbook, for heaven's sake," she said. "Search it if you want. There aren't any secret messages in it."

"Jim, hold up that light," Sergeant Gorham said, and he took the sketchbook, flipped through it, gave it a shake, and then presented it to her. "Looks harmless," he said.

"Thank you, Ernest," she said. "I'll get it back to you, along with a new-pad. Do you need some more pencils? Erasers?"

"I thank ye kindly, ma'am," Ernest said.

Another square intruded into the lantern's light, and Nail said, "Mr. Gorham, sir, I'd like her to have this too. It's just as harmless as that drawing-pad."

It was a book. A thick, heavy book. Sergeant Gorham took it and submitted it to the same treatment he'd given the sketchbook. Nothing fell out. It contained no letters or words other than the printed words. The guard gave it to her. He asked Nail, "What's it for?"

"It's just a ole book I'd like her to have. I won't be needin it no more."

"Nail," she said intently. "I'm going to save you. Ernest too."

"Well," he said, "there's just a part of that book I thought you might find interestin."

"Time's up, now," Gorham said, and put his hand on her shoulder. She shivered at the man's touch.

"Did you get my letter?" she asked Nail.

"Yeah, I sure did, and it was wonderful. I reckon you didn't get mine, but it wasn't much compared with yours."

"You know what I tried hardest to say in that letter?"

"It's hard to say," he acknowledged.

"I mean it," she said. "I can't say it again right here and now, but I mean it. Three words."

"Three words," he returned.

They took her back upstairs, and she picked up her purse at the warden's office. She gave T. D. Yeager the sack of cookies and said, "Share these with your wife."

"I don't have a wife, ma'am hee hee, but say, thanks a lot."

"I'll be seeing you again," she said, and offered him her hand. "And possibly again. Thank you for your kindness."

She went home and closed herself in her studio with Ernest's sketchbook and the book Nail had given her. It had a funny title, *Dr. Hood's Plain Talks and Common Sense Medical Advisor*. The book was grimy and smelled mouldy, reminding her of the smells of the death hole, which she would like to forget. It was well worn, as if Nail had read it again and again.

219

Why he wanted her to have this book she wasn't sure, but she understood one thing: it was probably the only reading matter he'd had, and his giving it to her was as if he were saying he had nothing more to give. She was touched. She flipped idly through it, and did to it what Sergeant Gorham had done: held it with the spine up and the pages flopping down, and flipped it and shook it to see if anything might fall out; nothing did. She leafed slowly through it, looking for a penciled message; there was none. The chapters covered such things as "Sexual Isolation" and "Prevention of Conception" and other matters dealing with love and marriage and childbirth and parenthood. Was he perhaps trying to tell her that this book dealt with a kind of life they could never have together? The pages were dirty and smudged; one even seemed to have a smear of blood on it, beside a definition of "Oil of Mustard," the significance of which she could not determine. She closed the book, a bit disappointed apart from being moved by his gesture of giving her his last possession.

Then she held Ernest's sketchbook beneath the studio's north light. The afternoon still had an hour to go before the light faded. The first drawing took her breath away. It was a landscape. Surely, it had been drawn from memory, in the poor light and confinement of a prison, but it had the authority and detail of a sketch rendered on the spot, the spot being the middle of a rushing mountain stream, looking upstream toward a tranquil pool overhung with great summer trees, themselves overhung by the crags of bluffs and the ridge of a mountain over which dramatic clouds gathered themselves. His clouds, particularly, were beyond her achievement. Her admiration for the draughtsman's skill was almost overwhelmed by her envy of it. All in black and white, the drawing yet evoked distinct colors, shade upon shade of green. There were effects here that she simply could not duplicate, try as she might. A native genius she did not possess. She was good, certainly she had skill and long practice, but she did not have . . . what was it? . . . she recalled Nail's words as quoted in the newspapers: "He's got a talent I could never hope to have: he can draw like an angel, although there's only one angel I ever saw do a drawing, and she's not here today, I'm glad to see."

As Viridis looked at Ernest's drawings, she suddenly understood how an angel would draw. But she was not one herself.

There was one drawing that she did not immediately recognize. After all the landscapes, the interior came as a different place, a confusing scene.

It took her a moment to shift focus from the outdoors to a room. A room containing a monster. But the monster, she recognized after deliberation, was the machine that was called—what had Ernest called it?—Old Sparky, the electric chair, but not the electric chair as she remembered it. Had Ernest Bodenhammer drawn the picture from memory? Or had he actually seen the chair? No, it seemed to be drawn from imagination, not just the imagination of a highly creative and fertile artist but that of a person inspired by the foreknowledge of his murderous sacrifice to that monster. The chair had a distinct personality, a menace and a malevolence that exceeded the sum of its various straps, panels, wires, and braces. It seemed to be alive and waiting. It carried a threat not just for the artist but for all humanity.

Almost with relief she turned the page. But the drawing she saw next stunned her. The sketchbook fell from her lap and lay shut on the floor for a long moment before she picked it up and forced herself to open it again. Viridis felt her face growing very hot, and she felt embarrassment as if she were a voyeur standing right beside the bed where the naked couple clenched in a tangle of arms, legs, elbows, knees, at the center of which their genitals seemed to be trying to devour each other. The man was Nail. There was no mistake, although his face was in profile. Nail, with a full head of handsome blond hair disheveled and matted by the sweat from his exertions. The woman . . . she certainly wasn't Dorinda Whitter, or anyone else Viridis could recognize, just a typical country girl, an earth goddess, very pretty and very shapely and very passionate. Had Ernest simply "borrowed" Nail for an imagined scene? Or had he re-created an actual event that Nail had described and narrated to him? Viridis was surprised at how grudging she felt; she turned three shades of green, jealous of whoever the lucky girl had been. And this answered, perhaps, her longstanding question, which she had vaguely worded to Nail's mother: "Did Nail ever have a girlfriend?" But as she stared in awe at Ernest's drawing, trying to forget the subject long enough to fully appreciate the draughtsmanship, she realized that it had the unexpected power to arouse her sexually. She was burning.

———

Not the *Arkansas Gazette* but its rival, the *Arkansas Democrat*, on pages 8 and 9 of the issue of Monday, April 26, 1915, carried Viridis' story about Ernest Bodenhammer, with two illustrations: a fuzzy photograph of the boy taken about two years before, and a fair reproduction of his master-piece, "Old Sparky." This was the first picture of the electric chair that had ever appeared in the pages of the *Democrat*, whose readership has always been more plebeian and democratic than that of the *Gazette*. A younger newspaper with an inferiority complex (it was founded at the time of the Mexican War in 1846, whereas the *Gazette* has been "the oldest newspaper west of the Mississippi" since 1819), the *Democrat* has occa-sionally resorted to sensationalism, if not outright yellow journalism, in its circulation rivalry, and Tom Fletcher himself suggested that Viridis try the piece on the *Democrat*, because he and his paper felt that the "Chism case" had already been given maximum exposure and readers were not interested in yet another story of "wrongful electrocution." In Europe, Germany was making war on Holland and invading Baltic Russia and preparing its submarines to torpedo the *Lusitania* (the ship Viridis had taken abroad), and the *Gazette*'s readers were beginning to turn their attention away from small local events to the international crisis and the growing issue of America's nonintervention, which most *Gazette* readers supported. Letters to the editor were preponderantly concerned with the war in Europe, and a total of only three letters had been received about the Chism case, two of them demanding to know why the governor didn't go ahead and pull the switch himself, "like he said he would."

Tom Fletcher said to her, "Very, this Bodenhammer piece is a serious mistake. It will only divert the public's attention from the Chism case."

Viridis' story in the *Democrat*, which an editor titled GIFTED YOUNG ARTIST MUST GO TO MEET HIS NIGHTMARE, was the only publicity that Ernest Bodenhammer ever received. She was disappointed that the *Dem-ocrat* showed only one of Ernest's drawings, but, as an editor candidly admitted to her, the typical *Democrat* reader "didn't know Rembrandt from Rumpelstiltskin." Viridis paid to have matted and framed behind glass a dozen of Ernest's best drawings (omitting of course *that* one), and tried to find a good place to show them concurrently with the appearance of her *Democrat* article, but the only place she could hang them was the Little Rock Public Library. She had photoengravings printed of those twelve drawings and mailed them out to her friends at Associated Press, as well as to the men who had come to Nail's thwarted execution and her party. She sent a special note along with the mailing to the *Houston Chronicle* man who had proposed to her. But if his newspaper, or any other newspaper in America, used her Bodenhammer story, she never received clippings or heard about it.

Art, she told herself, is dispensable.

The same issue of the *Democrat* that had her Bodenhammer story on page 8 had a front-page item under the headline Gov. HAYS INCREASES DEATH CHAIR'S PRIVACY, to the effect that the governor and his legal advisors were taking steps to reduce the number of witnesses required for an execution from twelve to six, and to limit strictly the attendance of newspapers. "An execution is not a circus," the governor was quoted as saying. "An execution must not be a public spectacle. Capital punishment is a remnant of barbarity, but as long as we practice it we must insure that it be done mercifully and with dignity, and this requires that we make it as private as possible, as silent as possible, as inconspicuous as possible."

When the *Gazette* also featured this story, Viridis asked Tom Fletcher, "What do you think he's up to? You don't suppose he'll start having secret executions, do you?"

"Wouldn't surprise me," Tom said. "That word 'inconspicuous' bothers me. The message to us is that we have to pool a man . . . ." (he lifted his eyebrows) ". . . or a woman, and let that one reporter cover the scene for all newspapers and wire services. No more parties." At her expression of dismay he pointed out, "That's really not so different from what we had been doing, is it? Weren't you the only reporter at the execution of that nigra, Skipper Thomas?" When she nodded, he assured her, "We're supposed to receive notice of all intended executions so that we can arrange with the *Democrat* and the AP to pool a man. Or a woman. I'll keep you posted."

But Tom's promise wasn't enough to make her comfortable. She went to the state capitol and asked to see the governor. This time he did not make her wait all day, but didn't she understand that, without an appointment, she couldn't just barge in on him? He apologized for keeping her waiting and offered her coffee, which she declined.

"And how was your tryst with the moonshiner?" he asked.

"I don't appreciate your failure to keep your part of the bargain," she said.

"I saved your life probably," the governor said, and then from the pile of papers atop his desk he lifted the issue of the *Democrat* that had her story. "And I see you didn't keep your part of the bargain either." He slammed the newspaper down on his desk. "That's a dreadful story, Miss Monday! My telephone hasn't stopped ringing! The telegrams are piling up! The letters are burying me!"

"Really?" she asked.

He laughed, then changed his tone from mock-indignant to coldly informative. "Do you want to know the sum total of public response to your story? Do you want to know how many people I've heard from as a result of that piece?" The governor made a show of propping his elbow on his desk top and then rounding his thumb and forefinger into a big 0. "Zero. None. Not a *blessèd* soul."

"So you're going to go ahead and pull the switch on him Saturday night?"

"That was dramatic oratory on my part. I could never pull the switch on a man myself. Mr. Irvin Bobo is a licensed electrician. I am not."

"But this Saturday night?" she said. "Three days from now?"

He did not respond. Instead he said, "I read your story. I was touched. I was impressed. The boy really is some sort of wizard with a pencil. Not that I know anything about art, but I recognize talent when I see it. I've never seen that chair myself, but he sure made it look petrifying, didn't he? I don't understand why nobody cares about him. Isn't that a shame, Miss Monday, that nobody cares?" She glowered at him, not knowing just how sarcastic he was trying to be. "Except you, of course," he amended. "*You* care an awful lot. In Ernest Bodenhammer you've found the perfect answer to the prayers of a lonely spinster. He's much better for your purposes than the moonshining rapist. Bodenhammer never raped anybody, except probably his sister and his mother. He's young and fairly innocent— all he did was kill a fat guard nobody liked anyway—and he's savable and malleable. You can make him into anything you want him to be, and everybody will live happily ever after . . . except the wife and children of Gabriel McChristian, the man he murdered."

She waited to see if the governor was going to say anything else. She told herself to try very hard to be polite, that the least show of anger would defeat her purpose. She took a calm, deep breath and said, as if it were the only thing she had left to say, "He's only sixteen."

"So? The state of Arkansas has executed murderers of fifteen and even fourteen. Once several years ago we hanged a thirteen-year-old nigra." The governor began to wave his forefinger back and forth. "But if you're asking me to show mercy for someone on account of youth, remember that Nail Chism's victim was only thirteen."

Calmly Viridis protested, "She recanted. She's willing to testify that she lied."

The governor picked up his telephone. "Martha, bring me that folder on Dorinda Whitter." Hanging up, he said, "Double perjury doesn't equal truth. Which is a fancy way of saying two wrongs never make a right." The governor's secretary brought to him a file, which he ostentatiously opened and displayed. "As I told you, I like to do a good bit of investigating of my own, in the interests of justice. I've attempted to find out all that I can learn about the victim, her background, her family, et cetera." The governor held up a small item. "I've even got her current report card at Fort Steele Elementary. Not doing so well, is she? Lies a lot to her teachers, doesn't she? And do you yourself have any suspicion that she may have struck the match that burned the school on April 5th? We know it was arson. But what concerns me more is her riffraff family. The girl's older brother, one Ike Whitter, was a murderer and ruffian who was executed by lynching, a manifestation of that community spirit and mob violence I keep trying to tell you about, Miss Monday, that has to accept capital punishment as a harsh but civilized answer to problems of justice. But the lynching of Ike Whitter isn't our topic. Our topic is that this girl, victim though she was, and an especially pitiful victim in view of the perverse, grotesque nature of the sexual crimes against her, is yet a girl of very low intelligence, with backward and inbred lines in a pedigree of coarse animals that even nigras would not consider of the human race. The girl has no sense of truth. She may or may not have lied when she told what Nail Chism did to her, but she is lying her head off when she tries to take it back!"

Viridis wanted to tell the governor of her trip to Stay More, she wanted to describe her meetings with Simon and Precilla Whitter, Dorinda's parents, whose poverty was the result not of inbreeding or lack of intelligence but of a series of misfortunes that had plagued Simon Whitter from his birth. But the governor did not have time to listen to her. She was not even here to rehash the "Chism case," as such. She knew there was nothing else that could be said to George W. Hays to alter his opinion of Nail Chism as a "moonshining rapist." She asked, "Would you consider postponing Ernest Bodenhammer's execution for a week or ten days?"

"Why?"

"I'd like to get an expert from a New York art museum to testify that Ernest's drawings are the work of a creative genius whose life must be spared."

"Testify to whom? To the state Supreme Court? They have already considered and rejected the automatic appeal that all capital cases must have. Testify to me? I've already told you, I consider Bodenhammer a creative genius. Testify to the people of Arkansas? Your New York expert would have to do more than testify. And you don't believe he could turn the people of Arkansas into connoisseurs of art in a week or ten days, do you?"

She clutched at a straw: "Governor, if you consider him a genius yourself, why couldn't you commute his sentence to life imprisonment so that he could go on making his drawings, even in prison? That would surely be preferable to breaking his pencil forever."

The governor shook his head. "If I did that, we would never again be able to hire a prison guard. This state must have a hidebound law that the killing of a law enforcement officer is automatically punishable by death. Otherwise, we wouldn't even be able to keep the policemen we've got."

Viridis felt her eyes beginning to get wet. While she could still see clearly through them, she looked at the paintings hanging on the walls of the governor's office, portraits of his predecessors, some of the state's more enlightened governors, such as Donaghey and Robinson and even the demagogue Jeff Davis. Her glance fell upon one portrait she recognized because of the clear family resemblance: Jacob Ingledew of Stay More. None of the portraits was a skillful painting. Each of them, by a different artist, was sloppy in brushstroke, muddy in color, unperceptive in interpretation of character. Her hand idly swept them. "Just to think," she said, "someday Ernest Bodenhammer might have been the very artist to do *your* portrait to hang on that wall, and he would have made you look much better than all of them."

His eyes, following her hand, gazed upon the clumsy likenesses of his precursors and seemed to reflect a mingling of veneration for their subjects' high position in history and a distaste for their second-rate execution by the semiskilled portraitists. He studied the portraits for a while, even

226

swiveling his chair around so he could contemplate them. Was he trying to imagine his own image up there someday? At length he swiveled his chair back to face her, leaned across his desk with his arms upon it, and said to her, "You really love Ernest Bodenhammer, don't you?"

She would not deny it. "I really love Ernest Bodenhammer."

"And you really love Nail Chism, don't you?"

As if intoning a litany, she said, "I really love Nail Chism."

The governor stood up. Respectfully or politely she stood too, wondering if he was not going to say anything further. But he did: "Miss Monday, I'd like for you to put yourself in my place. No, I'm going to do it for you: I'm going to put you in my place. As of this moment, I hereby authorize you, by executive order, to determine which one of the two men shall live, Nail Chism or Ernest Bodenhammer. *Decide.*"

It was almost as if he had struck her, and it took her a moment to recover from the blow. Her first reaction was to say, "You can't be serious."

"Oh, but I *am*. I am dead serious. Aren't you already beginning to feel the awesome responsibility that bears down on me? I am shifting that burden to you. *You* make that choice. The State decrees that both of them must die. There is no way on this earth that you, or I, or anybody, can save *both* of them. The State—call it public opinion if you will—would not allow it. But you may save *one* of them; just decide which one."

"You are simply trying to make a point," she declared. "You wouldn't let me do that, any more than you would let me enter Nail's cell and stay with him."

"I give you my solemn word of honor, Miss Monday. The choice is yours."

"It isn't fair!" she cried out.

"No, it certainly isn't!" he cried back at her. "But people ask me to make that kind of decision every day of my life! It's grossly unfair!"

For a moment she did understand, and she did feel some sympathy for the governor. It was a terrifying dilemma. But now, if he was playing a game with her to prove his point, could she meet the challenge? She thought of Solomon sitting in judgment on the two prostitutes arguing over a baby, and Solomon's determining the true mother by proposing to slice the baby in two. Could she find a Solomonic solution to this problem?

"Well?" the governor said at length, after waiting for her response.

"Give me your decision, and I'll have Martha come in here and draw up the executive order commuting the death sentence to life imprisonment for the man of your choice."

She shook her head. "I couldn't do it. Not right now. I would have to think about it."

"They don't give *me* time to think," the governor protested. "Oftentimes I have to make a judgment right on the spot."

"I'm sorry," she said. "Don't you realize I would have to live with the decision all the rest of my life?"

"And don't you, my dear, realize that *all* of my many decisions will haunt me the rest of mine?"

She turned as if to flee. She turned back. She turned again. "Could I have a couple of days? The execution is Saturday night?"

He nodded, to both questions. His last words to her were: "Unless you decide, *both* executions are Saturday night. We'll have a doubleheader."

His allusion to a sporting event did not escape her. There actually was a doubleheader baseball game on the afternoon of Saturday, May 1st, between the Little Rock Travelers and the Memphis Chicks, and that is where she found Mr. Irvin Bobo. The landlady of the rooming house where Bobo lived, on Asher Avenue within walking distance of the Arkansas State Penitentiary, told her that she would find him at the ballgame. And that was where he was.

Saturday morning, May 1st, she got up before five, when the first light of dawn came into her room. She had slept no better than the previous three nights and felt weary to the bone. She drank a pot of coffee and went outside and soaked her face in the morning dew, then went for a long walk up Arch Street past the Mt. Holly Cemetery, all the way to the beginning of Arch Street Pike, a road that ran to Malvern, her grandparents' home, forty miles away. If she had had Rosabone beneath her, she would have fled into the countryside and never come back. But she was on foot and had to make a very simple decision governing her simple walk: she could have turned west on to the Hot Springs road that led to the penitentiary, but she turned east and walked seven or eight blocks to Cumberland Street, then turned back north, toward town. Throughout her hike many dogs barked at her. A milkman stopped his wagon alongside her and asked if she was all right. The sun was well up in the sky when

228

her feet began to fail her, and she stopped at a small café on Third and Cumberland that had just opened for the day. She ordered breakfast and read the *Gazette*: there was a page 3 item, LITTLE HOPE FOR TWO MEN FACING SUNDOWN DEATH, and a subhead, EXECUTIVE SAYS HE WILL NOT INTERVENE WITHOUT 'DIVINE INTERCESSION.' Viridis asked herself, Am I "little hope," or am I "divine intercession"? but the answer remained stubbornly absent.

She read the entire issue of the *Gazette*, every one of its features: the significance of May, the fact that Robin Hood had died on May 1st, for whatever that was worth, the fact that in medieval and Tudor England everybody got up with the dawn and went "a-maying." Am I going a-maying? she wondered. Yes, in a way she was.

At Kavanaugh Park, the same park containing the baseball diamond where she would later find Irvin Bobo, one thousand girls of the Little Rock schools, Dorinda Whitter among them, staged an elaborate maypole winding for an audience of two thousand, Viridis among them. While the girls of the grammar schools continuously wound and unwound twelve poles with long ribbons, the older girls from the high school performed dances: the girls of the Thalian Literary Society gave the weavers' dance, the Red Domino girls did the Dance of the Roses, the Ossolean Literary Society did a Dutch dance, the junior-class girls did Spanish and Indian dances, and the girls of the "As You Like It" Society performed the Dance of the Foresters. When it was all over, Viridis managed to find Dorinda in the crowd and congratulate her on her pole-winding, and tell her that she was going to a baseball game and wouldn't be home until after dark.

"I never knew you keered fer baseball," Dorinda said. "Kin I come too?"

But Viridis explained that she had to meet some people there to discuss business. Dorinda rode home with the friends who had brought her.

The Little Rock Travelers, cellar-dwellers in the Southern Association, were losing to the Memphis Chicks at Travelers Field in Kavanaugh Park, and there were only about three hundred in the bleachers, so she spotted Irvin Bobo without much difficulty, sitting by himself behind first base. There weren't many women there at all, a few wives, and thus Irvin Bobo was surprised when she sat down beside him. He had swapped the familiar, grimy felt bowler he'd worn at all the executions for a more seasonal straw hat, but this one also had the band and crown stained with much sweat, and beneath it he wore the same green celluloid eyeshade he apparently slept in. Up close, in the sunlight, she saw that his dark, Chaplinesque mustache was stained yellow-brown by cigarette smoke. She had never seen his eyes before. Had anyone? They were tiny and dull and empty. "My goodness," she exclaimed. "Aren't you Irvin Bobo?"

He looked her up and down. "Do I know you?"

"Why, yes!" she cooed. "I'm the star reporter of the *Gazette*, and I've been to almost every one of your jobs." She laughed gaily. " 'Jobs' isn't the right word, is it?"

He was looking at her closely, and his tiny old eyes in their green shadow showed a spark of recognition. "Yeah, I 'member you! You was that lady jumped up and give me trouble when I was doing my duty on that white man."

She resisted the impulse to explain to him that he hadn't exactly been doing his *duty* when she had given him trouble. "Yes, you scared me," she confessed. "I thought you were supposed to wait until the warden got back, and you went ahead and pulled the switch. I didn't realize you were just kidding. Looking back now, I have to laugh." She did have to laugh, and she laughed, and then she opened her large handbag and took out the quart bottle of James E. Pepper bourbon, wrapped in brown paper. "Remember you offered me a drink?" she asked him. "Well, now I'm going to return the favor."

"Here's the pitch," Bobo told her and directed her eyes toward the field, where a man was winding up his body into a leg-lifted dance. The man threw the ball, and Bobo stood up, yelling, "That was a clean strike, goddammit! 'Scuse me."

She stood alongside him. He was actually shorter than her. "A clean strike, goddammit," she agreed.

They sat down, and she began unscrewing the cap on the bottle. Irvin Bobo was looking around to see if any neighbors were watching. "We aint supposed to drink in the ballpark," he informed her. "And I don't drink anyhow except before I have to do a job."

"You've got *two* jobs to do tonight," she reminded him. She brought out of her handbag two small metal jiggers and demonstrated how it was possible to hold and drink one inconspicuously.

In the course of the afternoon Viridis measured out nearly the whole quart of bourbon to Irvin Bobo, retaining only enough in her own jigger to give the semblance of conviviality. She even learned a few things about baseball: the manager has to decide whether to leave a pitcher in even if the pitcher is getting killed.

In the second game of the doubleheader Irvin Bobo began to lose interest, although the Travelers were winning. He tried to watch the field with one eye closed and then the other, but he could not see the field clearly. All he could see was the jigger in his hand, which she kept full. "You called me a monster," he mumbled.

She asked him what he had said, and he mumbled it again, and she recalled having said that. She patted his knee and left her hand there while she apologized. "I didn't mean you. I meant that awful boss of yours, Warden Burdell."

"Yeah, now he *was* a monster," Bobo agreed.

"He shouldn't have tried to make you kill a white man," she sympathized. "That wasn't fair."

"No, it sure wudn't. Burdell was a bastud."

"He's gone," she reminded him. "Yeager won't make you kill a white man."

Irvin Bobo made a sound that, she guessed, was the best approximation of a laugh he could manage. "I gotta choose who they tell me to choose," he said, or she thought he said, not hearing him clearly. Thinking about his words, she realized that he had not said "choose" but "juice." I gotta choose who they tell me to choose, she told herself.

The Travelers won the second game of the doubleheader, but Irvin Bobo was past cheering. He was even, she discovered, past standing. She had to hold him up. She hoped he had not driven to the ballpark; he had not, and intended to walk home. It wasn't far. Less than a mile. She offered to get a taxicab. He insisted on walking, but he fell down twice before he could get out of the park. She helped him up, dusted him off, called a taxicab, and took him home.

"Did anyone ever tell you that you look just like Charlie Chaplin?" she asked him.

"Who?" he asked, but she did not repeat herself. She realized he had never been to the movies.

In his room she offered to prepare some supper for him, but he said he wasn't hungry, he'd just like another little drink if she had any left, and if she didn't he had a pint somewhere around here. She told him that if he drank any more, he wouldn't be able to walk to the penitentiary, even though it was only a short distance down the road. He would have to eat something. In his cupboard she found a loaf of bread and a bologna sausage, which she sliced, and made three sandwiches, two for him, one for herself. She considered making coffee but then decided she didn't want him any more sober than he was now.

Making conversation to keep him paying attention, she asked, "How much do they pay you for a job?"

"Fiff dahs," he said.

"Only *five*?" she said.

"*Fiffy*," he said. "*Fiffy dahs.*"

"Oh," she said. "That's a lot. Tonight you'll make a hundred dollars."

"Doanwannit," he insisted. "Doanwannit."

She had to use the bathroom. When she returned, he was sitting on the edge of his bed, tilting up a pint bottle of his own whiskey and letting it run down his throat. "Hey!" she said, and moved to stop him. "You've had enough of that, now. You won't be able to walk to work."

"Doanwanna. Doanwanna." He groaned these sounds, then he fell over on the bed and passed out. She shook him, and shook him harder, but could not rouse him. She glanced at the clock on the table. It was almost five. Two hours to sundown. Probably, the executioner was expected to be on the job half an hour before. She made a pot of coffee but couldn't get him to wake up and drink it. She drank some herself.

She sat on the edge of the bed beside his flopped-out body, thinking. In all truth, in all *veritas*, Viridis Monday was no closer to a decision than when she had walked out of the governor's office. She sat on the bed of Irvin Bobo until she had determined he probably would sleep a long time. Then she knew what she had to do.

on

He protested when they tried to shave him again. Hell, it had only been ten days since they'd shaved him last, and he'd hardly had time to regrow anything but peach fuzz. He didn't mind so much being made bald as a doorknob for the third time, but he hated the goddamn trusty-barber, who couldn't hold his hand steady enough to keep from slashing his scalp. The barber had done a bad job on Ernest, Nail could tell just by listening. Ernest hadn't liked it at all. The kid wasn't the least bit vain about his mop of red hair, and he had surprised Nail with his ideas about facing death calmly because we all have to go sooner or later, but he yelled at Fat Gill, "I been a-cuttin my own hair since I was five year old, and aint nobody else never touched it! Give me that there razor, and I'll do it myself!" Fat Gill had guffawed at the thought that they'd be dumb enough to let the boy get hold of the razor. Nail, listening, had determined that Fat Gill and Short Leg were both required to hold Ernest down while the barber shaved him. They wouldn't have to hold Ernest when they put him in Old Sparky . . . not unless they did Nail first and made Ernest watch, and if they did that, Ernest might easily get mad or scared and start fighting. Nobody would tell them which one was going first. Maybe they'd flip a coin at the last minute. Nail hoped that he could go last, simply because he had enough experience to bear watching Ernest get it, in a way that wouldn't be so the other way around. But try explaining this to anybody. Of course there was always a chance that Viridis had got all of those newspapermen to come back again, but Nail doubted it. He had spent a good bit of time trying to imagine how Viridis might save him this time, but he hadn't been able to come up with a single blessèd notion, although he wouldn't put *any*thing past her: she might even set fire to the whole penitentiary to stop them. He was a little surprised at himself for being so inwardly calm, so resigned; it wasn't because he had any hope of once again being saved at the last minute but because he knew he would not be, and the only way to take it, this time, was to accept what Ernest had been preaching at him for several days now: "We ort not to fear nothin, not even that black thing they call death. Me and you will jist not *be* no more, but the whole world won't *be* neither. It will go with us, Nail. The whole world will die when we die, don't ye see? But it has to die sooner or later, I reckon, just as we'uns all do, so one time is about as good as another. That's all time is. One time is as good as another." The twelve witnesses, whoever they were this time, were sure going to be surprised to see both of them going to the chair so calmly. If the twelve witnesses were expecting any excitement from either one of them, they were going to be in for a letdown.

But there weren't going to be twelve witnesses, or even nine. When the head-shaving was finished, the new warden himself came down into the death hole. Yeager had impressed Nail as just maybe a *little* bit nicer than Burdell, although Nail knew that any man who had been the boss at Tucker Farm had to be plenty tough, or else numbskulled, and Nail hadn't seen enough of him to know which. Now Yeager was saying, "Good afternoon, gentlemen," and Nail couldn't tell whether he was saying "gentlemen" politely and friendly-like or just being sarcastic.

Nail heard Ernest say, "Howdy, Warden." Nail just nodded his head at the warden politely, and the warden could see him, because they now had electricity down in the hole; or at least they had wired up one bulb that gave some illumination to the basement. It was one of the new warden's "improvements." Now they learned of another: the warden was offering them a "last meal." "Just anything you want to eat hee hee," the warden said, the end of his sentence sounding like some kind of half-cough, half-laugh.

At neither one of Nail's previously scheduled executions had they offered him anything special to eat, or any special treatment, not even a final cigarette. He hadn't had a smoke now for six months, and no longer craved one. He wondered where the warden got this idea of a special "last meal." Probably he'd heard it was what they did in Tennessee or some civilized place. "Wal, I reckon I could set my teeth into a platter of chicken'n dumplins," Nail said.

"Me, I'd like a real honest beefsteak," Ernest said. "I aint never et me one of them afore."

"We'll see what we can do about them dumplins hee hee," said Yeager. "Now, you boys ought to know somethin about tonight's little entertainment hee hee. So I'm gonna tell y'all. First off, there won't be no pack of reporters like last time. Just one, from the *Gazette*. Second off, there won't be no twelve witnesses. New law says not but six, so that's all y'all will get, okay?" The warden waited to see if either of them would comment

234

on the new law, but neither of them did. "And third off hee hee," the warden resumed, "there is a real good chance that the governor hisself will show up. I can't promise nothin, but yes, I do believe he might appear, so I want you boys to behave yourselfs and be gentlemen, okay?" Nail nodded, and, since he heard nothing from the other cell, he assumed that Ernest was nodding also. "Now, if the governor does show up, I don't want y'all to start in to yappin at him about clemency or nothin like that. He's done made up his mind, and if y'all start beggin him and beggin him, it'll just embarrass all of us hee hee. So I want y'all to just keep quiet, okay?" Again Nail assented by nodding. "Of course hee hee, if y'all want to holler when the power comes on, y'all just go ahead and holler, won't nobody care. That's expected of y'all anyhow hee hee, aint it?" Nail took the question to be rhetorical and did not even nod. The new warden went on, "I aint never watched a execution before, myself. You have, aint you, Chism?" Nail nodded. "Don't you men that get executed generally start in to carryin on and screamin and all, hee hee?"

"Sometimes," Nail said, and then asked, "Which one of us are ye aimin to do first?"

"Good question, Chism hee hee," Yeager said. "I really aint given it no thought. Got any preference hee hee?"

"I'd 'preciate it if you'd do him first," Nail said.

Nail heard Ernest agree. "Yeah, do me first. I don't want to watch you'uns do Nail."

The warden looked back and forth between the two of them in their separate cells, trying to stand midway between them. He leaned toward Nail and asked, "You scared to go first? Or you still think somebody's gonna save you a third time hee hee?"

"Nossir, I jist don't want Ernest to have to watch me."

"Let me think about it," the warden said. "I caint promise nothin hee hee." He went back upstairs.

Later in the afternoon Jimmie Mac came, but he was still pretending that Nail didn't exist. He only wanted to see if Ernest was ready to be baptized. He had been working on Ernest all week, trying to baptize him. Jimmie Mac had even got to the point where he was willing to go ahead and baptize Ernest even if Ernest would not confess and repent. He wanted to make one last effort. "Son, just a few more hours and you'll stand there at those pearl-studded gates and they won't let you in," he said. Nail couldn't hear what-all Ernest was replying, but it took him a while. They went on talking in the next cell. Ernest had told Nail that up around Timbo where he came from everybody thought you had to be totally immersed in water to be saved, and there wasn't noplace around this pen where they could totally immerse you, and he didn't care to be sprinkled, although he didn't exactly mind it neither, it probably wasn't any worse than getting your head shaved. Finally Nail heard Jimmie Mac saying, "Son, you'll never regret this," and then some more talking, and then Jimmie Mac said real loud, "In the name of the Father, and the Son, and the Holy Ghost, amen," and then it was silent for a while before Jimmie Mac asked, "Don't you feel like shouting?" Nail didn't hear what Ernest answered, but it wasn't a shout.

At suppertime, sure enough, they brought Nail a platter of chicken and dumplings, and Ernest an honest-to-God porterhouse with all the trimmings. Those prison folks in Tennessee, or wherever it was, sure had the right idea. As Ernest put it, "By gonnies, I'd let 'em 'lectercute me ever night if they'd feed me like this aforehand."

They weren't given any time after supper to sit around on the porch and shoot the breeze or watch the hound dog chew his tail. Warden Yeager returned, accompanied by Fat Gill, Short Leg, and a couple of armed black trusties. Was it time already to go upstairs? Warden Yeager said, "Well now, gentlemen hee hee, not that I don't take your word for it that you'll be orderly during these proceedings, but just to be safe hee hee we are going to have to search you. Take off your hee hee clothes."

They opened the cell doors and made Nail and Ernest strip down naked. Of course Nail had anticipated this and had nothing around his neck except the tree charm. Warden Yeager fingered the tree charm, turning it over and even squinting at the inscription on the back of it. He decided to let Nail wear it but nothing else. They took away his clothes and turned the cell upside down looking for his blade. They tore up his Bible and ripped up the bed. It was Warden Yeager, maybe not so numbskulled after all, who realized it was inside the harmonica, where it had originated; he took the harmonica apart and removed the dagger and held it up in front of Nail's face and said, "Mister, does this belong to you, any chance hee hee?" Nail did not answer. The warden began to shake—out of checked anger, Nail thought at first, but then decided the warden was shaking the way you do when you've had a narrow escape. "Maybe we'll make you go first hee hee," the warden said, and Nail realized something else: whenever the warden made that sound "hee hee" it wasn't because he didn't know whether to laugh or to cough but because he was just real nervous. Yeah, T. D. Yeager was sure one nervous feller.

Jimmie Mac returned and said it was time for them to leave their cells. "Why, howdy, Nail," Ernest said at the sight of naked Nail standing handcuffed outside his door. "I aint seen you in a coon's age. Do I look as bad as you do?" Yes, it had been all of a month since they'd last laid eyes on each other, although they had talked so much they hardly had anything left to say, and yes, Ernest looked pretty awful with his red hair all gone except around his pecker. Now it was Ernest who began to protest to the guards, "Hey! Aint you gonna give us our clothes back? We caint go up thar nekkid as the day we was born! What if they's a lady present?"

"They aint no lady present," Fat Gill assured them. Nail sighed with relief, and soon saw what he meant: among the few witnesses there was no woman, no Viridis, not yet anyhow, and he hoped she would never come. Even if she did, they wouldn't let her into the room as long as he and Ernest had their peckers a-hanging down. There wasn't no governor neither. Just five strangers . . . well, one of them he had seen before, a newspaperman who'd been here the last time. He was the only one of the five who looked like he cared, and he was raising his eyebrows at the sight of these two convicts stark-naked. The death room was still illuminated only by the light from that one green-shaded bulb up near the ceiling, so it wasn't as if their genitals were exposed to harsh spotlight. In such darkness Nail didn't even feel naked.

Warden Yeager explained to the newspaperman, "We aint takin any chances this time hee hee. Were you here when the last warden had a little problem?"

"Yes, I was," the newspaperman said. "Well, 'Naked came I out of my mother's womb, and naked shall I return thither.'"

"What's that from?" the warden asked.

Jimmie Mac butted in. "The Bible. Book of Job, one and twenty-one. 'The Lord gave, and the Lord hath taken away; blessèd be the name of the Lord.' And the Good Book goes on, next chapter, 'Skin for skin, yea, all that a man hath will he give for his life.'"

The warden looked at Jimmie Mac uncertainly and asked, "Are you supposed to say a lot?"

"Just the final prayer," Jimmie Mac informed him, clearly liking the position of telling the new warden what was what.

"I aint been through this before," the warden declared, as if anybody needed to be told. "Do you say the final prayer now, or do we wait till Bobo gets here?"

The newspaperman spoke up. "We ought to wait till the governor gets here." He'd hardly said those words when the turnkey opened the guests' door, and in walked a man who surely was the governor, with another man who looked like he must be the local sheriff, and a third man who must be the governor's bodyguard.

"Good heavens!" said the man who must be governor, and accosted the warden, demanding, "Why are these men naked?"

"We found that blade, Your Honor hee hee," Yeager said. "I thought we would, and we stripped 'em and searched 'em to be sure, and Chism had a blade. I found it hee hee."

"Well, why are they just standing around like that?" the governor asked. He was more nervous than the warden, and looked like he was hunting for a place to relieve himself. "Why don't you do something?"

"We will, Your Honor," Yeager said. "We were just waitin for you to get here."

The governor looked around at the others in the room, squinting in the semidarkness to see how many were there. "If I'm saying there shall be only six witnesses," the governor said, "then there can be only six witnesses. Some of you men will have to go. Like *you*, Fletcher. Why don't you take off?"

The newspaperman laughed. "There has to be at least one of us poor ink-stained devils here, and it's me," he said.

The governor and his party evicted three of the other witnesses and took their seats, the governor sitting on the front row. The governor glanced at Nail's pecker and then at Ernest's, as if he were comparing them. "Do these men have to keep standing like that?" he asked the warden.

"Which one do you want us to do first hee hee, Your Honor?"

"Yeager, I'm not a courtroom judge anymore, you know. I'm not 'Your Honor' now."

The newspaperman, behind his hand but audible to everyone, said to Yeager, "He's 'Your Excellency.' "

"Yeah!" Yeager said. "Hee hee. Your Excellency, which one of these men should we fry—should we electrocute first?"

The governor turned around in his chair to speak to the newspaperman. "Fletcher, where is Miss Monday?"

"I have no idea, Your Excellency," the newspaperman said. "I haven't seen her for several days."

"Hmm," said the governor in a tone of disappointment. "I was hoping she . . ." The governor did not finish what he was about to say. Was he hoping she'd show up? From what Viridis had told Nail, the governor couldn't even stand the sight of her.

Jimmie Mac spoke up: "Warden, and Your Excellency sir, it's almost sundown. The law says a man has to be dead before sundown, and there's two of them to do this time."

The governor stared at Jimmie Mac. "Who are you?" he asked. "Are you Mr. Bobo?"

"No, he's the chaplain, Your Excellency," the warden said.

"Oh," the governor said. "You're supposed to comfort the men, right? Well, go ahead and comfort them, don't let me bother you." He seemed to expect Jimmie Mac to pat Nail on the back or offer him a handkerchief. After a long silence the governor said, "Well, make them sit down," and the warden motioned for his guards to get Nail and Ernest seated in a pair of the witness chairs.

A longer silence followed. Out of modesty and for the governor's sake, Nail and Ernest kept their handcuffed wrists over their genitals and sat with as much dignity as they could. It was so quiet that Nail began to hear it. He had wondered at what point, this time, he would begin to hear it again: the choiring of the trees. Now it was very faint: the trees were still up there on that mountaintop in Stay More, and their voices had a long way to go before they could be heard. He glanced out of the corner of his eye at Ernest, to see if Ernest was hearing it too. He had told Ernest all about the trees, to get him ready. Ernest was smiling, and was the calmest person in the room. The faint singing of the trees was interrupted by a spoken observation from the governor: "Well, it appears that . . . that nobody else is going to come." He began to look back and forth between the two condemned men again, comparing not their peckers this time but their faces, as if trying to make a decision between them. Finally his forefinger came up and pointed at Nail. The governor said, "Let's do him first."

Ernest spoke up: "Your Excellency, if it don't make a whole lot of difference one way or the other, I would sure appreciate it if you would do me first."

The governor gave Ernest a look that had a touch of compassion to it. Certainly, Ernest's words had been well chosen and fine spoken, but his voice had been that of what he was: a boy just sixteen years old. The voice was out of place, out of keeping with the other voices in this dark, still room. But the governor did not understand why Ernest wanted to go first; nobody, not even Nail, wanted to try to explain to the governor just how it was. The governor misunderstood. "That's commendable and brave," he said to Ernest, "but Mr. Chism was here first, and he's older, and he's going first." The governor gave an impatient flap of his hand, and the two guards lifted Nail out of his seat and walked him to the electric chair, and this time he was careful not even to show any sign of struggle as they strapped him in. This time they remembered to put the metal cap on top of his head, and this time, given the warmth of the merry month of May, the metal cap wasn't so cold as it touched the raw skin of his scalp.

Jimmie Mac prompted the warden: "Now you're supposed to ask him if he has any last words."

"Right hee hee," the warden said. "Mr. Chism, before we solemnly carry out the sentence of this state which has been imposed on you hee hee, would you care to address the gathering with any concluding remarks hee hee?"

Nail tried to smile. "Yeah. Where's Bobo?"

They had forgotten him. The warden was a bundle of nerves, the governor didn't know whether he was coming or going, Jimmie Mac was intoxicated with his sense of being in charge, and nobody but Ernest was still breathing normally. Now the warden really got flustered, and he said to Fat Gill, "Well, just where in hell *is* Bobo?"

Fat Gill shrugged; it was all new to him. Short Leg, the only experienced man here except for Jimmie Mac, spoke up: "He's probably out in the engine room fiddlin with the dynamo. Want me to go look?" The warden nodded, and Short Leg went out through the door that Bobo always came in through, that led to the power plant. Short Leg returned almost immediately, saying, "Here he is."

Drunk as usual—no, drunker than usual—Bobo shuffled in carefully as if trying to make sure he was putting his feet in the right place. The governor, for one, was shocked. "Is that man drunk? Has Mr. Bobo been drinking?"

Jimmie Mac, all-knowing, explained to His Excellency, "Yessir, he's always like that. It's a pardonable sin, wouldn't you say? Considering what he has to do . . ."

Bobo could barely lift a hand to the switch, but did, and stood there in a hurry to get it over with.

Jimmie Mac prompted the warden again: "Last words."

"Okay, here we go," the warden said, rubbing his hands together. "Last words, Chism?"

The trees were singing Nail's last words for him. They were in full voice now, rising and soaring in song. Anything he might say would be so feeble and earthly by comparison. He shook his head.

"No last words?" The warden looked to Jimmie Mac for guidance.

Jimmie Mac was mumbling the end of the Lord's Prayer, but he interrupted himself to say, "You're supposed to ask Bobo, 'Ready, Bobo?' "

The warden turned. "Ready, Bobo?"

Bobo nodded.

Jimmie Mac said, "You're supposed to raise your hand like this, and then drop it, like this."

Bobo did not wait for the warden to copy Jimmie Mac. Drunk and blind, Bobo took Jimmie Mac's gesture as his authority and threw the switch and closed the circuit.

But nothing happened. The governor, the newspaperman, all of the men in the room jumped an inch in their chairs and cringed and shivered, but nothing happened. The green-shaded ceiling light did not dim, the dynamo did not whine. In the silence—only it wasn't complete silence, because of the trees—the governor asked, "Who's singing?" and looked around trying to locate the choir. Everyone stared at Bobo. Nail turned his head and stared at Bobo, who still had the switch turned on but was looking down at his feet as if ashamed of his failure to make any current come to the chair. Then he staggered toward the chair itself and began fiddling with the wires one by one.

As Bobo began to examine the metal cap on Nail's head, Nail thought he heard him whisper into his ear, "I love you."

Nail was startled to hear this, and perplexed to find himself suddenly remembering that time in the visit room when Viridis had quoted his father's words 'Boy, don't ye never fergit, yo're a Chism, and Chisms don't never quit,' and almost exactly in the sound of his father's voice. Now it was as if Irvin Bobo had spoken those three words in the voice of Viridis! He turned to stare at Bobo, but Bobo was disappearing through the door into the engine room.

"Now what's the problem?" the governor asked in a quivering voice.

"Bobo's gone to check the dynamo, I guess," Yeager said.

They waited and waited, but Bobo did not return. Short Leg was sent to look for him. After a long while Short Leg returned alone. "It sure looks to me like he's done gone home," Short Leg said. "He aint anywhere around the powerhouse." He was shaking his head back and forth. "But he sure did fuck up that dynamo before he left."

"Fire him!" the governor said. He turned on the warden. "Goddammit, Yeager, there are going to be some changes made in this institution, and I am going to make them!"

"I've already made a few hee hee," Yeager protested.

off

One of the first things they did was fire Jimmie Mac. Or, rather, since Jimmie Mac had been just a volunteer to begin with, they replaced him with a paid, nearly full-time chaplain, an honest-to-God man of the cloth, the real Reverend Mr. Lee Tomme, formerly of the Colorado State Correctional System, who started in from his first day on the job correcting everything in the Arkansas system. Whether or not they fired Irvin Bobo, Nail couldn't find out right away. But one of the first "improvements" that the Reverend Tomme accomplished was getting the prisoners the privilege of reading magazines and newspapers, and just a few days after his third execution was aborted, Nail read an item in the *Gazette*, NEW ELECTRICIAN HIRED AT PENITENTIARY, which explained that G. H. Dempsey, of Arkadelphia, electrician for the past seven years at the Arkadelphia Milling Company, who had done the wiring at the Little Rock City Hall eight years ago, had been hired to replace Irvin P. Bobo, who was resigning for personal reasons. Near the bottom of the article Mr. Bobo was quoted as saying, "My memory isn't what it used to be. Sometimes lately people say I did things which I don't even recall ever having done." The new electrician, Dempsey, said he would have no objection to electrocuting any man whether that man was black or white. "A switch is a switch," he said. "It's all the same to me."

A day after that, the next issue of the *Gazette* was personally delivered to Nail's cell by the Reverend Tomme, who also offered Nail a cigarette. Nail almost accepted, but he said, "Preacher, I've gone this long without smokes, I can go awhile longer. Thank ye just the same. You go ahead and have one if ye want."

The Reverend Tomme (it was pronounced "Tommy") laughed. "I don't smoke, Brother Chism, but I want you men to be able to have a few pleasures in this life if you are able to obtain them. Look," and he handed the newspaper to Nail, pointing to an item. "Do you need me to read it for you?"

"I can read just fine," Nail said. The headline, a big black one, read: GOV. HAYS DEMANDS SWEEPING CHANGES IN PRISON SYSTEM. There was a smaller headline underneath: APPOINTS PRISON EXPERT AS NEW CHAP-

LAIN, and below that: WILL APPOINT COMMISSION TO INVESTIGATE CONDITIONS.

"The best place to start improving this prison is right here," the Reverend Tomme said, pointing at the dirt floor of Nail's cell. "The best person's condition to change is *yours*. I'm going to see if we can't find you a job upstairs."

"My God!" Nail exclaimed. He knew there was a law against requiring—or even permitting—condemned men to work.

"Yes, *your* God," the Reverend Tomme said, and smiled. "I'd like to think it's my God too, but I'll settle for your God."

Nail studied the minister. He had a pleasant face, not that of a man who couldn't take a joke. He wasn't much older than Nail, maybe thirty at most. Nail said, "My God is a Lady." He waited to see if this man would be different from Jimmie Mac.

The man didn't blink. "A beautiful One, I'll bet," the Reverend Tomme said. "And She must really love you. That God in Her goodness saved you three times from the electric chair. Would you tell me your thoughts about that?"

"Thoughts?" said Nail. "I think it's jist wonderful."

"Can you tell me what it's like," the minister requested, "to sit there one minute and think your life is over, and in the next minute to know that you'll live? I really can't imagine being in that chair. Nobody who has never been through that terrible experience could possibly imagine it. And nobody but you, Brother Chism, has ever cheated death three times."

"Well, sir," Nail began, and found himself becoming more talkative than he'd ever been in his life. He'd waited a long time to have somebody to tell it to. He would have liked to tell it to Viridis, but he never got a chance. He hadn't wanted to tell it to Ernest. Now Nail talked for a solid hour to the preacher. The preacher had a very lively face: he would smile or frown or scowl or laugh or just look like he understood completely what Nail was saying.

The preacher would sometimes say, "I see," as if he really did, or "Go on," as if he really enjoyed listening, or "Is that right?" or "No!" or "Yes yes," or whatever was required by what Nail was saying, but he didn't interrupt with any real comment until Nail was finished, and then observed, "It looks to me as if God in His wisdom—*Her* wisdom, I'm sorry—

has got something for you to do in this life that She wants to preserve you for, keep you for, let you do."

Nail smiled. "All I want to do, Reverend, is raise my sheep and watch after 'em as best I know how."

"That's just what our friend Jesus once said," Lee Tomme observed. " 'I am the good shepherd,' he said; 'the good shepherd giveth his life for the sheep.' You've come close three times to giving your life, but Jesus, or God the Mother if you think that way, has saved you from death because He or She, or both of them as One, has been put to death and knows what it's like and doesn't want you to have it, not just yet."

"That's fine spoke, Reverend," Nail said.

"Will you call me Lee?" he asked. "Just Lee. And I'll call you Nail? Good. We have much work to do."

"I aint had any work to do," Nail observed. "That's been my main problem. The whole time I've been in this prison, they've never given me a chance to do a lick of work."

Lee shook his head in sympathy. "It's an idiotic law that says a man condemned to die cannot be made to work, or even allowed to work. But that's their law, and I can only try to change it. Nail, would you tell me anything else you don't like about this place?"

Nail laughed. "Have you got all day?"

"I've got all day," Lee said, "and all night too, if need be."

The Reverend Mr. Lee Tomme did not spend the entire day and night with Nail Chism, but he stayed past suppertime and insisted on eating supper with Nail, the same cornbread and cowpeas. A couple of days later there was a front-page article in the *Gazette*, NEW PRISON CHAPLAIN BLASTS CONDITIONS.

"The food is not fit to eat, the living conditions are unhealthy beyond belief, and the unprovoked punishment is a hideous infliction of unspeakable pain," the Reverend Mr. Tomme was quoted as saying. "It is the same story at Tucker, the white men's prison farm, and at Cummins, the farm for black men and women. The whole prison system in the state of Arkansas is begging for change, and we are going to change it, even if we have to abolish the machine politician!

"Our prison system is at least fifty years behind the national standard, which is bad enough. The penitentiary and the farms are not self-sustaining, when they easily could be. The only mode of punishment known to the keepers, for any violation, real or imagined, of the rules, real or imagined, is the strap. And a terrible strap it is, which beggars description, although I intend to describe it if it is not immediately abolished.

"There is no self-respecting poor dirt farmer in the state of Arkansas who would permit his animals to dwell in the filth and the horror that surround these human beings, or who would flay them as these men are flayed. There are fewer deaths from natural causes than from preventable disease and from this corporal punishment which is in fact an illegal form of capital punishment.

"Where does the blame lie? The guards are only doing what they think is expected of them. The new superintendent, Warden Yeager, is an experienced penal administrator who is open to change, experiment, and improvement. The governor . . . ladies and gentlemen, I would not have the freedom to make these criticisms if the governor had not appointed me pastor to the poor oppressed captives.

"Who, then, is to blame? You are. And I am. Any one of us who learns of the brutal injustices of this system and does not act to stop them is in collusion with them! Let us put a stop to them *now*."

The very next day, Fat Gill escorted Nail upstairs into the engine room of the powerhouse and interrupted a big fellow almost as tall as Nail but thicker-muscled, who looked as if he could eat Fat Gill for breakfast and want a second helping. "Here he is," said Fat Gill.

"Take the cuffs off," the man said.

"But he's dangerous," Fat Gill said.

"Shit. He won't hurt me. Take the cuffs off and get out of here." Fat Gill obeyed. As soon as the guard was gone, the big fellow offered Nail a cigarette, and when Nail declined, he offered him a swig from a pint bottle, which Nail knew he could not successfully decline, so he made no attempt. While he was wiping his mouth with one hand, the big man grabbed his other hand and shook it, and said, "I'm Guy Dempsey, and one of these days I'm gonna burn your ass, but meanwhile you're gonna be my helper. You know anything about electricity?"

Nail shook his head. "The closest I come to learnin anything was when the feller who had your job let his hand slip and gave me a little charge before I was supposed to get the full dose."

"Okay, here's where we start," Dempsey said. "Pay close attention, and

246

they might even name something after you. They named the volt after a guy named Count Volta, they named the watt after James Watt, they named the ohm after a German physicist, and they named the ampere after André Ampère. They might decide to call the dose it takes to electrocute a man a chism. Unless you invent something better. Pay attention."

Beginning that day, and continuing every day afterward, G. H. Dempsey taught Nail Chism everything he knew about electrostatics, electrodynamics, and electromagnetics. At the end of that first day, Dempsey gave him a copy of Rowland's *Applied Electricity for Practical Men* and told him to memorize it. It wasn't nearly as thick as Dr. Hood, but it was twice as difficult. Thinking of Dr. Hood, Nail wondered if Viridis had ever noticed the "message," such as it was, that he had tried to smuggle out to her in Dr. Hood, wherein, on the page defining mustard oil, he had used his own blood to underline the definition. It wasn't fair of him, he realized, to have expected her to figure out what that meant. Even if she saw the smear of blood and read the definition, she wouldn't know that he was asking her to smuggle some mustard oil in to him.

He didn't have to wait for the morning light to read the Rowland book. Now he could read anytime because Dempsey had wired and illuminated the dungeon of the death hole, thanks to Warden Yeager, who had also put Ernest to work painting the walls of it. The job took him only a week, but he was allowed outside his cell all day in order to do it. That freedom and employment were a rare novelty to him, so Ernest happily painted while Nail did odd jobs upstairs in the engine room and took in Dempsey's lectures and demonstrations on electricity. Sometimes Dempsey had Nail come with him to the main building to do a job, or up to the guard towers to work on the new searchlights. Once Dempsey even took him into the warden's house outside The Walls to repair some wiring, and Nail reflected that he could have gained his freedom if he had overpowered Dempsey, something he didn't want to try. In the evenings Nail read Rowland while Ernest drew pictures with his new art kit. The ladies of the Arkansas Federation of Women's Clubs had put together for Ernest a box containing every conceivable type of artist's pencil, crayon, chalk, and a set of forty-eight colored pastels, including six shades of green: emerald, moss, olive, viridian, terre verte, and Paris; and he had enough paper, he told Nail, to wallpaper his cell, which he just might do if they didn't electrocute him soon.

247

After a week of this decent treatment, Warden Yeager himself came down into the death hole one Saturday morning and passed inspection on the new paint job, and then said, "Well, gentlemen, can I do anything else for you?"

"I want another one of them steaks," Ernest said.

"Yeah, and some more chicken'n dumplins," Nail said.

"Hee hee, hee hee," Yeager said. "Aint we been feeding y'all a little bit better lately?"

It was true. There wasn't any steak or dumplings, but the monotonous cornbread and cowpeas had been replaced by an occasional egg at breakfast, a sandwich at dinner, and a square meal at supper: hash or stew sometimes. They really couldn't complain about that. "We're happy, I reckon," Nail declared. "I only wish you'd change that rule about not lettin us ever go to the visit room."

"My goodness!" Yeager exclaimed. "I forgot about that. You haven't seen the visit room lately, have you, Chism? Come up and take a look." The warden himself, but with some help from Short Leg, escorted Nail upstairs, out across the Yard and into the visitors' room, where a few changes had been made: the dense screen had been torn out and replaced with a long table divided by a vertical board down the center of it, with chairs placed along both sides so that the inmates could sit on one side, the visitors on the other. And the table could accommodate up to six inmates and six visitors at a time, not just one of each. Two couples were using it at the moment: a black woman with her child was talking to a black convict, and a white woman was talking to a man Nail recognized as his old bunkmate Toy, who had such bad breath. The warden explained that they weren't allowed to pass anything across the board or touch or hold hands or anything like that, although one kiss at the beginning and one at the end were permitted. "If it's somebody you care to kiss hee hee," Yeager said. Nail wondered how the woman could stand to kiss Toy. And there were several other good improvements in the room: a visitor could bring you something, a present or some food or anything, so long as it got inspected first for anything illegal, and you could have a visitor not just once a month but once a week if you wanted.

"Well, I'll declare," Nail said. "Now all I need is a visitor."

The warden gestured toward the opposite door, which Bird was guarding in a new uniform that made him look like a hotel doorman. "She's in there hee hee," Yeager said.

"Huh?" Nail said. Then he said, "Oh. Warden Yeager, sir, you sure are a nice man."

"Don't thank me hee hee," the warden said. "It was the Reverend Tomme who made these improvements. Now, enjoy your visit hee hee. Bird, you let 'em talk all they want, just don't let her give him nothin except what's already been inspected."

"Yessir," Bird said, and saluted like some goddamn soldier, then opened the door. She stood there, in the doorway, in a green summertime outfit that was thin and silky, a shade of green that matched her eyes and made Nail notice how her hair caught the light in soft red sparks. She came in. Nail stood on his side of the table waiting for her. She came up to the table, studied the barrier-board between them, and raised her hands as if to make sure the screen was gone. She looked uncertainly at Bird. "Y'all can kiss, that's all," Bird informed her.

They both had to put their hands on the tabletop to steady themselves as they leaned toward each other across the divider. His hands were still cuffed together. It took what seemed to him like an awful long time to reach her, to get there. Seeing Toy out of the corner of his eye, he began to wonder if his own breath was bad and tried to keep his mouth clamped tight shut, but he had to make at least a little pucker of his lips. Nail had never kissed a girl before. Not once. As her face began the long journey across the tabletop, she was smiling, but as she came closer the smile vanished, and she seemed as if she were about to faint and closed her eyes. He kept his eyes open for fear he'd miss her completely. He realized their noses were going to get in the way, and he tilted his nose to his left, but at that instant she tilted her nose in that direction too, then opened her eyes to see why he hadn't made contact yet; seeing their noses in the way, she tilted her head back in the other direction at the same instant he was heading that way himself, and they had to stop and start all over again until they could somehow silently agree to tilt their noses in opposite directions and get them out of the way. They made a short, simultaneous laugh of self-consciousness. And then her lips were touching his. It was almost like that time Bobo had given him a quick little charge of current, not that it was painful but it jolted him like something he had never

249

expected to feel and wasn't ready for. He heard those trees, the same singing he'd sometimes heard in the death room. It was real nice. Sometimes, playing his harmonica, he had tried to imagine what it would be like kissing Viridis, but he'd never realized it would be as nice as this, or that it would make him tingle to the tips of his toes. He closed his eyes. The singing of the trees continued until finally it was hushed by Bird's harsh voice: "That's enough now." They disengaged and backed away from the middle of the table.

"Hi, Nail," she said, smiling.

"Howdy, Viridis," he said.

"Y'all sit down, now," Bird said, and they sat in their chairs on opposite sides of the table and looked at each other across the wooden board. The couples on either side of them went on talking. Toy's woman was saying something about a store burning in De Vall's Bluff, and the black man was asking his woman if the white folks she worked for were treating her proper. They paid no attention to Nail and Viridis.

"How are you?" Viridis asked, rather formally.

"I am real fine, I reckon," he answered, somewhat formally himself. "And how are you?"

"I am very hopeful," she said. "Everything is looking up. They're treating you decently, aren't they?"

"Compared with the way it was before," he said, "it is sure decent."

"You look good," she said. "You're putting on some weight."

He ran his hand over his bare skull. "My head don't look too good, I guess."

"Your hair's starting to grow back," she observed. "And they'll never shave it again." She repeated: "Never."

"I don't know how to thank you for what you done to stop that last execution, because I don't know for sure just what you done, but me and Ernest both are awful glad you did."

She smiled. She just smiled that real pretty smile of hers, like she wasn't going to tell him a thing about what she done. "I hear the . . . thingamajig in the power plant—the dynamo or whatever you call it, that powers the electric chair—was incapacitated," she said.

"Yeah. Incapacitated." He liked the sound of that word. "Dempsey, the new guy, that I'm workin for, he says he can't figure it out. Something's busted bad in that dynamo, but I might be able to fix it myself." He laughed. "Wouldn't that be something? For me to learn enough about electricity to fix the dynamo so they can go ahead and finish fryin me with it?"

She did not laugh. She leaned close toward the barrier and lowered her voice almost to a whisper. "Nail, the dynamo has a Number 12 cartridge fuse that has been removed and is hidden on the top shelf of the broom closet in the engine room. Leave it there."

Nail nodded his head. And then he nodded it again, and just left it nodding. At length he asked, "How did you know that's what it was?"

"It's written on the side of the fuse," she said.

"I didn't think Bobo was smart enough to read," he said.

"*Nail,*" she said. She just said his name, but the way she said it seemed to mean, Let's quit pretending we don't both know what happened.

He kept his voice down. "Where'd you git the fake mustache?"

She giggled. "It wasn't fake. It was his. I cut it off."

"How did he like that?"

"He was dead drunk, and he was still dead drunk when I put his clothes back on him and left him. I doubt he ever woke up until the next morning."

Nail felt his face getting red, and he knew Viridis could notice the blush. He observed, "You must've seen me and Ernest without a stitch."

"A stitch is a stitch," she said. "It's all the same to me." They both laughed so hard that Bird snapped to attention from his half-bored stance. "You do have a nice body," she went on. Did she enjoy keeping the blush on his face? "How did that *Post-Dispatch* reporter say it? 'Chism is a blue-eyed, light-haired, fair-complexioned man of splendid physique despite what harsh incarceration has done to it.' "

The blush stayed. "I never read no story of that kind," he said.

"I'm keeping a scrapbook for you," she said.

Trying to change the subject, he said, "There's something I can't figure out. How did you get inside The Walls if you didn't have Bobo with you?"

Very quietly she rapped out on the tabletop, *Shave and a haircut, two bits.* "That's the code for the door at the main gate," she said. "But to get into the powerhouse, I also had Bobo's key-ring on my belt . . . *his* belt, which I was wearing. That key-ring is the only thing of his I've kept."

Nail whistled, then whispered, "You still have Bobo's *keys?*"

She nodded. "He doesn't need them anymore. For instance," she lowered her voice even more, "did you notice there's a long ladder lying against one wall of the engine room?"

"Yeah, and it's padlocked on both ends to the wall," he said.

"The key to the padlocks," she whispered, "is in my hand. Before I have to go, I'll slip it into my mouth. Then, when I kiss you good-bye, I'll put it into your mouth. Okay?"

"Viridis," he said, "you are as good as they make 'em. I mean, you are really truly good as all gitout. But there's just one other thing I'd have to git . . ."

She didn't give him a chance to finish. "On the same shelf of the broom closet where the dynamo fuse is hidden," she said, "is Irvin Bobo's empty whiskey pint in a paper sack. Only it isn't empty. I filled it with mustard oil."

He shook his head. And then he shook it again and just left it shaking. "You didn't leave a railroad ticket up there too, didje?" he asked, laughing.

"Shh," she hushed him. "No, but I could tie Rosabone to a tree out by the swamp," she said, meaning it.

"I'll go on foot," he said.

"Where?" she asked.

"*Where?* Why, home, of course."

She shook her head. "That's the first place they'll look for you."

"Where else would I go?" he asked. "Mexico?"

She whispered again. "I could hide you up in the attic of my house." When he frowned and shook his head, she said, "I could really make a nice room up there, and you could have *anything* you want."

"Anything except mountains and meadows and creeks and country," he said. He shook his head again. "No, I thank ye kindly, but I'll light out for the back of beyond. I don't mean I aim to git my old bed back, in the homeplace. But there's some hollers I know up on the mountain where aint nobody ever been, except Indians. Places where nobody could find me."

"Could *I* find you?"

"Not if I didn't draw ye a map."

"Draw me a map."

"When the time comes. I aint leavin tonight. First I've got to figger some way to git upstairs from the death hole in the middle of the night."

"Whatch'all talkin about?" Bird said, and they looked up to see him leaning over them. Had he been listening? Had he heard anything they said? Would he snitch? Nail grew very anxious. But Bird was simply intent on announcing, "Y'all just got about five minutes left."

"All right," Viridis said. Bird backed away to his guard spot, and they went on talking. Viridis said, "I hope you don't mind if I visit with Ernest after you leave."

"Mind?" he said. "Course I don't mind. You know he don't have no folks to visit him from up home, where he comes from, up around Timbo. You gonna kiss him too?"

"I just want to talk about his drawings," she said. "Has he started using his pastels yet?"

"Those colored chalks? Yeah, he's covered a new pad with 'em. Did you bring back his old pad?"

She shook her head. "Does he need it? I had most of those framed to show to people to help save him from the chair."

Nail said, "There's one of them I hope you didn't have framed. Ernest forgot it was in the pad, and he sure was mortified at the thought you seen it."

It was her turn to blush. He was glad to see that she could. She'd caused him so many blushes. "No," she said. "I'm not showing that to anyone. Who is the girl?"

"What girl?"

"That he drew you in bed with."

"What makes you think it was me?"

"Nail. It looks just like you."

"He's shore a good artist, aint he?"

"Who's the girl?"

"Aw, she's jist some story I tole him. There wasn't never nobody like that. He jist made her up. I mean, *I* jist made her up, and *he* jist drew her."

"You've never been to bed with a girl?"

"Sorry, y'all's time is up," Bird said, and handed her a basket. "Lady, you can give 'im this now."

Viridis had brought him a basket of goodies, which had gone through an inspection by another trusty-guard in the anteroom. It contained fruit, cookies, men's hosiery, underclothes, handkerchiefs, books, packages of chewing-gum. Bird said to her, "You hid two things in there that's not allowed, and you can pick 'em up outside. He can't have that harmonica, and he can't have that letter."

"Oh, dear," Viridis said. "Well, that's too bad."

"You can just mail him the letter," Bird suggested. "But I don't know about that harmonica. They prolly wouldn't let him keep it, on account of *before*."

"I guess I'll have to say good-bye," Viridis said. "I can't say anything else." Nail saw why she couldn't say anything else: she had put something into her mouth. Pretending to wipe her lips in preparation for a parting kiss, she put the padlock key into her mouth. Bird wasn't paying much attention anyway; kissing seemed to make him squirm. They leaned across the table, and again Nail felt the spark of their lips meeting, and wondered if the Rowland book had any explanation for that. Her lips parted, and the key came through them, between his, into his mouth. Suddenly he was aware of a tightening in his pants. He took the key into his mouth and, unable to talk, nodded his head good-bye to her. Later he wished he had thought to tell her he loved her before he got the key in his mouth. He had planned to say so during the meeting but never did.

Ernest came back to the death hole from his fifteen minutes with Viridis more cheerful than Nail had ever seen him. He had got permission from the trusties to pass the new sketchbook across to her, and they had talked about his pastel drawings, which were considerably more complicated than the black-and-whites he had been doing. Viridis had made a few suggestions but mostly had just complimented him, and had said "Ooh" or "Ahh" as she turned the pages, and just made him feel real good watching her eyes and her face as she looked at his work. She had also brought him a basket, with pretty much the same things she'd brought Nail—"enough cookies to choke a horse"—as well as a couple of art books, *Advanced Pastel Techniques* and *Great Drawings of the Masters*.

That night Nail went through the basket Viridis had brought him. It was better than Christmas. He ate an apple and wanted to eat a banana too, but he saved it. He chewed some of the chewing-gum. He opened the books; there were three of them: a clean, revised edition of Dr. Hood, big and thick and fancy-bound, with new chapters he hadn't read before, on things like unhappy marriages and how to avoid them, how to raise children, and so on; there was a new book called *Tender Buttons* by a lady

254

named Gertrude Stein; and there was a slender little book of poems, called *Irradiations: Sand and Spray,* by John Gould Fletcher. Nail opened it to the flyleaf and read:

> To Nail Chism, a brave Arkansawyer,
> whose story will take more pages
> than this book.
> With ineffable admiration,
> John Gould Fletcher

Beneath the fancy ink of that inscription there was written in pencil in Viridis' hand: "He is the cousin of my ex-boss, and grew up in Little Rock, lives now in London, but has read all the newspaper stories about you, and thinks the world of you." Beneath that in blacker pencil someone had block-printed: WRITING STUFF IN BOOKS IS AGAINST RULES OF THIS PRISON.

Nail had been required by his teacher at the Stay More school to read poetry, but he hadn't particularly cared for it or had time for it. Now that he had a lot of time, he read Mr. Fletcher's verse cover to back, and then back to cover. There weren't any rhymes in it, and Mr. Fletcher seemed to get overexcited at times, but he had a good way of putting things, and Nail understood what he was saying. There was one long poem, called "Green Symphony," that was mostly about trees, and Nail appreciated such lines as:

> The trees splash the sky with their fingers,
> A restless green rout of stars.

and:

> The trees lash the sky with their leaves,
> Uneasily shaking their dark green manes.

A good poem, Nail reflected, ought to make you want to see it yourself, and he wanted to see those trees . . . or any trees. That time Dempsey had taken him to fix the wiring in the warden's house, Nail had glimpsed the trees on the warden's lawn, the first he had seen for eight months.

He wanted to watch some trees somewhere splashing the sky with their fingers and shaking their dark-green manes.

Since the painting of the death hole was all finished, they had Ernest build four more cells. They gave him the cement and the concrete blocks and the tools and finally brought him four ready-made barred doors, and all by himself Ernest built four more death cells, each of them only four feet wide by seven feet deep, and he painted those too, making a total of six cells for the death hole, and pretty soon three of the new cells were filled: there was Sam Bell, who had been convicted of killing four members of his divorced wife's family; and, briefly, two black men who had been convicted of killing their bosses, but they hardly stayed long enough for Nail to learn their names before the governor commuted them to life imprisonment and sent them to Cummins in order to make room for Clarence Dewein and Joe Short, two young white men not much older than Ernest, who had killed a storekeeper together, or one of them had done the shooting while the other robbed the man. The population of the death hole was five. There would have been even more than that, according to the *Gazette*, except for all the publicity about Nail, which had made juries all over the state reluctant to send men to the electric chair, exercising instead their new option for sentences of life imprisonment.

Warden Yeager summoned Nail to his office, had Short Leg unlock the handcuffs, and offered Nail a cigarette, which he declined. "Gettin kind of crowded down there, aint it hee hee?" the warden observed or asked.

"Yessir," Nail agreed. "I don't think that hole was meant to hold that many."

"But we don't keep you down there. You doin a good job upstairs with Dempsey, I hear hee hee. A good job, he tells me. Learnin a lot."

"Thank you, sir."

"Are you happy, Chism?" the warden asked. "Is there anything we could do for you?"

Nail thought. "Well, sir," he said, "you know that empty piece of the Yard on the east side of the powerhouse? Could I put me a mater patch in it?"

"A mater patch?" the warden asked.

"Yeah, and grow . . . to-maters? It's a shame to let a piece of land jist go to waste out there in the Yard, that the men don't walk on or nothin.

I could grow enough maters on that piece to feed the prison, come August and September, if you could git me the plants."

"Well, why not?" the warden said. "I'll get some niggers out there to spade it up for you. You need some fertilizer too. That's a good idea. How many plants you need?"

"I reckon fifty or so ought to be all it could hold."

"We'll sure do it, then, Chism. Would that make you happy?"

"It would help."

They gave Nail his tomato patch. It was really late in the year to be planting tomatoes, but the plants the warden got were kind of old and leggy anyhow, and Nail planted them deep. While Nail was cultivating them one afternoon, the warden came out there with three other fellows, all of them dressed in suits with straw hats. Nail was wearing a straw hat too, but it wasn't fancy, and he took it off. One of the men was a black man, and he was dressed the best. The only one Nail recognized was that local sheriff who had arrested Ernest and had come with the governor to his last execution.

"Chism," the warden said, "these here are some gentlemen would like to talk to you. This is Mr. George Donaghey, who used to be our governor, and this is the Reverend Dr. Alonzo Monk of the AME church, and I believe you've met Sheriff Bill Hutton. Now these men are gonna ask you some questions. Governor Hays has appointed them a commission to inspect and investigate the prison, and I want you to tell 'em just what you think, okay?"

The three men of the governor's commission stood around in Nail's tomato patch and asked him all kinds of questions about life in the prison. Warden Yeager stood there smiling, and his smile got bigger whenever Nail told how much things had changed lately, and how much better the food was, and all.

"Mr. Chism," said Governor Donaghey, "you have been, and still are, under sentence of death. Don't you think it's remarkable that you're allowed out here on the grounds to work in this garden?"

"Yessir, I reckon it is," Nail replied.

"Do you know the Reverend Lee Tomme?"

"I've met 'im."

"Do you think there is any substance to the charges he has made against this prison?"

"Well, sir, there was. Things was pretty bad around here before he spoke up. Of course, Warden Yeager was already doin his best to make 'em better, before the Reverend come along."

Later that afternoon, after supper (everybody got chicken and dumplings), the warden provided a little entertainment for the visiting inspectors: he turned Ernest loose. Nail didn't see it happen, but later Ernest told him about it. First thing, of course, they told Ernest that he would be pursued . . . and caught. They gave him a couple of extra pairs of pants (as protection, they said, but possibly also to impede his running) and opened the gate of The Walls and told him to take off, not toward the city but southward toward the swamp out behind the pen. They gave him a half-hour head start, and then, for the benefit of Governor Donaghey, the Reverend Monk, and Sheriff Hutton, they pursued him with the warden's pack of bloodhounds: Driver, Slim, Gloom, Dopey, Fetch, Nosey, and Lady. They had suggested the location of some telephone poles that Ernest could climb to get out of reach of the dogs' teeth, but he chose instead a sycamore tree beyond the swamp, a mile out, which was the farthest he could get before the hounds caught up with him, and he was returned, unharmed and unbitten, to the inspectors. The whole business was designed to prove how difficult it was to escape, and every inmate was told about it.

After dark, Nail was called out to help Guy Dempsey give the inspectors the "lighting ceremony," as Dempsey called it: a new searchlight had been mounted on a motorized swivel atop each of the four guard towers so that the guards could focus them on any spot inside the grounds or within a half-mile radius outside the grounds, and nothing within the reach of those lights remained in darkness. A half-dozen black trusties, dressed in prison stripes, were turned loose on the understanding that they would voluntarily come back after this demonstration. Apparently, the inspectors were greatly impressed and told the warden they would report that it was impossible, between the dogs and the lights, to escape from The Walls.

After the inspectors were gone, Warden Yeager invited Nail up to his office again and thanked him for the nice things he had said to the inspectors. "Is there anything else we could do for you to make you happy?" the warden asked.

"Yessir, there is," Nail said. "You know there's a awful lot of grass out there on the west side of the powerhouse. Could I maybe get a couple of sheep and put them out there?"

Warden Yeager laughed. "You used to be a sheep rancher, didn't you, Chism hee hee?" The warden shook his head in wonder at the idea, but also in refusal of it. "No, it wouldn't work. We can't even keep a flock of chickens here in The Walls. Now, if you were down at Tucker . . ." The warden snapped his fingers. "I got an idea. How about I get the governor to commute you to life and send you down to Tucker to start a sheep farm? I don't mean no two or even three sheep hee hee but a whole big flock of 'em. How about that?"

"I hear it's pretty bad down at Tucker," Nail observed.

"Not since that goddamn preacher, Reverend Tomme, started stirring things up. Hell, ole Tucker Farm is a country club now hee hee."

"Could you let me think about it?" Nail requested.

"Hee hee? *Think* about it? What's to think about? I'm offering you a chance at life instead of a fourth chance at the chair."

"Right now, Warden," Nail said, "I would have to tell you no, because I'd rather be dead than spend my whole life in prison."

"Aw, it don't mean your *whole* life. You'd be up for parole in fifteen, twenty years, maybe sooner if you did a real good job raisin them sheep hee hee."

"Let me think about it?"

"Better not think too long. I need to send the governor a list of names early next month."

That night Nail tried to tell Ernest about the warden's offer, but the other three condemned men in the hole overheard him. Nail and Ernest had no privacy anymore. The others jumped in on any topic that came up for discussion, even if it was the number of cockroaches keeping them company. The guy Sam Bell, who had murdered his in-laws, said he'd a lot rather die than go to Tucker for even fifteen months, let alone fifteen years. The two kids, Clarence Dewein (whom they called Dewey) and Joe Strong, were both of the opinion that a whole life of even eighty years in Tucker would be preferable to the chair, the thought of which gave them nightmares every night—apparently the same ones, because they screamed at the same time in their sleep.

Nail hated the thought of Tucker Farm, but it would have to be an improvement on this crowded death hole. Would Viridis come down to Tucker to see him? It was fifty dusty miles from Little Rock. Would she keep coming for twenty years? No, she had provided him with the means for escape, and he ought to try to escape, even if there was a severe risk of getting caught, as the warden had demonstrated for the inspectors. But maybe Nail would even lose his chance at a life-commute if he was caught trying to escape.

The next time the Reverend Mr. Tomme came to see him, Nail informed him of the choice the warden had offered him and declared he was having some trouble making up his mind.

Lee Tomme nodded. "I know. Yeager told me he wants to send you to Tucker. It would be a feather in his cap if you did a good job on a sheep farm down there."

"He says you've improved Tucker the same way you've improved The Walls," Nail said. "Is it really better'n it used to be?"

"For a while," Lee said, but sighed. "I'm not optimistic that the improvements will last. That governor's committee you talked to—Donaghey, Monk, and Hutton—they'll probably submit a report that things aren't nearly as bad as I said they were, and then everything will go right back to hell."

Nail frowned and considered that. "I sure hope I didn't say nothing to 'em that would make 'em do that."

Lee waved the thought away. "I'm not blaming you. I've got a suspicion these improvements are largely cosmetic: they pretty up the place for the benefit of inspection by the governor's committee, and as soon as the committee reports on how nice everything is, they'll take away the improvements."

"You think Tucker will fall back to what it was?"

"They'll have to fire me first," Lee said, "but I wouldn't be surprised if they did that too."

" 'They' or 'he'?"

"Okay. 'He.' Hays."

"And one of the first improvements they'll take away from The Walls," Nail conjectured, "is me and Ernest having jobs and a little bit of freedom. They'll try to put us in the chair again."

Lee looked sorrowfully at Nail. "I hope not. But I'd be a mealymouth to deny it could happen."

Nail debated with himself whether to tell the preacher he wanted to attempt an escape. He knew that Lee Tomme, who detested snitches, would not snitch. And maybe he could help. Or at least give him some spiritual advice. So Nail lowered his voice and said, "Lee, I don't think I'll take the warden's offer. I don't aim to spend *any* time at Tucker. I reckon I'll just go over the wall."

Lee smiled. "I wish you could."

"I can," Nail said.

Lee studied him awhile before asking, "Didn't you hear about that show they put on for the inspectors? This place is escape-proof."

"Not to me," Nail said. "I'm fixin to—"

"Don't tell me how." Lee held up his hand. "I don't want to know. I'll take your word for it. I don't want anybody accusing me of conspiring with you." The preacher smiled. "But you could tell me *when* you plan to go."

"Soon as I figger out a way to get upstairs in the middle of the night," Nail said. "That's the tricky part, as they say."

"Do you want me to let you know if I can figure out something?" Lee asked in a whisper. "Or would that be conspiracy?"

"Yeah, I reckon it would. I reckon you better let me figger it out by myself."

"Okay. Shall we change the subject, and speak louder? Do you know, when I worked in the Colorado prisons, instead of beating a man they would punish him by taking away his privilege of seeing the weekly motion picture."

Nail smiled. "That's nice. I aint never seen a motion picture."

"I thought as much. My next improvement to this facility—possibly my last improvement—will be to have movies shown, each Saturday night, and to suggest that violators of prison rules be punished not by the strap but by being forbidden to attend the picture show."

"The picture shows will be done at night?" Nail asked.

"Of course. The barracks will have to be dark."

"And somebody who knows something about electricity will have to help 'em run the projector?"

"You catch on very quickly, Brother Chism, but shall we change the subject?"

"Yeah. Tell me what it's like in Colorado. Do they raise a lot of sheep out there?"

A general prison announcement was made that the following Saturday at sundown there would be a performance of *The Absentee*, a great allegorical photoplay. The movie was projected onto four bedsheets sewn together on a wall of the barracks, from three reels on an old Edison donated by The Crystal, a Little Rock theater that was updating its equipment. It was the greatest event since Christmas. Nobody from the death hole was allowed to attend, but midway through the motion picture all of the power went out, and the old Edison began to smoke, and Fat Gill was sent down to get Nail and see if he could find out what was wrong. Nail was taken up to the engine room, without handcuffs, and guarded as he checked the generator and the fuses and the circuits. After replacing one of the fuses that had blown, he was taken into the barracks to check the projector. Nail found a wire loose in the Edison and twisted it back onto its contact, but not so tight that it wouldn't come off and short again before long. Then, because of the service he had performed, he was permitted to watch the rest of the picture show, in handcuffs. The show was difficult. As near as he could figure, it was about some character named Might, who took over a factory and lowered the wages of the workers, pocketing the difference for the betterment of his daughters, named Extravagance and Vanity. It was real strange, watching the people actually run around and do things, and move their mouths like they were talking, only their words would appear in letters when the screen went dark, and their words didn't mean very much. The workers went on strike, led by a man named Evil, but Evil got a heart attack and the strike fizzled out, and in the end the owner of the factory, Power, came home and discovered what a mess Might had made, and had him arrested.

Although the plot was confusing and the names of people ridiculous, the movie held the audience spellbound, and at the end the men applauded and stomped their feet and hollered and demanded another showing. Warden Yeager himself, who had enjoyed the movie along with his prisoners, got up and made a little speech and told them that if they all behaved themselves there would be another movie the following Saturday night. Almost immediately Nail could detect the men beginning to behave themselves.

Back in his cell, Nail reported to his fellow death-holers on the movie. None of them had seen a picture show before either, and Dewey and Joe said it sounded like one of their nightmares, while Ernest was somewhat apprehensive that motion pictures could make art obsolete, while Sam Bell said it sounded very interesting and tempting but he would probably see heaven or hell, one, before he saw a motion picture. But all of them, Nail knew, wished they had seen the movie and could be allowed to behave themselves too.

Nail spent a lot of time thinking about the way he had fixed the Edison projector and wondering if he had given the wire on its contact enough twist to hold it in place until the next movie started shaking the projector. He also spent a lot of time thinking about what Lee Tomme had told him of Colorado: a truly beautiful country with big mountains and lots of space, and thousands of sheep of all kinds.

He had pretty much made up his mind to go to Colorado when he broke out. Then he got a letter from me. Much, much later I learned that it was one of the few letters they had let him read, uncensored, in the original envelope. I have promised not to put myself into this story any more than is absolutely necessary, but I have the feeling my letter may have changed Nail's mind about going to Colorado.

Dear Nail,

Viridis told me I should write to you. She writes to me all the time and tells me everything that is happening, or not happening, to you. And then I tell everybody else in Stay More. It makes me feel important to stand around on the porch of Ingledew's store and tell everybody the news about you. You know, the Jasper newspaper doesn't say much, and that's because I guess Judge Jerram and them still run everything in Jasper. But that is changing. Which is what I'm writing to you about now.

Judge Jerram likes to sit on his brother Tilbert's storeporch as if he was still somebody important around here, but there is not one of us does not despise him and sneer at him and even his brother Tilbert does not like him because he's bad for business, Tilbert says to anybody who will listen. There's room on Tilbert's storeporch for Sull and Sheriff Snow and a deputy or two, and that's all, because nobody else will bother with them.

Your brother Waymon is not the least bit afraid of those fellows.

He will go right up to the edge of the porch, and turn his back to Sull and say over his shoulder, "You want to shoot me in the back again?" and Sheriff Snow will tell him to go away or he will arrest him for loitering, and Waymon will say, "It sure looks to me like you fellows are the ones who are loitering."

And they know they wouldn't dare try and arrest Waymon or they wouldn't be able to take him out of Stay More and put him in the Jasper jail. Your brother is fine and strong. I am sorry about your father, but I guess you know his health has not been good for some time. Your mother and Irene and Luther and all are just fine.

They all miss you, as does every one of us. I think your land misses you too. Yesterday I took me a long hike up through your sheep pastures. The weeds have taken over pretty bad. There's brambles too. From a distance those pastures are all pretty and green, and rolling, you know, and it's all so nice and peaceful up there, but when you try to walk through it, it's overgrown and lonely. The trees sort of sigh.

There's this one place, way up against the corner of your upper forty, where the two tree lines sort of converge at the edges of the pasture on what looks like a dead corner up against the mountainside, and is a real dark shade of green, like the mouth of a cave, and you feel sucked into it, or drawn up thataway, and when you get into it you see there's an old road there, just a trail, if you know the spot I mean, and if you follow that trail up through the woods for quite a ways, a mile or more, with the woods growing deeper and darker, you come to this glade where a waterfall comes down off the very top of the mountain, as if it was gushing up out of some powerful spring up there. The glade is sunny, with the sun shining right on the waterfall, but it's dark all around, and dark in these several sort of half-caves where it looks like Indians must have lived. It was kind of scary, and I didn't stay up there very long, but while I was there I thought of you, a lot, and I had a strange vision as if I could see you just living and dwelling in that hidden glade.

Of course I've had to look up some of these words in my dictionary to spell them right, and some of them to find out just what they mean or how they came to mean what they did, and I have to tell you that "glade" and "glad" are sister-words.

I'm glad that they haven't killed you, and I don't think they ever will. The glade and all of us are waiting for you.

Your friend,
Latha

It was almost, Nail reflected, as good as getting a letter from Viridis. He considered that the letters Viridis was writing to me must have taught me how to write a good letter, or even infected me with some of Viridis' way with words. But his main reaction to the letter was one of shock: that I should mention the very spot, the waterfall, where he had considered hiding, where indeed he thought about "living and dwelling." If I had discovered the spot, wouldn't other people discover his hiding-place? Not necessarily, because I had accidentally stumbled upon that trail whose beginning was almost concealed in the remotest corner of his highest pasture. The glen (and now I have to admit I was wrong: it was not so much a glade as a glen) is hard to get to, and it was the most secluded spot I'd ever been in, myself, and Nail knew it didn't lack anything he'd find in Colorado.

But what had I meant, he wondered, about his father? I realize I didn't word that part too well. I shouldn't have left it open like that, as if his father was already dead, not just on his way to the hereafter. Nail wanted to ask Viridis what she knew. Had she heard anything about his father dying?

And he got a chance soon: Viridis came for another visit. Once again they leaned across the table, meeting their lips above the dividing-board, and greeting, and sitting, and then Nail said, "I had a letter from Latha. Bless her heart. But why do they let me have her letter and won't let me have yours?"

Viridis smiled. "I suspect her letter wasn't nearly as bawdy as mine."

"Bawdy? You mean you used blackguardy words?"

"Blaggarty?" She laughed. "What kind of blaggarty word is 'blaggarty'?"

"Black-guardy," he pronounced it more carefully. "Aw, it just means smutty, you know. Dirty."

"My letters to you are very white and clean, but also very lurid."

265

"I wish I could read them."

"I'm saving them for you," she said. "I'm saving everything for you."

"It won't be long," he said.

Her eyebrows went up. "How long?"

Nail glanced at their tablemates, a couple sitting a few chairs away and engrossed in each other. Bird wasn't paying any more than his usual bored attention. Nail whispered, "Probably next Saturday night."

"Really?"

In a normal voice he asked, "Viridis, what did Latha mean in her letter when she said she was sorry about my dad? He's not left this world yet, has he?"

"No. Did Latha say that? He's very ill and ought to be in the hospital, but he won't go. I think the only thing keeping him alive is he wants to see you again."

"He'll see me soon," Nail whispered.

She whispered too: "No, Nail, his house is the first place the lawmen will watch for you."

"I'll find some way to see Paw," Nail reaffirmed.

"And me?" she said. "Will you find some way to see me?"

"I'll see you," he said, and realized it sounded as if it were just a polite leave-taking, and he didn't mean it that way. He said it again as if he really meant it: "I will see you."

"You were going to draw me a map, remember?"

He smiled. "No need of that. Just ask Latha."

"She knows?"

"Tell her she knows."

Viridis laughed. "I love the way you put that: 'Tell her she knows.' We would all like to be told that we know."

"Be told, then, that *you* know."

"Thank you. Now, here is something you should know." She lowered her voice to the point he had to watch her lips and try to keep one eye on Bird. "One mile southwest of The Walls, beyond the swamp, is a great big old sycamore tree. The newspaper mentioned it in connection with that awful story about how they demonstrated the bloodhounds on poor Ernest. That's the tree Ernest climbed to avoid being bitten by the dogs, but it's where they treed him and caught him. That's how I know about it, and that's how I found it. It's the only sycamore tree in the neighborhood, and it's so tall you'll see it silhouetted against the night sky, so you can't miss it, even if you don't hear the beautiful song it sings. At the base of that tree there is a flat rock, not too heavy for me to lift. Next Saturday afternoon I'm going to place beneath that rock a canvas bag containing a Smith & Wesson revolver, a box of bullets, a hunting knife, a harmonica, a pocketknife with a can opener attachment, and a few cans of food, corned beef and beans and such. I thought of including some sandwiches with fresh meat, but the scent would attract animals who might take the bag away before you got to it. I will also put in a hundred dollars in cash. Is there anything I've forgotten?"

"My God, Viridis!" he exclaimed. Bird looked up at them. Nail lowered his voice and asked, "What do I need all that money for?"

"You never know," she said. "You'll run out of food and need to stop and buy some more."

Nail thought of something. "Yeah, I might have another mouth to feed. For a while. You don't think I would go off and leave Ernest, do ye?"

"I didn't think you would," she said. "That's one reason I'm going to ask him, when we visit this afternoon, to give me all of his finished drawings, to take with me, since he can't take them with him, or leave them behind."

"But he don't know, yet, that I'm plannin to go," Nail pointed out to her. "I aint even asked him if he wants to go with me. I caint talk to him about it because of them other fellers down in the death hole. I don't want them hearin us, 'cause then they'd want to go too, and I shore don't aim to take everbody."

"You wouldn't want to take Sam Bell," she said. "He's a psychopath."

"A what? No, I don't want to take nobody. Just me and Ernest, and I wouldn't even take him except I caint leave him here to die or rot, whichever came first."

"I'm so glad you're taking him," she said. "Maybe I should put some extra clothing into the bag. At least some caps to cover your bare heads."

"But I caint tell him what I aim to do, not without them hearin us. So you'll have to tell him this for me. Tell him this Saturday night. Tell him Fat Gill will come down to git me to fix the fuse or whatever, and for Ernest to start countin, and when it's five minutes after Fat Gill takes me upstairs, for him to be ready to go without nobody else in the death hole seein us. It will be dark. I'm gonna kill all the power. He'll have to jist follow me upstairs in the dark without any word when I come down to git him."

"How will you unlock his cell?"

"Let me worry about that. Like I say, I aint even sure he would want to go. He'd be a fool not to, but maybe he'd rather take his chances with life at Tucker. If he does go over the wall with me, he caint go home with me. When we git out of Pulaski County, we split up: he can go home to Timbo or wherever, or go to Paris to study art like you did, or whatever he wants to do. But you better say your good-byes to him this afternoon, because you might not never see him again. So you jist tell him this: tell him that if he wants to go with me, for him to say, when we're back in our cells together, for him to say, 'Yes, it might be clear Sunday,' and I'll know he wants to go. Okay?"

"I'm so excited," she said.

"I'm so bored," said Bird, and they looked up at the trusty-guard looming over them. He added, "Y'all's time is about up."

"I wanted to thank you for the basket you brought last time," Nail said to her. "I 'preciate ever bit of it."

"Did you read the books?"

"Ever word," he said. "Except in Dr. Hood, I couldn't read *all* them words, and Dempsey give me this here electrical book to memorize that's givin me eyestrain. I'll need spectacles before long."

"Did you—did you have any trouble with Gertrude Stein, or the Fletcher poems?"

"Not a bit. That lady can really use words. I read some of it two or three times, just to make sure it was as good as I thought the first time. And you tell your ole boss, when you see him, to thank Mr. Fletcher for what he wrote to me in his poetry book, and to tell him that I think he ought to be back home in Arkansas where he belongs instead of over there in London."

Viridis laughed. "I agree. I'll tell Tom to tell him that." She glanced to make sure that Bird had moved back to his post, out of earshot, and she said, "I brought you another basket this time, and I didn't know you would be leaving so soon, or I wouldn't have put so many cookies in it. Don't try to take all the cookies with you over the wall. Nor the books."

"I'm takin Fletcher," he declared. He smiled. "And Ernest too, of course."

268

Before their lips met again in parting, he said, in a very gentle voice, as if he were still conspiring in his escape, "I love you, Viridis, and I'll see you soon in the great free world of trees."

"I love you, Nail, and I can hardly wait," she said.

Later, back in their cells after Ernest had been up and delivered his whole output of artwork to Viridis, Nail heard Ernest remark as if to the walls, "Yes, it might be clear Sunday."

"Who cares?" said Sam Bell.

"Going to a ballgame maybe?" asked Joe Strong.

"Naw, he's goin on a picnic," said Clarence Dewein.

"Don't save none of them cookies for it," Nail suggested. "Share a few with the other boys."

"You'uns want chonklit, pecan, or oatmeal?" Ernest offered.

On the Tuesday ahead of that special Saturday, it was announced that the movie this week would be a lively comedy photoplay on loan from a major downtown theater, The Gem, and would have six whole reels. It was called *Tillie's Punctured Romance*, and Tillie would be played by Marie Dressler, while the male lead was acted by the celebrated Charlie Chaplin, who everybody was dying to see. Nail himself was sorry that he couldn't watch the movie, because he wanted to see if it was true, as Viridis had told him, that Charlie Chaplin looked just like ole Bobo . . . or like Viridis herself that one time she had changed herself. Nail did a little bit of calculating and decided he couldn't just leave the circuits shorted while he went over the wall. It wouldn't be fair to the inmates, who by that time would be spellbound by the movie. He would have to figure out some way to turn the projector back on as his last act before taking off.

The next morning he asked Dempscy, "Does this here circuit draw from the same box the arc lamps are on?"

"No, that's on the free line down to the transformer," Dempsey pointed out, and chided him: "You ought to know that."

"Jist makin sure," Nail said.

Warden Yeager called him in once more, and once more the warden asked, friendly-like, "Is there anything more we can do for you to make you happy?"

"Nossir," Nail said, "I reckon I'm pretty happy."

The warden changed his tone, dropping the friendliness. "You aint gonna be much longer. I got bad news hee hee. Matter of fact, I got lots of real bad news. One, we got to take you out of that powerhouse and out of your tomato patch. It's against the rules for a condemned man to do any work, you know that, and we been letting you do it just on account of Reverend Tomme. They fired him. He was a nice fellow, and I'm kind of sorry to see him go, but he was really meddling a lot, and he don't know very much about how to run a pen. If you want to say good-bye to him, we gave him permission to make one last visit to the pen tomorrow. He said he wanted to see you especially, because he knows you're gonna die. That's the *real* bad news. There's three more men coming in this week to wait for the chair, and that's just too many. The governor has been getting a lot of trouble from everybody because of all the pardons and delays and commutations he's been throwing around like Santa Claus. So the word is out: we got to make room in the death hole. You and Bodenhammer and Sam Bell are getting transferred hee hee, to hell hee hee, in the chair this Saturday at sundown."

Nail was not too certain he had heard the warden correctly. What with all of those hee-hee's mixed up in there, it was kind of difficult to be absolutely certain that Travis Don Yeager had just announced that there would be a triple execution this Saturday, approximately two hours before Nail intended to go over the wall. "Sir?" Nail said, feeling bewildered. "What did you say?"

"You heard me," Yeager said in a voice so cold that Nail felt Yeager was probably having to force himself to sound mean. He really does like me a little bit, Nail told himself, but now he's got to try hard not to show it.

"This is awful sudden," Nail observed. "One day you're treatin us like human beings, and bein decent and kind to us, and then the next day you're puttin us right back where we were."

The warden lifted a folder from his desk. "You ought to read the report of the governor's commission of inspectors for the prison system."

Nail held out his hand. "Could I read it?"

"It don't mention you hee hee. Not by name, anyhow. It just says we've been coddling our prisoners and treating them like citizens, which they aint, not after conviction, and it says the governor—let me find it . . ." The warden opened the folder and ran his finger down several pages until he came to the words: " 'Governor Hays has been required to yield to

270

extraordinary outside pressures in order to stay executions, and this interference with justice works to the detriment of the whole system.' That's what it says, Chism hee hee. You can probably read most of it yourself in tomorrow's *Gazette*, along with the announcement of this Saturday evening's executions." The warden waited a full minute for Nail to comment, and when Nail did not, the warden said, "If you got nothing to say, you can get out," and waved him to the door.

Back in his cell, Nail still surprised himself by feeling no emotion. He was neither frightened nor disappointed, frustrated nor angry. He had been sent to the chair so many times, and nothing had happened. Maybe it was dangerous, he thought, to get to the point where you don't feel anything.

Ernest and Sam Bell apparently hadn't been told, not yet. But the next morning's *Gazette* was delivered not by a trusty but by the chaplain himself, or rather the ex-chaplain making his farewell appearance. Lee Tomme first visited the cell of Sam Bell and gave him the newspaper, and Nail listened to Sam Bell reading the item aloud for the benefit of the others. Then Lee visited awhile with Ernest, and Nail could not hear what they were saying. Finally Lee gave Nail his own copy of the newspaper. The report of the governor's commission was on the front page. The announcement of the executions was back on page 4, in a small item all out of proportion to the newsworthiness of the event: Arkansas's first triple execution since the days of Hanging Judge Parker of Fort Smith. It was almost as if there wasn't room for it on the front page, which was taken up with the commission's report.

"I'm sorry they sacked you," Nail told Lee.

"Who told you that?" Lee asked. Indeed, it wasn't mentioned in this issue of the *Gazette*.

"Yeager," Nail said, wondering if there was any chance that Lee himself hadn't been told. "Yesterday," he added.

"Then he had already told you about Saturday night?"

Nail nodded. "Yeah, he told me."

"The bastard," Lee said. "He promised to wait and let me tell you. How did you take it?"

Nail shrugged. "I'm an old hand at this now, ye know. It didn't trouble me."

Lee looked at him oddly, then moved closer and lowered his voice to say, "But the Saturday night movie is scheduled for *after* the executions."

"You think they'd go ahead and show a movie with the same juice they jist used to cook three fellers?" Nail asked.

"The men *want* that movie," Lee said. "They haven't been talking about anything else this week. All they're waiting for is that movie, and they're on their best behavior in order to see it."

"But the warden is cuttin back on all the privileges and improvements that you brought in," Nail pointed out. "Don't you reckon it's likely he'll do away with the picture shows too?"

Lee shook his head. "Not right away. If he tried to do it for *this* movie this Saturday, the men would go on strike or stage a riot. Sure, he'll abolish movies soon, but not this week. I went to a lot of trouble to persuade the theater people in Little Rock to loan us that first-run film."

"Well," Nail said. He didn't know much else to say. Out of genuine concern as well as politeness, he asked, "What are you fixin to do after you leave this job? Have you got another one?"

"Next week I'm interviewing for the position of chaplain in the Tennessee prisons," Lee said. He smiled wryly. "I seem to keep moving eastward, in the direction of civilization."

"I imagine you'll stir things up over there, too," Nail observed.

"I hope they won't need it as much as Arkansas does," Lee said. "This place really begs for help."

"It's too bad Hays wouldn't keep you," Nail said. "That governor can't seem to make up his mind about anything."

Lee laughed so uproariously that Nail wondered if he had unintentionally made a joke. "You've put him in a nutshell. Governor Hays *is* weak and indecisive. He changes his mind constantly. If only he could reverse himself just once more about executing you this Saturday, but he's changed his mind so often that now he lets other people change it for him, and the other people, this time, are the judges and the politicians who are raising a fuss about his clemency."

"I reckon I'm gone, this time," Nail allowed, and then he asked, "Lee, you believe in heaven, don't you?"

"Oh, yes, certainly," Lee said. "But not with clouds and pearly gates and golden streets and all that."

"But with trees?" Nail said. "Are there trees in heaven?"

272

"A tree," Lee declared, "has just as much right to go to heaven as a man does."

Nail decided that Lee Tomme was even a better man than he had already figured him to be. "I don't have no reason to go to hell," he declared, "so I imagine come Saturday night I'll be amongst them trees, and all of us singing."

"A cappella," Lee said.

"Pardon me?"

"No harps, no lutes, no mandolins, none of that," Lee said. "Just the trees singing as the voice of God."

Nail smiled and narrowed his eyes. "Will God be singin shaller or deep?"

Lee laughed. "Soprano or baritone? Now, *that*, Brother Chism, is a very knotty theological problem. But let's observe that in the very best of choirs, when all voices are loud and together, you don't notice the pitch of any one."

"I like that, Brother Tomme," Nail declared. "And maybe what you're sayin is that God aint a woman after all, nor a man neither, but God is all sexes, of all kinds and pitches."

"That's it," Lee said. "A pitch is a pitch. It's all the same to us."

They both broke up with laughter.

"Brother Tomme," Nail requested, "will you be around Saturday at the goin down of the sun to lead us to the chair? I'd 'preciate it if you could. I might even let you pray for me."

Lee Tomme abandoned his jovial face for a very sad one, and shook his head. "I promised the warden I'd be out of The Walls by sundown today. I think that for the executions they're planning to restore my predecessor, what's-his-name?"

"Jimmie Mac."

"Yes, I believe Reverend McPhee is returning Saturday."

"I hate to hear that," Nail said. He offered his hand, and when Lee took it, he said, "Well, Reverend, I want to wish you good luck and happiness wherever you go. When I see God under those trees, I'll tell Them to be sure and love you and keep you on this earth for a long, long time."

For once Lee was at a loss for words, and his eyes got moist. He did not let go of Nail's hand. Finally he looked down at their hands, which were just holding, not being shaken, and he placed his other hand on top on the two joined hands and said, "Look, this is my last day here at The Walls. But I think there is one thing more I could do. Yes, before I'm gone for good, I think I could persuade the Little Rock theater people to tell Warden Yeager that due to previous commitments they will have to move up the loan of *Tillie's Punctured Romance* from Saturday night to Friday night. How would that do?"

Ａnd behold, that old Edison shorted out right in the middle of the picture show. From his cell Nail could hear the three hundred men over in the barracks hollering, whistling, clapping, and stomping for several minutes before the lights came on in the death hole, and Fat Gill came down and said, "Okay, Chism, there's one more little job for you upstairs." He opened the cell door, then put the handcuffs on Nail.

Nail protested. "I aint fixin no electrical equipment with these here cuffs on me."

"Warden's orders," Fat Gill announced. "He says if you can't fix whatever's wrong with the cuffs on, we'll just have to forget it."

"Well, shit, let's go," Nail grumbled, and let Fat Gill lead him upstairs into the engine room. Nail had to get Fat Gill to do things for him because his hands were cuffed. "Reach up there and open the lid on that box . . . Now jiggle that little knob there and let's see what happens. Nope. Must be the other box." Purposely he led Fat Gill on a false trail of increasing difficulty until he was in a position to suggest, "If you'd jist take these cuffs off of me, we could git finished a lot faster."

"Sorry," Fat Gill said. "I'm just doin what the warden told me."

"Well, give that there knob—no, the next one—give it a sort of one-quarter turn anticlockwise." Fat Gill did as he was instructed and loosened the fuse to the projector's circuit, and of course nothing happened, not then. "I reckon we'd better go look at the projector," Nail suggested, and Fat Gill escorted him out of the powerhouse and up into the barracks, where the men were fidgeting until the show resumed. Warden Yeager himself was there, with Short Leg and some of his best black trusties surrounding his seat.

"What's the problem, Chism?" Warden Yeager demanded. "What's takin so long?"

"He put these here cuffs on me," Nail protested. "How the hell can I fix anything when I have to explain to somebody else what to do?"

"Take 'em off," the warden told Fat Gill. "He aint gonna try nothin with all of us around."

Fat Gill removed the handcuffs, and Nail went to work on the old Edison, opening it and fanning away the remaining fumes of the scorched short.

Sure enough, it had shorted exactly in the spot where he had twisted that wire before, and the wire's end had dissolved. He turned to the warden and guards. "Any of you fellers got a pocketknife I could borrow for jist a secont?"

The guards looked uncertainly at the warden, and Yeager said to them, "Well if y'all have one hee hee then *give* it to him hee hee." Short Leg produced a pocketknife. "Just take it easy with that thing hee hee," the warden said to Nail.

Nail scraped the ends of the wire and twisted it tight and firm around its contact. He stepped back dramatically as if expecting something to happen, but nothing did. He jiggled the projector's switch. He pulled out the plug, turned it around, reinserted it. Nothing happened. "Must be still a fuse or something down in the engine room," he declared.

By now the prisoners were whistling, clapping, and shouting, "Put a nickel in it!" and "Crank it up!" and "Turn on the steam!" and "Spit on it!" and they were stomping their feet and jumping up and down.

"Well, go fix the fuse hee hee," the warden said, and Fat Gill escorted Nail back downstairs.

Back in the engine room, Fat Gill wanted to put the cuffs on him again, but Nail protested, "The warden didn't tell you to."

"Aint takin no chances," Fat Gill said, and was holding the manacles open with one hand while he summoned with the other. "Come on, hold out your hands."

"Well, shit, *here*," Nail said, and brought his wrists together and thrust his hands right at Fat Gill, then suddenly raised them under his chin, snapping the guard's head back and stunning him long enough to throw a punch that caught him on the side of the head and slammed him against the wall. Nail didn't want to get into a boxing match. Before Fat Gill could recover from the blow, Nail picked up a length of lead conduit and brought it down on the guard's head, knocking him out. Then Nail took away his key-ring and opened the door leading down into the death hole. There were so many keys on the ring, and he didn't know which one would fit.

He turned out the lights in the death hole, groped his way down the stairs, and counted past the cells of Dewein and Strong and his own empty cell to Ernest's. He found the keyhole with his fingers and began inserting one key after another. A long moment passed, and Ernest knew he was there, and he knew Ernest was there, and apparently the other men in the death hole began to guess that something was happening.

"Nails?" said Sam Bell. "Is that you, Nails? What's up?"

It seemed it was the very last key on the ring that finally opened the bars of Ernest's cell. He felt Ernest's arm and gave it a tug. Only after he passed his own empty cell did he remember he'd intended to pick up the copy of Fletcher's poems, but he did not turn back for it.

"Nails!" hollered Sam Bell. "Is this a bust? Are you coppin a lam? What's goin on? Take us too! Dewey! You still there? Joe? Timbo Red? Who's bustin out? Who's stayin?" Dewey's and Joe's voices joined in and followed them all the way up the stairs. Nail shut the door on them.

Ernest looked at Fat Gill lying on the floor. "You kill him?" he asked Nail.

"Naw, I jist give 'im a knot on his head."

"We got a secont?" Ernest requested. "I want to say good-bye to Old Sparky."

"That door." Nail pointed, and Ernest went through it. Nail followed and turned on the one green-shaded overhead light that illuminated the death chamber. The familiar stage seemed strange, empty of all its actors . . . and its actress. The chair needed dusting. Ernest stood and stared down at it. Old Sparky looked far less menacing than Ernest had depicted it—as harmless, in fact, as some derelict piece of obsolete machinery. Ernest gave its leg a little kick with his shoe and said, "Mr. Spark, I hope you don't never git another customer. You won't git me."

"Come on," Nail urged, leading him out. "Let's git that ladder." Nail reached up into the top shelf of the broom closet and found the key Viridis had smuggled in to him, and the whiskey pint bottle filled with mustard oil. He gave the bottle to Ernest and said, "Carry this. Don't lose it."

"Can I have a drink of it first?" Ernest asked.

"It aint to drink," Nail said. "It's mustard oil."

"What's it for?"

Nail didn't want to take the time to explain. "Now look, Ernest," he said, more severely than he intended, "you let me do the talkin on this little trip. You jist do what I tell you and keep your mouth shut."

Nail unlocked the padlocks holding the ladder to the wall. He decided to return Fat Gill's key-ring to his belt. Then he tightened the fuse that ran to the circuit of the projector. They could hear the men in the barracks cheering as the motion picture resumed. It would be a few minutes before the warden or anybody else would begin to wonder why Fat Gill had not returned. And maybe a lot longer, if the movie was really interesting.

"Let's go," he said. The last thing he did before leaving the powerhouse was to open all of the circuits except the one to the main building, running the projector. The big lights in the guard towers went out. The guards up there would sound an alarm, but now the circuit powering the alarm was open too. By the time the guards could get down from the towers and into the barracks to notify the warden that the searchlights were dead, the searchlights would no longer be needed.

As Nail carried his end of the ladder through his tomato patch, he realized he and Ernest were trampling the young plants, but that couldn't be helped. He didn't mind that he would not be here for the harvest in July and August. When he had planted the tomatoes, he hadn't expected to share in the harvest himself.

The sun was down, but the sky still held some of its light. Nail could hear the guards up in the towers hollering at one another: "What happened to the lights?" and "You got a lantern?" and "Not me. You got one?" Slowly he raised the ladder against the high brick wall. As he had suspected, it did not reach all the way up. That was why he had attached a rope about eight feet long to the top rung: they would have to stand on that rung and reach up and pull themselves up onto the top of the wall and then pull the ladder up after them.

Which they did. Nail went up first and balanced himself carefully on the wall, discovering it wasn't as broad and thick at the top as he had expected. He straddled it and reached down as Ernest handed up to him the end of the rope.

Then came the really tricky part, as they say. Ernest and Nail had to move apart, straddling the wall, so that there would be enough space between them to pull up the ladder and turn it and lower it to the outside of the wall. Without exchanging a word, they gingerly performed this maneuver, Ernest lifting the bottom of the ladder over his head and pointing it toward the outside, while Nail held the top rung and the rope.

In his months of thinking about the escape, Nail had often wondered if the ground outside the wall, on the east side, would be lower than inside. He had no way of knowing. It stood to reason that the levels would be the same, that the wall stood on firm, flat ground. But from his one trip with Dempsey to the warden's house, Nail had observed how sharply the land on that side, the north side, sloped downward away from the wall, and he was prepared to find that the slope was similar on the east side. But in this darkness they could not see the ground down there beyond the wall.

With Ernest steadying the ladder and letting go of it rung by rung, Nail lowered it until he was holding the end of the rope. The ladder still twisted and swayed. Nail's forehead broke out in sweat. "Goddamn," he said, just loud enough for Ernest to hear him. "I caint touch ground. The ladder won't reach."

"Must be a *long* way down there," Ernest said in awe.

Could there be, Nail wondered, some kind of dry moat running around that end of the wall? The eight-foot rope was attached to a ladder of about thirty feet. So was it over forty feet down to the ground? He kicked out behind him with his legs until he lay on his stomach flat across the ridge of the wall. "Hold me down," he told Ernest, and he leaned and stretched as far down the outside of the wall as he could, with the rope in his fist . . . until finally it seemed he could feel, through the rope, that the shoes of the ladder had touched ground. He tugged the rope end against the wall, but the contact he'd made with the shoes seemed to vanish. He could only hope the shoes would hit ground and the side rails would lean the right way against the wall when he let go of the rope. He let go and waited.

Then, after a time, they heard the ladder crash to the ground.

"YOU HEAR THAT?!?" a voice in the tower called, and another voice answered, "THERE'S SOMEBODY OUT THERE!" and from a third tower another voice tried to substitute for the dead alarm bell by yelling at top volume, "JAILBREAK! JAILBREAK! JAILBREAK! JAILBREAK! JAILBREAK! JAILBREAK! JAILBREAK! JAILBREAK!" The lights in the barracks, on the same circuit as the projector, came on, and Nail knew the movie was aborted.

"Lord God!" said Ernest. "What do we do now?"

"We shore caint jump fer it!" Nail said. "We'd break our fool necks."

"We gonna jist sit here till they come and git us down?"

Nail pointed. "See that?" Down toward one of the guard towers, about five feet out from the wall, there was the silhouette of a smooth cypress pole of the electrical system, carrying power to and from the engine room.

It occurred to Nail that this pole, intended to help bring in the current that would have extinguished his life and Ernest's, now offered the only hope of saving them. "Jist watch me," Nail told Ernest, "and see if you caint do what I do." Nail raised himself and stood up on the wall, balancing carefully, trying to feel the slightest warning in the delicate balance mechanisms within his ears as he placed one foot in front of the other until he was as close to the power pole as he could reach; he bent at his knees as if about to squat, then sprang up and out toward the cypress pole, slamming his body against it painfully but throwing his arms around it, and then his legs. Slowly he slid down the pole until his feet touched ground.

He wanted to kneel and kiss the ground, the free earth of the outside world, but he stood and watched Ernest teetering along the top of the wall toward the same leaping-spot. Ernest swayed and nearly toppled but caught himself, fighting the air with his arms for balance. "Come on," Nail called. "You can do it, son." Ernest reached the spot of springing but hesitated, as if trying to measure the distance, to determine consciously what had been instinctive for Nail moments before: the exact amount of effort necessary to reach the power pole without slamming into it and knocking yourself out.

Still unsteady, Ernest hesitated as he stared at the power pole and then pantomimed the first tentative flexing of his knees in order to leap. Nail realized that it might have been like this if he had gone first to the chair: watching Nail get electrocuted might have made it all that much harder for Ernest. Here Nail only wanted to show him how it was done. But was he leading the boy to attempt an act beyond his strength and ability?

Nail wanted to pray. But he did not. He heard the trees praying for him. Out there, beyond The Walls, they were all over: real trees, saplings and old ones, hickories, oaks, scrub pine and white pine, blackjack, all kinds of trees crooning to Ernest the song to get him out to that pole and down to the ground.

The singing stopped. Light shone on Ernest. The tower guards had obtained lanterns. "THERE HE IS!" a guard yelled, and another guard yelled, "HOLD THAT LIGHT STEADY AND LET ME GIT A SHOT AT HIM!"

"Jump!" Nail yelled up at the boy. "For godsakes, jump and grab the pole!"

Ernest flexed his knees once again and sprang out for all he was worth.

For *more* than he was worth: he jumped much too hard and almost caused the pole to bend with the force of his body slamming into it, stunning himself so brutally that he could only make the most clumsy grabs at the pole with his hands before he fell the forty feet to the ground, flat out.

Nail knelt quickly beside him. Ernest moaned. He was alive and conscious. Nail smelled something and realized it was the mustard oil: Ernest's fall had broken the bottle. "Can you move?" Nail asked, and tried to get him to sit up or roll over.

Ernest shook his head and groaned weakly, "I reckon I've done busted ever bone in my body." Nail tugged at his arm. "Ouch! Naw, I caint move. I've had it, Nail. You git on. Git on out of here."

Nail fished the bottle of mustard oil out of the waistband at the side of Ernest's trousers. The bottle was only cracked, and there was a good bit of oil left. He began smearing it on Ernest. "I'll rub this stuff on ye so the dogs caint smell ye, and I'll drag ye off in the woods and—"

"You aint got time!" Ernest protested. "Please, Nail, git yoreself out of yere while ye still got a chanst!"

"I caint jist leave ye!" Nail told him.

"The hell ye caint! You'd be a damn fool not to. You'd regret it all the rest of the days they'd keep ye back in those walls before they fried ye! Go, goddamn ye, git and *go*!"

Nail heard the warden's bloodhounds, who already knew Ernest's scent, being taken out of their pens. Nail said, "I shore hate this."

"Don't make me baig again," Ernest begged. "Jist go."

Nail began to smear the mustard oil on his shoes and legs and arms and hands. Then it was all gone. "Ernest . . ." He tried to say some last words.

Then the lanterns of the tower guards found them, and he heard a guard yell, "THERE HE IS! THERE'S *TWO* OF THEM!"

"*Go*," Ernest said, weakly. "Go, go, go on and go."

"Good-bye, son," Nail said. "Somebody will take care of you." Then he sprang up and began running.

He heard the rifles firing. Were they shooting at Ernest? Would they kill a fallen boy?

In the dark, Nail could not keep running. It had been a long time since he had taken a good walk, and much longer since he had run. The dogs would be able to outrun him because they could see much better in the dark. But finding Ernest would slow them down. He hoped the guards handling the dogs would stop them before they started into gnawing on Ernest . . . if they hadn't already shot him.

Nail paused at the edge of the swamp to catch his breath and listen. He heard the dogs behind him, in the distance, trying to find his trail. He had so much mustard oil on him they couldn't possibly sniff him out unless the scent of him in the night vapors was enough to give them a lead. He turned and skirted the edge of the swamp and began looking for the sycamore tree. He hoped he was pointed in the right direction, to the southwest of The Walls. He could still see the penitentiary looming high on its knoll in the distance, and he saw how the ground dropped off sharply on every side. That was why the goddamn ladder hadn't reached.

If he could find the sycamore and get that revolver loaded (or maybe she had already loaded it for him), he could shoot those dogs if any of them traced him, and shoot any man who tried to come after them. He plunged onward, and in the dark he could not keep the edge of the swamp clearly in view. He made a misstep and suddenly found himself up to his waist in water. For a moment the shock of the water took his breath away, but then he laughed, because it was the first time he'd been in water since his arrest nearly a year ago. This was his first bath in ages, and he loved deep water. He splashed briefly and then swam hard and fast until he reached the opposite bank of the swamp, and climbed up, and found himself within view of the tall sycamore tree splashing the sky with its fingers, shaking its dark-green mane.

He shook the water from himself; he was wet all over but would soon be in dry clothes. He was concerned that the water might have washed away the mustard oil, but a deep breath told him he still stank of it. He wanted to run up and hug that tree. So he did.

Viridis had told him there was only one tree in the vicinity; this one certainly dominated all the others around it, and at its foot he found the flat rock she had described to him: an ideal place for hiding something. But nothing was underneath it, and his groping did not discover any other flat rock nearby. Nail heard the dogs—running closer, he thought—and the distant voices of men.

Abruptly he remembered that this was Friday night, and Viridis had not planned to hide the cache until Saturday afternoon. If this had been Saturday night, he might not be alive. He was alive, but there was no cache: no canvas bag, no gun, no food, no money. He thought how hard it was going to be without those things that Viridis had meant for him to have. Would all of his planning, and all of hers, come to nothing?

Nail ran on. Or stumbled on; his wet trousers and debilitated condition kept him from running. He had a sense of direction. The sycamore tree was southwest of the penitentiary, but his destination was to the northwest. He veered. As he struggled onward, around the edges of other swamps, through some of them, getting wet again, he kept pressing to his right, turning slightly without, he hoped, starting a great circle that would take him right back where he came from. Eventually he came out on the cement of the Hot Springs highway, one of the first paved roads in that part of the county, and far up it he could see the headlights of automobiles approaching from the penitentiary road.

Quickly he crossed over the road and found himself in a lumberyard, among stack after stack of sawed and kilned boards. He remembered that many of the men in the barracks were sent out to work in this lumberyard and came back to the barracks smelling of the same fresh-cut wood that now surrounded him. He realized that all these boards had recently been trees in the forests, and those trees had died and stopped singing to make these piles of wood. Or maybe they had not stopped singing: maybe these piney, pitchy, turpentiney fragrances were the continuing song of the trees, who never died as long as they could still broadcast their odors. He moved among the stacks, finding himself in a labyrinth of lumber. The butchered trees imprisoned him. He hadn't helped fell them or cut them, but now they menaced him and would not let him out. He thought of turning back to the highway, but the sound of the automobiles kept him from even turning that way in his frantic threading of the maze. It seemed to take forever to reach the back side of the lumberyard, where he broke free from the stacks of boards and found a high wire fence. He couldn't get a toehold in the links of the fence to climb it. If he followed the fence, he would probably come back to the highway, where the cars patrolled. He gathered up some boards of different lengths and leaned them lengthwise against the fence, their butt-ends forming steps for his feet to get him to the top, where he threw a leg over and hauled himself up, and then fell blindly into the darkness beyond. The top of the fence was not barbed, but the sharp ends of the meshed wire snagged and ripped his clothes, and cut a gash the length of his trouser leg, which left him lightly bleeding.

From the fashioned timber of the lumberyard he plunged into a wild, virginal forest on hills that dipped and rose for several miles northward to the Arkansas River. Along the south shore of that river ran the tracks of the Rock Island Railroad, almost parallel to the Iron Mountain tracks on the north shore that Viridis had taken. The Rock Island tracks were his immediate destination: if he could reach them and get aboard a freight train and ride westward as far as Ola or Danville, he'd then be in a position to head north toward a crossing of the river that would get him to the vicinity of either Russellville or Clarksville, jumping-off places for Newton County.

For now, he had this forest to get through. He was already tired enough to drop, and growing hungry, and thirsty almost enough to risk drinking stream water, but although he found and crossed several rivulets and a creek, he would not risk drinking any water he could not see. Unless it was a spring and he could tell just from its feel or sound that it gushed or oozed directly from underground, he would not drink running water, let alone the still water of the swampy places.

Toward the first light of morning, when he figured he must have covered at least eight miles from the penitentiary, and no longer heard any automobiles or dogs or other sounds save the nocturnal soughing of the forest itself, his thirst drove him to dig an Indian well. It would slow him down, but he needed it badly. Near a still pond of water, downhill from it, using a piece of jagged sandstone for a shovel, he excavated a hole about two feet across, until the water began to seep in slowly from the pond. With the scoops of his hands he bailed it out. He let it fill again. He bailed it out again. The third time it filled, and had settled for a few minutes, it was full of filtered water, safe for drinking and for washing his bloody leg. His pants and shirt were still soaked, but he couldn't tell, and didn't care, if they were still wet from his plunge in the swamp or from his sweat or from both. He took them off, along with his underwear and his socks, the white cotton ones Viridis had given him. Naked, he dunked his clothes into the hole of water and stirred them around and squeezed them and dunked them again and took them out and wrung them, then hung them over a limb where the morning sun would hit them.

The sun rose about 4:30. A little over eight hours before, he had been a prisoner. Now he was free, and with his thirst slaked and his clothes washed, he began to appreciate his freedom for the first time. Naked, he did a little jig. He laughed. The morning birds watched him oddly. "Howdy,

Mr. Sun!" he yelled, and heard his echo off in the woods. He was in a glade, and remembered my letter, and yelled aloud, "I'm glad!" but then he told himself to shut up, even if there was nobody to hear him or see him cavorting naked in the sunshine. He jumped into the pond and scrubbed himself, although without soap there was no way he could get all the mustard oil off his skin.

He gave his clothes a couple of hours to dry in the sunshine while he wandered around looking for something to eat. He was hungry enough to eat dandelions, and he did. But he also found a small stream, and from beneath its rocks he picked crawfish, then cracked open their tails and peeled them and ate them raw. It was the first fish he'd had in over a year and the first crawfish he'd ever eaten, cooked or raw; between that and the dandelion salad, he decided, he'd had an elegant little breakfast. And that filtered pond water was as good a beverage as any he could remember.

His clothes weren't quite dry, but he put them back on and resumed his journey. Coming down out of the forest, he saw a house in the clearing and skirted it, but came to another house in a clearing beside a road and had to stay out of scent-range of whatever dogs were there. As near as I can figure by studying maps, he was approaching the Twelfth Street Pike, which today they call Kanis Road, due west of Little Rock. That part of it even today isn't yet developed, and back then you'd scarcely believe that this rural scene was just about seven miles, as the crow flies, from the bed where Governor George W. Hays was sleeping. When Nail crossed the road, he neither saw nor heard anything coming. People were having breakfast; the odors of coffee and cooking bacon drifted to him and renewed his hunger. But the odor of him drifted to their watchdogs and started them barking. On the other side of the pike he entered another woodland and saw no more houses for another two hours of hiking.

The sun was well up in the sky before he came to another road. There was a small village that still bears on maps the name it had then, Ivesville, and he emerged from the woods to the west of it, saw it in the distance, and kept away from it as he approached that last highway he would have to cross before reaching the railroad tracks. Beyond the road on the horizon he could see the bulk of the volcano-like hill that is called Pinnacle Mountain. This road was traveled. He crouched in a ditch behind tall weeds to watch a wagon and team of horses going by, a farmer taking his family to Saturday market. An auto came along, and he stayed crouched down. The car was an open Ford, filled with city folks heading for the country. He waited until it was completely out of sight before he rose up. But then, from the direction the car had disappeared, a horse and rider approached at full gallop. He ducked down into the ditch again and hid and waited. The horse, a great roan mare, came into view; the horseman was wearing riding-breeches and whipping the mare's hind end with a riding-crop . . . but as they came abreast of Nail, he saw that it wasn't a horseman but a horsewoman, her red hair blowing out behind. Nail stood up abruptly and wondered if he was dreaming: it was Viridis! Horse and rider flew on past, toward the city.

He leaped out of the ditch. "VIRIDIS!" he hollered after her. He stood in the road and waved his arms. Horse and rider disappeared into the distance. He wanted to run after them but knew he couldn't run. "VIRIDIS!" he called once more, but the noise of the horse's hooves had deafened her.

What was she doing out here? Looking for him? If so, why hadn't she been *looking*? She had been staring straight ahead, as if in a big hurry to get somewhere . . . or as if being pursued. Nail looked in the direction from which she had come, the west, to see if anybody was coming after her, but the road remained empty for a long time, and finally he crossed it.

He was almost certain it had been her. If she knew, as she ought to, that he was on the loose, and she was searching for him, why hadn't she *looked*? No, he decided: just as she hadn't known he was escaping Friday instead of Saturday, and thus had left nothing under the sycamore tree, she still did not know he was free. He knew that she took that mare of hers—what was her name? yes, Rosabone—she took Rosabone for rides out to Pinnacle Mountain. If only he had recognized her an instant sooner.

Soon enough he reached the tracks of the Rock Island, and followed them westward to a place where they began a curve and upward grade. There was a trestle across a small creek (my map calls it Isom Creek, flowing into the Little Maumelle River), and Nail sat beneath the trestle and waited patiently. Large fish lost their fear of him and swam within his view. He could have grabbed one with his hand, or flung it onto the bank, but he had no way to cook it and wasn't about to eat raw bass. Noon came. He broke off several cattail spikes and ate them; he'd had them before and knew they were as good as wild asparagus, or better, raw. At a place along the creek bank where a spring flowed into the creek and he could easily separate the pure water from the creek water, he scooped up enough to wash down the cattails. While drinking, he heard the train coming.

Slowed by the curve and the upgrade, it was a long freight consisting almost entirely of empty gravel hoppers open to the sky. The first dozen hoppers went by before he decided that no open boxcars were coming. In a burst of energy he ran alongside the train, trying to match its speed, then grabbed on to a hopper's ladder and climbed up. The empty gravel hopper had high metal sides and a bottom that sloped toward the center, where Nail saw a chute for unloading the gravel and a metal beam broad enough to sit on. He hopped down and gripped the beam tight with both hands, as if he were riding a bucking horse; his knuckles stayed white and his hands grew tired.

The rough ride lasted less than a hour before the train stopped. Nail stood up on the beam and could just see over the side. A water tank loomed ahead down the tracks, but the train had not stopped for water. A sign beside the tracks read simply HOUSTON, and Nail remembered that the famous man had been an Arkansawyer before he went to Texas. Three men were walking down the track from one direction, and the brakeman was coming to meet them.

Nail ducked back down and heard a conversation:

"Seen any riders?"

"Aint looked for none."

"What's in these cars?"

"They're empty. Caint you tell?"

"Wouldn't be somebody ridin one of those empties?"

"Take a look if you want. You huntin hoboes?"

"Fuck hoboes. We're huntin for a man escaped the pen last night."

"Any reward on him?"

"A hunderd dollars."

"Jesus! I'll help you look myself, but there's sixty-three empties on this train. Take you all day to climb up and look into each one of 'em."

"Tell you what. See that water tower up yonder? We'll just climb up on that, and y'all drive under real slow, and we'll look into each of the cars that way, and if we see anybody, we'll wave you down."

The voices stopped. Nail cautiously raised his eyes above the side of the car. The brakeman was heading for the caboose, and the three men were going the other way, toward the water tank. Soon the engine puffed steam and the train lurched and began to move. Nail climbed over the opposite side of the car, hung from the ladder for a moment, watching the tracks in both directions, then jumped down to the roadbed and tumbled into a ditch. He clambered into a stand of weeds and crawled low a good distance from the tracks before he stood up and got as far away from them as he could.

But he continued in the direction of the tracks, because it was a generally northwestward course and that was his inclination. He hiked up through Copperas Gap, keeping the tracks in view, but when he reached the point where they veered sharply westward, he began to think that he ought to abandon his plan to take the train part of the way home. And his sense of direction, which kept wanting to turn north toward home, disliked the train's westerly course. He wanted to get across the Arkansas River and up into the Ozarks. Once in the Ozarks, even the foothills, he would feel as if he were back in his own country, and that would give him strength to walk another week, if need be, to reach Stay More.

Just to the north of Copperas Gap is a place where the Arkansas River, plunging southward and running into a mountain, narrows dramatically and bends eastward. It is one of the river's narrowest passages in Arkansas, and it was there, probably, that Nail decided to cross.

In trying to find that spot on my map, I was astonished to discover something very strange: that the hamlet, or settlement, or maybe just a riverbank landing, on the north shore of the Arkansas River, where the current would take him or his body after his attempted crossing at Copperas Gap, was named Nail. Yes, that's what the map said. Now, from my years as postmistress of Stay More and my many dealings with the Post Office Department, I know that two towns of the same name in the same state can't both keep their name very long, and that we already had a town named Nail in Newton County, although in that year, 1915, it wasn't a post office yet and wasn't shown on that same map that showed Nail as a town in the southern part of Conway County, due south of Plumerville, on the Arkansas River. I doubt very much there's anything left of *that* Nail now, but it was there then. And that's more or less where Nail was headed. Maybe it had been founded by distant kinsmen of his. And maybe it had already passed into oblivion, being one of those river towns, like storied Cadron downstream and legendary Spadra upstream, which had once been busy but were now dead. Or maybe, I sometimes think, it existed only as a locale on a map, a name just to show me that this was where Nail would have landed.

He stood on the south bank and measured the river's breadth with his eye, its narrowness at this point compared with its broadening expanse downstream. Just recently, in late May, the river had flooded severely, and now, in June, although the water level had dropped and the banks were more or less back in their original locations, the river was still wide and swift and roiling brown, cluttered with debris.

But Nail was an excellent swimmer. He had swum the Buffalo several times when that wilderness river was at its worst. On calmer pools he had raced his brothers and the friends of his youth, and had never lost. He could swim better and faster on his back than most people could on their bellies. He could swim in the pitch dark . . . although it was still before sundown when he entered the river. In fact, it was just about the time of day that Saturday they would have been coming to take him to another appointment with Old Sparky.

He was aware of this, and he knew that if that had happened, with just him against all of them, his chances would have been slight. Now it was just him against the river, and he was free and proud. Oh, he was foolhardy too, and hungry and tired and weak. And he did not know that no man, however good a swimmer, had ever swum the Arkansas at Copperas Gap when it was as swift as this.

But he was almost sure he could swim that river.

off

When she decided to take Rosabone for that run out to Pinnacle, it was to prepare the both of them for a return to Stay More. And her insomnia had been worse than any night since that night before the governor was going to let her (or make her, he thought) get into Nail's cell. She needlessly rose from bed more than once and climbed up to her studio to recheck the contents of the canvas bag she had prepared for Nail and Ernest, to make sure she had remembered it all and to try to determine if anything else might come in handy. What if they needed a compass? How about a few yards of mosquito netting? Maybe a bar of soap? Could they use some salt and pepper casters? A pocket watch? At one point in the wee hours she suddenly realized that she *had* forgotten an important item: *matches*! They would need to build a fire, if not to keep warm, to cook. She tiptoed downstairs to the kitchen and wrapped a handful of sulphur matches in oilcloth and added them to the other items in the canvas bag, which once again she inspected and checked off her list. Maybe she ought to include a box of raisins. Did Nail and Ernest like raisins?

At sunrise she gave up brooding about the contents of the canvas bag and realized that it would be useless to try to sleep any longer. She got up and dressed, almost automatically donning her riding habit without realizing that was what she intended to do: take Rosabone out to Pinnacle and back. She did not bother with breakfast. She took a few of her own cookies from the cookie jar and an apple for Rosabone.

She rode hard out and harder coming back. "We've got to get in shape, Rose girl," she explained to the horse. "We're going back to Stay More. You liked it there, didn't you? Well, we're going back again in just a few more days."

Usually when she rode out to Pinnacle, she would rest the mare and herself at the foot of the mountain for a while before returning to town. She told herself this time to take it easy, that she wouldn't need to start for the sycamore southwest of the penitentiary until midafternoon at the earliest, but she was too impatient and eager. If nothing else, she could spend the rest of the day finishing her letter to Nail, which she would enclose in the canvas bag, even if it was already too long and, she feared, too candid.

She scarcely gave Rosabone time to dry her sweat before heading back for town. More than once she met or passed an auto painted with the insignia of the Pulaski County Sheriff or the Little Rock Police, and more than once an officer waved at her; one time a deputy honked his horn at her before waving. They all grinned as if they would like to give chase but had more important things to do. She did not think there was anything unusual about so many lawmen being on the roads on Saturday morning, but later she would remember them.

When she returned to her house, her father was sitting on the porch in his favorite wicker chair, reading the *Gazette*, as he always did Saturdays and Sundays. He motioned her to sit in the wicker chair next to his, but she said, "No, thank you, Daddy. I've got an awful lot to do today."

"Meeting someone?" he asked.

"No," she said. "I'm not meeting anyone."

"Are you sure?" he asked, and then he turned the paper so that she could see the front page. There was her original drawing of Nail, with his head shaved for his first appointment with the chair, with a caption: NOTED CONVICT WHO MADE ESCAPE. Her eyes shifted to the headline to the left of it: NAIL CHISM SCALES WALLS AT 'PEN' AND ESCAPES. Viridis snatched the paper out of her father's hands and sat down with it in the other wicker chair.

There were no fewer than four subheadlines, one right under the other: NOTED NEWTON COUNTY MAN, CONVICTED RAPIST PREPARED THREE TIMES FOR ELECTRIC CHAIR, TAKES FRENCH LEAVE, and the second one: ACCOMPLICE IN ESCAPE, YOUNG BODENHAMMER, THWARTED AND CAUGHT, and the third one: $100 REWARD OFFERED FOR CHISM'S RECAPTURE, and the fourth one: NEWTON COUNTY ALERTED; FULL MANHUNT PROMISED.

The accompanying story pointed out that Nail Chism was only the second man ever to escape from The Walls since it was erected; but the first one, J. F. McCabe, had made his escape long before the recent "improvements" that had supposedly rendered the prison escape-proof.

The article even carried a reference to her, not by name, in its fifth paragraph: "A Little Rock woman who had conducted a long campaign to liberate Chism, whom she felt had been unjustly accused of the crime, will be sought for questioning later today by the sheriff's office."

"Well, thanks for warning me!" Viridis said aloud.

"I wasn't warning you," her father protested. "That story has already done it."

"I was talking to the story," Viridis said. She resumed listening to it; it told her that Ernest Bodenhammer was in St. Vincent's Infirmary, where doctors had been required to place most of his body in a plaster cast. It was feared that he might be permanently paralyzed, although his neck was not broken. Apparently, he had sustained his injuries in an attempt to imitate Chism's successful leap from the top of the prison wall to a power pole. While Chism had evidently slid down the pole to freedom, the youth, only sixteen, had missed the jump and fallen to the ground.

"Oh, *damn!*" Viridis said.

"Where are you meeting him?" her father asked.

"St. Vincent's Infirmary," Viridis answered.

"Not *him*," her father said. "Not the boy. Aren't you meeting the man somewhere today? Or is it the boy you're really interested in?"

"Daddy, listen, I've got to—" she started to tell her father, but they were interrupted. Two autos pulled to a stop in front of the Monday house. The first one contained two men she recognized, Sheriff Bill Hutton and Warden T. D. Yeager, and the second one carried one man she recognized, a reporter from the *Gazette*.

These men, followed by several others, climbed the high front yard and the high porch of the Monday mansion. The sheriff spoke first: "Good morning, ma'am, and Mr. Monday. I see y'all have done already read the paper." Neither of them responded, although her father nodded when the sheriff said to him, "We've got to ask the young lady a few questions, if it's okay with you."

They asked her more than a few questions. But she maintained, truthfully, that she had not expected Nail Chism's escape. Of course she felt that his conviction and incarceration were wrongful, and he certainly *deserved* to be out of prison, but she knew nothing about his escape other than what she had just this moment read in the newspaper. She was aware that he had been imprisoned and tormented by the threat of death as long as he could stand it, so she could certainly understand how he might be desperate for freedom on the eve of an unprecedented *fourth* attempt at executing him; but still, his escape came as a total surprise to her.

"You have no idea where he might of could gone?" the sheriff asked.

"Your guess is as good as mine," she said.

"Ma'am, *my* guess," the sheriff said, "is that you just might be hiding him up in your house somewheres. Mind if we look?" He addressed this question to her father, not to her.

And her father, bless his heart, said, "No, but you will have to get yourselves a search warrant to go into my house."

"We done already thought of that, sir," the sheriff said, pulling the search warrant out of his hip pocket and showing it to her father and then to her. She felt some panic. Would they find the canvas bag? Or, for all she knew, maybe they would find Nail: maybe he had reconsidered her offer to hide him in her attic and had already hidden himself up there. She did not want these men to go into her house. The sheriff looked at her again and said, "If you'll just lead the way, ma'am."

Her mother and Cyrilla and Dorinda were having breakfast in the kitchen, and the servants, Ruby and Sam, were also there, and the lawmen just said, "Excuse us," and went in and out of the kitchen quickly, and spent little time on the first floor of the house before heading for the stairs. They gave only a perfunctory search to the bedrooms and closets of the second floor before the sheriff asked her father, "Where do those doors go?" Her father explained that one door led to the attic storeroom, and the other two led to the south turret playroom and the north turret, where Viridis had her studio. The sheriff instructed his deputies to split up and try all three doors. He himself would accompany her up the north turret stairs, to her studio.

There were no closets or cubbies or hiding-places in her studio. Just her easels and her supplies and the cabinet in which she kept her drawings, its flat drawers much too narrow to conceal anybody, but the sheriff pulled them out anyway, one by one, and asked, "What's all this stuff?"

"Do you mind?" she said, not answering him. "You won't find Nail Chism in there."

The sheriff moved around the room, looking at its contents; he studied her most recent painting on its easel, a winter landscape of Stay More done from her sketches. She expected him to ask her if that was the village of Stay More, but apparently he did not recognize it as a village or as a landscape. His glance moved onward and came to rest upon the canvas bag, loosely closed atop her table. He picked it up, hefted it, asked, "Mind if I look in this?" and started to open it.

She did not have to lose her temper; it lost itself. "Sheriff Hutton! You

have a warrant to search for a man, not to pry into my personal effects!"
She lowered her voice: "Especially not items of . . . of feminine hygiene."

"Of which? *Oh.*" The sheriff blushed and gingerly replaced the bag.
"Sorry," he said. He moved on around the room. "Never can tell," he said.
He headed for the stairs and went back down.

As the men were leaving the house, having satisfied themselves that she
was not hiding Nail Chism, Warden Yeager said to her, "You'll let us
know hee hee if you run acrost his pawmarks hee hee, won't you?"

"Don't count on it hee hee," she said.

The warden gave her a wounded look as if she had failed to return a
favor. Come to think of it, she realized after the men were gone, she had.

They would not let her see Ernest at St. Vincent's. She had to wait at
the hospital and speak with the mother superior to request permission and
explain that, while not related to Ernest Bodenhammer, she was the only
person who had visited him regularly in the penitentiary. The mother
superior was kind and considerate but had to inform Viridis that Ernest
was under guard and also under heavy sedation. Possibly, Viridis could
see him tomorrow, but she would need written permission from Warden
T. D. Yeager.

All the rest of that day she stayed in the newsrooms of the *Gazette*. If
any word came in of Nail's having been spotted or recaptured, or anything
at all, she could learn it faster in the newspaper office. Tom Fletcher did
not mind her being there, but he advised her that several days might pass
before any news developed.

And he was right. Many days would pass before she heard the first
rumor that any trace of Nail had been seen, and even that would turn out
to be a false lead. She was impatient to get on to Newton County and wait
for him there. She had anticipated, when she planned to leave the canvas
bag for him, departing Little Rock herself within a few days to go back to
Stay More. She had been in correspondence with both me and the old
woman in the Jacob Ingledew house who had been her friend and hostess
during her previous visit to Stay More.

I had kept her informed of the swelling local sentiment against Judge
Sewell Jerram and his gang. Strangely, his crony Judge Lincoln Villines
remained popular enough to be touted as a possible candidate for governor
(only in the event his friend George Hays chose not to seek reelection),
but Sull himself was so unwelcome that a joke went the rounds about his

having to pay Duster Snow time-and-a-half overtime wages to serve as his personal bodyguard. The good sheriff we'd had before Snow, W. J. Pruitt, had let everybody know that he intended to oppose Snow in the November election, and almost everybody planned to vote for him.

Viridis had written me to ask if I thought it was safe for Dorinda to return home. The school term in Little Rock had already come to a close when Nail escaped, and Dorinda was honestly homesick, or that's what Viridis said; I had sort of been hoping that Rindy herself might write and tell me how much she missed us, but I suppose her penmanship lessons hadn't got that far. I had told Viridis, after asking the advice of my parents, Rindy's parents, and even John Ingledew, that Sull would have killed Rindy by now to silence her if he was ever going to do it; besides, the man was smart enough to realize that the point had long since passed beyond which her silence meant anything at all. He probably wished she did not exist and wished even more that she had never existed, but there wasn't much likelihood he would be any further threat to her. Bring her home, I said.

Now Viridis was ready to do just that. She had taken Rindy out and bought her a fancy suitcase to take all of her nice new clothes and belongings back home with her. She did not intend to return Rindy to Stay More by the same means she had taken her out: riding double on Rosabone. No, she was going to arrange for a wagon in Pettigrew to meet their train and take them and their luggage (she was bringing more than one trunk herself, and hatboxes), with Rosabone tied behind, the miles across the mountains to Stay More.

I knew she was coming. But I did not know that Nail had escaped. That news didn't reach us at all until the following Thursday, when we read it in the local newspaper. On the second page of the *Jasper Disaster*, under a small headline, NAIL CHISM MAKES HIS ESCAPE, was a brief condensation of the same story that had appeared in the *Gazette* five days before, now stale and unstirring. Remember, we had no telephones in Newton County, no electricity; all we had was the U.S. Mail, which wasn't even the Pony Express. Later Viridis would apologize for not having written us a letter, which would have arrived several days before the newspaper. She had been too busy to think of it.

She was busy trying to get in to see Ernest without written permission from T. D. Yeager, who at that point wouldn't have given her permission to breathe. On the third day after Nail's escape, Tom Fletcher "smuggled" her into Ernest's room as a *Gazette* reporter, and she was permitted to "interview" the boy for half an hour. He was awake and fairly cheerful, all things considered: all things such as having nearly every bone in his body broken: compound fractures of both arms and one leg, eight broken ribs, six broken fingers, a cracked pelvis, and a dislocated hip. Miraculously, his whole spinal column from neck to tailbone remained undamaged, and he would not be permanently paralyzed, as had been feared at first, although at the moment, and for the next six weeks, he wouldn't be going anywhere, not even back to the penitentiary.

He enjoyed pretending it was a real interview. "Yeah, quote me as sayin these yere nuns feed me real good; I aint et like this in my whole life."

"Mr. Bodenhammer," asked the lady reporter, Viridis, "did Mr. Chism say anything to you about your intended destination?"

"Nome, he never. Tell ye the truth, I never even give it no thought whereabouts I was goin myself. I didn't aim to light out for Newton County, whar he was a-fixin to go, but I never thought none about goin back home to Stone County neither. I aint got no friends up in them parts."

"Did he say anything at all to you about his intended route to Newton County? Where and how did he plan to cross the Arkansas River?"

"Ma'am, he never hardly said a thing to me about nothin. I didn't even know we was breakin out until you—until that there other lady who is his ladyfriend, she told me to be ready. But from the time he come down to git me out of my cell, until we said our good-byes, we never said nothin much atall."

"I can't imagine Nail Chism abandoning you like that," she said.

"Aw, *hell*, Viridis, I mean, Miss Ma'am, he never *abandoned* me! I made him do it. I tole him to. It was hopeless, the way I'd done botched up my chance and fell forty feet, a-hittin that pole, and there wasn't nothin he could do for me. Hell, I had to baig him to save his own skin and leave me alone."

She put her hand on his cheek, which reporters don't do. She left it there as she said, "I'm so sorry you didn't get to go with him."

"Look at the good side of it," he said. "I was sposed to die Sattidy night, and I'm still alive. People are takin real good keer of me, and I don't hurt too bad."

"You won't be able to draw again for a while," she observed.

He wiggled the four fingers of his left hand that were not bound in splints or casts. "Didn't you know I was left-handed?" he said. "I still got some fingers I can draw with."

"I'll see to it you get some materials," she said. "I'll arrange for you to get all you need to keep on drawing." She paused. "I'd bring them to you myself, but I . . ."

He finished it for her, nodding his head to say yes, he knew. "You're takin off for Newton County," he said quietly.

She raised her chin into a modest nod. And then she did something that reporters don't even think of doing: she bent down and kissed him lightly on the mouth.

"You'uns live happy ever after," he said.

"You too" was all she could say.

Taking leave of her father was not quite as easy: he insisted on going with them to the train station. When she protested, he observed that from the looks of all the luggage she was taking with her, she intended to stay for quite some time.

"I'll be back," she said.

"But I doubt *she* will," he said, indicating Dorinda. "I'd just appreciate the honor of seeing you two ladies off."

So he went with them to the station. Viridis had made arrangements to have Rosabone transported on the same train, which would involve two transfers: one at Van Buren, from the Iron Mountain to the Frisco, and another, at Fayetteville, to the Frisco's spur toward Pettigrew. Cyril Monday took the morning off from his job at the bank to see them catch their train.

At the station he drew her apart from Dorinda for a moment to ask, "You got all the money you need?"

What kind of question was that? For several years now, since her return from Europe, she had not been required to depend upon her father for any assistance beyond a place to live. "Enough," she said.

"Never can tell what emergencies might come up," he said. "My daddy always told me, you never know when you might meet some fellow selling two elephants for a nickel."

She remembered Tom Fletcher's old jokes about elephants in the Ozarks. This time Tom Fletcher hadn't made any jokes, except one, of sorts: if she ever wanted to write a column called "An Arkansawyer in Stay More," he had told her, he would pay their usual rate for it. When she had only smiled, not laughed, he had prompted, "It's nearly as remote as Yokohama to me." She had told him he ought to visit her there sometime.

She told her father, "Thank you, Daddy, I've got all I need."

"Just never can tell," he said. "Here," and he thrust a roll of bills into her hand. "Put this in your purse and forget about it until you need it." She tried to protest, but he touched his finger to her lips. "Better take it now instead of having to ask me for it later, when I might be in a bad mood."

He had a point there. She put the thick roll of bills into her purse. "You're sweet," she said.

"I hope you'll remember me that way," he requested. And he had one other request: "Cyrilla wanted me to ask you, she said she couldn't ask you yourself, but if it's okay with you and you don't think you'll need it anymore, can she have that studio of yours up in the north tower?"

Viridis raised her eyebrows. "Does she want to take up art?"

"Sewing. She wants me to buy her a sewing machine."

Viridis smiled. "None of y'all expect me to come back, do you?"

"From the looks of it, no," her father said, and then he moved back to where Dorinda stood, to tell the girl that he had enjoyed having her stay at his house and was sorry they hadn't got better acquainted. He wished her a pleasant trip and good luck and a long and happy life.

"BOART!" hollered the conductor, and the three said their good-byes and exchanged hugs.

Viridis Monday left Little Rock.

———

Take any day in June in Stay More. School's been out awhile, Mr. Perry the schoolteacher has left town to find a summer job in Harrison, the crops have been planted and are growing, nothing is ready to harvest yet except the snap beans and first spinach, nobody is really busy except the men cutting the hay and the timberjacks who keep on logging into ever more remote stands of the white oak forests.

My father never lost a chance to tell us girls that when school let out he expected us to help more on the farm, but every year school let out and he couldn't seem to find enough to keep us busy. He complained to Ma and anybody else who would listen that if he'd only had him just *one* boy to help around the place, instead of all three of us worthless girls, he might be able to turn the farm into a cash proposition. As it was, he could only raise enough to feed us. We weren't starving, not by any means, but we never had any cash money.

As the youngest of the three unwanted girls, I felt least wanted, so I tried hardest to help out around the place. While Barb and Mandy wouldn't have been caught dead doing a lick of work outside the walls of the house itself, I got myself the job of tending the garden patch. I wouldn't let a weed grow loose in that garden patch, and I spent a good bit of my summer out there in the broiling sun, underneath my sunbonnet but my dress all soaked through with sweat. I was pretty young when I discovered something important about the way the brain works: your thoughts are always better, more interesting, more lively, while you're working than while you're just sitting. I knew that the worst part of Nail Chism's experience in the penitentiary was all the hours he had to do his thinking just sitting or lying around: the thoughts he had in those times must have been drab shades of gray.

Take any day in late June in Stay More and it's apt to be real hot. Generally, I'd try to get my garden work done right after sunup, without even waiting for breakfast. There would still be dew glistening on the vines and sogging the greens. The dog Rouser would trot behind me out to the garden, which wasn't but as far as from here to there the other side of what passed for Paw's barn, and Rouser would just sit and watch me, or the morning birds, while I chopped weeds out of the garden. Then he would go with me afterward up in the holler behind our house, just a quarter-mile or so, to the falls. It wasn't really a waterfall; it didn't fall more than maybe five feet from the ledge to the pool; it was more of a cascade than a waterfall, but I called it the falls, and I was the only one in the family who used it. Barb and Mandy drew just enough water from the well to fill an oaken sitz tub about once a week, Saturday evening usually before they stepped out, and they'd share that water, Barb first because she was oldest and because she'd drawn the water, and stand, not sitz, in the tub and splash enough to get off the worst dirt and smells. But me, take an early morning in June in Stay More and you'd find me getting wet all over beneath my little waterfall up the holler. No, you'd not; because neither *you* nor anybody knew where I was, and I was stark naked and only a little bit uncomfortable that Rouser, who was watching me, was a male.

If anybody or anything had come along and spied on me, Rouser would've barked. He never did. And also, I took my .22 rifle with me, just in case. Not that I was afraid, being back up in that dark, mossy, woodsy holler. It was real cool after a couple hours of chopping weeds out of the garden patch, and the water that trickled over that ledge was almost cold.

Of course I never stood under that waterfall when I was having my monthlies. Everybody knew that would be a terrible thing to do, almost suicide. Anybody could tell you of a fool girl or two who had got tuberculosis or a stroke of paralysis from taking a bath at the wrong time of her month.

I have been called superstitious, but I know some things which have never been known to fail. This is not boasting but observation. There are plants that work wonders and always have for thousands of years. I never got chiggerbit, because I knew where the pennyroyal grew, and I rubbed it on my legs, and when the chiggers were chewing my sisters alive, they didn't bother me at all. Now, is that superstition?

Take the common mullein, which some folks call the velvet plant because of its velvety leaves, a shade of green so pale you'd think the plant was worthless. And it is, for most things; cows won't eat it, and although I've heard of some outlandish remedies concocted from the seeds, I've never known one that honestly works. The mullein stalk grows straight up, sometimes as tall as eight or nine feet. The yellow flowers are small and moderately ornamental, and I've known a few folks' yards where they let the mullein grow just for decoration.

In late June the mullein hasn't even started to flower, and at most it's just a few feet high, and inconspicuous, and totally worthless . . . except for this: if somebody, or something, is lost, you can name a mullein plant after him, her, or it, and then bend the stalk down to the ground. Likely, it will stay bent down. It will surely stay bent down and keep on growing that way if the lost person or the lost thing remains lost. But if that mullein stalk straightens back up, the lost will be found.

This never fails. At least, I have never known it to fail, and I have lost a lot of things: recovered some and never found the others.

Because somebody who has left Stay More is, in a way, "lost," the mullein is also good for letting you know if they are ever coming back. When I saw the first mullein of June that was tall enough to bend down, on my hike back up into the holler to my bathing-place, I named it Viridis and bent it down. Not too long after that, another mullein started growing tall right near it. I bent that one down too, after naming it Nail.

Each morning, after two or three sweaty hours in the garden, I would hike up to the waterfall to clean up, and I would pause to notice that both mullein stalks were still bent down. I would greet them and tell them I hoped they would straighten up.

When I had bathed and put on a fresh dress, I would mosey on down into the village and hang around Ingledew's store at the time of morning when everybody was there to get their mail. I never got any mail, except from Viridis. But she never wrote to tell me exactly when she was coming.

The men would sit on the furniture of Ingledew's storeporch like it belonged to them. The women and girls would have to stand around, not on the porch but off to one side, or out in the road, or sometimes inside the store around the dry goods, which was an exciting place to be, especially after Willis Ingledew received a new shipment of bolts of cloth, clean and bright and smooth. Nothing smells better than fresh cloth. But while I enjoyed hanging around the dry-goods department, more often I stood outside off the edge of the porch near enough to the men to listen to their stories or their talk about current events. The main current event now was Nail's escape. How long would it take him to get home? There was no doubt in any man's mind that he was coming home; there were only two questions: how long did it take a feller to walk from Little Rock to Stay More if he was careful not to let himself get seen? and how soon after coming back to Stay More would Nail do something to Sull Jerram?

Every man was of the opinion that Nail would do *something* to Sull Jerram. If he didn't kill him, he'd mutilate him beyond recognition or something equally terrible, and Sull knew it, and the men who'd been to Jasper lately reported that Sull was . . . I thought they said "scared spitless" and figured they meant he was so frightened he couldn't work up enough saliva inside his mouth to take a decent spit, because a man in that predicament was practically unmanned. From my observation, every male human being above the age of twelve or thirteen had to be able to spit at least once every fifteen minutes or he risked being mistaken for a female.

I had to watch where I was standing when I eavesdropped on the porch loungers; I had to be ready to jump to one side quickly.

I told nobody about my mullein stalks. You don't ever tell, which would break the magic. Nobody in Stay More except me, and I suppose the old woman who lived at Jacob Ingledew's (although her house was directly across the road from Willis' store, she hardly ever crossed the road; I never saw her), knew that Viridis might return to Stay More any day now.

One morning in late June on my way to the waterfall after working in the garden, I paused to observe the two mullein stalks and noticed that one of them, the one I'd named Viridis, was behaving like a pecker ready for love. I was so excited I could scarcely take time to go on to the falls and take off all my clothes and get real wet. Later, on my way to the store, and at the store itself, I couldn't understand why all the rest of the world, except that mullein stalk, remained so normal and unexcited. It was a typical dull, slow morning in Stay More. The mail wagon came out from Jasper, and Willis Ingledew sorted the mail, and folks saw what they got and read it, or read it for those who couldn't read, and I didn't get anything, but I didn't *need* anything, because I knew she was coming!

And sure enough, she came! Mullein stalks are *never* wrong. That very morning, while we were all still there, in or on or around the Ingledew store, the twenty-odd porch regulars loafing in their chairs or on their kegs and keeping the dust of the road down with their spitting, ankle-deep in the shavings from their pocketknives, the children playing in the road without fear of traffic, for there was none, the women mostly inside around the dry goods, and myself leaning up against one of the posts that held up the corner of the porch roof, a slow-moving wagon came into view, coming not from Jasper but from the schoolhouse road that goes westward up the mountain toward Sidehill, Eden, and places beyond. There was an additional horse tied behind the wagon, trotting briskly. I think I recognized that horse, or mare, before I recognized the passengers in the wagon. I could tell by her gait. It was Rosabone.

I let out a yell. Everybody turned to stare at me briefly before returning their gazes toward the distantly approaching wagon. To the few who continued staring at me, I explained my outburst: "It's Viridis. She's here." Then I started running toward the wagon. I was barefoot, as I always am when the weather's warm, and the gravels of the road bit into my pounding feet, but I scarcely noticed. Rouser chased after me and commenced barking. Other dogs picked up his cry.

So there was a great hubbub as Viridis returned to Stay More. As soon as I started running, others followed me, not all of them running but moving as fast as they could to keep up with me. We didn't give the wagon a chance to arrive and stop at its destination, whatever its destination was: I still don't know whether Viridis had told the driver she wanted to go to Ingledew's store, the old woman's house, my house, or the Chisms', or the Whitters', or where. We stopped her right there in the road. Rindy jumped down from the wagon like she expected a big hug from all of us at once, but it was Viridis I hugged first, and then I hugged Rindy, and the way other people were hugging Viridis, she might have been kinfolks and long lost . . . or at least the heroine that all of us knew her to be.

Women were exclaiming, "Did ye ever!" and "I swan!" and "Lawsy sakes!" and men were saying, "I'll be a son of a gun!" and "Wal, dog my cats!" and "What d'ye know about that!"

Then all the commotion ceased as suddenly as it had begun, and it was absolutely silent for a time, so quiet you could hear the trees behind Willis' store whispering. Waymon Chism broke the silence by declaring, "He aint showed up yit." We all knew who "he" was.

Viridis had been smiling that great smile that made her mouth look so pretty, but now she frowned and bit her lip. Then she said, "Well." That's all that was said for a while by anybody, although they were all looking at one another and exchanging expressions. Then Viridis declared, "We'll just have to wait for him, won't we?" In response there was a chorus of men's and women's declarations: "He'll turn up" and "Give him time" and "Any day now" and "Shore as shootin" and "You bet ye" and "Shore thang."

Then came a dozen different offers from a dozen different women, my mother included, for Viridis to stay with them. They were all disappointed that she had already promised to stay, for the time being, at least tonight, with the old woman who lived in the Jacob Ingledew house right yonder. Men fought each other for the privilege of carrying her luggage to that house. Viridis paid the driver, a young man, or just a teenager actually, and thanked him for bringing them all that distance from Pettigrew.

As it turned out, the young driver, whose name was Virgil Tuttle, did not intend to turn around and head back to Pettigrew, not right away. It had taken them a night on the road to cover the distance (they had put up at a sort of hotel in Sidehill), and during the long trip and that night Dorinda had become real friendly with Virgil, or just Virge as she called him, and now he accepted her invitation to stay at least tonight, and maybe longer, at the Whitter cabin, where, before sleeping with two or more of

Rindy's brothers, he might be permitted to "sit up" with her. She was sweet on him, and I could see why: he was sightly and strong, and he could talk the hind foot off a mule.

He drove Rindy and her new suitcase on toward her house, with her mother riding in the back of the wagon to chaperone them, and I hung back to watch Viridis and the old woman at Jacob Ingledew's house greet each other and then disappear inside. One by one the other citizens of Stay More returned to their accustomed places in, on, or around Willis Ingledew's store, or they drifted on home for dinner. I was alone except for Rouser at the foot of the steps leading up to the porch of the big fine house where Viridis was staying with the old woman. I looked at it sadly, disappointed I'd scarcely had a chance to say more than hello to Viridis. But I figured she was tired and also wanted to visit with the old woman, who was her friend, after all, and had just as much claim to her as I did, or more.

But while I was standing there looking at the house, the door opened and Viridis reappeared, coming out on the porch and smiling at me. "I didn't mean to walk off from you like that," she said. "My hostess wants me to ask you if you would have a bite of dinner with us. Will you?"

"Gosh, *sure!*" was all I could say, and I joined them for dinner in the kitchen of the Jacob Ingledew house. I had never been inside of that house, and I was thrilled. Oh, in the years since then I've seen some finer houses in other places, and looking back I have to think that my world was awfully small that I would consider that house such a palace, when, by comparison with any good city house, it was just a country shack. But to me, then, going inside that house was like stepping into another world.

And both women treated me not as some child eavesdropping on their grown-up conversation but as an equal, almost. I was drawn into their talk as if I really was grown up and had something worth saying and worth listening to. The only times I felt a little left out were when the old woman and Viridis would refer to what had apparently been a lengthy correspondence between them, longer and more continuous than mine with Viridis. One of them would say, "As I mentioned in my last letter . . ." or "You'll recall when I wrote to you in early April . . ." or "But you said to me in your letter of May 15th . . ." and I couldn't help feeling a little jealous. But the more I thought about it, the more I felt I ought to consider myself privileged that such an intelligent and beautiful and heroic woman as

Viridis would have bothered to write to me at all, let alone as often and as lengthily as she had. And I got a chance, too, to throw in a couple of expressions like "Remember what you said to me in that letter about . . . ?"

We talked for most of the afternoon, and I suppose Rouser got tired of waiting for me to come back out of the house, and he went on home by himself. Finally Viridis looked back and forth between the old woman and me and asked the question that she had been putting off. "You don't suppose he might actually have come back but is hiding and doesn't want anybody to know he's here?"

I thought it was a kind of desperate question, as if she couldn't quite face the possibility that something had happened to keep him from coming home. After all, terrible as it was to contemplate, he *could* have drowned in the Arkansas River. Or he could have been recaptured, and we wouldn't know about it until the next week's issue of the Jasper newspaper. Or he could have changed his mind about coming home and gone to Colorado.

"Aw," I said. "If he was home, he'd of told his folks he was here."

"But what if," she asked, "what if he'd made them promise not to tell anyone else?"

That was possible, I considered. But I protested, "Waymon wouldn't have lied to *you* like that."

"With all of those people standing around?" Viridis said. "Maybe he couldn't take any chances that somebody he didn't want to hear it would hear it? Maybe he's waiting until he can tell me in private?"

The more she talked in that vein, the more desperate she sounded, so I wasn't surprised when finally she declared that she wanted to ride Rosabone up to the Chism place for a private talk with the Chisms. She changed from her dress into her jodhpurs and saddled Rosabone and rode off, telling me she'd stop by my house on her way back to the village.

But she didn't, although I waited up past bedtime. Maybe, I thought, her suspicion might have been right: maybe Nail was hiding out at the Chism place and had made his folks promise not to tell anyone, but once Viridis had gone up there, they couldn't keep it from her. And now, I thought, as I lay in bed trying to sleep, they are in each other's arms at last.

The next morning I worked for only an hour in the garden before heading for my waterfall to bathe. The mullein stalk named Viridis was standing proud and tall. But the one named Nail still drooped to the ground. I took

305

a real quick shower bath, returned to the house and had a quick breakfast, and was sitting on the front porch of our cabin when Viridis rode up on Rosabone.

"He wasn't there," she said.

"I know," was all I could say. But I *did* know, from the mullein stalk, that he had not come back to Stay More.

The Chisms of course had been so delighted with her visit that they hadn't easily let go of her. She'd had to stay with them through supper, and until it was scarcely light enough to see her way home, and by then she had been too tired to remember her promise to stop by my house. She was sorry. I said that was okay, that I was sorry she hadn't found Nail.

"You don't suppose," she started again with those familiar words that sounded sort of desperate, "that he could be somewhere up in the mountains or lost hollows, hiding out?"

I shook my head. I couldn't break the magic and tell her about that mullein stalk named Nail, or it would pop right up and pretend he wasn't lost when he actually was.

"You don't suppose," she asked, "that he might not even want his own parents to know that he has come back?"

"Viridis," I said, with a little exasperation, "I know that Nail's not anywhere around Stay More."

"How can you be so certain?" she said, not really asking it so much as accusing me for my cocksure conviction.

"I just know," I declared. "Believe me." I nearly added, by way of consolation, I'll tell you the minute I see the mullein straighten up again. But you can't tell anyone about the mullein.

She said, "Latha, Nail told me that you could tell me where he would be hiding. Do you know where it is? Would you show me?"

Then I remembered what I'd written to him in that letter about the lost glade, or glen, of the high waterfall, way back up on the mountain beyond his upper sheep pasture. I was flattered that my telling him about it would have made him want to use it as a hiding-place. For a moment, even, I wondered if the range of my mullein's magic extended that far into the wilderness. Could it be that my mullein didn't know he was already there? But no: the mullein will tell you if something or someone is lost even if it or they are a thousand miles away. "Sure, I could show you," I said, "but I don't think you'll find him there."

"Can we go there?" she asked, and that note of desperation still gave an edge to her question. She observed, correctly, that I was just sitting in the rocker on the porch, not doing anything, and she asked, "Are you free to go right now?"

I looked around as if somebody might try to detain me, or as if to see if anybody was spying on us, but Viridis and I seemed to have the morning all to ourselves. "Let's go," I said.

And we went. Rouser tried to follow and I told him to stay home but Viridis said he could go with us, so we let him trot along after Rosabone as she carried the two of us up the road toward the Chism place.

But somebody *was* spying on us. I should have guessed, I should have been able to put myself inside of Sull Jerram's crooked mind and figure out that if he and his courthouse gang were determined to keep Nail from returning, or to capture him as soon as he showed up and turn him back over to the authorities in Little Rock, they'd likely post a watch on Viridis and trail every move she made. By now everyone knew she was here. By now Sheriff Duster Snow had had plenty of time to tell his deputies to put Viridis under surveillance. Two deputies, we later learned, had taken up residence in Tilbert Jerram's General Store, from which they could watch any comings or goings from the old woman's house, and it was one of these deputies who was now following us, on his horse, as we rode Rosabone in the direction of what had once been Nail's sheep pastures. Rouser caught wind of him and growled a little bit to attract my attention. I looked over my shoulder and saw the man on his horse, a good distance behind us. "Viridis," I said, "we're being followed."

She stopped and turned Rosabone. When she stopped, so did the distant rider. "Do you know who he is?" she asked.

I couldn't see him well enough to recognize him or even to know for sure that he was one of Snow's deputies. "No, but I reckon he's one of the law," I said.

"We'll have to lose him," she declared. "Where can we go to shake him off?"

"That way," I directed her, not pointing but just nodding my head slightly in the direction of a byroad that diverged from the Chisms' lane and dropped down toward Butterchurn Holler. We rode Rosabone along the Butterchurn Holler trail for a mile, with the deputy still coming along behind us, hanging back but definitely following us. I knew there was a sharp bend ahead in the trail, and I told Viridis, "When we reach that big hickory up ahead, right past it let's cut quick into the woods."

She spoke over her shoulder: "I'm afraid I don't know a hickory from an elm. You'll have to say when."

I told her when. We left the road and plunged into the deep woods that rose up the north side of Butterchurn Holler. The climb was steep, and we both dismounted and led Rosabone up to the top of the ridge, where we paused and waited for fifteen or twenty minutes to see if the deputy had discovered which way we had gone. But there was no further sign of him. He must have followed the Butterchurn Holler trail onward. We remounted Rosabone and rode across the ridge until we could double back and regain the Chism lane and cross it into Nail's sheep pastures. As we rode across the pasture, I watched carefully in every direction for signs of any other deputy or spy.

The pasture rose, rolling, through the high weeds and brush that had taken over the place since Nail's sheep had died. The Chisms ought to have bought a few sheep or goats just to graze it and keep it from going back to the wild, or at least they should have mowed it for hay. "What is all this ferny stuff?" Viridis asked, and I explained that it was yarrow, which Nail had planted for his sheep to supplement their diet; but it had grown tall and its leaves, a grayish shade of green, were rank. "Yarrow's a pretty name for a plant," she said, and I told her that some women and girls used yarrow as the main ingredient in a love medicine. "Love medicine?" Viridis laughed, and I had to explain to her how you could concoct beverages that had the power to influence the man of your choice.

She didn't take me very seriously. Then as we went on she asked me to identify other weeds and grasses, and I told her the names of all the pretty ones: chicory and butterfly weed, coreopsis and oldfield toadflax. "Really? Is it really called oldfield toadflax?" she asked, and I said that was what I'd always known it to be called.

Then we were drawn into that uppermost corner of the field, where it nestles against the side of the mountain, lined on two sides by thick, close hardwoods that seem to make a cul-de-sac in the corner but actually open into an old trail. But I didn't direct Viridis toward that trail opening, just yet. "Let's wait here a bit," I suggested, and dismounted from Rosabone. "You just sit there on her for a while, and I'm gonna check to make sure nobody's watching you."

Viridis did as I told her, and I crept over behind the tree line at the edge of the field and followed it for a good ways back along the slope of the pasture, with Rouser at my heels. I moved from tree to tree, keeping myself hidden and looking out across the field to catch sight of anyone else. But there was no one. We were alone up there. "Smell anybody?" I asked Rouser, and he planted himself and raised his nose into the air as if he understood my question. I wouldn't have been surprised if he had shaken his head in reply, but he just gave me a blank, dumb, doggy look as if to say no, he didn't smell anybody. I went back to Viridis and motioned for her to follow me, and we crossed the tree line and entered the deep woods.

There had been some logging activity not too long ago in this part of the woods, which had all second- or third-growth trees, not very tall, and thin. The earth here was still gouged by wheel ruts from the heavy-laden lumber wagons. But after following the main logging-trail for less than a mile, we found ourselves in a holler that had no path except what remained of some ancient passage, perhaps of Indians. The deeper we got into this holler, the taller the trees stood, until we were in rare virginal woodland: towering stands of oak, ash, and hickory, hung with huge grapevines and blackjack vines that had given up trying to climb the trees and made the place look like a jungle. Either these trees were too hard for the loggers to get at or whoever owned the land had not permitted logging. I didn't know who owned the land. Not the Chisms, whose acres we had left far down below.

If these virgin trees were singing, they sang only with fragrance, not with sound. It was eerily quiet and still in this forest, a silence matching the darkness: although it was well past midmorning and the sun was high in the sky, the canopy of the forest shaded everything except a random patch of sunlight here and there.

A small branch meandered through the holler, and its gentle gurgling was the only sound besides the clop of Rosabone's hooves on an occasional slab of chert. The branch was the runoff of the falls, which were still out of earshot. Along the banks of the branch grew wildflowers, and Viridis asked me to name them for her: my voice seemed to have an echo, nearly a boom in the silence, as I pronounced, "Bee Balm, Mallow, Lady Slipper, Fireweed . . ." We were deep into a rich, woodsy fragrance that was only partly flowers; the rest was moss and leaf mold and fern and the silent singing of the trees. I mentioned to Viridis in passing that the lady slipper's roots are used in concocting one of the most powerful love medicines ever known, a surefire aphrodisiac . . . although I didn't know that word, not then. "It makes a body right warm and lusting" was the way I put it, blushing furiously in the effort.

It was almost eleven o'clock when we came to the glade, or glen, which was illuminated by the full sun: the northeast end of the holler terminated in cliffs, and over the lowest ridge of the bluff spilled the waterfall, a white square fifteen feet high, dazzling in the sunlight. On both sides of the waterfall the cliff was deeply undercut into caverns, sunless grottoes in which Indians once had lived and which still contained the shattered relics of their habitation: bits of woven stuff, shards of pottery, bones. Viridis was entranced. Rouser was having a field day, sniffing around.

"Here we are," I declared.

"Nail?" she softly called, but of course there was no answer. She tested the water of the falls with her hand, and so did I; it was much, much colder than my shower bath falls. "Is it safe to drink?" she asked. We were both very thirsty from our ride and hike. Rosabone had not waited for my answer but was already lowering her head to drink from the deep, blue pool at the base of the falls.

"It's springwater," I said. We knelt and cupped our hands to drink. The water was delicious: cold and fresh and pure. There wasn't even a minnow swimming in it, nor a waterbug. A flitting dragonfly was the only creature besides us around the pool. But in the mud at the edge there were some tracks, of more than one animal. I wasn't very good at recognizing animal tracks, and some of these I'd never seen before. Rouser was practically rooting his snout in the tracks and holding his tail very still, which he does when he's trying to think.

Viridis didn't seem to notice the tracks, and I wasn't going to scare her with the thought that we might be surrounded by wolves, bears, or panthers, not to mention gowrows, jimplicutes, and snawfusses. The latter three were just as real to me as the former three, but I had never seen any of them, although I'd heard wolves howling at night far across the ridges.

We were sitting now on the log of a fallen tree, while Rosabone with her reins loose wandered around the pool and Rouser went off out of sight to pursue the trail of one of the animals. "It's so peaceful here," Viridis observed, smiling and taking a deep breath as if the air were peaceful too.

"This would be a perfect place for Nail to hide if he—" Her voice caught, she choked, then sobbed once, loudly, and I thought sure she was going to cry, but she stopped herself and sniffled, using her wrist to rub away whatever had been ready to run from her eyes or nose. Then sadly she said, "Maybe he'll never see it."

"He's already seen it," I said. "He knows every inch of this mountain." I thought of what I'd said to him in my letter: "I didn't stay up there very long, but while I was there I thought of you, a lot, and I had a strange vision as if I could see you just living and dwelling in that hidden glade." I told Viridis, "If he's alive, and if he goes anywhere, he'll come here. He might even be on his way here right this minute."

We waited. It was almost as if we'd been told he'd come at high noon and we had just a few minutes to wait for him. Meanwhile Viridis asked me to identify everything that I could see from where I was sitting: she wanted to learn the names of everything visible that could be named. There were some ferns growing around the pool that were so uncommon I didn't know their name, and there was even a flower, some kind of twayblade, that I couldn't identify, but I told her everything I knew in that green glen.

And she knew things I didn't, that every shade of that green had a name, some shades of green I'd never heard of before, that she pointed out to me: cinnabar, Aubusson, smaragd, cobalt, Hooker's, palmetto, Véronèse, teal, gamboge, shades of green that only an artist would know but that would come in handy if you wanted to remember the difference between a frond of fern and a bough of cedar. Cinnabar is a very reddish green, and I didn't even know that green could be red, its complement, until Viridis pointed it out to me.

We were learning things from each other. But it was past noon now, and we were both hungry for dinner, and I hadn't brought my .22 with me to shoot something to eat, and even if Rouser had trotted back with a possum in his mouth I wouldn't have known how to cook it. It would be way past dinnertime before we got back home, and we'd be starved.

A blue lizard frightened Viridis into leaving the place. It was just a harmless little skink that crawled out from under a rock and flicked its tongue at her, but maybe she had never seen a lizard before: she jumped up with a squeal of terror and ran several feet before stopping. Of course by then she'd scared the daylights out of the poor skink, who'd slunk back to his hidey hole. "It was just a lizard," I said. "They won't bite."

"Up close he looked like a small dragon," she said, recovering herself, and then, apologetically, "Well, we'd better go, don't you think?"

I nodded and called for Rouser. He came back from wherever he'd been tracking whatever, and Viridis took Rosabone's reins and said, "I wish there were some way I could let him know that I was here, in case he comes."

"Well," I said. I began picking up small rocks, and I arranged them beside the pool of the falls into a large letter V. "If he sees that, he'll know it stands for you."

Viridis studied my handiwork, and then she bent to gather some other stones and make beside the V another letter, a large L.

I was flattered, but I protested, "He won't know what that stands for."

"If he doesn't," she said, "let him think it stands for love."

I blushed red.

———

Each morning thereafter Viridis went to that remote glen of the waterfall, but without me. I understood. Sometimes I guess I overstood: I let my imagination run away with me in picturing the first meeting between Viridis and Nail, the first time they'd ever been allowed to touch without someone watching them. What kind of touch would it be? They sure wouldn't simply shake hands. And it would probably be more than a hug. It would probably be more than even my imagination could guess, and I understood why Viridis did not invite me to go back with her to that glen. But there was another reason: she could ride Rosabone a lot easier and swifter without me behind. She had to elude those deputies who watched her every move from their lookout at Tilbert Jerram's store. Both of those deputies had good horses, but they weren't jumpers like Rosabone, and that mare would really give them chase. Viridis would point her west, or north, or south, or any direction except her northeastward destination, and then lead those poor deputies on a pursuit that would take them all over the Stay More countryside before they quit and realized they had long since lost her. Without me riding behind, Rosabone could jump pretty near anything that stood in her way: fallen trees and fences and creeks and brush piles that would impede or completely stop those men trying to follow her. Not once did those deputies come anywhere near discovering Viridis' actual destination in the green glen of the waterfall.

Viridis would go on alone into the glen after shaking off her pursuers. It scared her a good bit, going alone through that dark forest to that place where possibly fiercer creatures than blue lizards dwelt. On the forest path once, Rosabone shied and reared up and nearly threw Viridis: there was a copperhead in the path, and those snakes are sure enough a lot less harmless than lizards: a copperhead's bite can kill you.

When she got to the glen, Viridis would give herself and Rosabone a good long drink from the pool and then just hang around awhile, looking for signs that Nail or any other man had been there. Each time she went there she would take something and leave it, in the largest cavern beside the falls, like a bird building a nest: she would pack in a blanket one day, another blanket the next day, and eventually all of the things she had meant to leave under the sycamore tree behind the penitentiary: the hunting knife, the harmonica, the pocketknife with can opener attachment, and the few cans of corned beef and beans and such, as well as the compass, the pocket watch, soap, salt and pepper, and a few yards of mosquito netting (the mosquitoes were getting bad). On each trip she would check carefully to see if any of these items had been used or even touched. Disappointed, she would just sit for an hour or so listening to the trees, and waiting, before heading home.

Only one item that she had intended to leave for Nail and Ernest she did not place in the cavern but carried with her at all times: the Smith & Wesson revolver. Having the gun with her allayed the terror of encountering a panther, bear, or wolf. Against a pack of wolves the gun wouldn't be much help, but it was better than nothing. She kept it in a small saddlebag attached to the back of Rosabone's jumping-saddle, where she also sometimes carried a sandwich, in case she was gone past dinnertime.

Returning from the falls, she would be just as careful as she had been going to them, to make sure that she wasn't watched or her route discovered. She would take a circuitous path that brought her out north of Nail's sheep pastures, and then she would come back across those pastures to the Chism house and stop to say hello and perhaps make sure that he hadn't shown up there.

On one of these visits to the Chism house she discovered that Seth Chism was in pretty bad shape. Nail's father had been ailing for quite some time, and now it appeared that he might not survive. Doc Plowright had been to see him, but now the Chisms had sent for young Doc Swain, who was there when Viridis arrived and who later talked to her alone back in town.

"They call it heart dropsy," Doc Swain said to her. "Leastways, that's what . . . my colleague across the road yonder calls it." He gestured toward Doc Plowright's clinic. "I reckon that's what he's always heared it called, and he keeps on callin it that even though he must know it's actual a pericarditis. Or maybe he don't know that. Anyhow, ole Seth's heart is shore to fail. Now, I reckon if Nail was to show up, he could get better. But if he don't, his heart is bound to fail."

"Mine is bound to fail too," she said.

Doc Swain, who wasn't any older than she was, looked at her with compassion. "It better not," he said gently. "There aint nothin I could give ye for your heart."

The old woman had a visitor that night. Or maybe he meant to visit Viridis, but the way he acted, it was the old woman he had driven all the way from Jasper to see. Judge Lincoln Villines drove the car himself, and he came alone. He must have left early in the afternoon, to drive that car over all the ridges and through all the creeks between Jasper and Stay More. He arrived just a bit too late for supper. The old woman and Viridis were taking their coffee out on the porch when he pulled into the yard. Of course they recognized him from the previous time he'd been on that porch: it was almost as if those five or six months had not intervened since he had last stood there in the company of the sheriff and the county judge; it was almost as if they could still hear him snapping at the latter, "Shut yore fool mouth, Sull! Aint you done made enough trouble already? Jist shut up, afore ye go and make it worse!"

But now he spoke mildly, although the subject of his speaking had not changed: "Ladies, good evenin and howdy. I trust ye aint had no trouble lately from . . . my colleague, Jedge Jerram?"

"He knows better than to show himself in my sight again," the old woman said.

Lincoln Villines smiled at her and waited to see if she would offer him

314

a chair. She did not. He turned to Viridis. "And you, young lady? Has he given you ary bad time?"

"Not directly," Viridis said. "I haven't seen him. But his deputies are trying to stalk every move I make."

The circuit judge smiled. "Them is Sherf Snow's deppities, ma'am. They don't work for Sull."

"Does it matter?" Viridis said testily. "Aren't all of you in cahoots together?"

The judge coughed. "That aint a pretty color to put on it," he said. "I don't have no sympathy nor friendship with the sherf. And I don't have no feller-feelin with Sull Jerram neither."

"You're both judges," Viridis pointed out.

"He aint no *judicial* jedge, ma'am. Don't ye know that? He's jist a *administrative* jcdge." Villines turned to the old woman. "Iffen ye'd be so kind as to offer me a cheer, I'd set and explain the difference to y'uns."

"We know the difference," the old woman said. "But pull you up a cheer and set, if you've a mind to."

He sat. He rubbed his hands together as if washing them. He started to spit over the porch rail but decided not to. "Fairly cool for this time of June, aint it?" he observed, but neither of the women commented. Then he said, "No, I'm sorry to say it, but Sull Jerram don't know beans about law. Iffen he'd of knowed the first thing about the law, none of this mess would have started nohow." When that brought no comment either, he addressed a conversational question to Viridis: "How's ever little thing at the *Gazette* and all, these days?"

"I'm no longer with the *Gazette*," Viridis informed him.

"Is that a fack?" he said. "Wal, I do declare. Times change, don't they. You aint a reporter no more?"

"I never was a reporter," she said. "Just an illustrator."

"I see," he said, uncertainly. "George Hays told me you was a reporter."

"There are many things that Governor Hays does not understand."

"Wal, I don't make no promises, but I do believe that if I was to be elected governor, I couldn't do no better."

Both women attempted to figure that one out. They looked at each other. Had Lincoln Villines just intimated that he intended to run for governor, or hadn't he? Viridis had heard the rumors, that the so-called Jeff Davis faction of the Democratic Party, named after a demagogue who had served

315

as governor early in the century, was touting Lincoln Villines as their likely candidate in the event that George Hays chose not to seek reelection. Villines' only qualification for the nomination, apparently, was that like Jeff Davis he was an Ozarks mountaineer. "Are you going to run for governor?" Viridis asked him. "Has Hays decided not to seek reelection?"

"I was hopin you could tell me that one," the judge said. "I was hopin maybe you'd heard if George is made up his mind yit."

"There are rumors he won't run," Viridis said. "Just rumors."

"Do Little Rock folks expect him to?"

Even if she could answer that, why should she? She owed no favors, of information or anything else, to this man. She shrugged her shoulders. "He probably won't run," she declared, and realized that she was encouraging the judge, for some motive she didn't yet understand herself.

"Is that right? Wal, I suspicioned it myself, although George hasn't told me. You'd think he'd tell me. We're real good friends from way back. You'd think that I'd be the first person he'd tell when he makes up his mind, on account of several fellers have told me that I'd be first choice to step in and take his place if he didn't run." Judge Villines rambled on, talking aloud to himself more than to the two ladies. The two ladies smiled at each other. Neither of them could guess the real motive of the man's visit, and they waited patiently for him to reveal it. The sun was on its way down. Judge Villines squinted at it as it sank behind the mountain that walled in Stay More on the west.

Finally he did spit. The old woman knew, as she would later explain to Viridis, that ordinarily a man spits only in the presence of his fellow men; when a man spits in the presence of women, with no other man present, it can mean only one thing: he is nervous about having something important to say. He said it: "No, the governor, ole George, he aint said a word to me about whether he plans to run or not. He did say one thing, though. He said, and I quote him, that I better take care of this Nail Chism business. It could hurt what chance I've got to be a candidate for the nomination for governor. It's real bad news that Nail is runnin around loose. I shore do need to have a little talk with him."

Viridis interrupted. "If you're trying to get me to tell you where he's

316

hiding, I'm afraid I don't know anything more about that than you do."

The judge studied her to determine if she was telling the truth. "I jist want to talk to him," he said. "I don't mean him ary bit of harm. In fact, if I can jist git myself nominated for governor, one of the first things I aim to do is give him a full pardon." The women swapped skeptical glances. "All I want to do," Judge Villines went on, "is talk to him and tell him that I aint been mixed up in no way whatsoever with those men that he thinks framed him."

Viridis laughed. "*You*," she said. "You tried and convicted him and sentenced him to the electric chair. You refused to recommend to Governor Hays a second trial. You refused to sign a petition with six thousand other residents of Newton County, who believe Nail is innocent."

The judge held up his hands as if she were raining blows down on his head. "Whoa, lady!" he begged. "All I was doin was my duty as the court! The court makes mistakes! Don't ye know? The court kin only listen to the evidence and listen to the jury, and that there jury of twelve honest men convicted Nail, not me, and I jist had to impose the sentence prescribed by the law and voted by that jury!"

"Did I hear you confess you made a mistake?" Viridis asked.

"I reckon you did! I reckon I did! Everbody makes mistakes, and I'm here to tell ye that if I had to do it all over again, I would've found some way the court could've let him off! That's all I want to tell him! If you'll jist tell me whar's he's at, I'll crawl on my knees to him and tell him I'm sorry!"

The judge sounded as if he were about to break down. Viridis almost felt some sympathy for him. "You really believe that I know where he is?" she asked, and when he nodded, she said, "Well, let me tell you: if I knew where he was, that's where I would be, right now, instead of here listening to you!"

"You honestly don't know?" he said.

"He could be dead for all I know!" she said, admitting it to herself now at last, and began to cry.

The judge was uncomfortable, and he stood up and prepared to leave. "Well, if he shows up, I jist want you to know that it would be greatly to his advantage, and yourn, if you'uns would jist let me have a few words with him before he does anything rash."

317

Because Viridis could not reply, the old woman spoke for her: "We'll tell him what you said."

In the last days of June, Stay More eases into the slow rhythm that will stay with it throughout July and into August: just enough rain, not very often, to settle the dust and keep things green; just enough work to keep everybody from being idle but not enough to keep them from enjoying what summer was mainly meant for: the casual contemplation of the inexorable passage of time. Summer is a season for endurance and abidance. It is too hot to enjoy life but too green not to. And green is cool. The color alone sustained us, and was all around us, in every conceivable tint and hue.

The men sat on the storeporch and tried to make grist for conversation out of Viridis' occasional comings and goings and whether or not there would ever be another coming of Nail. After a while it seemed that even that grist was depleted, and nobody spoke of Viridis or Nail, either one. Even the two deputies spying from Tilbert Jerram's store seemed to be bored and at loose ends, and one of them, at least, got up his nerve to come down to Ingledew's store and sit with the other men and whittle and chew and spit and hem and haw and cough and spit and whittle and kick the dog off the porch and watch what there was of the world go by. The deputy allowed as how he sure would like to get on back home. None of the Stay More men asked him why he didn't just do that; they knew he had a paid job of work he was required to do, whatever it was, keeping an eye on that lady, and he'd just have to do it until Sheriff Snow or whoever told him he could quit.

The deputies gave up trying to follow Viridis to her destination on her daily rides. They didn't have to apologize to anybody that their horses weren't made for jumping the way Rosabone was. They had seen that mare jump clear across Banty Creek at a spot where it must have been all of twenty feet from one side to the other. Now, did you ever know ary horse or mare hereabouts to do a thing like that? No, it was no use trying to find out where that lady went. If Nail actually had come back and was hiding out wherever the lady went, there just wasn't going to be any way to find him.

But I knew he hadn't come back, even if Viridis hadn't kept me informed on her progress, or lack of it. Every day I observed the mullein stalk still

318

bent down when I went to my own little waterfall to take a bath after working in the garden. Rouser always went with me, but, like I say, I carried my .22 rifle as an extra precaution, and also in case I saw a fat squirrel or a partridge that was ripe for the pot. Sometimes I hit one, and we had a little variety on the table to replace the pork that was usually our only relief from a diet of greens: with every meal except breakfast, we had spinach, turnip tops, wild poke, lamb's quarters, or some other wild green. I've always been fond of greens, cooked not too long if I could get Ma to move the pot off the stove before they cooked brown, but even the best mess of greens got tiresome by itself and was greatly improved by the little bit of fresh critter I sometimes shot.

Seth Chism took a turn for the worse. Nowadays, if he were still living, he'd be rushed in an ambulance to the hospital and put in the ICU, but back then nobody'd ever heard of an ambulance, and although there was a kind of hospital up at Harrison, thirty miles off, it was an all-day ride on a road so bad it'd kill you if your disease didn't, and once you got there the bed wasn't any different from what you had at home. So Seth Chism lay dying in his own bed, and all Doc Swain could do was send Waymon Chism to Harrison to bring back a prescription for some heart medicine, which Doc didn't carry and which couldn't be had in what passed for a drugstore in Jasper.

Waymon hired out one of Willis Ingledew's best horses to ride to Harrison for the heart medicine. He hoped to leave early enough and ride hard enough to get back in the same day, and he was already gone when I was out in my garden patch before sunrise. I had my bath, and on my way back from my little waterfall I spotted a fat red squirrel sitting on a tree limb and hit it with the first shot from my .22, and Rouser retrieved it for me, and I promised him the bones from the stew pot that night. I noticed the mullein named Nail still bent down to the ground, and I stood and talked to it for a while, but it wouldn't even twitch. Then as I was returning to the house, not yet close enough to the house to have a good view of the road, I saw Viridis and Rosabone go by; I could tell it was them by the mare's gait. They were just trotting along, not running.

They were scarcely out of sight when here came another rider. I figured at first it was just one of those deputies. But I'd seen both of them, and their horses, often enough to know, even from a distance, that this wasn't either one. The trouble was, I was close enough to the house, and running now, trying to get closer, to tell it wasn't a deputy, but not close enough to recognize the man.

When I reached the house, I threw my squirrel into a pot and covered it, then kept on running after them with Rouser at my heels, and I had to shush him when he commenced barking because he sensed my excitement. It was uphill, and I couldn't run fast enough to keep up with them. I realized I was still carrying the .22 in one hand, and I was tempted to leave it so I could run faster, but something made me hang on to it.

I didn't come within sight of Viridis or the horseman until, much later, I reached Nail Chism's sheep pastures and could just make out the figures of Viridis and Rosabone disappearing into the far corner where the upper pasture dissolved into the woodland trail. I knew that Viridis always waited there, as she had the first time we'd gone there together, to make sure that she wasn't being followed. But now the man who was following her had disappeared, or was hiding, and I didn't see him again until a few moments after Viridis disappeared into the woods; then he and his horse came crashing out of the trees at the south end of the sheep pasture and took out across the pasture at a gallop, headed toward that far corner where she had gone.

For a wonderful long moment, I thought it was Nail. I wondered where he had obtained such a big fine horse, but he could have stolen one somewhere along his travels from Little Rock to Stay More. And yet I knew that my mullein stalk wouldn't have lied to me. It could not be Nail. I was reminded of that time, a June ago, over a year, when I had been at the playhouse with Rindy and had seen the man far down below in the field, the man who, everybody would try to get me to say, was Nail, but was not Nail, was the man who had actually assaulted Rindy: was Sull. Was this Sull too? He was too far away for me to tell, but I was determined to find out, and I paused breathless and heaving for just a minute before resuming my climb up through that weed-infested sheep pasture toward the obscure entrance to the woods where now the man and his horse had disappeared in pursuit of Viridis.

By the time Rouser and I reached the entrance to the woods ourselves, we were far behind them. If the man was following Viridis, he had surely caught up with her by now. If he was only trying to find out the location of the hideaway that she visited daily, he had found it by now. If he intended to do her some harm, to rape her, even to kill her, he was well on his way to doing it. Once I'd reached the woodland trail and it leveled off a bit and I could run faster, I began running again, and as I plunged deeper into the woods I ran until I thought my heart would burst or my lungs explode.

I tripped on a root and flew: I was airborne, and my rifle left my hand and flew farther than I did before I slammed down to the ground and got all the wind knocked out of me and my dress ripped up and dirtied and could only lie there whimpering for a while until the air came back into my lungs and I could bend and kneel and get my feet up under me again and then, painfully, stand. I hadn't broken anything. I found my rifle off in a pile of old leaves, nearly hidden. I ran on, watching my feet.

I still had a ways to go to reach the glen of the waterfall, when I saw the horse. It was the man's horse, but he was not in the saddle, and the horse was just standing there, not tied. Suddenly I stopped, thinking the man was bound to be near. My heart was already pounding in my ears from my run; now it was pounding harder from fright. I raised my rifle and held it ready to use. I crooked my finger around the trigger. But I did not squeeze it. That I am sure of.

And I am *almost* sure that the rifle wasn't loaded. It was a cheap single-shot .22, and I don't recall putting another bullet in it after I killed that squirrel. But I would ask myself, in the hours and days following: was it at all possible that in my excitement and distraction I did reload, and then when I tripped on that root and the rifle left my hand, it hit the ground and fired itself? Could that be? I had slammed into the ground so hard that I might not have heard the rifle go off. Could it, by sheer chance, have landed in that pile of leaves pointed so that its bullet, accidentally discharging, would find its way through hundreds of yards of thick woods and hit a man in the back of the head?

Because he had been hit in the back of the head. It was, Doc Swain declared later, a .22 bullet. It had been fired not from the Smith & Wesson revolver that Viridis possessed but from a .22 rifle such as the one I carried.

There have been a few times in my long life when I was not at all certain just what was happening to me, or what I was doing, but unless, as I conjectured, my rifle shot itself off after flying out of my hands, *that bullet was not fired from my rifle*. I know this!

And yet there he was. I found him near his horse, lying face up, already dead, I knew. I wouldn't touch him, I just looked at him.

And then I spoke to his dead body the kind of thing a murderess might have said: "Well, Sull Jerram, you won't never hurt another soul."

on

"**Y**ou didn't do that."

She had not ridden Rosabone all the way into the glen of the waterfall, and thus she did not know if Nail had finally come nor if the contents of the cavern had been touched. When she heard the rifle fire, she pulled back on Rosabone's reins and waited, listening, for a long scary moment, then turned back in the direction of the sound without even knowing who had fired the rifle. She had not ridden very far back when she came upon the strange scene: a dead man lying on the ground beside his horse, a girl standing over him with a rifle. "You didn't do that," she said to the girl.

"Uh-uh, I sure didn't," I said to her.

Viridis jumped down from Rosabone's back and peered closely at the face of Sull Jerram, the eyes squeezed tightly shut as if in pain, the mouth clenched, an ugly face making its last grimace. She had to turn the face to one side, gingerly, to find the bullet hole: just behind the right ear at the base of the skull. I don't see how a .22 bullet fired from such a distance could have penetrated the head of such a thick-skulled man. But it did. Except that at that moment I didn't know it was a .22 bullet. And he was as dead as you are allowed to get in this world. Viridis put her ear against his chest and listened for a heartbeat but shook her head. She felt for his pulse but found none. "He's dead," she told me, as if I needed to be told.

"He was following you," I told her, as if I knew something she didn't.

"And you were following him?" she asked, and then pointed to my rifle. "Could I see that?"

I handed her my rifle. She examined it, sniffed it, looked into the chamber, where a spent cartridge lay. "I killed a squirrel," I said.

She gave me a strange look I hadn't had from her before. "Where's the squirrel?" she asked.

I attempted to explain. The squirrel, I said, had been killed some time before and was now in a pot on the porch of my house. I hadn't reloaded the gun but was just carrying it, I guess with that spent cartridge of the bullet that had killed the squirrel still in it. I sure hadn't shot Sull Jerram with it. Much as I would have liked to. Heck, I didn't even know it was him until I found him dead. I swear. "Don't you believe me?" I begged.

"I *want* to believe you," she said, and she commenced looking around at the woods on all sides of us. "But who else could it have been? Unless . . ." She stared so fixedly off into the woods that I thought she must be looking right at him, and I looked in that direction too but didn't see anyone. "*NAIL?*" she shouted.

I really hoped he was there. Despite my mullein, which never lies, I hoped he was there, so that he could take the credit, or the blame, for shooting Sull Jerram, and so that we could all live happily ever after. It was time for him to come. But he had not come. The woods were deep-green and silent.

At length she said, "Well, I guess we've got to tell somebody about this."

I offered, "I could run home and fetch Paw's shovel, and we could just bury him right here and nobody would know about it."

She gave me that strange look again. "And bury his horse too? No, they'd find him, sooner or later. We'd better report this. Who should I report it to?"

We discussed it and decided that the best person to tell would be Doc Swain. But while we went off to fetch him, we couldn't just leave the body and the horse to the mercy of wolves or buzzards. One of us would have to stand guard until Doc Swain got here.

"Can you ride Rosabone?" she asked.

"Sure, but she knows you better. You go, and I'll stay with the body."

"You won't be scared?"

"A little, but I can manage."

"All right, we'll be back as soon as we can." She climbed up on Rosabone and turned her to go. "You'll be here when I get back?" she asked uncertainly.

I nodded, and she was gone. It wouldn't take her half an hour to run down to the village, and if Doc Swain wasn't too busy he'd saddle his horse and be back with her within an hour. But it was going to be the longest hour I ever spent. My first thought, when I was alone with the corpse of Sull Jerram, was that whoever had killed him might still be lurking in the woods and take a shot at me. My second thought, as the all-overs began to creep up on me, was that maybe I was the killer and had no one to fear except myself.

Rouser kept me good company and didn't wander off.

I had never seen a dead body before, much less been all alone with one.

It was worse than being alone in a cemetery at night: at least the bodies there are all covered up so you can't see them.

I thought of reloading my rifle, for protection, but decided I'd better just leave it the way it was.

I tried what Viridis had tried: I called out, "*NAIL?*" and heard my voice echoing up in the glen but didn't get any reply.

If I hadn't killed Sull, and Nail wasn't anywhere around, who had done it? Waymon Chism? But Waymon was gone to Harrison, or was supposed to be.

I began to worry about something else, something important: Doc Swain would be discovering these woods, this intended hiding-place, and if he brought the law up here, they might even go farther up the holler and discover the waterfall and the caverns. What good would it be as a hiding-place if everybody knew about it?

Or maybe it wouldn't ever be needed as a hiding-place. Maybe Nail wasn't ever going to come.

When that long hour had dragged out to its close, and the morning was long gone, Viridis returned. There were two other men on horses with her, neither of them a sheriff's deputy. One was Doc Swain. The other was his father, old Alonzo Swain, who, I realized, was still our justice of the peace, as he had been for many years. The older Doc Swain, who had given up his practice to his son Colvin a few years after the son got his medical degree from a St. Louis mail-order college, was also still deputy coroner for Newton County. So he could serve several functions here.

The younger Doc Swain helped the older down from his horse. Both men first said politely to me, "Howdy, Latha," and then began to examine the corpse. Doc had a notebook with him, and he made some notes and drew a couple of diagrams showing where the body lay in relation to the trees around it, and then he took a sharp stick and traced an outline of Sull's body in the dirt, and then he and his father lifted the corpse and slung it over the saddle of Sull's horse like a sack of meal.

We Bournes had never been able to afford Doc Alonzo Swain, and Doc Plowright had always been our doctor, so the older man didn't know me too well. Now he looked at me, and the first thing he asked was "How old air ye, gal?"

Of course he hadn't delivered me. A midwife had done it, without even any help from Doc Plowright. "Goin on fourteen," I said.

"Do ye want me to question ye out yere in these woods, or do ye wanter go have ye a bite of dinner and then come to my office?" He asked this kindly-like, and I appreciated it.

"I don't keer," I said. "Might as well do it here."

"I've done et my dinner anyhow," he announced, "and so's Colvin. But you ladies mought be hungry."

I was flattered he called me a lady, without any of the condescension that one hears in "little lady." "I can hold off eatin till you're done with your questions," I declared.

"All righty," he said, and motioned for us to sit together on a fallen tree trunk. "Well, number one. Would ye have any reason fer killin this man?"

I laughed. "Do you know anybody who wouldn't?"

"Please jist answer the questions, Miss," he said.

"Sure," I said. "I had all kinds of reasons for killin him. He raped my best friend. He sent a good man to prison and nearly to the 'lectric chair. He was follerin this lady, Viridis, and Lord knows what he aimed to do to her. Sure, I had all of kinds of reasons for killin him, and I wish I had. I really wish it was me who had done it. But it wasn't. I didn't."

"Who else do you think it might've been?" old Doc Swain asked.

"It could've been any man . . . or woman . . . or child old enough to hold a rifle. Anybody who knew Sull Jerram and knew what he was like and what he done." I pointed at the old doctor's chest. "It could've just as well been *you*."

That didn't fluster him. He chuckled and glanced at his son and said, "She's shore right about *that*. Or you, either one, Colvin."

"Don't I know it?" the young Doc Swain admitted. "But ask her whar she got this yere Winchester." He held up the .22.

"Well?" the older man said to me.

"I bought it from Sears, Roebuck through the mail," I declared truthfully, and added, "Four dollars and twenty-five cents, plus postage."

"Whar'd you git the money?" he asked. The question contained an insinuation I didn't like: the Bournes were too poor to afford Doc Swain, too poor to buy their least daughter a shootin-arn.

"Same place you got yours," I said. "Honest toil."

The old doctor grinned, and for a moment I thought he would ask me what kind of honest toil, and I was prepared to answer that one too, but he took up a different line of questioning: "You said that Sull . . . the deceased . . . was a-follerin this lady. How do you know he was a-follerin her?"

So I started at the beginning: how I had seen a man on a horse riding after Viridis, and how I had followed them, and everything that had happened, including me tripping and falling and dropping my rifle. "I'll show you where it was," I offered, and I led them back through the woods to the place where I had been running, and I pointed out the root that had snagged my foot and sent me flying, and I showed them the pile of old leaves where my gun had landed. The younger Doc Swain measured off the distance from this spot to the spot where Sull Jerram had lain dead.

"Hmm," said old Doc Swain. "Still and all, you've got a empty cartridge in that rifle."

So I told them about the squirrel too.

"What did ye do with the squirrel?" old Doc Swain asked.

"I put it in a pot on the porch," I pronounced, unmindful of the alliteration.

"I reckon we better go see if it's still there," declared the old doctor/ j.p./coroner.

We left those woods. As far as I know, the two doctors Swain never did go any farther back up into the glen where the waterfall was. They never did learn of the hiding-place and trysting-place that was still waiting for Viridis and Nail to use, if he ever showed up. They questioned Viridis about what she had been doing, where she was going when Sull was following her, and they checked to make sure that her Smith & Wesson was a .38, not a .22, and for that matter hadn't been fired anytime recently. But she never said anything about her destination at the waterfall, which was beyond sight and earshot of the place where Sull Jerram fell dead.

And that old squirrel was still in that old pot, where I had left it. I figured it sure had been lucky that Rouser had gone with me; if I'd left him at home, he'd have worried the lid off that pot and got that squirrel. But it was in the pot. The younger Doc Swain took his pocketknife and dug out the bullet and matched it up with that spent cartridge in my rifle, and he looked his father in the eye and nodded. The old doctor said, "Wal, Latha, it looks like you aint a suspect no more. I don't reckon we even need to tell the sherf that you ever was a suspect. We'll jist say you was the one who discovered the body, and the sherf might want to ask you some questions too, but you jist tell the truth, 'cept you don't have to say nothing about no rifle you was carryin. No need to do that."

I wasn't invited to ride any farther with them. Viridis did; she rode Rosabone onward with them and the body of Sull slung across the saddle of his horse into the village, and said she'd see me later. My folks were dying of impatience for me to tell them everything, which I did. Nearly everything.

We had that squirrel stewed with dumplings for supper, with a mess of greens, and some fresh biscuits, and even though one fat squirrel won't feed five people, it was the best eating I could ever recall.

Before nightfall everybody in Stay More knew that Sull Jerram was dead, dead, dead, so it was decided to have some kind of celebration and party. The Stay Morons threw a big square dance up to the schoolhouse, and it was a Wednesday besides. Nobody could recall when they'd ever had a square dance that wasn't on Saturday, or leastways Friday. A Wednesday night square dance was really a special event, and although nobody came right out and said it was being held in celebration of the demise of Sull Jerram, everybody knew that was the reason for it, and Luther Chism showed up with a whole keg of private-stock Chism's Dew, and even some of the ladies sampled it. I had a taste myself. Old Isaac Ingledew, the champion fiddler of the country, got his instrument out and dusted it off and gave one of the last performances that anybody could ever after recall hearing him play.

Among the revelers and dancers were Rindy Whitter and her new beau, the young driver Virge Tuttle, who still hadn't gone back to Pettigrew but appeared to have moved in with the Whitters. Rindy was so busy seeing him, which she did all the time, near about, that I had never got the chance to renew my friendship with her. But I had been too preoccupied myself to care.

Waymon Chism still hadn't returned from Harrison with the medicine, but while the square dance was in progress, pretty far along in the night, he came riding up; he'd brought the medicine and Doc Swain the younger was up at the home place right now administering it to Seth, who was already pretty cheered up with the news of Sull's passing. Now Waymon was ready to join the celebration himself.

But those two sheriff's deputies, who'd been participating in the square dance along with everybody else, and had their own share of Chism's Dew, told Waymon that he was under arrest. Despite his alibi of having gone to Harrison, despite the evidence of the medicine he'd obtained there, he was still the number-one suspect in the murder, and the deputies had instructions from Duster Snow to bring him in. Poor Waymon spent the night in the Jasper jail. The square dance celebration fizzled out about the time they took him away.

Usually when there was whiskey at a square dance, the party was over when some of the men got so drunk they started a fight. There wasn't any fight this time, just a big argument: no less than six different men, all of them intoxicated, each claimed that *he* had shot Sull Jerram. But nobody awarded the honor and the prize to any one of them.

And that was the end of June. Next morning July was upon us. Hot, and humid, but heavenly because the worst man who ever came from Stay More was no longer among the living. Folks said they weren't going to let Sull Jerram be buried in the Stay More cemetery. Tilbert Jerram, his next-of-kin in town, said he figured Sull would be just as happy to be buried in Jasper, so that was where they were going to bury him, and Irene, who was still his legal wife, let it be known she didn't plan to attend whatever funeral they were going to give him.

That same July morning was a scorcher, and my labors in the garden left me lathered with sweat. I was so eager to get washed off at my little waterfall that something along the way scarcely caught my eye, and I had to turn back and look again to make sure: the bent-down mullein stalk, the one I'd named after Nail, was standing proud and tall.

off

He had reached the point of no longer expecting to get to the opposite shore. The current of the swift Arkansas had been more than he had bargained for or could have struggled against. Within a minute after plunging in from the south bank, with his shoes tied together and wrapped around his neck, he suffered a bad cramp in his left calf and had to stop swimming and try to get the cramp out: several repetitions of pulling up on his foot and bending his toes back and then kicking his leg straight out finally removed the cramp from his left calf, but then a cramp in his right foot stopped him, and while working on that foot, he noticed the log coming swiftly at him, nearly upon him before he saw it, and thrashed wildly to get out of its way, just in the nick of time, or perhaps not soon enough: a jagged limb on the log raked his hip and cut deep into his skin.

He had not even reached the midpoint of the narrow river crossing before beginning to wonder if he would be able to make it. Each time he paused for breath or to turn over and swim on his back for relief, he found himself dodging a log or limb or being spun around and sucked under by a whirlpool. Once when he had resurfaced, disoriented, after fighting a sucking whirlpool, he swam a good distance back toward the closer south bank before realizing his mistake, and he was tempted to continue in that direction.

But he reversed himself and kept going, although aware that the current had forced him far below the narrow crossing, out into the broadened expanse of floodplain. He alternated between breaststrokes, backstrokes, and sidestrokes, the last especially whenever a wave of the current hit him and he needed to keep watching where he was going. He had reached what seemed to be midway of the broadened river, beyond which there was no turning back, before realizing that he simply had no energy remaining, no strength, that his months of incarceration without exercise had left him totally out of condition for such a marathon. By then it was too late. Out in the middle of the broadened channel the current was still so strong that he had ceased to make more than a feeble effort at fighting across it, not really making any progress but continuing to swing his arms overhead, just to keep himself from surrendering to the river.

Finally he had no choice but to grab hold of the next large log that came floating past, and to cling to it for a long time, as it carried him downstream. He wanted to hang on to that log forever, or until it carried him to New Orleans or wherever it was headed. But he knew it would eventually reach Little Rock, a place he never wanted to see again, so he let go of the log and continued swimming toward the impossibly distant north bank. The brief respite of clinging to the log had renewed his strength enough to swim with mighty strokes.

If only he had been able to keep that up. But as the north shore seemed to come closer and he felt all his muscles failing him, he lashed his right arm over his head with such desperate energy that a terrible pain shot through his shoulder. He screamed. He knew it was no mere cramp or muscle spasm; he had thrown something out of joint. From then on, he could not move his right arm at all, and the pain was all he could think of.

With his left hand he paddled several more strokes to keep afloat, until another log came drifting within reach and he caught it with his left hand and hung on. He did not know how long he clung to that log, conscious of nothing but the terrible pain in his shoulder and the darkening of the sky; the sun must have set. Seized with frantic thirst, he was almost tempted to drink the brown water but dared not. Then he roused himself from his pain to observe that the log was not in the midcurrents of the river but was caught in an eddy swirling toward a bend in the river; his log was headed for a great raft of snags. He kicked free from it just before it crashed into the pile of other logs, but the currents of the eddy had been too turbulent and confusing for him to fight with only one hand.

He must have lost consciousness—briefly, blessèdly—because he had stopped screaming from the pain. It was fading twilight when he found the world again and discovered his situation: he had been wedged into the pile of debris, clear of the water except for one leg and his useless right arm. He pulled himself up and got into a sitting position from which he could get his bearings: he had reached the north shore! Or not the shore itself, not dry land with earth beneath his feet, but this vast tangle of logs and limbs shunted into a bend of the shore. He crawled from one log to another, trying to hold his dead arm against his stomach, trying to hold his balance with the other hand, slipping, falling, from log to log, trying to extricate himself from the brush pile. It took a long, long time. When he had at long last reached solid earth, or sand, and thrown himself exhausted upon it, it was full night, full dark, and he slept.

331

Mosquitoes awakened him. Those biting him on his right side, or anywhere below his waist, he swatted and killed with his good left hand, but he could not swat at any mosquito alighting on his left arm or his left side. He spent most of the rest of the night battling the mosquitoes, too tired to get up and move away from the riverbank.

The first light of morning found him moving again: he walked away at last from the river, heading north across a sandbar, wading an eddy beyond the sandbar to climb a steep bank of clay and reach the first stand of cottonwood trees, who seemed to be singing him a welcome. He slaked his terrible thirst by using a handful of grass to mop up the morning dew from plants and rocks and squeezing the drops into his mouth: the beginning of his practice in doing things with his left hand alone. But the left hand soon began to fail him when he neared the first human habitation and a dog came to meet him, shattering the stillness with vicious barks; with his right hand he reached down to pick up a rock, and the searing pain reminded him that he couldn't use that arm; he switched to the left hand and attempted to throw the rock at the dog but missed so badly that the dog itself seemed amused and drew even nearer. Finally he picked up a heavy stick and lashed out repeatedly until the dog withdrew. Leaning toward the left, instinctively toward the northwest, he went on, avoiding the dog and its master, and whatever remained of the settlement of Nail, Arkansas, as it once had been called.

The pain in his shoulder did not let up, but he had grown almost accustomed to it. Still, it distracted him entirely from the wound in his hip until he unfastened his pants to relieve himself and looked down to see the mass of coagulated blood along his hip and leg. He realized he needed to clean the wound, and the next thing to find, even before something to eat, was fresh water, water safe enough to clean the wound.

He came to one of the abandoned homesteads northwest of Nail, in a stand of cottonwood trees and briars. Hardly a homestead: just a cabin, a squatter's shack, clearly long abandoned, although the rope on the well bucket was not fully decayed and the bucket itself, even rusted through with holes, held enough water to be drawn and inspected and found to be pure enough for washing the wound. Once the wound was cleansed, and freshly bleeding, he discovered it was deep enough to need stitches. Beyond the perimeter of cottonwoods he found what he needed: a yarrow plant, like those he'd fed his sheep, but this one wild, whose leaves he crushed to smear on his wound and slow its bleeding; and a common plantain, whose leaves mashed to a pulp made a mild astringent; and a lone loblolly pine, whose pitch he transferred from one of its wounds to his own. "I need this more than you do," he had said to the tree, realizing these were the first words he'd spoken since greeting the sun the morning before. The pine would have answered him if it could: it would have gladly contributed a bit of its pitch to disinfect and protect his open wound.

Then he returned to the cabin and searched it for something to dress the wound, but there was no cloth, save the fragile, grimy remnants of curtains on one window. The interior was bare of anything but the twisted remains of an iron bedstead, and some discarded kitchen items: a battered blue enamel washpan, a broken fork, a bent tableknife. In one corner of the floor was a small pile of walnuts still in their husks, perhaps gathered by squirrels or chipmunks, but Nail had not noticed a walnut tree in the vicinity. There was a small fireplace in a chimney at one end of the room, and Nail considered making a fire in it. He considered staying awhile, letting his wound close and hoping his shoulder would stop hurting, snaring some small game to cook, taking advantage of the supply of well water. He was impatient to keep moving toward home but felt the need to recover from the river crossing.

He had to dry his soaked shoes. Even untying their laces, which had held them together around his neck during the river crossing, was nearly impossible using only one hand and his teeth. The cottonwood tree, or eastern poplar, has branches easily broken by the wind, and the yard surrounding the cabin was littered with an abundance of firewood. The brown seeds of the cottonwood have clusters of white, cottony hairs, hence the name cottonwood, and these, when dry, make good tinder. He spent the rest of the morning just preparing his fire: in the fireplace he arranged a pyramid of cottonwood sticks and branches over a pyramid of kindling: twigs and bark and some splinters from the wood of the cabin itself. Then on the hearth he carefully assembled the little mound of tinder: first a layer of cottonwood seed fluff, then some woodworm dust on top of that. He had to walk barefoot for an hour around the neighborhood, but avoiding the direction where he'd met the dog, until he found a small piece of flint, not indigenous to the spot but washed down by a flood from some higher elevation. He took the flint back to the cabin and held it down with his right foot beside the mound of tinder while holding the tableknife in his left hand and striking the flint until sparks brought the first wisp of smoke from the tinder, and then he knelt and blew the sparks into flame and shoved the tinder pile beneath the kindling. By noon a fire was going in his fireplace. He stepped outside to examine the smoke rising from the chimney: it was not conspicuous. The nearest neighbor might not see it.

The day was hot; he did not need the fire for warmth, but all afternoon he built up a pile of coals in the fireplace to roast whatever he could find. For lunch he cracked some of the walnuts out of their husks; every other one was dried or rotten, but the edible ones made him a meal. It had been a lot of work, with one hand, to crack the nuts beneath a rock and to pick their meat.

For dessert there were no end of wild raspberries. He was careful not to overindulge and give himself indigestion. Later in the cabin, noticing the shard of mirror still hanging on the wall, he brushed the grime from it and took a look at himself: a fright, but a comical one, with the red all around his mouth. He made no attempt to wash it off.

He fashioned himself, from a limb of Osage orange, or bois d'arc, a digging-stick, an all-purpose pointed tool for turning up roots or for spearing: he spent part of the afternoon digging up a mess of wild onions, slowed by having to use the stick with only one hand: it was more a poking-stick than a digging-stick. But he quickly acquired dexterity in wielding it, so that once, when he stumbled upon a rabbit hole just as the animal was emerging, almost by reflex he stabbed it with the digging-stick, enough to maim it, and then administered the coup de grâce by using the stick as a club. He gutted the rabbit by venting it and squeezing its innards toward its middle and then holding it high overhead with his good left hand and swinging it with great force downward and between his legs, causing its entrails to be expelled. He saved the heart, liver, and kidneys, roasting those too in the fireplace, for a supper of both raw and roasted onions with rabbit meat, washed down with good well water, and another dessert of wild raspberries.

But before roasting the rabbit he had carefully stripped away and saved the tendons of the muscles, planning eventually to dry them and twist the sinews into the cord of the bowstring for his bow and arrow. He was that optimistic: that he would somehow regain the use of his right hand and arm.

Sitting in front of the cabin after supper, watching the sun go down, feeling free and safe and contented, and even burping a few times, he did not even hear the dog sneaking up on him until the dog, the same one he had encountered earlier, was within a few feet. The dog began to bay, as if it had treed a coon. It did not come any closer, within reach of his digging-stick, but continued baying until, moments later, its owner appeared: a man with a long beard, face hidden beneath a floppy fedora, and cradling in one arm a double-barreled shotgun.

The man did not raise the shotgun to point it at Nail but carried it loose in the crook of his arm. He regarded Nail quizzically for a while before saying, "What's yore name?"

Nail was tempted to answer truthfully but paused. Could this man know that there was a wanted escaped convict by his name? Was this man's house, hereabouts, within reach of the news of the escape? For that matter, where was he? Nail had no idea, except that it was near the river; the drifting logs might even have carried him beyond Little Rock. "Where am I?" he answered.

The two questions remained there in the air between them, exchanged, unanswered, for a long moment. Did they answer simultaneously, or was the man just a step ahead of him? No, it seemed that both answers, in the form of that one word, were spoken by both men at once.

"Nail."

Then they just regarded each other with further cautious surprise for a spell until, again simultaneously, they spoke: "What?"

"I ast ye, what's yore name?" the man said.

"And you jist said it, didn't ye?" Nail said.

"Why'd ye ast me whar ye are, if you done already knew?" the man asked.

"What?" Nail said again. "You aint said, yit. Where am I?"

"Nail," the man said. "What's yore name?"

"I aint about to tell ye my last name till you tell me where I'm at."

"I done did. You need to know the name of the state too? Whar'd you float down from? This here's Arkansas."

"I know it's Arkansas," Nail said impatiently. "What part of it?"

"Nail," the man said again. "I don't need to know yore last name. What do folks call ye?"

"Just Nail," Nail said.

"That's right," the man said.

And so it went until it dawned upon first Nail and then the man that they were speaking at cross-purposes, each giving the same answer to a different question. It was Nail who finally got it figured out enough to ask, "You mean the name of this here place is Nail?"

"What I been tellin ye the last ten minutes, dangdurn it. Don't tell me yore name if ye don't wanter. I don't keer."

"My name is Nail," Nail said.

"Huh? Is that a fack now? I thought ye was funnin me." The man studied him more closely. "You got any kinfolks hereabouts?"

"Not as I know of, but you never kin tell, if it's got that name. It's a ole fambly name."

"Yo're the sorriest-lookin feller ever I seed," the man said. "What happened to yore haid?"

It struck Nail that his shaved head and his face smeared with raspberry juice made him look either injured or comical, or both. His faded and torn chambray shirt and trousers would not have given him away as a convict; and now he was glad that being in the death hole had not required him to wear stripes like the other convicts. "I had the mange," he said, rubbing his head. And then, running his hand down his cheek: "And this aint nothin but berry stain."

Gesturing with the gun barrel toward the chimney, the man asked, "You got a far burnin in thar?"

Nail nodded and asked, "This place don't belong to nobody, does it?"

"Belongs to me," the man said. "You wanter buy it?"

"Naw, I'm jist a-passin through," Nail said. "I jist aimed to stay a night or two."

"Aint no bed in thar, I guess ye noticed," the man said. "But you jist come over to my place. Aint far from yere."

"I don't want to trouble ye," Nail said.

"No trouble, and I got a spare bed fer comp'ny. Come on."

So Nail went with the man, first banking the coals in his fireplace and retrieving his shoes, which were pretty much dried by now. As Nail put them on, with difficulty using just one hand, and unable to tie the laces, the man observed, "Swum the river, did ye? What happened to yore good hand?"

"I reckon I must've th'owed my shoulder out of joint," Nail said.

That night, in the man's cabin, which wasn't any larger than the abandoned cabin Nail had taken up residence in, but was in reasonably good condition, the man urged a tin cup full of some strong, fiery whiskey upon Nail, who, being the equal of any of his forebears as a connoisseur of corn liquor, coughed and gagged and declined a second helping, but the man said, "You'd best swaller all of that stuff ye kin hold, or it'll kill ye when I fix yore arm."

"You've fixed arms before?" Nail asked apprehensively.

"A time or two," the man said. "Drink up." Nail swallowed as much of the bad booze as he could force down his throat; his stomach was feeling giddier than his head. The man said, "Let's take off that shirt," then unbuttoned and removed it from him, as a valet might have done. Then he asked, "You ready? Better take one more big swaller."

Nail drained his tin cup, with deliberate speed that left both his head and his stomach lightened, while the man probed and poked Nail's upper arm and shoulder, and then, quicker than Nail could think, threw a strange, complicated two-arm lock around his upper body and lunged and pulled and jerked.

Nail screamed. The pitch and volume of his agonized bellow would have surprised him had he not momentarily blacked out. When he had resumed awareness and could still feel the searing torture in his shoulder joint, he became aware of the man's words: "Jesus! I reckon they could hear ye all the way back at the stir."

Nail groaned and sighed at length, and then asked, "The where?"

"The big house," the man said. "Whar ye came from. The Walls."

Nail eyed the man, at the same instant discovering that he could again move his right arm, although painfully. "How'd ye know?" he asked.

The man held up Nail's shirt. "Use to wear one myself."

"You break out too?"

The man nodded. "But before they even finished buildin her."

Nail spent that night, and three more nights, with the man, who never told him his name. Nail knew that the only man who had ever successfully escaped The Walls and was still at large was named McCabe, so he assumed this man was McCabe, but he never asked. The coals of the fire that Nail had so carefully built in the other house were allowed to go cold. The man fed him well, catfish one night, duck the second night, more catfish the third, and the swelling went down in Nail's shoulder until he could use his right hand again. They fished together: the catfish of the third supper was one that Nail had caught, a monster. They did not talk an awful lot; they made some casual conversation about the progress of the war in Europe and casually debated whether or not the United States should join the fight. The man was pro, Nail con.

But on the fourth day the man began to reminisce about The Walls and to ask Nail questions. "Is ole Burdell still runnin the place?" he asked, and Nail told him what had happened to Burdell and how T. D. Yeager had come in and taken over, and what sort of man Yeager was. The man eventually asked, "Is ole Fat Gabe still workin in thar?" and Nail related in detail the death of Fat Gabe at the hands of Ernest Bodenhammer, privately grieving anew over Ernest's fate. But the man became so elated at the news of the death of Fat Gabe, whom he had loathed more than any man he'd ever known, that he decided to celebrate, and produced from some hiding-place a quart of genuine bottled-in-bond sippin-whiskey, James E. Pepper, which he had been saving for a special occasion or serious illness, whichever came first, and the two men consumed the whole bottle in short order and became loud and boisterous. With his shotgun and the help of his dog the man killed a possum, and they had for the fourth supper a wonderful meal of roast possum and sweet potatoes and hot biscuits, the meat fat and greasy and filling and delicious.

On the fifth day the man offered Nail the gift of the other house. The man pointed out its advantages, which were already obvious to Nail: seclusion, peace, privacy, an abundance of fish and game, and, for whatever it was worth, the man's companionship and assistance. Almost with sorrow, Nail explained why he had to get on home to Newton County. There was, he said, a lady waiting for him.

The man regretted being unable to furnish Nail with a firearm, since he had only one, his shotgun. But he gave him a hunting-knife with a sheath that could be attached to the belt. And a bota: a water bottle made of goatskin. As well as a small wad of string, some matches, and two fishhooks, and finally a paper sack containing a dozen biscuits and some bits of leftover possum meat. Nail said, "I wush there was somethin I could give ye in return."

The man pointed. "How 'bout that thar gold thing on yore chest?"

Nail fingered the tree charm almost as if to hide it. "Not this. This here was given me by that lady I spoke of, and it's all that's stood between me and goin off the deep end."

"Wal, say howdy to her for me," the man suggested, and clapped him on the back and walked him as far as the beginning of the trail that led to Plumerville. He told him how to get around the west side of Plumerville and over the old Indian boundary, toward the flatlands of northern Conway County.

Nail said in parting, "If you ever find yoreself up in Newton County, come to Stay More and visit with us."

Then he followed the directions the man had given him, skirting the edge of Plumerville without being seen by a soul. When he got to the tracks of the Iron Mountain Railroad, the same tracks over which Viridis and Rindy and Rosabone had traveled en route to Stay More just that morning, he was tempted to wait for a freight he could catch and ride to Clarksville, but his experience on the Rock Island freight had made him leery of trains, and the stretch of track between Plumerville and Morrilton was too open and straight and exposed. He headed northward from the tracks and then crossed some low hills and picked up his stride across the flatlands leading into the village of Overcup.

His shoes were not of the best: soaked by the river crossing, dried too fast by the fireplace, they had shrunk, and were too tight and pinched for him to walk in them as fast as he had hoped, and even so had given him blisters.

He camped that night on a ridge overlooking Overcup, which is the name of an oak tree, so called because the husk, or cup, of its acorn nearly covers the rest of the acorn. The overcup is not a common oak, but there is an abundance of them around the village named after them. From his camp Nail could watch the lights of the village come on, and since he had been too busy hiking to stop and hunt, he considered sneaking up to the edge of the village to grab a chicken. But that would be theft, even if the chicken was running loose, not penned in somebody's coop. Nail had never stolen anything in his life; he had never committed any crime, unless you consider his bootlegging a crime. And he was not starving; the previous night's supper with McCabe was still fresh in his mind, if not his stomach, and he had a bit of it left in his paper sack.

He ate another of McCabe's biscuits and finished off the possum as he watched the village until its lights had one by one gone out, and then he lay down on the soft earth beneath an overcup and gazed awhile at the sky and its vast expanse of starlight. A nearly full moon had begun to rise.

The night was warm and clear and entirely silent except for the occasional distant baying of some dog. Nail began to sense for the first time the extent of his freedom: there was that enormous firmament of stars overhead, almost enough light to illuminate this enormous firmament of earth that surrounded him and in which he was free to roam or to lie still, as he chose, and he chose now to lie still. Then he slept.

The next morning, after two more of McCabe's biscuits for breakfast, he climbed down from the ridge and sought a good place to skirt the village undetected and gain the trail that led to Solgohachia, his next landmark. Of course he did not know the name of Overcup, nor would he come to learn the name of Solgohachia, but those were the two villages I found on topographic survey maps I used to trace his probable route. None of those villages he would skirt or pass through—Round Mountain, Wonderview, Jerusalem, Stumptoe, Lost Corner, Nogo, and Raspberry—would ever become known to him by name, except the last, because he did not encounter anyone after leaving McCabe, and, even if he had, would not have stopped to ask questions.

Solgohachia happened to be the hometown of Sam Bell, who was Nail's inmate in the death hole, sentenced there for killing four members of his divorced wife's family (Viridis had called him a psychopath), but Nail would not have known this, for he would not have known it was Solgohachia he was stopping through, nor known the Indian legend surrounding the well where he had paused to draw himself a drink of water: a chief's daughter had been married to a great warrior at this spot, and according to popular belief anybody who drank from this well would have a long and happy marriage; consequently, thousands of couples had come from miles around to Solgohachia to solemnize their weddings at this very spot, where Nail, unknowing, paused for a drink of water. Coming to and going out of Solgohachia, he found an abundance of usable arrowheads for his future bow and arrow, so he should have known that this had once been an Indian place.

Crossing through a gap of the hills between Solgohachia and Point Remove Creek, he nearly stepped on a large snake, whose checkerboard pattern might have misled a woods novice into thinking it a diamondback or a copperhead, but Nail recognized it for what it was, a nonpoisonous hognose, or spitting adder; and he took some time to observe and study it, hunkering motionless on his heels, so still the snake lost its fear of him.

It was the first resumption of his nature study. All those months in the penitentiary, of all the pleasures of freedom he had missed, he had missed most his loving attention to the variety of the natural world. Nail was a naturalist of no small merit, but until now he had been too busy escaping the prison to stop and notice the welcome that nature was giving him on every hand. Almost as if Nature Herself had sensed his return to the watching of Her, She let loose a magnificent falcon, a red-backed male kestrel, what Nail would have called a sparrow hawk if he'd had anyone to call it to, and he dallied on his trek for nearly an hour near the tree in which the kestrel had its nest, watching it, and watching too the eventual appearance of the female.

Not long afterward he began the construction of his bow and his arrows. He fashioned the four-foot bow from a long stave of Osage orange, or bois d'arc (the same words from which "Ozark" derives), and the arrowshafts he made from willow. For three nights, in the lingering light after supper, he slowly trimmed and shaped the bow, careful not to whittle it with his knife but just to scrape it into shape. He had saved all the sinew from each animal he'd eaten, rabbits and squirrels alike, and had carefully dried and twisted it into a long bowstring. Leftover sinew went into wrapping the nock ends of the arrows and into tying the arrowheads to the foreshafts. For fletching, he used the feathers of a wild turkey he had surprised with his digging-stick used as a spear, having given up any attempt to hit a quail or partridge, both abundant but elusive.

When he had finished the construction of his bow and arrow, he spent an entire day practicing with it, slowed down on his hike by the necessity to stop and take aim and experiment with ways of holding his bow and his arrows and crouching in a shooting position.

The number of miles he covered each day diminished as the terrain became rougher and steeper: he had reached the Ozarks, and the uplifts had risen; some folks say everything above the village of Jerusalem is technically in the Ozarks; beyond that point he would certainly encounter no more flat plains. Between practicing with his bow and arrow, actually hunting with it, and struggling with the rugged inclines of Van Buren County, his progress slowed to no more than fifteen miles a day. His shoes had begun to fall apart, and he resewed them with sinew and a needle made from one of the fishhooks straightened; they still gave him blisters.

But with his new weapon he was able to kill anything alive and edible

341

that crossed his path, or whose path he crossed: a raccoon, a pheasant, and even, while fording a stream, a large bass. He did not want for food, and he used the pheasant feathers to fletch more arrows and made himself a cap from the raccoon's fur: although the heat of summer made a fur cap unnecessary, his still-bare scalp was often chilly, and he feared getting sunstroke while walking in the broiling sunshine at midday without a head-covering. But the pheasant and the coon had been small game; he did not feel that his marksmanship with the bow and arrow were yet sufficient to risk an encounter with a buck deer or a bear. He saw plenty of the tracks of both, and once he even saw a mother bear with her cubs, at some distance, upwind, and avoided them. Crossing over into Pope County from Van Buren County, into the wilderness near New Hope, he encountered an entire family of deer and crept up on them, upwind, and took careful aim at the buck from not more than twenty paces; he missed it with two arrows but hit it with the third, right behind the shoulder, wounding it enough to catch it and finish it off with the hunting-knife. It was a seven-point buck. He butchered it of its haunches and stuffed himself on spit-roasted venison, and then, too full to move for many hours, used the time of digestion to carefully skin the animal and prepare its hide for some future use. He carried the deerskin wrapped around his neck like a big cape thereafter, transferring it to his waist as the heat of each day came on, while he gained the headwaters of Illinois Bayou, a trackless wilderness of forest that left him feeling like a pioneer.

I have not been able to find out how the mountain settlement of Nogo got its name. I'm sure there are legends, or apocryphal attributions to some settler who penetrated as deep into the wilderness as the wilderness would allow, and who gave up in frustration because it was "no go" beyond that point. For Nail, it would become no go as well.

In a wild place called Dave Millsaps Hollow, just to the west of Nogo, Nail was picking blackberries when he discovered that he had some competition for the berry patch: a black bear. Almost simultaneously he and the bear happened to look up from their labor of picking berries and stuffing their mouths and looked directly into each other's eyes from a distance of not more than thirty paces. Nail's first instinct was to shift his eyes about quickly to ascertain that there were no cubs around, because a female with cubs would have attacked him instantly. As it was, she . . . or he . . .

just snorted, as if to challenge Nail's right to the berry patch. Nail stood his ground. The bear growled and lowered itself from its hind legs to all fours, and from that position commenced swaying to and fro while continuing to growl, its eyes locked upon Nail. He made a sudden shooing gesture with his arms and hollered, "Git!" but the animal did not git. Nail, who had encountered bears in his explorations of the Stay More countryside, guessed that the bear was about two years old and probably male, although he could not understand why the bear was not retreating at the sight of him, unless it was so possessive toward the berry patch that it did not intend to relinquish it. Again by instinct, Nail found himself reaching behind to take his bow and arrows, but even while bringing an arrow up and attaching the bowstring to the arrow's nock, he attempted once more to frighten the bear. He stomped his feet and yelled, "Git outa huh-yar!" and then lunged toward the bear and waved his arms and his bow and shouted, "Go home!" For one instant the bear turned as if to flee, but then it changed its mind and, growling, charged Nail.

Nail knew that he would not have more than one shot, as he had with the buck, so he aimed carefully for a spot immediately below the bear's chin, toward his shoulders, toward his heart, and waited the extra fraction of a second for the charging bear to get close enough to feel the full impact of the puncturing arrow. Almost in the same instant as he released the arrow, point-blank, with the bowstring pulled back as far as it would go, Nail fell to one side, lunging really, to dodge the bear's charge, but he did not escape the bear's reach. The bear swiped at Nail with claws that would have torn his face away had it not instantly felt the confounding pain of the sharp flint transfixing its vitals, and thus the full force of the bear's swipe had been arrested. As Nail fell, the bear lunged onward a few steps before crashing to the earth, howling in pain and attempting clumsily to grab with its paws the shaft of the arrow. As the bear completed its death throes, Nail watched for what seemed long minutes, his heartbeat and breathing so rapid that he had not noticed that blood was coursing from his forehead down his cheek. He had not even attended to his own wounds before he assured himself that the bear was, if not entirely dead, immobilized enough to be finished off with the hunting-knife.

But as Nail kicked the bear with his foot and prepared to plunge the knife into it, the bear made one last defense, raking a claw into Nail's leg.

When the bear had become at last motionless, Nail realized he had blood covering his face and more of it running down his ankle, and he had to stop his own bleeding before he could bleed the bear any further.

Later he dragged the bear's carcass into the mouth of a cavern, or undercut bluff ledge, in Dave Millsaps Hollow, where he was almost too tired to build a fire and butcher the bear and roast some of its meat. While the bear meat was cooking on a spit over the coals, he settled down to prepare the bear's hide, although there was so much of it, the thick furry hide, that he couldn't conceive how he would need it for anything in such hot weather. But the bear's fur seemed more important to him than the meat; he was not particularly fond of bear meat, and he kept telling himself that he had only shot the bear in self-defense.

But if he wondered what earthly use he might have for a thick bearskin, he would soon discover a desperate need for it: the next morning he awoke before sunrise, feeling severely cold. He jumped up and attempted to warm himself by hopping around and clapping himself, and then built up his fire and held himself close to it, and then added more and more fuel until it was blazing and roaring, and then wrapped the bearskin tight around himself, but still it was awful cold! He could not understand: the sun had risen and the day *looked* just as bright and hot as any late-June day ought to be, but here he was freezing! There was nothing in the appearance of Nature to indicate that the temperature of the air had actually dropped so drastically. He considered that there might be a cold draft blowing up from some hidden crevice inside the cavern, and he moved out into the sunshine, surrounded by warm air in the morning sun, but still he began to shiver; then, increasingly, to tremble helplessly. He lay down beside his roaring fire wrapped tight in both his deerskin and his bearskin and shook so violently that he felt his chattering teeth would knock themselves out of his mouth, that every bone of his body would splinter.

His terrible chill lasted for almost an hour and then abruptly stopped, and he scarcely had time to catch his breath before he became overheated. He threw off the deerskin and bearskin and crawled away from the blazing fire into the cool recesses of the cavern, but still he felt as if he were burning up. He was tempted to hike down into the holler to search for a stream of cool water to immerse himself in, but he lacked the strength to hike because the awful heat seemed to be afflicting his brain and his energy; he felt of his forehead: it was still caked with blood from the bear's blow, but the skin was hotter than any fever he had ever had. He considered that possibly he had not cleaned and stanched his wounds well enough to prevent infection, but even the worst infection would not so suddenly give him a high fever. Would it?

His fever continued to immobilize him in agony for several hours, for most of the morning, and then, sometime in the afternoon, he began to drip with sweat. Hot as he had been all morning, he could not understand why he had not sweated during the morning, but it was afternoon before the cooling perspiration began to form in his pores and then gradually to soak him and his clothes. He wondered which of the three conditions was worse: to freeze, to burn, to sog. The same bear fur that had warmed him he now used to blot up some of the flood of lather from his skin until the fur had become as soggy as he was.

Was it beginning to darken so soon? The day was ending, and he had accomplished nothing except the helpless attention to his changes in temperature: first too cold, then too hot, now too wet, but now also too weak to do anything but lie upon the floor of the cave and collect his wits and try to imagine what had happened. This was not, he assured himself, the fever of an infection from the bear's wounding him. Had he eaten something bad? Had the bear meat contained some poison? Or had he perhaps unknowingly been bitten by a poisonous snake or reptile?

He got himself painfully up from the hard earth to search for his bota, and found it, but the goatskin bottle was empty. Had he drunk it dry during his fever? He stepped outside the cavern to begin a hike in search of water but realized he could not go anywhere; he was not just weak but increasingly dizzy. His head began to spin. Darkness was falling, not just from the setting of the sun but from something inside his head.

He fell to his knees and remained thus for a long time, he did not know how long: too tired to stand but too proud to fall over. His vision clouded. Then he saw the bed. The bed! Right over there in one corner of the cavern. How had he missed it before? Well, it wasn't any four-poster or even any kind of bedstead as such, but it was a neat stack of quilts and blankets and comforters and pillows, and even had some fresh white sheets on it! Somebody had made a bed inside the cavern. He crawled to it and heaved his body up onto it and felt his body sinking into it, and it was the most comfortable bed he'd ever been in, even if it didn't have any springs or slats or frame or anything but just this thick pile of stuffings. His hand gripped the white sheet with wonder, and then, gripping it further, he discovered that he was also gripping paper. Not just a white sheet of cloth but a white sheet of paper. He picked it up and had to hold it very close to his eyes to make out that it had letters written on it.

He squinted and managed to make out: *Dear you (I cannot write your name for fear somebody else might find this), I have been coming to this cavern every day in hopes of finding you here, and I have prepared this bed for you, bringing each time I came a blanket or two, and these pillows, one for you, one I hope for me, this bed for us, when you come here. You will come here, won't you? I know you will, it is just a matter of time, but as I write these words two weeks have passed since I came to Stay More and began to wait for you, and you have not come. This is the place that Latha said you would come to. I hope. Please come. If you are reading these words, it means you are here, and it means I will soon be with you. Lie still. Be here. The trees will sing for you until I join you. With all my love, The Lady.* And there was a P.S.: *Your new harmonica is under this bed.*

How could this be? Although Nail had had only the rising and setting sun as his compass, and had known that he was pointed in the right direction, he had a good idea of how far Newton County was from Little Rock, and there was simply no way he could already have reached it; he had to be still somewhere in Pope County, northeastern Pope County by his calculation, with maybe fifty miles, three or four days' travel, separating him from Stay More.

But now he groped beneath the pile of blankets and quilts until his hand touched metal, and he withdrew the harmonica: an M. Hohner Marine Band Tremolo Echo, identical to the one he'd had for years and had destroyed to make a dagger. He raised it to his mouth and kissed it, and then he began to play it, and he played it through the dark hours of the night until the trees, roused from their slumber, joined their voices to his music.

Then was it morning? Or did she appear with a lantern? Or was it neither morning nor lantern but her own light, the light that emanated from her goodness? He opened his eyes, realizing he had not slept but having no idea how long he had lain with his eyes closed: he opened his eyes and there she was, kneeling beside the bed she had made for him. She was smiling but also frowning: she was shocked at his appearance, at

346

the blood on his face from the bear's clawing him mixed with the red of the berry juice and his two-week growth of beard.

You made it! she said. *But are you all right?*

"I reckon not," he said. "I must be real bad sick, 'cause I don't have the least idee how I managed to git here."

She felt his brow. *You're real cold*, she said. *Cold as death.*

"Yeah, I've been either too cold or too hot or too wet for quite a spell." These words came out almost like stuttering, because of the chattering of his teeth and the trembling of his body.

Before he could protest that he looked awful and smelled worse, she climbed beneath the covers with him and held him tight and attempted to warm him. The thick quilts and coverlets piled atop them imprisoned her body heat and divided it with him, but that was not enough for both of them: she became cold herself. Together they trembled for a long time until each of them removed or parted enough of their clothing to make contact and penetration possible, and the pleasure of the contact and the penetration was so great as to make them oblivious to any cold or sickness or loneliness, and they continued it even beyond the point where they ceased being too cold and became too hot, beyond that to the point where they were both drenched with sweat, as well as the bed, and still neither of them reached the endpoint of the exertion.

Finally they had to stop, and they lay panting in a pile of wet bedclothes. She was the first to speak: *I guess you can't get over the mountain.*

He observed, "You caint either."

Let's rest, she said. *Let's nap and then try again.*

He napped. More than napped: he fell into a deep sleep without knowing that he slept, then fell out of a deep sleep without knowing that he had never slept, then discovered that he was neither shaking with cold nor melting with heat nor dripping with wet but had resumed a stable temperature and humidity. Light came from the mouth of the cavern, with full sunshine in it. There was no bed. If he had somehow got through the night without sleep, it had happened upon the bare earthen floor of the cavern: his arms and face were caked with dirt.

He had no energy whatever, not even enough to heed the urge to make water. He rolled over to one side, opened his fly, and urinated upon the dirt beneath him, shifting his body to avoid the dark puddle. He had no hunger but did have a mighty thirst; he recalled that he'd had it the previous evening but had done nothing about it, and now it was worse. He managed to get to his knees and crawl to where the bota lay, but discovered that it was empty and remembered that he had already tried it and found it empty. He attached the bota to his belt on one side and attached his hunting-knife in its sheath to the other side, donned his three furs, the coonskin cap, the deerskin cape, the damp bearskin robe, and then took up his bow and three remaining arrows and left the cavern. Downhill from it he looked back at it, and stared long at it as if he half-expected that she might appear, and then he gave his head a vigorous shake to clear it and staggered on down and out of the hollow and into the middle fork of the Illinois Bayou, where he removed his clothing and his furs and lay in the water for a long, long time.

Just soaking all that dirt from his body lifted his spirits, and afterward, resuming his hike, he felt lighter, light enough even to make a joke about it to himself: "I ought to feel lighter; I've washed off ten pounds of dirt." He even laughed, and his laughter helped him begin to climb the mountain ahead, which, before the morning was over, would be the hardest mountain he'd ever climbed, although it couldn't have been very high. He spent nearly all the morning on his hands and knees, or rising enough from his knees to lurch upward and grab a sapling trunk to pull himself another foot higher. He reflected that if he had been totally well, he could have stood up and hiked to the summit in less than an hour, but as it was it seemed to take him all day, reaching its summit with the last of his strength, unable to stand, crawling onward. He was too tired to notice, as he attained the plateau at the top of the mountain, that he was crawling through the garden patch of a homestead. By the time the dog bounded up to him and commenced barking, it was too late to find a way around.

"Jist hold it right thar!" a voice yelled at him, a high-pitched, trembling voice trying too hard to sound stern. He looked up into the muzzle of a shotgun held by a woman standing beside the barking dog. He raised his hands, one of them holding the bow and the arrows. "Drap thet bone air!" the woman ordered him; he complied and continued to hold his hands over his head, kneeling. She approached closer. "You kin understand English, huh?" she said. "Yo're a smart Injun, huh?"

"I aint no Injun," he said.

"Take off yore hat," she ordered, and he removed the coonskin cap, revealing his close-cropped scalp. Enough of his hair had grown back in two weeks or so to show that he was blond. The woman moved even closer but kept the shotgun pointed at his chest. "You aint, air ye?" she declared, in wonder. She appeared to be a youngish woman, or . . . it was hard to tell . . . she had lived a hard life that made her look thirty when she was hardly into her twenties. He reflected that she looked more like an Indian than he did. "What're ye doin creepin aroun in my guh-yarden with thet thar bone air?" she asked.

He looked down at his knees, and, sure enough, he had been crawling among squash vines. "I'm right sorry," he said. "I didn't notice it was yore guh-yarden."

"Whar ye from?" she demanded.

"Stay More," he said, but her blank look told him she had never heard of it, and he added, "Up in Newton County."

She inclined her head over her shoulder. "That's a fur piece up yonder," she said.

"How fur?" he asked.

"You don't know?" she challenged.

"I aint never been in this part of the country afore," he said.

"Wal, it's ever bit of seven mile to the county line," she said.

He laughed, partly with pleasure. "That's all?" he said. And then he exulted, "I'm jist about home!" But by then exhaustion, from having climbed the mountain and encountered a stranger, had taken hold of him: he abruptly lost his balance on his knees and fell over and then just lay there on his side, unable to rise.

"Air ye porely?" she asked, with some solicitation, dropping the muzzle of the shotgun. He could have reached up and yanked it out of her hand if he had wanted.

"Jist tard," he declared, weakly. "Jist real tard."

"Come sit in the shade of the porch, and I'll fetch ye a drink," she offered, and with surprising strength for a woman lifted him up from the ground so that he could stagger onward to her house.

He stayed to supper. More than that: he stayed the night. The woman—her name, she said, was Mary Jane Thomas—had two children, a girl of five named Elizabeth and a boy of three, Edward Junior, who were fascinated with this strange visitor wearing coonskin, deerskin, bearskin, and carrying a bone air. Edward Thomas Senior had been killed in an accident down to the sawmill two years before, and Mary Jane had stayed on at the homeplace, making a decent enough living off the land. This place was called Raspberry; there were two other families down the trail not too far, and that was it: Raspberry, Arkansas, population eighteen.

From Raspberry to Ben Hur, which was in northernmost Pope County, almost on the Newton County line, was indeed only seven miles, and this closeness to home (even though Ben Hur was still a good thirty or thirty-five miles from Stay More) was the reason Nail resisted Mary Jane's suggestion to stay awhile, or even forever if he had a mind to. She served him a magnificent supper: chicken and dumplings with sweet corn on the cob, a mess of fresh greens, snap beans, sliced tomatoes, and for dessert a blackberry cobbler with real cream. After putting the children to bed, she used the rest of the cookstove's heat to warm up some water for a good bath for Nail, with real soap, and a shave if he so desired (he did), and a change of clothes: he could help himself to what was left of her late husband's wardrobe, such as it was; Eddie Thomas had been roughly the same size, not quite as tall, as Nail. But before Nail put on his fresh shirt and trousers, she insisted on inspecting his wounds. She wanted to know how he had got each of them, and without going into detail about his crossing of the Arkansas River he explained that this wound had come from the sharp stob on a log and this wound had come from the claws of a bear, and so had this one, and these were tick bites or chigger bites, of course, and these were just blisters from his shoes, which were too tight. She gave him a pair of her late husband's boots, which fit too. She concocted a salve or ointment of some herbal or vegetable matter (he could only make out the smells of polecat weed and mullein leaves), which she insisted would help his cuts and bruises and scabs, and put it on the bad places for him. It was soothing. She offered him the makings of a cigarette, some leftover papers and a tobacco pouch of her late husband's, but he thanked her and declined. She asked if he would mind if she read the Bible aloud, and he didn't mind. She read some of Leviticus, and some of Job, and this of Matthew: "For I was an hungred, and ye gave me meat; I was thirsty, and ye gave me drink; I was a stranger, and ye took me in; naked, and ye clothed me; I was sick, and ye visited me; I was in prison, and ye came unto me." From the way she looked at him after reading these last words, he suspected she knew, or guessed, that he had been in prison.

It grew late. She yawned and told him, "I aint got a spare bed. You'd

350

be welcome to mine if this weren't jist the first night and I hardly know ye. Tomorrow night maybe we could jist sleep together."

"That's all right," he said. "I'm much obliged. I'd be jist fine on a pallet on the floor, and tomorrow I've got to be gittin me a soon start on back up home."

But the next morning, before breakfast, after a whole day of not bothering him at all, the chill hit him again. It shook him, and kept on shaking him violently for nearly an hour, although the woman piled up every quilt she owned on top of him, after getting him up off his pallet and into her deep, warm featherbed. At first she blamed and berated herself, thinking the chill had been caused by his sleeping on the floor, but soon she saw it was something much more severe than any lack of hospitality could have been blamed for.

"I do believe you've got the swamp fever," she told him, and then, after the chill had ceased and the burning fever had started, she was confirmed in her suspicion: "No doubt about it, you've got yoreself the bad malaria." She became almost happy at the prospect of keeping him another day, or longer, tending his fever with towels soaked in cold well water, and later, when he began to sweat profusely, lovingly blotting it all up with rags. She sent the girl, Betsy, down the trail to the neighbors' to see if she could borrow a little bit of whiskey, and the girl returned carrying the glass jar as if it held frankincense or myrrh.

Mary Jane put something into the whiskey; she refused to tell Nail what, but he, who could judge whiskey well enough to smell the feet of the boys who'd plowed the corn, knew the whiskey was adulterated. "I aint sposed to tell ye," she insisted, "or it would take the spell off." Whatever she put in (and I can only guess it probably was three drops of the blood of a black cat; Nail had observed a number of cats around the place) helped, although it tasted so awful he nearly gagged on it. He could not eat the fine dinner, or the leftovers at supper, but she forced him to drink some boneset tea, which is also very good for malaria, and to have another dose of the whiskey-with-cat's-blood every two hours, or as often as he could stand it. And at bedtime she crawled in beside him. "Do what ye want," she told him, but he had no strength to do anything, although he appreciated her closeness and softness and willingness.

Early the next morning, while she still slept, he awoke to find that enough of his strength had returned that he could take her if he wanted, but he had made his choice: whatever strength he had, he would use for the hike. He was fully dressed and ready to go before she woke up, blinking at the sight of him in her late husband's clothes in the pale light of dawn, and he protested that he didn't need any breakfast, but she begged him to stay and have a big plate of bacon and eggs and biscuits and jam, and the first real coffee he'd had in nearly a year.

And while he was pausing to eat before departure, the two children appeared and watched him eat, and Betsy asked him, "Don't ye wanter be our daddy?"

He could not finish eating. "I don't know how," he said. "I aint got any experience in that line."

"You're a fool," the woman said to him. "You don't know a good thang when it's lookin ye right squar in the face."

"I'm a fool, I reckon," he admitted.

"Have you got a woman waitin fer ye?" she asked.

"I shorely hope so," he said, and thanked her for everything and several times protested her insistence that he stay.

When it became apparent that she could not persuade him to stay, she gave him one more thing of her late husband's: a .22 rifle and a box of bullets for it. Nail had declined, but the woman had displayed her late husband's entire arsenal: two shotguns, three rifles, even a handgun. She had offered him his pick, and he had decided on the .22 as most convenient. He would not be needing the bone air anymore, would he? she asked. "Could ye leave it for Eddie, when he grows up? I druther he learnt to use it than ary arn."

Nail presented his bone air to Eddie. Eddie swapped him his dead father's felt fedora for the coonskin cap.

She walked him as far as the trail and pointed the direction toward Ben Hur.

"I'm shore much obliged," he said.

"Obliged enough to kiss me?" she asked.

And he took off the hat that had been her husband's, and he kissed her on the mouth and put the hat back on and did not look back, knowing that she'd not be watching him disappear, because it's real bad luck and even worse manners to watch somebody go out of sight.

Well, he told himself later on the trail, he wouldn't never forget where Raspberry was, and if things didn't work out between him and Viridis, he'd know where to find Mary Jane. Then he smiled and said to himself, But things is bound to work out between me and Viridis.

It was in 1880 that General Lewis (Lew) Wallace published a historical romance called *Ben Hur: A Tale of the Christ*, which became one of the best-selling novels of all time, and popular even in the Ozarks, where somebody discovered it about 1895 and decided to name a community after it, or, rather, after its title character, a Roman-educated Jew who converts to Christianity and does good deeds. There was no post office of that name until about 1930, when the boundary between Pope and Newton counties was redrawn and Ben Hur became a part of Newton County. As late as 1963, Ben Hur was the last community in Arkansas to receive electricity, and even today the eastern approach to the town remains the last stretch of unpaved state highway in the Ozarks.

When Nail Chism passed through Ben Hur, he did it openly and even waved at a few people he encountered. He could have been taken for a foot traveler on his way to Moore or Tarlton, which is exactly what he was, carrying the deerskin and bearskin folded up under one arm, not wearing them in the heat, and the .22 rifle in the crook of his other arm was no more or less than any traveler might have carried.

He was determined to reach the Newton County line before nightfall, and, while there were no signs along the road indicating the county line, he seemed to know when he had reached his home county: his pace slackened, his step faltered, and he stopped, knowing he had reached the end of the day's journey: just a little less than nine miles, which, in his weakened condition, had utterly exhausted him. For supper, he had only the fond recollection of his last supper at Mary Jane's, and then he went to sleep on a pile of leaves beneath a rock shelter in a place called Hideout Hollow.

The next day he awakened once again with severe chills and knew then, conclusively, that he had the "two-day ague," the form of malaria that recurs every other day. This third attack of the sequence of chills, fever, and sweating did not have the help of the medicine Mary Jane had given him; once again he was immobilized all day, and again he had the hallucination, or delirium, that he had reached Stay More and found a rock shelter in the glen of the waterfall prepared for him by Viridis. But this time when she appeared to him, she berated him for having slept with Mary Jane and told him he might as well go on back to Raspberry. On

353

the next "good" day, in between the recurrent sick days, his first waking thought was that he ought to turn back to Raspberry and just stay there, if not forever at least until he was wholly recovered from the malaria.

But he went on. For the duration of his next good day, he made no attempt to keep hidden in the woods but walked on the cleared wagon trails that connected Ben Hur to Moore, and Moore to Tarlton, and Tarlton to Holt. I calculate that he covered another eleven miles or so along those wagon trails, stopping only once to pass the time of day with an inquisitive driver who was hauling a load of hay from his lower meadows to his barn and wanted to know who Nail was and where he was headed and what he thought of this terrible drought. Nail almost relished the chance to chat casually with a countryman, a fellow hillman, and he even told the man the truth: what his name was, where he had been, and where he was heading. "Shore, I've heared of ye," the man acknowledged. "Matter of fact, I signed that thar petition to git ye off. Leastways I put my X on her."

As Nail politely declined (three or four times) the man's invitation to stay the night, the man asked, "Wal, air ye fixin to shoot Jedge Jerram?"

Nail laughed. "I'd shore lak to do it, but all I kin think about right now is gittin myself on up home."

"Don't take the right fork yonder," the man suggested. "That'd take ye down Big Creek towards Mount Judy. Cut back over yon mountain and ye'll come down to Tarlton. Stay More aint but about twelve, thirteen mile past thar. But you'd best jist come go home with me and stay all night."

"I'm much obliged," Nail said, and then, remembering his manners, counteroffered, "Why don't ye jist go to Stay More with me?"

"Better not, I reckon," the man said, and let him go, but called out from a distance, "I was you, I'd shore slay Jedge Jerram."

For the next several miles Nail thought about that. He had been bent, all these days, only upon reaching the hills of Stay More, making contact with his folks, and seeing Viridis without a screen or a table separating them. He had not given much thought to revenge upon Sull Jerram. He hoped he would never even have to encounter the man; if he did, he didn't intend to start anything; if Sull started something, Nail would be obliged to finish it. Certainly, he hated Sull, but he had not spent much time thinking about murdering him.

As that good day ended, somewhere short of Tarlton, Nail wished he had accepted the man's offer to spend the night. He knew that the next day promised another attack of chills, fever, and sweats, and he'd have been better off at the man's house; maybe the man had some quinine or something that Nail could have taken. But it was too late, he was miles past the man's place, and he needed to find something for supper that would tide him over the bad day, and to find a sheltered place to spend it.

His weakness, his fatigue, his sense of being so close to home that he could almost smell the air of Stay More overwhelmed him, made him giddy, staggered him. Late in the afternoon he found himself, he thought, in a sheep pasture! Real sheep, or at least tangible ones: he called to them, a flock of less than a dozen, "Sheep! sheep! sheepsheepsheep!" and they came to him, and he sank his fingers into their regrowing fleece, although they were skittish, smelling the bearskin he still carried. He inspected them carefully; whoever owned them did not know much about the care of sheep and was not feeding them right or keeping them happy. Nail could not see any near farmstead or signs of a trail leading to one, and if the owner of the sheep had a sheepdog, the dog was busy elsewhere. Nail decided to spend the night with the sheep, and he did. For his supper, he shot a squirrel with the .22 and roasted it over coals. The sheep watched him and sniffed the smoke of his campfire and made puzzled sheep's-faces.

When the chills seized him the next morning, he attempted to snuggle up against a ewe to keep warm, but she did not understand what he was doing and ran away from him. The bellwether, a castrated ram, led her and the other sheep off down the hill, away from Nail, who could not get up from the ground and follow them. He covered himself with his deerskin and his bearskin and shivered violently for what seemed longer than the usual hour. All day he watched for the sheep to return, but they did not, although he called them again when the sweats had cooled him enough to restore his ability to shout, and eventually he decided that the sheep were only part of his delirium.

Did he get up from the ground and move on? Or was that just another part of his delirium? It seemed to him that he was walking, but he could not actually feel his feet touching the ground; it was more like the kind of wayfaring that we do in dreams, moving soundlessly and effortlessly from place to place, maybe even leaving the ground and flying. He must have flown over a few of those mountains. Journey within a journey: fish leaping for him on the still pools of a richly imagined creek that looked so much like the west fork of Shop Creek near the village of Spunkwater, just over the mountain from home. Even the distant chimneys and schoolhouse bell tower of Spunkwater, where he hadn't been in longer than he could remember, he remembered still as looking like that, or created them to look that way: familiar and comfortable and welcoming. The village had been named by some early drought-stricken settler after the lifesaving rainwater that remains in the cavities of trees or stumps, from the Scottish "sponge-water." The drinking of spunkwater is supposed to cure you of wanderlust or make you handsome, one or the other or both, just as the waters of Solgohachia give you marital success.

If Nail actually stopped at Spunkwater for a sip of the leftover rainwater, then he was cured of his roaming and would never do it again, and was transformed back into a good-looking man. If he only imagined that he had reached Spunkwater, the last community before you approach Stay More from the east, then he was a beggar riding his wish and spurring it on beyond its endurance.

He would never afterward have any clear memory of the . . . hours? days? . . . of the following long passage of time. His last reasonably clear memory had been of the sheep disappearing, and that sheep pasture had been miles and miles from home, and then of his feeble efforts to find a shelter for the duration of his day's sickness, where he could lie still and pretend he was hiking through Spunkwater, and up the steep eastern slopes of Ledbetter Mountain above Butterchurn Holler, and down, down into the glen of the waterfall. If we are only going to imagine things, we may as well imagine them as we have known them.

The waterfall seemed so very real that he could almost use the help of the last time he had visited it, not the help of my letter but his memory of the last visit, before the trouble had started, in June of the previous year, just a little over a year before, and nothing had changed much since then, except that maybe the volume of the falls, springfed though it was, did not seem quite so full. That time he had explored again the caverns beneath the ledges on both sides of the waterfall and inspected their meager contents, the bits of woven stuff, shards of pottery, bones. This time he staggered into the larger cavern expecting to find exactly what he found: a bed. That bed was the best creation of his fevered brain, the product of his most burning fancy.

He fell into it, that pile of blankets, quilts, comforters, and pillows, topped, as he had known it would be, with fresh white sheets, but he forgot to grope around for the fresh white sheet of paper with her handwriting on it that would tell him there was a harmonica beneath the bedpile; nor did he think to grope for the harmonica and play it all night. Nor did he think to notice even if it was night or day. His eyes closed as soon as he hit the bedpile, and he spread his arms to embrace the bedpile, and his overworked imagination failed him and dropped him into a deep, deep slumber.

I was on my way to my own little waterfall when I spotted the mullein stalk standing upright. Looking back, it is a wonder how I managed to keep on going to my destination. My first impulse was to fetch Viridis immediately with the news that the mullein stalk was up! But two things stopped me: First, I really needed that bath; it was an exceptionally hot morning, and I'd sweated more than a girl should, and I wasn't about to go off to meet my hero with garden dirt on my face and dried sweat all down my sides. And second, I could just see myself hollering, "Viridis! Viridis! The *mul-lein* has risen!" and her saying, "The what?" and me trying to explain and even forgetting an important fact: you can't tell anyone about the magic of the mullein, or it's sure to spoil the magic. If I told Viridis, or anyone, that the mullein had announced the safe return of Nail Chism to Stay More, provided they didn't think I was crazy or just a silly, superstitious girl, I might be embarrassed to discover that my act of telling had wiped out the act of his coming.

So I did two things: I went on up the holler and calmly took my bath . . . well, maybe not calmly, but deliberately enough to make sure that I got thoroughly washed off from head to toe, and even washed my hair, which would mostly dry in the sunshine before I could get home and brush it. And then I went on up to the glen of the waterfall alone, or alone except for Rouser, whom I couldn't persuade to sit or stay. I even paused at the house, before trying to persuade him to sit or stay, to change from my faded gingham dress into my better blue calico, and then to brush my hair as best I could to get most of the kinks out. I thought of maybe a little rouge but decided against it. I did powder my nose, although it would become unpowdered again by the time I got to the glen of the waterfall. I wanted to wear my good shoes, but it was a long hike, so I made up my mind to wear my ugly working-shoes and take them off before I got there.

"Where you goin in that dress?" my mother yelled as I was sneaking out the front door. "This aint Sunday, you fool."

If she'd been more civil, I would have answered her. Instead, I kept on going, and told Rouser to sit, but he wouldn't. I told him to stay, but he wouldn't. I nearly took a stick to him.

Finally I just tried to ignore him, and he followed me all the way up the mountain to Nail's old sheep pastures, and across them to the forest, and through the cool, dark forest to the bright glen of the waterfall. I kept telling myself that all I wanted to do was find out if my mullein had been lying to me. There are, after all, a few known instances when superstitions didn't do a bit of good, they only made you feel better or they out and out refused to cooperate, for some perverse reason of their own. It was just possible that my mullein stalk had mistaken Nail for somebody else, or else was a botanical freak that couldn't stop growing straight anyhow. If by some small chance the mullein stalk had lied, I would be the first one to know it, and the last and *only* one to know it, and then I was going to tromp the heck out of that mullein and start over with a fresh one. If, as I devoutly believed, my mullein stalk was being honest and trustworthy, I intended to summon Viridis immediately and tell her that by accident I'd discovered that Nail was back. Well, of course I'd have to say howdy to him before I ran back to the village. I couldn't just sneak up and make sure it was him and then run like the dickens.

These were the thoughts that were running through my head while I hiked as fast as my legs would carry me. But there was another thought too, and I'm not ashamed to admit it: I had a kind of proprietary interest in Nail Chism. From the moment the whole trouble had started, a year before, I'd scarcely gone a day without thinking about him. I wanted him to be okay. I wanted him to escape the prison, as he had done, and I wanted him to make it safely back home, and I wanted him to live happily ever after. Sure, I wanted him, period. But that was something else. I knew Viridis deserved him a thousand times more than I did, and I knew she was going to have him, and I knew they were going to live so happily ever after that it would be like a fairy tale, and I knew in my bones that ever after was about ready to begin. But for a little while, just a little while, he was mine.

Yes, I took off my ugly shoes before reaching the glen of the waterfall and walked the last hundred yards barefoot and stopped where the water was still in a pool, away from the plunge of the falls, to look down into it and see my reflection: my face was red, not from any rouge, and both hands could not arrange my black hair the way I wanted it, but at least I had on my best dress, and a strand of artificial amber beads around my neck. I wasn't beautiful like Viridis, but I wasn't ordinary either.

In the mouth of the cavern, as my eyes adjusted to the darkness, the first thing I saw was the rifle. A .22, lying on top of a big wad of black fur: the skin of a bear, I figured out. Neither the rifle nor the bearskin was among the items that Viridis and I had steadily been furnishing the cavern with. Viridis had considered leaving the Smith & Wesson revolver in the cavern but had decided to keep it with her, for her own protection. She had left no firearm here, or at least she hadn't told me about any firearm, and she told me virtually everything.

And then I saw him. I knew it was him, and yet I was afraid. Who else could it have been? Since that last time in court I'd nearly forgotten what he looked like, except for his body: no man of my acquaintance, then or after, ever had a body as splendidly put together and held together as Nail Chism did, all the parts of it in perfect shape and accord. The body was sprawled out face up on the bed that Viridis and I had prepared for him. His eyes were closed, and I had to study his chest for a long time to determine that it was slightly moving with his breathing. He was not dead. But he was sound asleep at full day, nine o'clock in the morning. I'd expected to see him in prison clothes, something of which I had only a vague idea, zebra stripes and such, nothing like what he was actually wearing: just a man's light-blue chambray shirt, some gray cotton trousers, a pair of boots that didn't look like he'd hiked all the way from Little Rock in them, and a felt fedora hat, fallen upside down behind his head as if he'd dropped to the bed without bothering to take it off.

I resisted the impulse to shake him and see if he would awaken. I sat cross-legged on the floor of the cavern near him and studied him and felt a wild mixture of feelings: exultation that he was home, pride in my mullein stalk for being accurate and straight-up-and-down, admiration for his rugged and battered but beautiful features (the blond hair was growing back rapidly), befuddlement at his deep slumber in broad daylight, and, most of all, growing certainty that he was the one who had killed Sull Jerram. I didn't understand why my mullein stalk had not announced his return on the same day that Sull Jerram was killed, but the ways of mullein are as mysterious as they are magic and infallible, when they're not just being ornery.

I had to get Viridis, and yet I could not. First I had to see if he would wake, and let him know that everything was all right and that I would fetch Viridis right away. I wanted to somehow thank him for accepting my suggestion that the glen of the waterfall would make a good hiding-place. I wanted him to know that I'd helped put all of these things in the cavern for him, which, I saw by looking around me, he hadn't yet used: the cans of corned beef and beans and such were unopened, the pocketknife with can opener attachment untouched, the bar of soap still wrapped, the yards of mosquito netting neatly folded up, the hunting-knife still sheathed. He had not disturbed any of these things . . . except, I noticed, the harmonica, which now lay on top of the pile of bedclothes, near his open hand, as if he had held it and maybe even played on it but let it drop.

For the rest of the morning I stayed with him, waiting for him to wake. It must have been getting on toward noon. Rouser had wandered off after giving a good long sniff to the bearskin and to Nail's body. Maybe Rouser had gone back home; he wasn't all that faithful. I was getting hungry, and thought of opening a can of something to eat, but the sound of the can opener might wake him, so I waited. I felt like an intruder, in a way. I was invading Nail's privacy, or the privacy of his sleep: in sleep the body does things to us that we don't know about but wouldn't want to share with anyone else: in sleep Nail's most private part distended and bulged mightily within his trousers, and fascinated me but reddened me all over with embarrassment or guilt at watching or . . . yes, reddened me with a kind of lust. I was not, for going on three years now, a virgin, and I knew the meaning of that thickening and extension inside his pants, but I had never actually *observed* it, even if my observation now was impeded by the covering of his trousers. I knew it could happen in dreams: sometimes I'd seen Rouser asleep, when he wasn't chasing rabbits in his dreams, chasing some imaginary bitch and letting his pink thing swell and pop out of its furry sheath and drool. I wondered if Nail was dreaming about Viridis, even dreaming about something he'd never done, because, to the best of my knowledge at that time, in twenty-seven years he had never succeeded in doing what I had done nearly three years before, when I was only eleven. While studying him, I amused myself by imagining that I was reaching out and unbuttoning the fly of his trousers and liberating from the prison of its clothes that big convict.

This daydream was so real and diverting that I was shocked to realize his eyes were open and looking at me as if I had actually done it. Or maybe in my lust I really had done it while thinking it was only a daydream. One of his big hands abruptly covered his groin. He stared at me and began to tremble. Was he afraid of me?

I was smiling as big as I could, but also frowning, at his trembling. "Howdy, Nail," I said. "It's just me, Latha."

"Where am I?" he asked.

"You made it!" I said. "But are you all right?"

"I reckon not," he said. "I must be real bad sick, 'cause I don't have the least idee how I managed to git here."

I reached out and put my hand on his forehead. At the real touch of his skin I knew that I had only imagined touching him down below. Reality is always more touchable than imagination. "You're real cold," I said. "Cold as death."

"Yeah, I've been either too cold or too hot or too wet for quite a spell." His words came out almost like stuttering, because of the chattering of his teeth and the trembling of his body.

I drew a blanket up over him. And then another one. And yet another one. And then a quilt. I draped and tucked more covers over him than I'd ever had myself the coldest winter night of my life, and still he shook so mightily that I thought he'd pop right out of the bed. I couldn't understand how anybody could be so cold on such a hot morning. Well, it was cooler in the cavern than out in the sunshine, but not all *that* cool. I touched my own brow, and I felt normal; no, I felt a good bit hotter than normal. I considered that his conscience might be giving him a nervous chill: that he had killed a man and now feared the consequences. But nobody ever shook like that simply from guilt or fear. He was, I understood, sick. I wanted to run and fetch not Viridis but Doc Swain, but I was afraid that Nail would shake himself to death and freeze while I was gone.

So, almost without thinking, I did what I did: I climbed beneath the covers with him and held him tight, trying to warm him with the heat, the plenty of it, from my own body. The thick quilts and blankets piled atop us imprisoned my body heat and divided it with him, but that was not enough for both of us: I became cold myself. Together we trembled for a long time. We didn't have our arms around each other, not all four arms anyhow, but we had our bodies pressed as hard together as they could get, and that big bulge down there in his pants had never gone away, and my mind was filled with wild thoughts and fear and chill and lust and everything.

Then we were not side by side, exactly. In an effort to still his shaking, I had pressed down on him, mashed him to his back, and I lay hard atop him, the whole length of him, mashing down, and then he did have both arms around me, around my back and my waist both, holding me tight to him. We squirmed and shook and squeezed in that position for so long that somehow the bulge in his britches worked itself directly beneath the juncture of my thighs so that our most private places were not just touching but mashing very hard and rubbing harder, and before I knew it I had begun a different kind of shaking, not of nervousness or chill but of fulfillment of the exertion and labor of love. I cried out. Maybe, even, I passed out, because the next thing I was aware of, and it seemed time had gone by, he was no longer trembling at all. He was perfectly still, except for his breathing, and he had thrown the covers off us, and I wondered if the weight of all of me on top of him was mashing him uncomfortably, but he didn't seem to mind, and I didn't want to move from that position just yet, because I knew that once I did, I would never find myself like that with him, ever again.

At last I rolled off and lay there beside him, not touching him anymore, giving him up to whoever would claim him that he belonged to. I just looked at him, with love but also with a little wondering: had he maybe just faked his shaking in order to get me to do what I'd done? Because he wasn't shaking the least bit anymore. He was smiling, and I know it was just a smile of being friendly and maybe a little embarrassed, but it also seemed like a smile of having tricked me into that enjoyment.

Then he said, "You went over the mountain."

"Yeah," I said, as if to let him know that I knew what he meant saying that. "I got over the mountain."

"You're not Viridis," he said, as if he'd just noticed.

I had to laugh. "I wish I was," I said. "I sure truly wish I really was. But don't you even know me?"

He smiled again. "Some ways, you're better than Viridis," he said.

"What ways?" I wanted to know.

"You're home folks," he said. "You wrote and told me about this hide-away. And I do honestly misdoubt that she'd have warmed me up the way you jist now did. Or gone over the mountain."

"Aw, I had to climb that mountain," I said.

"I know you did," he said. "I shore appreciate it, what-all you've done."

"You're not shakin no more," I observed.

"No, you see, Latha, I've got the two-day ague, and the way it works is, I shake like crazy for an hour, and then I'm burnin up, like I am right now, for another little spell, and then I commence to sweat like a stud horse—'scuse me, Latha—I get soppin wet for a time, and then I'm okay for another twenty-four hours, and it hits me again the next day."

"I've never had that," I declared, "but I've heard of it. You've done been skeeterbit."

"Yeah, that's what causes it," he said. "Skeeters."

"You'd best let me run and fetch Doc Swain," I told him. "And of course Viridis too. She'd be real mad at me if she knew I'd come up here by myself."

"You don't have to tell her nothin," he told me.

"I'll make up a story," I said. "I'm pretty good at that, don't you know?"

"I reckon," he said.

I stood up and straightened my dress and patted my hair into place. "Can I get you anything 'fore I go? A drink of water? Anything to eat?"

"Just maybe a sip of water is all, right now," he said, lying there in the pain of his high fever.

"And we'd better hide that .22 before Doc Swain sees it," I announced, and tried to think of a safe place to hide it.

"How come?" Nail wanted to know.

"*How come?* Well, his dad is still justice of the peace, don't you know, and they've already been up here checkin when they came to get Sull's body, so naturally Doc would put two and two together and know it was you." Nail just stared at me as if he hadn't the faintest idea what I was talking about, and I began to wonder if maybe he really didn't. "That *is* your rifle yonder, aint it?" I asked.

"Yeah," he said.

"How long have you been here? What day did you get here?"

He shook his head. "I honestly aint got the foggiest notion." Then he asked, "What did you say about Sull's body?"

Somehow, the way he asked that, I knew he really didn't know anything about it. Maybe he had done it in his delirium, but maybe he hadn't done it at all. "Nail," I said, "day before yesterday morning, right down the trail yonder, Sull Jerram was shot off his horse with a .22 bullet."

The way Nail looked, I knew he was, if not innocent, ignorant of the act. "What was he doin up here?" he asked.

"Followin Viridis to find your hidin-place, I reckon," I said.

"Who shot him? Did she do it?"

"No, I thought it was you, but maybe it wasn't, if you weren't even here day before yesterday."

"Where was he hit?"

"Right yonder, jist beyond that big white ash tree."

"No, I mean where in his body did the bullet hit him?"

I touched a spot behind my ear. "Right here," I said.

Nail shook his head. "Was he hurt bad?"

"He's dead, Nail."

"No."

It got awfully quiet up there in that cavern; all you could hear was the sound of the waterfall. Finally I made some conversation: "They buried him this mornin up at the Jasper cemetery, but your sister wasn't even plannin to go to the funeral, and I don't reckon nobody else went neither, 'cept the preacher and maybe the sherf." Nail didn't comment on that, so I went on: "You never saw such a happy bunch of folks as everbody in Stay More. We threw a big squar dance up to the schoolhouse to celebrate." Nail managed a smile but didn't say anything about that either. "The sherf locked up your brother Waymon at the Jasper jail, but Waymon has got a good alibi because he was gone plumb to Harrison at the time it happened, to get some medicine for your dad."

"How's my dad?" Nail asked.

"I reckon Doc Swain can tell ye all about that," I said. "I better go git him right now." Then I suggested, "Why don't I jist take that .22 with me and hide it somewheres off from here?"

"No," Nail said. "Leave it where it is. I want Doc Swain to see it."

"You're crazy," I said.

He smiled. "So are you, Latha. Comin up here like ye done. Takin keer of me. Warmin me up like ye done. Weren't ye scared there was a danger I could've raped ye like they thought I done to Rindy?"

364

I smiled. "I wush ye *had* done somethin to me. And now I won't never git me another chance. Good-bye, Nail." I turned and fled.

———

I wondered who to tell first: Viridis or Doc Swain. As it turned out, I didn't have to decide, because when I went into the village looking for one or the other, I found them sitting together out on the porch of Doc Swain's clinic, enjoying the shade and the afternoon breeze. I don't know what they'd been talking about as I strolled up, but they'd become pretty good friends and could have been talking about anything under the sun.

"Howdy, Latha," Doc Swain said.

"Howdy, Doc," I said.

"Hi, Latha. How are you today?" Viridis said.

"Hi, Viridis. I'm pretty good. How are you?"

"Fine."

"I wish it would come a rain," Doc Swain said.

"We could use one," I allowed.

"I wish it would come a man named Nail," Viridis said.

"We could use one of them too," I said. I timed a few beats before adding, "And it looks like we've done finally got one, sure enough."

Doc and Viridis both raised their eyebrows at me. "How's thet?" Doc asked.

"He's back," I said.

Doc looked up and down the main road of Stay More. "Shore," he said. "On a big fine white horse, in a full suit of steel armor and chain mail."

"No, he's flat on his back, with alternate-day malaria," I said.

Doc said, "Huh?" and Viridis said, "Where?"

"At the waterfall," I said to her. And then I had my story ready for her: "I thought I'd seen you on Rosabone riding by, heading that way, and I figured you'd looked for me and not found me, so I ran off after you, but I couldn't catch up, and so I went on to the waterfall by myself, and there he was, in the cavern."

Viridis jumped up. "Really?" she said.

"Yes, and he's got a bad case of alternate-day malaria, and this is the alternate day, with chills and fevers and sweats."

Doc Swain jumped up. "Really?" he said. "That's shore enough the symptoms. Where is this cavern?"

"Just beyond where you went day before yesterday morning."

Doc and Viridis exchanged looks, and I knew they were thinking what I had thought, and I said, "But I don't think it could've been him who done it. I don't think he even got here until sometime last night."

Viridis was leaving the porch. "I'll saddle Rosabone," she said.

Doc was leaving the porch. "Let me get my bag, and then I'll get my horse too."

I was not leaving the porch. They hadn't invited me. I waited to see if either of them would think to invite me. I didn't have a horse, and I'd slow them down if I rode behind Viridis on Rosabone, and I was prepared to refuse the offer if she made it. But she didn't. She reappeared very shortly, astride the mare. She hadn't bothered to stop to change into her jodhpurs but was still wearing her dress and had hiked it up immodestly to get her legs over the mare's back. Doc Swain appeared on his horse, with his gladstone bag strapped behind the saddle. His dog tried to go with them, but Doc said, "Sit, Galen. Stay," and the dog obeyed.

At least, both Doc and Viridis thought to wave good-bye to me.

I was hungry, I hadn't had any dinner, but I just sat there on Doc's porch. The least I could do, I thought, was act as his receptionist; in case any patients came, I could tell them the doctor was out on a call and would be back shortly. How shortly I didn't know, but I sat there for a long time on Doc's porch. Galen slept. No patients came. Some of the men who gathered every afternoon over on the porch of Ingledew's store drifted into the village and took their places, sitting on crates, nail kegs, and odd chairs, whittling with their pocketknives and spitting, and scarcely throwing me a glance. Doc Plowright, who had his clinic practically right across the road from Doc Swain's, stepped out on his porch and stared at me for a bit, wondering what a patient of his was doing sitting on the porch of his competitor. Then he went back inside. He didn't have any patients today either.

The afternoon passed. Rouser showed up from wherever he'd been, following my trail and finding me. Rouser and Galen argued for a while but decided it was too hot for a fracas. They lay together on the porch floor and went to sleep. To entertain myself, I had a few pretty good daydreams, with real people in them, Viridis and Nail, the woods, the trees, the moon and the stars, forever.

By and by Doc Swain returned, stopping his tired horse in the yard of his clinic and getting down. He came up and sat with me on the porch.

"Latha," he said, "I do believe you were absolutely right. It shore enough *is* the two-day ague, or alternate-day malaria, as you call it. But he's gonna be all right. I gave him some quinine and some advice. He's gonna be all right. Them two are gonna live happy ever after."

on

The trees are singing. She notices it as soon as they reach the tall white ash beneath which Sull Jerram fell. She hears the ash itself, who starts the chorus. As she and the doctor ride between or beneath them, those last hundred yards, the trees one by one pick up the song until all of them, white ash, oak, hickory, maple, walnut, beech, chinquapin, elm, locust, and even cedar are harmonizing in their serenade of her. The smaller dogwood, redbud, persimmon, and sassafras try to join in but are almost drowned out.

"Shore is purty way back up around in here," Doc observes. "Listen at that waterfall."

"That's not the waterfall, Colvin," she tells him.

He stops his horse, dismounts, listens. A smile of pleasure comes to his face. "I do believe you're right," he says. "It's something else. Angels, maybe."

The late-afternoon light from the west breaks into long rays through the boughs of the high trees; the black hole of the mouth of the cavern is illuminated as if by spotlights. The singing swells. Doc's halloo overrides it, cuts into it.

"HELLO THE CAVE!" he calls. "Nail! It's us. It's Colvin Swain and yore ladyfriend."

The singing of the trees muffles whatever reply comes from within, a feeble acknowledgment or welcome.

She walks behind Doc, partly afraid. If the sight of him is truly awful and causes her to stumble, she can stumble against Doc's back and he will turn and catch her.

But it is Doc who stumbles, on the scree or talus of the cavern's lip. She is thoroughly familiar with every step of the way, but he is not, and falls. She helps him up. He is embarrassed. "Kinder pre-carious there," he remarks. She waits to let him go on ahead of her.

It takes a long moment for their eyes to readjust from the spotlight beams of afternoon light to the cavern's dim interior. While the two of them are blind, the trees, seeing her disappear, muffle their cantata to a murmur. She is aware of the quiet and the dark and the nearness of Nail. Then she sees him: he is making a great effort to get out of the bed. He has his feet outside the bed, on the ground, but the bed is not much higher than the ground itself, and he cannot rise up. Colvin Swain moves to him quickly and puts a hand on his shoulder. "Here there, boy, jist lay easy! Don't ye try to git up." The doctor forces him to lie back down but notices the dampness of the bedclothes and exclaims, "Woo, you shore wet the bed!"

"Sweat," says Nail. It is his first word, but as he lies down he fixes his eyes upon hers and smiles. "Howdy, Miss Monday," he says, with mock formality. "Glad ye could make it."

"Good afternoon, Mr. Chism," she returns, with careful politeness. "I'm proud to be here."

"Heck," says Doc Swain. "I thought you two knew each other better'n *that*. Don't ye even want to shake hands? I could turn my back, I reckon, if ye want to do more than that."

"We can wait," Nail says.

"Wal, let's take yore temper-ture," Doc says, and sticks a thermometer into Nail's mouth. Then he begins his examination, palpating the spleen. After a while he removes the thermometer and studies it and says, "Hmm," and begins asking Nail several questions. How many days now has he had this trouble? Has he had any diarrhea? Has he lost consciousness?

Viridis only half-listens to the conversation, the questioning. She is still trying to hear what the trees are singing, but it is soft and distant. She takes note of the careful array of supplies she's left for him, all of them untouched. She opens the bag containing the spare bed linen and takes out fresh sheets, to replace the damp ones, and a fresh pillowcase.

"This is shore some layout ye got here," Doc observes, to Nail. "You say you think you jist got here last night?"

Viridis explains, "I put all of this here, for him." And she thinks to add, "With Latha's help."

"I see," Doc says. "Been plannin a hideaway, huh?"

"He couldn't very well go right straight to his folks' house, could he?" she says.

"Reckon not," the doctor admits. "The sherf would shore to haul him off to jail purty quick."

"You won't tell where we . . . you won't tell anybody about this place, will you?" she asks.

"Wal now, that depends," Doc says. "You'uns know that my dad is the justice of the peace, and I shore couldn't tell my own dad a lie." The doctor opens his gladstone bag, rummages around in it, brings out a pair of bottles. "These yere pills is for yore fever," he says. "Take a couple of 'em whenever ye git to feelin too hot, but not more'n six or eight a day. Now, this here blue bottle is the quinine, and I want ye to take a spoonful . . ." (he turns to Viridis) ". . . is they a spoon here? okay, a spoonful ever four hours or so, till it's all gone, and then you . . ." (he turns to Viridis) ". . . you come and git me and I'll come and give him some more of it, if he needs it, and he probably will. Now, this quinine will probably make ye start hearin things, funny noises that aint real. It's called tinnitus, and it aint as serious as it sounds, but I figured I'd better warn ye. You'd better jist rest and stay off yore feet and get good and well afore ye try to do anything."

"Anything?" Nail says.

Doc Swain coughs. "Anything *real* strenuous. Anything that you'd have to git out of bed to do. You can do anything ye want as long as it's in bed." He coughs again.

"Right," Nail says. "When can I go see my dad?"

"Not till I tell ye," the doctor says. "I don't want ye to go no further'n that white ash down the trail yonder till I give ye permission."

All three of them glance at the white ash, whose pianissimo murmuring seems audible only to Viridis. She understands the significance of Doc Swain's reference to it, and her eyes shift, as theirs do, from the white ash to the rifle lying atop the black bearskin.

"I aint never used that on a person," Nail says of the rifle.

"Who said ye did?" Doc challenges.

"You're makin hints," Nail observes. "I jist want ye to know right here and now, I never kilt Sull."

"How'd ye know he's been kilt, if ye didn't do it?" Doc says, almost cocky with the knowledge that he'd tripped him up and caught him.

"Latha tole me," Nail says.

"Damn that gal!" Doc swears. "Why couldn't she of waited and let me do it?"

"You couldn't tell me as nice as she did," Nail says.

"That's a .22, aint it?" Doc demands.

"Yeah, but I aint never used it on a person. I swear."

"How you gonna convince a jury of that?"

"I done already failed to convince one jury," Nail says. "I hope I don't never have to try to convince another one."

"Boy," Doc says sternly. "If this aint a mess. If this aint the beatenest kettle of fish ever I seed. Damned if I want to be a goldarned *accessory*, or even accused of one, but I am gonna take that rifle with me, and I am gonna keep it where nobody can find it, and if you'uns have to have you a firearm for keepin off the wolfs and bars at night, I'll bring ye a different caliber next time I come up here."

Surely, she thinks, the other two, the two men, can hear what she hears, the rising chorus of the trees. "Colvin Swain," she says, "you are a very nice man."

"Heck, shoot," the doctor grumbles. "I got to git on back to work. I got to drop in on another patient, Nail's dad, and give him the word. The word is gonna make him well, jist wait and see if it don't. While I'm at it, do you want me to send yore brother Luther up here with anything you need? No, wait, I aint gonna tell nobody whar yo're at, not yet anyhow. Not even yore folks. But they'll be mighty proud to hear the news." The doctor snaps shut his gladstone bag and lifts it. He stares at Viridis for a moment before finding the words he wants to say to her. "You take good keer of him, now, hear me? See to it he takes his medicine. Keep him off his feet."

"Yes, sir," she says.

The doctor steps over and takes the rifle in his other hand. "You'uns be good now, hear?"

"Don't be rushin off, Doc," Nail says formally, in the code of backwoods politeness. "Stay more and spend the night with us."

"I'd shore lak to, but I better be gittin on down home. You'uns come go home with me."

"Better not, I reckon," Nail says. "Stay and have supper with us."

"Caint do it, this time," Doc says.

Viridis listens in wonder as the two men invite and counterinvite each other until finally Nail says, "Wal, come back when ye kin stay longer," and the doctor is allowed to leave.

She walks him to his horse and thanks him and repeats Nail's invitation. Then she asks, "When you told us to be good, just how good did you have in mind?"

371

He grins, and blushes a bit. "I was jist tryin to be silly," he says. "I didn't mean nothin by thet."

"So it wouldn't hurt him if we . . ." she begins, but can't quite find the words.

"Lak I said, don't let him do nothin that caint be done in bed," the doctor says. He climbs up on his horse and turns to go. His parting words are spoken down to her. "But I imagine there's quite a heap of things a body can do in bed, besides sleep." He starts to ride away. She waves. He stops the horse, reins it, holds it; he sits there listening, looking not at her but off at the forest. "Do you hear that?" he asks. He glances at her for confirmation, and she smiles and nods her head. "What d'ye reckon is makin that purty sound?"

"The trees," she says. "They're singing."

"Is that what it is?" he asks. "Wal, how 'bout that? Don't that beat all?"

"It surely does beat all," she agrees, and the good doctor, shaking his head in wonder, rides away.

And as soon as she gets back to Nail's bedside, she wants to know: "Don't you hear them?"

"Yeah, but the doc tole me this medicine would cause that."

"You haven't taken the medicine yet," she points out. "But you're going to, right this minute." And she fetches a spoon from the implements she hoarded for him and makes him take his quinine.

Some of it dribbles down his chin, and he raises his hand to wipe his mouth, but she stops his hand and licks up the dribble herself. It is very bitter; both of them make faces. She explains she did that to see what it tastes like.

He is looking all around, as if searching for something. She asks him what he's looking for. "Bird," he says.

"What bird?"

"The guard, Bird. I caint believe he's not watchin us. I caint believe we're all alone."

She gives him a long kiss, a very long one, longer than any she'd ever done with Bird watching. He tastes of quinine, but she's already tasted it, and it doesn't bother her. When finally she breaks the kiss (realizing it would be up to her to start or break anything), she asks, "Would Bird have let us do that?"

"I reckon he must be off-duty," Nail observes, grinning.

"There's not even a table between us," she remarks.

"Just these soppin bedcovers," he observes.

She squeezes the fabric of the quilts and blankets, which are wet from his perspiration, although he has not been sweating for some time now. She whips the bedclothes off him. "There's not much sun left in the afternoon," she observes, "and I'd better hang these out to catch the last of it." She starts to carry out the bedcovers but turns. "Are you cold?"

"Not right now," he tells her.

She takes the wet blankets and quilts outside the cavern and drapes them in sunlight over the boughs of the cedars. She talks to the trees while she does it, and Rosabone thinks she's talking to her and lifts her head to listen. She talks to Rosabone too. When she returns to the cavern, Nail asks her, "Who were you talkin to?" and she tells him the trees and her horse.

She kneels beside the bed and, with him still in it, begins changing the sheet: this technique she learned years ago when her mother was bedridden: you roll them to one side to remove the old sheet partway, roll them to the other side to get the rest of it, roll them back when the fresh sheet's in place. But Nail is heavy; rolling him toward her, her hand slips and snags in the string around his neck, and she lifts it till her fingers hold the charm, the tiny golden tree. She's nearly forgotten her little Christmas present to him, and hasn't seen it since the day she bought it at Stifft's Jewelers and took it home and wrapped it in a wad of tissue to enclose in her first letter to him. Thinking of that, she remembers that somewhere in Rosabone's saddlebags is the bundle of all the letters she wrote him which they never let him have at the penitentiary, or which she has written in her idle hours in Stay More while waiting for him. More than a hundred pages, no, closer to two hundred: the story of her life, or all the parts of it she wants him to know, for now: her childhood in the big house on Arch Street, her brothers, her sister, her mother, and as much of her father as she can mention, for now. The story of her art lessons with Spotiswode Worthen. The story of her travels: an Arkansawyer in Chicago, in New York, in Paris, in London, in Arles, and then around the world with Marguerite Thompson Zorach. The story of her first visit to Stay More. The story of her visits to the governor. The story of the day she went to the ballpark to meet Irvin Bobo, and what happened that evening.

All the stories. One of the letters contains a story of what was not actually allowed to happen but was only imagined: the night that the governor permitted her to spend in Nail's cell. Another one of the letters, written in the future tense and the second person, contains the story of what will not yet have happened: the first night they will actually spend together. But she did not know, when she wrote it, that he would be ill with malaria, so that story is overly romantic, although the setting for it is actually this exact place and time, this cavern, this night, this July.

Should she let him read it? It would tickle him, amuse him, and any good humor would be sure to help him get well. But it was rather immodest and even frank in its details. Wouldn't he be shocked? Wouldn't he consider her brazen or indecent?

"Why do you keep on holdin it?" he asks, trying to see her hand wrapped around the golden tree beneath his chin.

"I'm thinking," she says, and puts the tree charm back against his chest. Nestled there in the golden hair of his chest, the golden tree is like a mighty oak in a thicket of brambles. "I have a letter for you, if you'd like to read it."

"You bet," he says.

"But it's nearly two hundred pages long."

"What else have we got to do?"

She gives him a sidelong glance, and then she gives him a mock punch in the ribs. "*You*," she says. And then she says, "We've got lots else to do. For one thing, we've got to eat. I'd better start supper. What would you like?"

"Chicken'n dumplins," he announces.

"Sorry," she says. "The eggs haven't hatched yet. And besides, I don't know how to make dumplings. But tomorrow I'll go get your mother to teach me."

Nail laughs: the first she's heard him laugh in a long time. "You honestly *would* do that, wouldn't ye?" he tells her, delighted.

No, not only have the eggs not hatched, but there are no chickens to lay them. She wonders if they could keep a flock of fowl in this glen of the waterfall. Would the varmints of the woods get them? But she has seen no varmints. If there are wolves or bears hereabouts, they haven't made themselves visible.

374

For their first meal together, she is obliged to put together a light supper of crackers, cheese, and a tin of sardines. But she discovers she has no appetite at all, not because the offering isn't appetizing. And he discovers he hasn't any appetite whatsoever, not because he's ill.

Love has no stomach.

The supper uneaten, they keep close, she sitting cross-legged beside the pallet of his bed, he lying. After a while he suggests, "You could read it to me."

"What?"

"The two-hundred-page letter."

"Oh," she says, and again: "Oh." The light in the cavern is just enough to read by, but it won't remain that way long. She'll have to get up and light the kerosene lantern after a time. "Well." She thinks awhile, then says, warningly, "I'll blush terribly over parts of it."

"I'll like to see ye blush," he says. "I bet it makes your pale skin look healthy."

She laughs, but also warns, "I don't think I could even stand to read parts of it. Parts of it I wrote thinking you'd not even be near me when you read them."

"If you love me," he tells her, "you could read it all."

That's true. She says, "That's true, but parts of it are going to make me sound most unladylike."

"Those will probably be my favorite parts," he says. "Let's have it."

"Promise you'll never laugh."

"Aint there no funny parts?"

"Not deliberately funny," she says.

"Well, I won't laugh unless I hear ye laughin first."

She could always, she realizes, skip some of the parts. She could always censor part of it, and he'd never know . . . until the time came that he might want to read it over to himself, and then if he found the parts she'd censored and wondered why, maybe he would understand. Nail Chism, she honestly believes, will always understand.

So she gets up, and from one of the sacks in the cavern she fills her straw hat with oats, and takes it out to Rosabone, and sets it down where the mare can eat the oats. "Don't eat my hat," she says. Then she gets the bundle of letters out of the saddlebag. She pats the mare's neck and speaks some last words to her: "You'll hear me talking, Rosabone. All night long you'll hear me talking, but I won't be talking to you. You get some sleep, and we'll go back to the village in the morning."

All night long the mare hears her mistress talking. But surely, sometime in the night, the mare dozes off.

Viridis Monday holds nothing back. She reads it all. Once, after lighting the lantern and resuming, she asks him, "Is this boring you?"

"I thought you'd know me better than to ask a question like that," he says. "Don't stop."

But once again, much later, she interrupts herself to ask, "Does that shock you?"

He is smiling, not with mirth but with pleasure. "I reckon I can stand it," he allows, offhand.

And again, when she comes, in time, to the story of the night she thought she was going to be allowed to spend in his cell, and is describing in detail what she anticipated, she hears his breathing quicken and what might be a gasp, and she stops to say, "Of course I'm just making up this whole part. It's just what I had *imagined* might happen."

"It happened," he says. "If you wrote it, it happened."

His saying that, his way of putting it, eases her, makes her more comfortable and confident with her own telling and her own invention. But it also perhaps leads to, or at least explains, what eventually happens this night, which is of course only written but also happening.

A strange thing: at some point she ceases to distinguish between what has been written and what is happening.

She has reached the present in her narrative: she has discovered that her narrative itself has switched from the past tense to the present tense and she is describing time as it occurs. She is surprised to discover herself reading a letter in which she describes what she is doing right now: sitting cross-legged on the floor of the cavern beside Nail's bed, reading him a letter in which she describes herself sitting cross-legged . . .

Tiredness might be a contributing factor; for Nail, it could be the effects of the quinine: a strange tinnitus that makes him hear not what she is saying but what he wants her to be saying. Is that it? Is she actually continuing to read from her actually written letter or simply describing aloud what happens as it happens? This is very strange, and no sound comes from Nail, except once when she stops and asks, "What am I saying?

What am I *doing*?" and he observes, "You're asking yourself, What am I saying? What am I *doing*?"

All this night she has held nothing back from him. Her whole life, and every thought she's considered of any importance, has been laid bare to him. Her most secret and private imaginings have been put so clearly to him that they have become his own. Not just with candor, because candor implies a conscious opening up, and she has not been closed to begin with, but with total truth, she has turned herself inside out to him, and as the night wears on she discovers that she is naked and unashamed.

Never before, since her mother first clothed her, has she been naked to anyone except herself. But the nakedness of her body is as nothing; it is almost anticlimax, almost redundant. Especially because she has already written this in the letter too: I have on no clothes now. Now in the glare of coal oil light I am without a stitch. It does not bother me that he is not following suit, because I have already seen him without a stitch, in the death chamber, and because his time to be as bare as me will come later. Now is mine. His turn is later, after I have nothing left to reveal to him.

His turn comes at dawn. On this morning, the beginning of the alternate day of his two-day ague, the day he will not shake from cold or burn from fever or drip with sweat, he realizes that it is his turn, because she has told him everything she has to tell, given him everything she has to give, done for him everything that can be done.

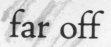

far off

"Well, I'll be!" I'll say, seeing Every Dill come walking up to my front porch, carrying a big earthenware bowl with a lid on it. It will be the first time I'll have had a good look at him since that night when I was eleven and I had to stay at his folks' house while everybody but me and him went to a funeral, and we wound up in the same bed.

"Good mornin, Latha," he'll say, and hold the big bowl out to me. "Maw said fer me to give ye this."

"Jist set it down there with them others," I'll tell him, and gesture toward the porch floor, where there will already be twenty-three assorted bowls, pots, tureens, casseroles, and other containers, each of them steaming with what I know is the same thing that's in his: chicken and dumplings.

"Yore dog will git it," he will object, nodding his head toward Rouser and continuing to hold the bowl out to me.

"Rouser's done et one of them, and licked the bowl clean," I will point out. "Caint you see how his belly's all pooched out? He won't eat another'n before suppertime leastways, and maybe by then we'll figure out what to do with that many bowls of chicken'n dumplins."

"Huh?" Every will say. "You mean everlast one o' them bowls has got chicken dumplims in 'um?" When I nod, he will say, "Wal, heck, Nail and that lady could never eat all of them in a month of Sundays, could they?" When I will shake my head, he will say, "Wal, heck, mize well take this'un on back home."

"Suit yourself," I will tell him.

"But Maw tole me to leave it, I'd better leave it, don't ye reckon?"

"Whatever ye think."

He will set the bowl down on the porch, but in front of the others so that it might get taken first when the time will come. He will study it. "Wal, heck," he will say, "it aint even dinnertime yet, but I wouldn't mind havin a bite or two of that myself, if ye'd lend me the borry of a fork."

"I'll git ye a plate," I will tell him and go into the house for a clean plate and a fork and a big spoon for him to serve up a pile with.

"Who's that out there?" my mother will ask.

"Every," I'll tell her. "Now we've got twenty-four bowls of chicken'n dumplins. But I think he's fixin to help eat part of one."

"Law sakes," my mother will say. "I never thought them Dills had a chicken around the place. Must've been a ole rooster."

I will take the eating equipment to Every, and I will watch him eat. He will eat as if it has indeed been a long time since he's had anything as good as chicken and dumplings, and I will reflect that given a chance he might even grow up to look and sound a little bit like Nail Chism. But right now he'll be just a fourteen-year-old towhead who's pretty well earned his nickname Pickle. I will scarcely be able to convince myself that I, who came awfully close to making love to Nail himself just yesterday morning, already lost my virginity to this boy a couple of years before.

This boy will pause in his chewing and ask, "What're ye thinkin about, Latha?"

I will manage a smile. "Us," I will say. "I aint hardly seen you since."

He will blush furiously. But he will pretend not to know what I'm talking about. "Since when?" he will ask.

"Since that night you crope into my bed."

"I never!" he will protest. "It was more lak you crope inter mine."

"The bed was in your house, and your folks owned it, but it was *my* bed at the time."

"But it was the bed I slept in every night of my life," he will point out.

"But you were sposed to sleep on a pallet in th'other room," I will remind him. "Don't you remember?"

"Yeah, but I reckon I was kind of groggy and conflummoxed," he will observe. "Heck, maybe I was even sleepwalkin."

"Every Dill," I will accuse him, "don't you even remember what you and me *did*?"

"Was you awake?" he will ask.

"Silly! We talked for an hour before we did it. Don't you re*mem*ber?"

"Yeah, it kinder comes back to me," he will admit.

"I'm sorry to hear it ever left you in the first place."

A silence will ensue. He will be just standing there in the dirt yard beside my front porch, shuffling his bare feet in the dirt, hanging his head bashfully, poking his hands into the pockets of his overalls, and taking them out again. At length he will ask, without looking at me, "Did you not mind what we done?"

379

"It hurt some at first," I will admit. "And you were awful impatient. But it was a heap of fun."

"It was?" He will lift his eyes and search mine.

"Sure was."

"You got all limp and still, like I'd kilt ye."

"I reckon I must've just swooned for a bit."

"Because I was hurtin ye?"

"No, because I'd done went and gone over the mountain."

His look will tell me that he does not understand and that it would be no use, yet, for me to try to explain it. He will give me that look for a while before changing it to another look with narrowed eyes and a question: "Would ye lak to do it again?"

I will look around me as if we are being observed, and of course we are, because you, dear reader, will be observing us. In a hushed voice I will say, "Not right here. Not right now."

He will laugh. "I never meant that. I jist meant sometime."

"Okay," I will grant. "*Some*time. But you ought to know, when we did it before, I was still a little too young to get . . . to have . . . to make a baby. I aint, anymore. I could make one now. You ought to know that."

"We'd have to be real keerful, wouldn't we?" he will allow. I will observe that just the talking about it, just the implication that we *might* do it again sometime, has given him a noticeable bulging in the fork of his overalls, which I will recognize from having seen on another male just the day before. For a moment I will be possessed of a wild urge to grab his hand and lead him off to the barn, until I recall that I am custodian of twenty-four pots of chicken and dumplings and have not yet decided how I am going to transport even one of them up to the glen of the waterfall. And I will realize that, possessed as I am by this urge, I have not been listening carefully, and that Every has asked me a question.

"What did ye say?" I will ask.

"I ast ye, *when?*" he will say. "When can we?"

I am about to reply, when we are interrupted by the arrival of the twenty-fifth bowl of chicken and dumplings. It will come by automobile, the first one to enter our yard in quite a spell. The driver of the car will be a man I haven't seen in quite a longer spell, but I will remember him from his trip to Stay More with the sheriff and Judge Jerram, and I will certainly remember him from his courtroom, where I had to testify. It will

380

be Judge Lincoln Villines, alone again like the time he came to pay a call on Viridis and the old woman.

He will stand in the yard, holding the fancy china serving-dish and looking at me and then at Every. "Howdy," he will say, and then squint his eyes at me again. "You shore are Latha Bourne, aint ye? I seem to recall you from once I seen you afore." When I nod my head in acknowledgment, he will say, "I was tole that you was the one could take this yere bowl of victuals up to Nail Chism and his ladyfriend." When I nod again, taking the bowl from him and setting it among the others, he will glance at Every and say, "But I don't believe I know you."

"I was just leavin anyhow," Every will say, and start shuffling off. "See you later, Latha," he will say.

I will be a little put out with Every, that he has taken off like that and left me alone to deal with the judge, who will now watch as Every disappears and turn back to me to ask, "Your brother?"

"My beau," I will say.

The judge will snort a laugh but then cover his mouth with his hand. "Aint you kind of young to carry that bowl way off through the woods to where they're hidin?"

I will point at the hodgepodge of bowls filling the porch. "No, but I reckon I'm too young to figger out some way to get all them other bowls up to 'em."

The judge will finally notice the great assortment of other bowls and look at them like a suitor appraising the crowd of fellow suitors for a lady's hand. "What's in them?" he will ask.

"Same as what's in yourn," I will say.

"Chicken'n *dumplins*?" he will ask.

"Yep," I will say.

"My, my," he will say, and will meditate upon the fact, like a suitor discovering that his competition is just as strong and handsome and rich as he is. "News shore travels fast, don't it?" Then he will ask, "Wal, how air ye figgerin on gittin even one of them bowls up the mountain to 'em?"

"I got two hands, aint I?"

"Yeah, but it's a fur ways off," he will say. "Real fur off."

I will begin wondering how he happens to know just how far off it is. His reference to "the woods where they are hidin" and "up the mountain" will indicate to me that he has a pretty good idea of where they are. I will wonder if the news traveling fast has told the whole world not only that Nail Chism has a hankering for some chicken and dumplings but also just where he's hiding. But nobody else will know, except me and Doc Swain, who surely will not have told anybody.

It will suddenly dawn on me why, or rather how, Judge Lincoln Villines knows where Nail and Viridis are. But I will pretend ignorance and innocence and will tell him, "The reason I aint taken any of these bowls up there yet is that I'm not too sure just where it is they're hiding."

"You're not?" he will say. "I was tole that you was the only one that knows."

I will gesture vaguely northward. "I jist *think* it's somewheres up yonder."

He will correct my gesture, pointing properly eastward. "Naw, it's over yonderways, up that mountain."

"Could you show me?" I will ask.

"Well, I don't want to go right up to the cave with ye, but I could lead ye part of the ways."

"As far as where Sull Jerram was shot?" I will ask.

"Shore, I could take ye that—" Abruptly he will stop and change what he's saying to: "Everbody knows whar that is, don't they?"

"Nossir," I will tell him. "Jist me and whoever it was kilt him."

———

Will it matter, in the end, who killed Sewell Jerram? I think that what will matter, what will be of any interest to anybody, will be not so much the identity of the culprit as, rather, the motive. The reason that Sull Jerram was shot and killed was not because he was about to molest Viridis, not because he had raped and abused Dorinda Whitter, not because he had sent an innocent man to prison, but because he alone knew how much Lincoln Villines had to do with the bootlegging operation that had started the whole thing.

Arkansas has had a number of governors who were less than brilliant, less than capable, less than gubernatorial. George Washington Hays himself, despite his corruption, was not without intelligence, was a man who made many mistakes but was at least smart enough to realize when he had made a mistake. In this story Governor Hays will not last much longer, not as governor. In November he will announce that he will not seek reelection. He is intelligent enough to know that he would probably be defeated if he did seek it. Lincoln Villines was not intelligent enough to realize that he could never have been elected to the office even if he had not been stupid enough to get involved in a bootlegging operation.

A professor of political economy at the University of Arkansas, Charles Hillman Brough (the name rhymes with "tough"), will decide to campaign for the 1916 Democratic nomination for governor, opposing not just Hays, if he chooses to run again, but Hays's entire machine, especially the Jeff Davis faction of the machine, which will appear so eager to hand the nomination to hillbilly Lincoln Villines . . . until suddenly Villines will not only be revealed to have a shady past but also be suspected of, and then indicted for, murdering a fellow judge, Sewell Jerram, who had threatened to expose that shady past.

The scandal will shake the Democratic Party but not to the extent of preventing its nominee, Brough, from swamping the Republican and Socialist nominees in the general election, by almost a hundred thousand votes.

As one of his last acts in office, as the very last of a long string of sometimes questionable pardons, Governor Hays will grant a pardon to Lincoln Villines, then under a relatively light sentence of ten years, a Newton County jury having convicted him not of murder, reasoning that it isn't murder to do away with a bad man, but of "voluntary manslaughter," as the foreman attempted to classify it.

Governor Hays in retirement will keep a law office in Little Rock and will publish a number of articles in national publications, arguing his continued advocacy of capital punishment as the only alternative to mob violence. During Prohibition and the Jazz Age he will remain a staunch supporter of Alfred Smith as the Democrats' candidate for president, because, he will point out, "It was the Republican Party that tried to force the social equality of the Negro upon the Aryan people of the South." But Hays will not live to see Smith win Arkansas while losing most of the South and the election. Hays will die as another advocate of Aryan supremacy, an Austrian named Schicklgruber, is rising to power in Germany.

Governor Brough, an erudite and persuasive man bent upon prison reform and better roads and education, will as one of his first acts of office consider extending a pardon to Nail Chism, unconditional except for one little condition: that Nail Chism come to Little Rock, give himself up directly to the governor, and receive his pardon. That offer will be something for Nail to think about.

───────

But there will be many other things for Nail to think about before then. At one point he will have to decide whether or not he and his lady should relinquish their sylvan sanctuary and move back to society. It will become clear, after a while, that nobody is really trying to find them. Nearly everybody will know that they are up there, somewhere, high on Ledbetter Mountain in a cave or cavern near a spectacular waterfall. They will know that I have made countless trips up there myself, each time carrying a bowl of chicken and dumplings, and I myself will have heard of the men on Ingledew's storeporch making bets on which will happen first: the remaining chicken and dumplings will spoil, or Nail will grow tired of them. And sure enough, those wagering on the former contingency will be victorious.

What will bring Nail out of hiding, eventually, will not be my continued reassurance that nobody, especially not the law, or what is left of the law in Newton County, is actively searching for him, but Doc Swain's sorrowful announcement to him that his father has taken a turn for the worse. On one of his visits, a week or so after Nail's return, Doc Swain will examine Nail and pronounce him almost recovered from his malaria, and then will sadly tell him that his father is dying.

That will bring Nail home.

He will never again return to the cave, except, oh, years later on a kind of nostalgic pilgrimage to it, he and Viridis will take their little boy to see the spot where the boy was conceived, although of course they won't try to explain to a kid that young what "conception" means. And I will be getting far ahead of my story.

[Although my story, that is, the story of my own life, will tend to fade off, far off from here. I will not immediately, or soon, honor my assent to Every's request; for one thing, my mother will constantly remind me that he cannot be my beau, for two reasons: he's a cousin, even if twice removed, and the Dills are the lowest of the low on the Stay More social ladder, such as it is. Raymond Ingledew, youngest son of banker John Ingledew, will begin to take notice of me, or take a letch for me (is there a difference?), and my mother will think Raymond makes a far more eligible beau, but the story of all of that, and what will happen between Every and Raymond, will have to wait until you, dear reader, can tell it.]

Nail will attend his father in his last hours. Nail will move back into his father's house, and he and Viridis will sleep there, not together of course, because even though everybody will assume that Nail and Viridis have been sleeping together in the cave, it would be improper and unseemly, not to mention immoral, for an unmarried couple to sleep in the same bed in the house of decent folks. And besides all that, it would not be nice for a man to have relations with his girlfriend while his father is dying. Seth Chism will hang on for nearly a week after Nail moves home, and Nail will sleep in his old bed, and his brother Luther will be sent to Waymon's house so that Viridis can have Luther's bed. And everything will be proper while Seth is dying.

When Seth dies (happy, Doc Swain assures everybody), Nancy, Seth's widow, will move in with her oldest son Waymon, who lives down the trail a ways in the old McCoy place with his wife Faye, and young Luther, her least boy, still a teenager, will go with her, leaving the old Chism place entirely to Nail and to Viridis, and even though they will not be married yet, it will be nobody's business whether they resume sleeping together. It will be their house. Nancy will deed that house and eighty acres to her son Nail, who will add to it the forty acres of his own that had been a pasture for sheep. Now he will have a hundred and twenty acres on which to raise sheep . . . if he cares to.

Will he care to? One of the biggest things he will have to think about is not whether he wants to raise sheep again, because that is really all he honestly wants to do, but whether he ought to ask Viridis if she'd mind if he resumed shepherding. He will brood about asking her this question much longer than he will later brood about asking her the other question: whether or not she might be interested in getting married to him.

He should not need to brood so; she will understand him. She will know him through and through, what makes him tick, what winds him up and makes his pendulum swing, and whether he is midnight or high noon despite his hands being the same at both times. Viridis will almost want to ask him herself, Aren't you thinking about getting some more sheep? but she will decide to wait, because she will know he is.

And he will start a new flock. Not right then, because late summer isn't the best time, but soon. Within a year he'll have his hundred and twenty acres up to capacity with sheep, more than he's ever had before, and Viridis will set some tongues to wagging because she'll do something that most wives hereabouts (although she won't be a wife yet) never do: she'll help with the stock. She'll learn the ways of sheep. She'll become, for heaven's sake, a *shepherdess*.

Won't that be pastoral? I will come across them once, on my rambles. I'll ramble a lot. The day that Dorinda Whitter elopes with Virge Tuttle and is taken by him back to Pettigrew to live, I'll go up on the hill to shut down our playhouse. Not just shut it down but destroy it, I guess. Then I'll keep on walking until I happen to find myself in Nail's sheep pastures, and I'll catch sight of them: Nail and Viridis, sitting on the hillside, under a singing hickory, surrounded by grazing sheep. Nail will be playing his harmonica to the hickory's singing. Viridis will have her sketchbook in her lap, drawing, I'll suppose, a pastoral landscape.

They will catch sight of me and wave. That ought to be my last picture in this story, the two of them there on that hillside, waving good-bye together, waving to signal that the story is over, that everything's fine, that I can go my way and they can go theirs, that the sheep will be happy and grazing, that all'll be right with the world.

But they will also be waving hello as well as good-bye, and I will go on up and visit with them for a little bit. It will bother me to be that close to Nail, and I guess I'll blush. I'll still be in love with him. I'll still have dreams, waking and sleeping, about what it would've been like if I'd, that morning with him in the cave, if only I'd . . .

"Could I see your picture?" I'll ask Viridis, and she'll show it to me, the landscape she's working on. When the time will come that Governor Brough will invite Nail to come to Little Rock and give himself up and receive the governor's pardon, and Viridis of course will go with him (and the two of them will conspire to get Ernest Bodenhammer a Brough pardon too), she will have a whole bunch of pictures to take with her, not just the very best landscape sketches ready to be framed but a number of canvases too: oil paintings of the Stay More countryside and of the people. She will not by any means be the first to have depicted the village and its inhabitants on canvas, nor by any means will she be the last, but to me she will always be the one whose pictures never fail to capture my eyes and my heart, both.

Viridis Monday will always be the one, and I'll get through a lot of the rough places of my life just by thinking of her, and wishing I were like her, and trying to be like her, and only sometimes envying her for having taken Nail. I'll never find a man to save. Not like she saved him. But I'll keep my eyes open.

———

Far off, the day before yesterday, I will attend Dorinda Whitter Tuttle's funeral. My grandson Vernon will drive me the fifty-three miles to Pettigrew for it. Pettigrew, to my sorrow, will be all run down from its former glory as the terminus of the Frisco Railroad, which will have been gone from it for some fifty years. Pettigrew will be just a wide place in the road, both sides of the road clotted with junked automobiles: a vast junkyard. At least it's not in Newton County, but over the line in Madison County. Vernon will not stay for the funeral; he will have business in Fayetteville. Rindy's daughter Latha will have agreed to drive me home afterward; I will be uncomfortable, not so much because Rindy has named her daughter after me and it will be awkward having two Lathas in the same car, as because Latha Tuttle will be seventy years old herself and only a little bit better a driver than me, and I will not be able to drive at all. At least, I will be somewhat relieved to discover that Latha Tuttle at seventy will have no resemblance to myself at seventy. We will not talk an awful lot. She will not be particularly grieving or mournful; she will have been living in Russellville, a widow herself, for many years largely out of touch with her mother, especially in the last years, when Rindy's body was consumed by cancer. Nor will Latha Tuttle have much interest in the old lady she was named after, and even less interest in the remains of the hometown of that lady. Strangely, it will be her first visit to Stay More and her last. She will be eager to deposit me at my home and get on back to her own. I'll have time for just one question: "Did your mother ever say anything about Nail Chism to you?" Latha Tuttle will ask me to repeat the name a couple of times; her hearing will be very impaired.

"Was he one of her beaux?" she will ask.

"No, he was a man who was wrongfully sent to the penitentiary because of her."

"Law, me," she will say. "You'd think she'd of tole me somethin about that, wouldn't you? But no, she never said no word about no Nail Chism."

She'll shake her head at the mild wonder of it and ask conversationally, "Did he ever git out?"

"He got out," I'll tell her.

———

Now will I even need to say that Doc Swain was right: they will live happy ever after? Do I have to tell the rest of it, let you know whether or not they will actually get married? Or how many children they will have? Or about the times when Viridis will get bored and lonely and restless? Or the bad years that all of us had together? Will I have to mention the droughts and the floods and the fires?

And should I tell how Nail Chism will eventually, with poetic justice, become Newton County's first electrician? Although by the time poor Newton County finally gets around to being electrified, won't Nail Chism be too old even to remember the fundamentals of electrical mechanics?

No, I will think back to the picture I began this story with: a red-haired newspaperlady sitting in the death chamber at the state penitentiary and sketching a head-shaved convict waiting to die. The making of that sketch was what started the saving of him, and started this story, and I will let this story end with another sketch by Viridis, which she will show me that afternoon: a dale of green pasture grasses, so many shades of green that even though she has done them all in black and white, I will feel the many greens, the white bodies of the sheep dazzling in their whiteness because of the green that surrounds them, their heads down to eat the green, while a man in a straw hat and blue denim overalls plays his harmonica and watches them, and sitting close beside him a woman draws the whole scene in a sketchbook held in her lap: the man and the sheep and the dale and, out across the dale, far off up on the lilting mountain above the village, a farmplace that is their home, beneath a fat maple and a gangling walnut, both singing. But the woman in the picture will have already finished drawing that: now she adds a final touch, with her kneaded eraser she makes room for the final touch: a girl, not quite yet a woman, walking through the green grass out among the sheep, coming to join the man and the woman, and to be in the picture, forevermore.

Books by Donald Harington available from
Harcourt Brace Jovanovich, Publishers,
in Harvest/HBJ paperback editions

The Architecture of the Arkansas Ozarks: A Novel

The Cherry Pit

The Choiring of the Trees

Lightning Bug

Some Other Place. The Right Place.